RETURN
TO GRACE

KAREN HARPER

RETURN TO GRACE

MIRA®

ISBN-13: 978-0-7783-1481-3

RETURN TO GRACE

For questions and comments about the quality of this book please contact us at Customer_eCare@Harlequin.ca.

www.Harlequin.com

Printed in U.S.A.

For all the friends and family
who love Ohio Amish country, especially to Don
for all the great trips there.

1

October 31, 2010

HANNAH ESH HAD SPENT TIME IN THIS AMISH graveyard but never to host a party. She would have given anything not to be here now, especially with her four goth friends, who didn't even have to dress for Halloween to look weird. But she should talk, because she'd been one of them for nearly three years. Yet more than ever she wanted to go home, and home was the farmhouse just across two fields from here.

"Awesome!" Liz Bartoli, her roommate, said with a shudder as she saw how dark it was without car or neon city lights. There weren't even electric lights from the nearby Amish properties. "Maybe after we have a bash here, we can all go through that corn maze down the road. An amazing maize maze," she added with a snorted giggle. "It wasn't fair of you guys to run through it without us."

"Kevin and Mike have already seen that. Besides," Hannah said, "the sign said it's closed after five and you have to make special arrangements with the owners to go in there after dark." She'd been upset when Kevin had driven right up to the entry of the corn maze. Then he and Mike had gotten out to tear a ways into it—and come crashing back through one wall of it when they got lost. "And each of us would have to leave a donation," Hannah added as she opened the unlocked, squeaky gate in the wooden fence surrounding the hillside acre of graves and grass.

"Listen to you!" Tiffany Miles, who worked with Hannah at the recording studio, scolded as she got a blanket out of the trunk. "You can take the Amish girl out of the country, but you can't take the Amish out of the girl. Rules and regs out the wazoo!"

Kevin Pryor, Tiffany's guy, found that really funny as he and Mike Swanson, Liz's friend, hauled the cooler from the trunk of Kevin's black car. But Hannah wasn't laughing. Ever since her family's barn had burned last spring, she'd been more than homesick. She missed her folks, even her *daad,* the local bishop she'd had a huge falling-out with. She longed to see others, too, but she couldn't think of that now. Somewhere she'd heard the expression "You can't go home again," and it scared her to death that it might be true.

Oh, why had she let her friends talk her into this tonight? Worse, Halloween fell on the Sabbath this year, and that bothered her, too. She should have just given them directions but she figured she'd better keep an eye on them. Since she'd recently broken up with her boyfriend, she'd tried to get out of coming along, but they'd insisted they could cheer her up. Yet being back here, all she wanted to do was cry.

"Perfect place," Mike said with a tip of his velvet

top hat, "for a booze and boos party. Boo! We goths have finally gone ghosting!"

"There are no ghosts here," Hannah insisted, feeling defensive as they passed her grandparents' simple tombstones. "Everyone buried here is at peace." But the truth was she felt haunted by all she'd loved and left behind.

Mike cranked up the volume on his MP3 player. Deathrock music spewed out, heavy drums and synthesizers to a tribal beat, pulsing but sad, so different from the music Hannah had in her head of singing a country song or a hymn, her own voice blending with Seth's, now as lost to her as all the Amish.

Suddenly, she wanted to strip off the heavy, draped chain necklaces she wore, the fishnet stockings under the ankle-length, purple ruffled skirt and black velvet jacket. To wash off her heavy eye shadow and black lipstick, to hide her spiky, red-dyed hair under a black bonnet.

The guys plunked their stuff down pretty much in the middle of the graveyard before she read the name on the closest tombstone. Oh, no! Not Lena Lantz's grave, but it was too late to make them move and no way was she going to explain why. Lena had died almost a year ago, so Hannah had not been here then and had only heard indirectly about the tragedy. It was so hard to believe she'd been away from the Home Valley for nearly three years.

Kevin passed around wineglasses and poured. Clumps of clouds hid the moon, but he pretended to howl at it. They clinked glasses and drank the bloodred wine.

"Vampires got nothing on us tonight," Mike teased,

and pretended to bite Liz on the neck while she screamed and giggled. Tiffany got to her feet, twirling the parasol she always carried, even after dark—what an attention-getter, as if goths needed that. She did a jerky dance around the low, matching stone markers with only the deceased's name, birth and death dates.

"Stop that. Not funny!" Hannah protested when Tiffany pretended to be digging up Lena's grave with the closed parasol as a shovel. Kevin got up to cavort with her. Suddenly, it was too much. Hannah pictured herself standing nearby with her family and friends when they buried her grandparents…and here lay a young mother, even though she was the woman Seth dumped her for. Hannah hated herself for bringing her friends here where they didn't belong—and neither did she.

She stood and yanked the parasol out of Tiffany's hands and shoved her back from Lena's grave. Then, ashamed that she'd used violence, she turned her back on her friends as tears spilled down her cheeks. Hands on her hips, lifting her gaze up the hill, she stared at the dark woodlot, trying to get control of herself. *I will lift up mine eyes unto the hills. From whence comes my help?* The words ran through her head.

"Chill out, Hannah!" Kevin protested. "We're just kidding around."

"Sorry, Tiff," Hannah told her friend, turning back to face them, "but please don't even pretend to do that—disturb the dead. We—we shouldn't be here."

Hannah sat back down and took a big swig of their bitter wine—another mistake, for she soon felt sick to her stomach and her very soul. She flopped back on the grass, wondering if she was going to throw up, wishing again they were not so near Lena Lantz's grave as her four friends whispered and stared at her.

Then… Was that sound a clap of thunder? No, there was no storm. A shot?

The music—the voices—another sharp sound! Tiffany flew back, fell at Hannah's feet, holding her shoulder, screaming. Everything happened at once. *Bang, bang!* The gravestone Hannah had been lying near splintered, exploded, peppering her with stone shards. Kevin shouted, "Gun! Someone's got a g—" before he threw himself back flat on the ground so he wouldn't be hit. No, he was hit, right in his forehead, where blood bloomed. Tiffany kept screaming as she lay flat on the ground, and Liz and Mike cowered.

On and on went the beat of the music and a new staccato of shots. Ignoring a sharp pain in her wrist, Hannah belly-crawled for her black macramé bag a few feet away. Cell phone. Get help. Tiffany hurt. Kevin staring at the sky. So dark. Loud blackness.

She found her phone, punched in 9-1-1, thinking the shooter would come closer, but no more shots. Pulse pounding. In shock? Still alive, still moving, thinking. Terrified but energized. Her own voice frenzied, answering the calm questions on her phone. "Yes, that's what I said. Some people have been shot at—shot… Yes, with a gun!… The Oakridge Road Amish graveyard northwest of Homestead. Send help quick!"

It was only then she saw the left sleeve of her velvet jacket was torn and wet and that her wrist was ripped open and slick with blood.

Seth Lantz couldn't believe someone was hunting after dark—or had a car misfired…more than once?

It was rolling country here; maybe a car would come roaring over the next hill. No, a woman was screaming. A hunting accident? Maybe *Englische* kids were playing some sick Halloween prank on the Amish because they ignored this worldly holiday. It was the Sabbath, and he wouldn't even have been hunting today if it didn't help to keep meat on the table. In this far-reaching recession, big building jobs were hard to come by, and he'd been doing pickup repair work lately.

He reined in his horse as he approached the fenced-in graveyard on Oakridge. His mare, Blaze, tossed her head, upset to be stopped in the middle of nowhere while heading home. That screaming and loud noise: it was from the graveyard.

He giddyupped Blaze to the gate and saw a black car parked there, though this was an all-Amish *graahof.* His young wife was buried here, as were his grandparents, including his dear *grossdaadi* Gideon, who had taught him to build barns. He threw Blaze's reins over a hitching post and, hunched low, went around the outside of the fence instead of through the gate.

Some sort of loud-beat music thudded on. Amid other voices, the woman's screams had turned to gasping sobs. He put one hand on the wooden fence and vaulted it sideways. No place to really hide in here, no tall monuments, trees or bushes like in English cemeteries, but at least the darkness hid him.

Then, despite the noise, he picked out a voice he thought he knew, the one that sometimes still danced through his dreams. If it was Hannah Esh, who was she talking to in a one-way conversation?

"Yes, in the head. He's not moving, not breathing.... Pulse. I—I'm not sure.... Two others wounded—losing blood, a lot.… Her shoulder and my wrist.… Yes, just visiting.… I—yes, I said my name is Hannah Esh, and I used to live near here. I'm dizzy—faint.… Yes, thank you, please hurry because Kevin might be dead.…"

Seth rose to his full height and strode forward, nearly tripping over a prone body. A scarlet cape was splayed out under him, matching the blood that covered his face and white, ruffled shirt. He saw one woman, her arm and chest soaked in blood—a woman with dark-lined eyes. A horror movie he'd seen once in his *rumspringa* days darted through his mind: ghouls robbing graves and feeding on corpses.

He saw another woman sobbing, bent over on the ground. And then the one he sought, though he hardly recognized her, hadn't seen her for more than three years, had only heard what she'd done to herself after what he'd done to her.

"Hannah," he choked out, "it's Seth. Are you hurt?"

Tears streaming black lines down her ravaged face, the woman who had once been the love of his life looked up at him. "Seth? Sorry. I—we—I called for help. He's dead, I think, and I just want to die from pain and shame."

She looked like something from the depths of hell, as he bent to rip the purple velvet ruffles off the bottom of her long skirt. Using his pocket knife to cut the material, he made a tourniquet for her arm and wrapped her bleeding wrist. He made a pressure pack for the other girl's shoulder and told the unharmed girl to keep her hand on it, even though it hurt the one who had been shot. He put two fingers to the blood-slick side of the young man's neck, then flipped up the edge of the blanket over the lifeless body.

Striding back toward the huddled group, he asked the man who had not been shot, "What happened here? Did one of you do this?"

That man's eyes were wide, his face expressionless. He, too, wore dark-eyed makeup and was dressed fancy, old-fashioned. After a moment, as if it took time for the question to sink in, the man shook his head. "From out there," he said, pointing up the slant of hill toward the back of the graveyard. "From the dark."

"Turn that music off," Seth said. Looking dazed, the man fumbled with the MP3 player, and silence finally descended. Seth hurried up the hill, ran the entire fence line, seeing no one, though someone could be hiding, watching in the woods higher up. It made the hair on the back of his neck prickle.

He heard distant sirens and went back to hold the blood-soaked velvet to Hannah's wrist. "Why are you all here? What in the world…?" he started to ask, then bit off the rest when he saw that Hannah lay almost on his wife's grave and that her marker had been blasted to bits.

Hannah's pain got worse, worse. Cold waves, then sizzling hot in her wrist, hand, arm. Twirling now, floating. Seth could not really be here. Had her thoughts summoned him? Had he come to be with Lena? His handsome face sported a blond beard now. Well, of course it did…married man, even if widowed. And with a child, a girl, Lena's child, must be two years old now, named Marlena. How it had hurt to hear all that, but she'd asked her friend Sarah to keep her informed, anyway.

What in the world? Seth's words kept revolving

through Hannah's head. She had gone to the world, left her people. Seth's fault? Lena's? Her own? Because of the terrible argument she'd had with her father? Forgive Seth? She could not. She'd jumped the fence, left the Plain People, tried to have a singing career, tried to fit in, but really didn't.

Bright blinking lights, a siren that went silent. People to help, medics. A little beam of light in each eye. Voices, words flying by she tried to grab. Seth's voice, then these strangers' words.

"…Can't transport him…deceased…bled out. Bullet to the head. Crime scene. Sheriff Freeman should be here soon. He can call the coroner."

"Wooster, E.R., we're going to transport two females with gunshot wounds, shoulder, wrist…starting IVs…sending vitals…"

"Did you see what happened here, Mr. Lantz?"

Muffled words in and out of her head…

Lifted onto a gurney, carried, made the pain worse. IV in her arm, wrist bandaged. Two emergency vehicles, bloodred lights piercing the night, but so bright inside where they lifted her, slid her in. The sound of a buggy, a single horse's hoofbeats coming fast, a voice she knew. *Daad! Mamm,* too! Was she dreaming?

"We saw the blinking lights from our house. Did a car hit a buggy? Can we help?" her father asked in English.

In their German dialect, her mother said, "Seth, Naomi's with Marlena, so don't you worry for that. *Ach,* what happened here?"

Before Hannah could hear an answer, with great difficulty, she lifted her head to look out past her feet. If she was going to die, to bleed out or never be allowed back here again, she was going to get a glimpse of her parents.

"Bishop Esh," Seth was saying, "Hannah was here with worldly friends. She's been hurt—shot, and she's inside that one, right there."

Her mother peered into the E.R. vehicle. It had been so long since Hannah had looked into her pale blue eyes. More wrinkles than Hannah remembered. *Mamm* looked grieved. Grieved for her.

"Oh, *Mamm,*" Hannah got out before bursting into tears.

Her father, white beard, intense stare, squinted into the brightness at her, and choked out his childhood nickname for her. "Hanni!"

Mamm climbed right up, came in and bent over her, holding her other hand. "I'm going with her," she called out to *Daad* with Seth standing so tall behind him, though Hannah could barely make out their silhouettes in this brightness. "You tell Naomi to take care of things, Joseph."

"Naomi," Hannah heard herself repeat her younger sister's name. "How is…Naomi?"

"Planning her wedding to Joshua Troyer in two weeks," *Mamm* said, close to her ear. "You can help her with things when you come home and let that painted scarlet hair grow out to your real blond." She stroked Hannah's forehead, brushing her gel-spiked hair back. With her unhurt hand, before she remembered it was tethered by IVs, Hannah seized her mother's wrist and held tight. If she did die, she thought as she began to slip away, she could at least go grateful: she'd seen Seth and he had helped her; *Mamm* and *Daad* at least still claimed her; and sweet Naomi was going to be married...going to be married.

Someone slammed the door and her thoughts went black.

2

HANNAH SWAM INTO THE LIGHT, THEN PLUNGED to darkness again, thinking, Naomi's going to be married, going to be married.

Hannah had been certain she was going to be married, too. Seth Lantz was the only man she had ever loved. They'd been scholars together at the one-room schoolhouse. He had been her come-calling friend for years. They'd survived their rebellious *rumspringa* years and had planned to be baptized into the church at the same time. Whether they sang duets of the old hymns or "Take Me Home, Country Roads," their voices blended beautifully, and their lives would, too. Hannah's best running-around friends, Sarah and Ella, knew she and Seth were privately promised to each other. And then…and then…

She had been certain Seth was going to propose to her that sweet spring evening at the pond. He was so nervous, the big six-footer, one of the tallest men in the Home Valley. One of the handsomest, too, with his blond hair and sky-blue eyes, his square chin. Then came the words that had turned her well-planned life upside down.

"Hannah, I—I don't know how it happened. I mean, I know how but not why," he'd faltered. "I realize you and I have been waiting for each other—waiting to join the church, to bed together, to build a life, start a family, but I... It only happened once, but—I hope you and the Lord and the brethren can forgive me—but Lena Miller's going to have my child. She's sure—and I'm going to have to...to marry her."

She had just gaped at him. The words didn't register at first, but his stark, stunned expression did. She'd wanted to drown herself in the pond—she wanted to drown him!

"I—I will always love you," he'd stammered, "and I hope you can forgive me...."

She had become so hysterical she was never certain what she'd said to him that night. She'd hit him, too, pounded on his big, broad shoulders when violence was not their way. But this was brutality. He might as well have beaten or killed her. Running back home across the fields, past the Kauffman farm to her own, blinded by tears of pain and fury, she'd wished the fresh-plowed earth would simply swallow her. Then that argument with her father, the bishop, no less.

"No, I can't forgive him—never will!" she'd shouted. "Even if I could forgive, I could never forget! Don't tell me I have to accept that and go on, see them together, see their children over the years, Lena in his house, in his buggy—poor Hannah, the castoff. He's the one who should be sent away, but I'm the one who's going! I'm going to sing for a career, I don't care if say I can't. At least I won't be shunned, becau never joined the church, never been baptized, never been betrayed like this, either. I don't care if both of them admit their sin before the church or the entire world, because I won't be there. I won't be anywhere around here!"

Her mother's pleading, her sister's tears, nothing stopped her. In her deepest, darkest dreams, she could still hear her father's calm voice calling after her as she charged up the stairs to pack. "Hannah! Hannah Esh, you come back here!"

"Hannah. Hannah," a voice called now, pulling her from heavy, sodden sleep. With great difficulty, Hannah slitted one eye open. Her mother, wearing a black bonnet and cape, was sitting by her bed. A hospital room. Hannah saw she was tied to tubes and monitors.

Her mother stood and leaned close over her, putting a warm palm on Hannah's cheek. She spoke in their German dialect. "I thought you were waking up, dear girl. You lost a lot of blood, but they operated to patch you up and put some metal pins in your wrist. They say with physical therapy, you'll recover most of the use of your hand, but it will take months. At least it's your left one and not your right. I was praying you'd come back to us, back to life and come home to your family now. The police, even a government FBI man, are going to find out who shot at you and—and your friends. I'll stay with you, stay right here in your room, and then you come home with me, oh, *ya.*"

Hannah tried to say, *"Danki, Mamm,"* but her throat felt raw, and nothing came out. What a mess she'd made of things. It all came back in a rush: Kevin dead, Tiffany and her shot while they were defiling the graveyard with their boos and booze. She'd lived through it, but whatever life she'd once had among her Amish family and former friends was surely dead, too.

Hannah floated in and out of strange sleep—pain pills, that was causing her problems, she told herself. When her thoughts settled, she wished she could take medicine to mute her mental pain, as well.

Once *Daad* was even here. They didn't talk, even though they had so much to say. He mostly paced the floor, frowning, muttering to himself, even hitting his forehead with his hand now and then, as if he was blaming himself for the state she was in. But he'd also lifted a glass of water to her lips, and the strangest scrap of scripture had popped into her head: *If your enemy is hungry, feed him; if he is thirsty, give him a drink; for in so doing you will heap coals of fire on his head.* Would all she'd said, all she'd done, make her father turn against her? He was an upright, stern man. Would he believe she had caused not only her own punishment but the harm that came to Tiffany and Kevin? Tiffany was recovering in a Cleveland Hospital, *Mamm* had said, and Kevin's body had been autopsied and would be released by the authorities and buried in a few days. Liz and Mike had gone home to their families.

Later, Hannah wasn't certain when *Mamm* told her that Sheriff Freeman had come to see her. "You sure you're strong enough to talk to him?"

"Yes. I want to help any way I can. To know who would do such a thing and why."

"Perhaps God only knows. I'll sit in the chair in the corner, and you tell the sheriff or me if you get too tired or too upset to answer his questions. He's been keeping some folks away from you, so we are grateful."

"What folks?" Hannah asked, wondering if Seth had tried to see her.

"Newspaper and TV reporters. Don't you fret, because there is a police officer outside your door to keep them away."

If that was meant to be comforting, it only made Hannah more nervous. This was a double nightmare: not only had people's lives been ruined because of her, but she was evidently in some danger. Surely a policeman wasn't just to keep reporters away. Did the police think she could identify someone? Her people lived private, plain lives and now look what she'd done by bringing trouble to them.

Tall and straight, Eden County's sheriff was an imposing man in his crisp black uniform. The Amish didn't trust government officials much or even vote in worldly elections. But Jack Freeman, who was elected, got along with them just fine, although the Amish did not approve of his divorce. Still, word was, his wife had left him when he didn't want her to, so maybe that wasn't all his fault.

His brown eyes assessed Hannah, then took in the room as he thanked *Mamm* for her help. He pulled up the chair next to the bed and put his big-brimmed hat on the floor and a white bakery box on the bedside table.

"From Ray-Lynn Logan," he said, referring to the worldly woman who ran the Dutch Farm Table Restaurant in Homestead, the biggest town in the Home

Valley area, though that wasn't saying much. "She remembers you liked whipped pies."

"Oh, you mean whoopie pies. They're more like cookies, like Amish Oreos with filling." She couldn't believe they were making small talk when she feared what was coming. "Please thank her for me—you, too, for bringing them."

"She said she hopes you're coming back home. Your family and friends want you to."

She still had friends at home? The Amish might be great at forgiving sinners, but could they ever forget the things she had done and now had caused? Her dearest friend, Sarah Kauffman, had remained close, but she'd left for Columbus and was going to marry an outsider. Sarah had said that Hannah's other once-upon-a-time good friend Ella Lantz, Seth's sister, had been very critical of Hannah's worldly life. Or could the sheriff possibly mean Seth had said he was still her friend? He must have also interviewed Seth about the shooting.

"Still, I can't wait around for you to come home to get your statement," he was saying as his voice tightened and his face became more intent. "Hannah, we got us a cold-blooded murder on our hands, and you two women shot. We don't need any of this, not after the media mess with those barn burnings last spring."

"I know. I'm sorry I brought my friends here—there, I mean. I just thought it would be a private picnic."

Frowning, he took out a small notebook and flipped it open. "How 'bout you tell me everything you remember happened at the graveyard?"

She went through things, step-by-step—why they came, their arrival, the loud deathrock music...

"Deathrock?" he interrupted, looking up from his scribbling. "That's its name?"

"Yes, it's very popular with goths."

"Yeah, I been researching that. Black clothes is about the only thing you goths have in common with the Amish, far's I can tell. Go on."

You goths, he'd said. She'd rebelled against her people by casting her lot with something shocking, something even more *verboten* than going to the world. Now she'd brought deadly violence, which the Plain People avoided and abhorred, to them.

"The music must have covered any sounds until the gunshots," she admitted. "I don't know what kind of gun."

"Not your worry. A high-speed rifle, like some folks hunt game with. You could have been killed. Your wrist would have been completely shattered if the bullet that hit you hadn't been partly slowed and deflected by a gravestone that was busted up instead."

Lena Lantz's tombstone, Hannah thought. She should have made everyone move away from her grave. Growing up, she'd known Lena Miller well and liked her. Lena had lived on the next farm to Seth and Ella, and they'd all gone to singings and frolics together. The Lantz and Miller children had gotten especially close after Lena's parents were killed when a car hit their buggy. But she'd never suspected that Lena had her cap set for Seth—or he for her. It took two, oh, yes, she knew that, and in a culture where birth control was forbidden...

"So, you strong enough to talk to Agent Armstrong now?" the sheriff was asking as he flipped his notebook closed. "I promised him I'd cut this short so as not to tire you out. I'll do a follow-up later on whatever else you might remember."

"I—sorry, what did you ask?"

"I know this is difficult, Hannah, but with this being a murder investigation, I called in the FBI, and they're working with the State Bureau of Criminal Identification and Investigation, the BCI. Ever since those young Amish girls got shot and killed in their schoolhouse in Nickel Mines, Pennsylvania, a couple of years back, the FBI like to swoop in real quick if there's something like this—something that could smack of a hate crime against the Amish. From a distance, you all might have looked Amish with your long skirts, the guys in hats and such."

"I— Yes, I understand."

"So, FBI Special Agent Linc Armstrong would like a few words with you. Now, he stays too long or pushes too hard, you just tell him, but he's a pretty take-charge guy. This is the third day I've kept him away from you. You okay with this?"

"I want to do everything I can to help."

"Good girl. 'Preciate it. Oh, Ray-Lynn also said, if you're coming back and—" he nodded to *Mamm,* who stood and came closer "—if you won't be working in your mother's Amish cap-making business, Ray-Lynn can always use a good hand in the restaurant kitchen or waiting tables."

"Tell her one good hand would be it for a while, Sheriff, and thanks for all you're doing to unscramble the mess—the tragedy—I made."

"Not all your fault by a long shot," he said. "Well, didn't mean that about a long shot, but I tell you we'll find whoever put bullets in some visitors to my baili-

wick. Even though you were in the wrong to be carous-
ing there, you didn't force your friends to come along
and you sure as heck didn't fire a rifle at them." He
lowered his voice. "Now, don't you let Linc Armstrong
get you down," he said, and made for the door.

"I'm already down," she whispered to her mother.
"I guess I haven't been myself since that night I argued
with *Daad.*"

"*Ya,* I know," she said, bending over the bed. "You
just be brave with this government man now, because
he already gave Seth a good going-over, and he's been
prying into everyone's past, especially yours."

Seth shoved his roofing hammer through a loop in
his leather carpenter's apron and heard the nails in it
jingle as he scooted a bit higher on Bishop Esh's farmhouse roof. The roof had been scarred by the Esh barn
fire, set by an arsonist, and he was putting down new
shingles. Seth was a timber framer, a barn builder, by
trade. He'd overseen work crews erecting big buildings from churches to rustic state park lodges, but he
picked up odd jobs between projects. Like everywhere
in America, times were tough.

He could see the hilly sweep of much of the Home
Valley, where he'd lived all his life. The woodlots were
every hue from scarlet to gold, the wheat harvest was
in the big barns or silos. Shucked corn was in the Yoder
grain elevator, waiting to be hauled out in boxcars.
The stalks in the corn maze delighted both Amish and
Englische kids and adults as they ran through it. The
white farmhouses and smaller *grossdaadi hauses,* the
big red or black barns—three of which he'd built—
stood strong and tall in the autumn sun, punctuated

by occasional silos and windmills. From this vantage point—he loved heights—he could see the pond where he used to swim with Hannah, a place he had never gone with Lena, and then the graveyard beyond....

That brought his thoughts back to earth. When the authorities took away that bright yellow tape they'd strung along the fence there, he intended to replace Lena's shattered stone grave marker. He'd been questioned by both Sheriff Freeman and that FBI go-getter, Lincoln Armstrong, interviews he'd expected and accepted. He'd even weathered Armstrong's implications he might have had a motive to shoot at Hannah, and the fact he'd asked to see his gun to check his ammunition. What he hadn't been prepared for was being called a hero for helping the wounded women.

His people knew better than to label him that, because such a thing was prideful, but two newspapers and three TV reporters had tried to interview him and take his picture. It was a blessing that the local paper had recently closed and had not been picked up by a new buyer, because it would have been all over this. But up here, he felt safe from his new, sudden fame. Bishop Esh, working in his barn below, had said he'd head off anyone else who came looking for the Amish Hero Saves 2 Lives, Finds Man Dead in Graveyard.

Seth turned and gazed past the chimney, toward his boyhood home, the next farm to the northeast where his brother Abel helped their *daad* farm. The Miller farm beyond that, Lena's childhood home, was owned by her only brother. At the far edge of his parents' property, Seth saw his own small house, which he'd built, where he still lived with little Marlena and where Lena had died suddenly on their kitchen floor of a burst aortic aneurism. She'd had the condition since birth, and no one knew it. He was grateful he didn't have to add Marlena to the brood of kinder at his parents' place as usual, but had brought her with him today, thanks to the Eshes' kind offer to let her play here. Mrs. Esh was at the Wooster hospital with Hannah, but Naomi was keeping an eye on his girl.

Again, though it was the last thing he wanted or needed, his thoughts turned to Hannah. When he'd first seen her in the graveyard, lying almost on Lena's grave, her hair had looked so scarlet that for one split second he'd feared she'd been shot in the head, too, and was bleeding from her skull. Now why had a pretty woman like her done those things to herself? Black eye paint around those blue-green eyes and dark strokes covering her blond, arched eyebrows. Her beautiful hair, once long and honey-blond, hacked off, dyed the hue of martyr's blood and stuck up in spikes. The clothes—well at least they covered her lithe, lovely body, so she wasn't flaunting that to the world.

He shifted his weight on the ridgeline of the roof, the very roof where the Lantz and Kauffman kids used to play Andy Over, heaving a ball up and letting it roll down the other side of the roof, where your opponent had to run and catch it, wherever it suddenly appeared. How clearly he recalled once when they were fifteen that, with both of them looking up, Hannah had bounced into him. They both went down and rolled in the autumn leaves together, with him on top, pressing her down with his knee between her legs, touching her breast, laughing and then kissing for the first time before their friends ran back around and they'd jumped to their feet....

He shook his head to shove that memory away. It really annoyed him how the mere thought of Hannah against him, in his arms, under him, made his body go tense with desire. He missed the pleasures of the marriage bed, even with a woman he had not chosen. Now, he knew two willing Amish *maidals* who would make him a good wife, and he needed to decide which one to pursue and get to courting so Marlena could have a mother and so he could stop this stupid longing.

"You coming down for noon meal?" Bishop Esh's voice sliced through his agonizing. He stood below with his hands cupped around his mouth. "Your little girl's waiting with Naomi. I see any more of those media folks, I'll get rid of them for you, sure I will."

"Coming right down. Just taking a breather."

How long has the bishop watched him sitting up here? And how long before Hannah—if she returned at all—would be brought here, so he could at least see her again?

3

ALTHOUGH FBI SPECIAL AGENT LINC ARMSTRONG'S
taut mouth smiled, Hannah noted that his sharp gray
eyes did not as he assessed her. He was sinewy, angular
and seemed tightly coiled. His brown hair was only
about an inch long, short compared to Amish and goth
men. His ears were so close to his head that his face
seemed even longer than it was, a serious, angular face.
He was dressed in black slacks, white shirt, striped tie
and a dark blue jacket with FBI scripted in gold thread
over the pocket. Though Hannah, who had just turned
twenty-five, was not good at guessing people's ages,
she figured him to be in his mid- to late thirties.

"I appreciate your time while you're recovering," he
told her, then introduced himself. He even held out his
badge to her, in a sort of wallet he opened. The badge
flaunted an eagle holding arrows in his talons over a
line which read Federal Bureau of Investigation, U.S.
Department of Justice. Under that was Armstrong's
photo; his face had a serious, even pained look. When
he still held the wallet open—perhaps he didn't realize how fast an Amish woman could read—she reread

the other words near his photo: "Lincoln Armstrong is a regularly appointed Special Agent of the Federal Bureau of Investigation and as such is charged with the duty of investigating violations of the laws of the United States in cases in which the United States is a party of interest."

A party of interest? That sounded so cold, and the badge looked so...so commanding. No wonder the Amish never wanted to be involved with government agents, even though they were not arresting and executing the Plain People for their beliefs like in the old days in Europe.

Lincoln Armstrong's words were clipped; he talked fast. He said he was Assistant Special Agent in Charge assigned to investigate violent crimes in Northeast Ohio. He was from "the Cleveland office," but would be staying at the Red Roof Inn on the interstate eight miles from Homestead until his investigation was finished.

"I want to help in any way I can," she told him. "Those were—are—my friends, though I shouldn't have brought them here—there—that night."

The man made her very nervous. Even seeing a State Highway Patrol or police car when she was driving bugged her and she slowed way down, but then she'd never really liked driving the car she and Tiffany had shared. But she told herself again that this man was here to help, and she was going to help him.

Still with bolt-upright posture, Agent Armstrong sat on the bedside chair and asked question after question, while she answered as best she could. She could tell that sometimes he was asking the same question but in a different way. No, she didn't think they were followed that night. No, she'd told no one else where they were going.

"To the best of your knowledge," he said, looking up narrow-eyed from where he'd been taking notes, "did you or your friends have any enemies who might want to scare or harm you? For instance, I understand you broke up with your boyfriend, Jason Corbett, recently. Though he has an alibi, you never know that he didn't send or hire someone."

She just stared at him. *Mamm* was right, this man had been checking into her past. And he'd had three days to interview everyone else.

"He wouldn't do that," she insisted. "We really weren't that serious to start with, a friend of a friend kind of thing, and breaking up was a mutual decision."

"Okay, that fits what he told me. It's ironic, isn't it, that Seth Lantz, your other former boyfriend, came along just after the shooting in time to find and help you? And I understand your breakup with him was not a mutual decision."

Hannah pushed the button that raised the top of her bed higher. She was fairly tall for an Amish woman and wanted to stand up to this man's height and rigid posture, but in bed like this she felt at such a disadvantage.

"Thank heavens, Seth came along!" she said, a bit too loudly. She lowered her voice. "Although I managed to call 9-1-1, he saved Tiffany and me, even if it was too late for Kevin. And he tried to spot the shooter, though he must have gone by then."

"He or she or they. It's best not to assume or construe. But we can surmise the shooter went back into the woods above the graveyard, then down to wherever a vehicle or buggy was hidden. Unless the shooter lived close enough to walk home."

Buggy? Walk home? She'd never considered it could be someone Amish, but she and her friends had been disturbing the peace, desecrating hallowed ground. She had no doubt that Seth must have been upset by that.

"We were in the dark, so he, she or they must have been a good shot."

"You didn't glimpse any movement from higher on the hill, did you? I realize the music kept all of you from hearing anything until the shots."

"You know," she said as the memory came back to her, "I did glance up the hill, just to calm myself because I was upset that Tiffany and then Kevin were dancing on the graves. But no, I saw nothing, no one."

"And then Seth rode up—though not on a white horse—from the other direction."

He had interviewed Seth, hadn't he? "No. You must know he was in a buggy. And Blaze, his horse, is chestnut-colored with a white mark only on her face and chest."

Something she'd said amused him, but she wasn't sure what. Had he been trying to trap her in something? Agent Armstrong—no way was she going to call him Lincoln or Linc—leaned closer and lowered his voice, too.

"Considering your and Seth's past, I'm sure he hurt you more than you did him when you broke up, Hannah, but I have to examine all possibilities, even that an apparent rescuer was the perpetrator."

She sniffed and shook her head.

"It happens," he went on. "Seth was out with a hunting rifle, but our forensics have shown that wasn't the weapon involved. Still, I can tell from talking to him that he is upset that you 'jumped the fence,' as he put it, and hung out with the goths. He's still upset with you about that."

She didn't like the direction this was going, but it scared her even more how much she wanted to defend Seth. She blurted, "Then you'd better put about everyone in the Amish church under suspicion, Agent Armstrong! They were all pretty upset when the bishop's daughter left, though of course we—they—are all pacifists and would never shoot someone!"

"But that was a pretty big stretch for an Amish girl, wasn't it? Not only leaving the only life you'd ever known, but going goth?"

"That's just the group of friends I fell in with when I went to my 'Cleveland office,' to try to start a singing career."

His eyes seemed to light, and the corner of his mouth twitched as if he would either grimace or smile at her subtle jab. "I like backbone in a witness and a victim," he said, standing. "Good move to call 9-1-1, and good job giving all that information when you were shot and your friends were bleeding around you. I think you're being released to go home tomorrow, Hannah, so I'll see you then, because I want you to walk me through exactly what happened at the crime scene. It's been secured, photographed, sketched and searched. I've questioned your remaining three goth friends, but I think your visiting the site with me would be invaluable. I take it I can find you at your parents' place."

It was a statement, not a question. Did he imply she

was being confined there at least until she returned to the scene of the crime with him?

"If they'll take me in for a while, yes, then I—"

"Take you in?" *Mamm* said as she peered around Agent Armstrong's shoulder. "It's your home. You are coming home, *ya*, at least till your wrist is better. Then we can all discuss what comes later."

"Yes," Hannah said as tears she could not stem blurred her view. "Agent Armstrong, I'll be there—at my parents' home."

He tapped the edge of her mattress twice as if she were being dismissed, at least for now. "Thank you for your time and help, and thank you, Mrs. Esh," he said with a nod *Mamm*'s way as she stepped to the side of the bed. "And thank you and Bishop Esh for feeding me so well yesterday."

This government officer and law-enforcing *ausländer* had eaten at her house—that is, at her parents' house—when she hadn't been inside for years? It made her homesick all over again.

It was strange, Hannah thought as Agent Armstrong left the room, to have to deal with a man who knew things you didn't and, even though you were both an eyewitness and a victim and he was going to help, who made you feel like you were under surveillance, too.

It was a couple of hours after dark that night when Sheriff Jack Freeman pulled into his driveway. Hearing an engine, Ray-Lynn Logan went to the kitchen window over the sink and cracked the curtains to make sure the headlights slashing through the night were his. Yes, his black sheriff's cruiser with the gold logo on the side. He no doubt saw her van in the driveway. They had keys to each other's places now. She wondered if he could possibly be as excited as she was each time they were together, but he was probably exhausted investigating the graveyard shooting and working with that hard-driving FBI guy from Cleveland.

Using the window glass for a mirror, she quickly checked her appearance. Pretty good for a woman who was almost fifty, she thought. She knew Jack liked her full breasts and hips, even though he'd admitted he was a "leg man."

Ray-Lynn had seen little of Jack since the shootings three days ago, and just when things were really getting comfortable between them. So she'd left the restaurant the minute it closed tonight to bring them a meat loaf dinner to share—brought him his favorite raisin cream pie, too. She was getting familiar with his kitchen and this spacious brick ranch house, though she didn't like the fact he'd lived here and decorated it with his ex-wife. Besides, it was two miles east of town, and there was a woodlot right out back, when some idiot was shooting people from trees in the dark. Maybe, she tried to tell herself, the shooting had been just some Halloween prank, an aberration, a one-night freak thing, and goths sure looked like freaks. Dealing with the Plain People was one thing, but no way did she want strange outsiders around her adopted town.

Ray-Lynn met Jack at his own back door with a big hug he returned so hard it made her toes curl. A Southern girl by birth, she'd almost chucked all the good manners her mother ever taught her to finally get this man to notice her as more than the source of good country cooking at her restaurant in town. Jack was divorced and had been sort of a loner, married only to his job since his wife had left him to move somewhere out west several years ago. He'd admitted that his ex was the only woman he'd loved, and he'd been heartbroken when she said she was done with him and rural, small-town living. But Jack had finally added, "That is, she was the only one I ever wanted before I fell in love with you, Ray-Lynn."

Jack, who was just a year older, stood tall and ramrod-straight, maybe a leftover from his days as a marine. His auburn hair had a touch of gray at the temples, but with all that had gone on around here lately, he'd kidded her that he'd be all silver-headed soon. He'd bailed her out of a financial crisis earlier this year by investing in half of her restaurant in town, though he sure had more than fifty-percent of her heart. She loved it that they were partners in business, and she longed to be partners in life, too.

"Something smells good, but you smell better, honey," he said, closing and locking the door behind him, then burying his face in her hair before giving her a long, openmouthed kiss that made her want to forget supper. She held tight to his leather jacket. He smelled of crisp autumn air and, as ever, both of safety and sexiness.

When they came up for a breath, she asked, "Progress here for sure, but any progress on the graveyard case?"

"Luckily, forensics cleared Seth Lantz, or at least the rifle he had in his buggy that night. Witnesses have been interviewed by either Armstrong or me—in some cases by both of us. Both wounded women are being released tomorrow, and Hannah Esh is coming home, at least for a while, so—as ever—the Amish see a blessing even in a tragedy."

He hung his jacket, gun belt and hat on pegs by the back door, then, with a playful pat on her rear, went to use the bathroom. All dreamy-eyed—she had to admit, that's what this man, in or out of uniform, did to her—Ray-Lynn jumped when she accidentally touched the hot pan she was warming the meat loaf in as she took it out of the oven. She yanked back about as fast as she had when she'd come across an old photo of Jack and his ex while she was looking for candlesticks today. It had been shoved, facedown, under some candles and matchbooks in an end table drawer.

As she ran cold water over her burn, she pictured their faces in the photo again, though it was the last thing she wanted in her head right now. They'd both looked so young and happy. Lillian Freeman was a pretty blonde, big-busted but not fat. Hopefully, Jack preferred Ray-Lynn's real red hair to that bleached blond, but sometimes men couldn't see through that and a blonde was a blonde. In the pic, they were sitting on a fence somewhere, grinning like all get-out, him in his marine uniform, her flaunting great legs in shorts and her breasts in a skimpy top.

"Smells like meat loaf!" Jack said when he came back in. "You okay, honey?" he asked when he saw her holding her finger under running water.

"Just a little burn."

He came over and hugged her from behind. "I'm starved, but willing to kiss it—kiss you—to make it better."

"And who said the way to a man's heart is only through his stomach?" She turned in his arms to face him as he pressed her against the sink and kissed her again. They both ignored the running water, though they could have used a bit of a cold shower right now, she thought as she kissed him back hard again and slid her hands, burn or not, in the back pockets of his pants.

She was surprised when he broke their embrace, leaning past her closer to the window over the sink. He cracked the curtains and squinted out into the November night. Her head cleared. She heard something outside, too.

"Bad timing," he said. "Headlights from someone pulling in. Hope it's not the G-man, but someone might be in trouble. Don't recognize the car."

"If they come to the back door," she said, straightening her blouse and smoothing her hair, "it must be someone who knows you."

To her dismay, he strapped his gun belt back on as someone knocked hard on the back door. He motioned for Ray-Lynn to step out of the kitchen, and she did, hovering in the hall where she could see the back door in the hall mirror.

As Jack opened the door and a blast of cold air rolled in, Ray-Lynn gasped and pressed both hands over her mouth to stifle a shriek. Though she'd never met the woman, she recognized her image in the mirror the minute Jack opened the door. "Lily?" he asked, sounding shocked, but excited, as well. "Lily!"

"Jackman!" his former wife cried. "I've come home! I've missed you so much, baby, but I was scared to call ahead in case you said not to come!"

Lillian Freeman—if that was still her name after four years away—threw her arms around Jack's neck as he took a step back in surprise, then hugged her as she burst into tears. Ray-Lynn fled into the living room, grabbed her jacket and purse and cried, too, all the way to her car.

She fumbled with the key in the ignition and backed down the driveway before remembering to turn her headlights on. Jack ran out and shouted something to her, but she spun her wheels and roared off into the dark night.

4

HANNAH WAKENED TO THE MUTED *THUD-THUD*
of *Mamm*'s hand-operated pressing machine that put
the creases in the stiff, white prayer *kapps* she made
in the old sunroom at the rear of the house, a familiar
sound that always carried up the back wall. She opened
her eyes, then closed them again. It was bad enough to
have to look at the wrapped gauze and taped bandage
on her left wrist and the array of pills on the bedside
table but worse to feel she was in a time warp. Except
for moving her twin bed to the guest room and storing
some wedding supplies here, Naomi hadn't changed
much of their shared back-corner bedroom after Hannah had left.

From the top of the familiar maple dresser, Hannah's bonneted childhood doll seemed to stare at her
for all the things she'd done wrong, despite being eye-
less and faceless. Strange to have the feeling she was
being watched in this private, second-story bedroom
in the middle of open fields.

Despite her pain pills, she hadn't slept well because
she'd heard some sort of unfamiliar flapping, like bird

wings, from time to time. Maybe it was a loose shingle on the roof in the brisk wind that had now calmed a bit. If Seth was working up on the roof today, she hoped he'd be careful. Amish men didn't use safety harnesses, for whatever happened was God's will, one thing she'd learned to question during her days in the world. After all, sometimes people's injuries were their own stupid fault.

But one huge change in this spot of her happy childhood and *rumspringa* years were the signs of Naomi's coming wedding adorning the room: a treadle sewing machine with a nearly completed, sky-blue wedding dress, bolts of burgundy material for her four attendants' dresses, boxes of favors and inscribed napkins stacked in the corner by the closet. The talk at supper last night had been all about the Esh-Troyer marriage. Well, of course, Hannah could see why. It wasn't just to avoid talking about the mess she'd made of her life. Amish weddings were planned and prepared quickly after the announcement in church of the betrothal. With so many invited, lots of people pitched in, preparing to feed nearly four hundred guests at a wedding feast with a traditional, home-cooked meal.

In the emotion of her reunion with Naomi yesterday—Hannah knew her younger sister had looked up to her just as she had to her older, now-married sisters, Ida and Ruth—she had promised not only to attend the wedding but to help with it. Nothing like facing the entire Amish community she'd let down. At least she had until a week from today to prepare herself for that.

Hannah groaned, sat up carefully and gasped to see a small, round face staring up at her over the side of the bed. So that's why she felt she was being watched.

It was a darling little Amish doll—a living one, with a pert mouth and wide, azure eyes.

"Where Naomi?" the child asked in their German dialect. Then Hannah knew who it was. Not the niece whose birth she'd missed while she was gone, but Seth and Lena's little daughter, Marlena, now around two and a half years old.

"I'm Hannah," she told the child, and her voice broke. Like an idiot, she blinked back tears. The little girl resembled Seth more than Lena. "I—I can help you find Naomi."

"*Daadi* go up," Marlena said, pointing at the ceiling or, more likely, the roof since Seth was reroofing the house, though she hadn't heard one hammer or nail when it must be midmorning. "*Mamm* go up, too," Marlena added.

"Oh, there you are!" Naomi cried, rushing into the room and scooping up the child. "She was playing in the hall when I went to use the bathroom."

"Naomi," Hannah said as she swung her feet carefully to the floor, "you do not have to move out of your room for me, especially not with all you have going on here."

"It was our room for years and still is!" Naomi insisted. "And now it can be yours, because after next Thursday, we'll be living with Josh's folks for a while. I'm fine in Ida and Ruth's old room."

"*Daadi* go up," Marlena said again, pointing. "Up to the sky." The child squirmed to be put down, toddled to the back window facing the barn and craned her neck to peer skyward.

"I'll have to tell Seth you're up, and he can pound away on the new shingles now," Naomi said. "He didn't want to wake you, so he's helping *Daad* stack firewood. As for this little one, she thinks her *daadi* goes up on the roof looking for her *mamm,* who is in heaven."

"Oh, that's what she meant. But Seth or anyone else does not have to work around me."

"You know it's our way, whether you're a guest or family, and you're both," Naomi said with a nod. Taking Marlena's hand, she started from the room. "Oh," she said, turning back, "someone else is waiting for you to get up. Special Agent Armstrong will be here right after noon meal to take you to the graveyard to walk through…through what happened. Sorry, but that's what he said when he came by earlier. Give me a shout if you need help getting dressed," she added, and pointed toward the chair in front of the sewing machine as they left the room.

Hannah gasped. Now she saw why Naomi's wedding dress was only partly done. It was not just because they were letting Hannah sleep in this morning. She saw, laid out over the chair back and arranged on its seat, a new Amish dress in emerald-green, a good color for a *maidal;* black undergarments, no bra of course, which would take some getting used to again; a new pair of white, laced walking shoes like the women wore; a new cape—no, it was one of her old ones—and a new black bonnet. But no prayer *kapp* for her red-dyed, short-cut head, the sign of a dedicated Amish woman. All this kindness and generosity—but the lack of that precious *kapp*—spoke louder than Naomi's words.

Tears blurring her vision, Hannah walked slowly to the small oval mirror they kept turned to the wall unless it was absolutely needed. After all, it was prideful to preen and to change the appearance God gave to each of His children. The true reason photographs of Amish faces were forbidden was that it could lead to individualism and conceit in one's appearance, even though it also defied the Biblical warning "Thou shalt make no graven images."

Hannah turned the mirror outward and jolted as her image stared back. Scarlet hair, though it now lay flat and looked softer after *Mamm* had washed and brushed it in the hospital. A face plain and naked without the dramatic mascara and black lipstick. Just Hannah Esh's Amish face again, only one now lined with pain, perhaps fear, eyes narrowed, full lips pressed together, and the lower one trembling. She realized she was shaking all over and not just because she'd risen from a warm bed.

Was she scared to be home? Afraid of having to face everyone, especially Seth, again?

She thrust out her lower lip in defiance and walked to the clothing. One-handed, she reached for it to get dressed. It was only then she noticed that the screen to the side window behind the sewing machine was cleanly slit along its edge. Maybe that was what she'd heard flapping last night. But it was so unlike her *daad* to leave something not repaired. She leaned closer and gasped. Long, dark marks on the sill inside of the screen made it look like some sharp object had tried to pry the window itself open.

"You didn't lean a ladder at the driveway side of the house, even to carry the shingles up, did you?" Bishop Esh asked Seth as he sat at the far end of the dinner table from Hannah, with Marlena in a high chair beside him. Seth was pleased to see Hannah at the table and dressed Amish, though she hadn't covered her head. As ever, she seemed for him some sort of magnet and he the compass needle pulled to her true north.

He had to focus on the bishop's words. "No," Seth answered. "I've kept the ladder between the flower beds in back, near where the shingles were unloaded. Since the peak of the roof is on the driveway side, my ladder wouldn't reach it. Is there a problem?"

"Yes, one we will have to run by Agent Armstrong, that's for sure," the bishop said, frowning.

Naomi, sitting on the other side of Marlena's high chair, put in, "Someone cut the screen in the side window to my bedroom—now Hannah's—and it wasn't my Josh, that's sure. He wouldn't do that, even if the ladder marks were under the cut window. And someone tried to pry it open, too, but it sure wasn't Josh and me!"

"We know that, Naomi," Mrs. Esh said, and reached over to pat her youngest daughter's hand. "You've always done things on the straight and narrow, *ya,* we know that."

Seth saw Hannah's cheeks color, as if that was a reflection on her, maybe on him, as well. Sure, Hannah used to slip out to meet him once in a while after the house went dark but not through a sliced window screen. Hannah and her friend Sarah, next farm over, had sneaked out in their *rumspringa* years to listen to the radio and fool around. But this news upset him, and not because he'd been indirectly asked if that ladder and the cut screen was his doing. If it wasn't him, who was it? Could Josh have done it and not told Naomi?

Once Linc Armstrong found out about it, he'd probably question anyone within miles who had a ladder.

"Could someone have been trying to break in?" Seth asked, his fork halfway to his mouth. He hadn't so much as tasted the chicken on biscuits yet, since he'd been making sure Marlena ate well.

"Naomi's sure the window wasn't that way yesterday," the bishop said. "It could be those nosy reporters with their cameras, not taking no for an answer."

Or it could be something worse, Seth almost said. That thought hung in the air while people went back to eating. Finally, Hannah spoke.

"I don't want Agent Armstrong trampling all over my private life, but he's going to have to take a look at the window and the ladder marks."

"Right," Seth put in. "One more thing. He asked me to go with you to the graveyard this afternoon. Not to hear what you tell him, but to pick up the story where I came in. To talk to us about the crime scene."

He said no more and tucked into Mrs. Esh's delicious dinner, though he hardly felt hungry anymore. He'd bet a new barn that part of the reason Agent Armstrong wanted him to go along was so that he could see how he and Hannah would act when they were together. Actually, he'd like to see how they would, too.

Hannah noted how tense Seth and Agent Armstrong were around each other as they stood under her bedroom window after dinner.

"Those imprints look identical to your ladder's feet, Seth," Armstrong observed as he rose from a squat after a close examination of the imprinted soil between the bare rose canes. He'd already taken photos of the feet of the ladder, the cut screen and the scratches he called "jimmy marks" on the bedroom windowsill upstairs.

Hannah hugged her cloak tighter around herself with her good arm as she, Seth, Naomi and *Daad* watched the agent's every move. His eyes had seemed to take in everything inside and outside the Esh home, just like he tried to see inside people's heads.

"Of course," Agent Armstrong added, "whoever it was could easily have borrowed your roofing ladder, though I don't see any footprints back there but yours."

Hannah watched as the two very different men looked at each other, eye-to-eye. Neither blinked or flinched.

"It's the why that will lead us to the who," Seth said.

"Lead us? But I get your drift. Motive. Easier said than done, but I'll get to the bottom of it," Armstrong countered.

"But what I don't like," Seth went on, "and what you didn't mention is that if someone was trying to get to Hannah, he had to know what bedroom she was in, had to be some sort of insider. Bishop Esh and I checked, though I don't think you did, to be sure no other windows in the house had a random cut screen or screwdriver marks."

"Who said it was a screwdriver?"

"I— We, especially her family, just want Hannah protected," Seth insisted.

Bishop Esh put his shoulder between the two men to make them step farther apart. "I'm going to buggy into the hardware store in town," he told them, "get a new screen and bolts for both Hannah's windows and extra ones for the windows and doors downstairs. Hannah told her mother in the hospital that she could not think of anyone who was her enemy, but I know Agent Armstrong has considered that, too, Seth."

"Daad," Hannah put in, "I'm sorry to cause so much trouble again for y—"

"Ya, you have, my girl!" he said, frowning at first before he cleared his throat. Hannah jolted at his tone. Since she'd been back, she'd seen *Daad* had a bee in his bonnet over her leaving and defying him. Maybe he still resented the way her hair looked. She'd tried to just ignore and smooth over the tension between them. After all, she could hardly blame him after what she'd put him, as her father and as bishop, through. "Just be grateful," he went on in a calmer voice, "you are where you should be now, that's for sure." He shot a side glance at Seth she could not read. "You two go on now, help Agent Armstrong."

Though Hannah could tell Seth didn't want to get in the black car Agent Armstrong drove, she got in the backseat when he opened the door for her. "Watch your head," he told her, and put a hand on her hair, then leaned over her to fasten her seat belt, evidently so she wouldn't have to do it one-handed. She smelled a tart pine scent on him, and his hand touched her hip hard through her cape and skirt as he clicked the belt closed.

"You want to ride shotgun, Seth?" he asked. "You know, up front?"

"I'll ride with Hannah," he said, and walked around to sit next to her in the rear seat behind the cagelike divider that separated the front seats from the back. It was, she thought, a wide seat. Agent Armstrong was across the screen, but Seth seemed so away from her.

"Listen," Armstrong said as he drove slowly out of the Esh driveway past clothes blowing on the line in the brisk November day, "I've been calling both of you by your first names, so I'd appreciate it if you'd just call me Linc. My dad named me Lincoln for our Civil War president, Honest Abe, and that's my motto—straight talk, full disclosure. I expect that from both of you. We're working together on this, okay?"

"Fine," Hannah said only. She did want to help in any way she could, including getting along with this man. She looked at Seth's frowning profile.

"Fine with me," Seth muttered. "You going to make straight talk a policy with everyone you question, such as Josh Troyer, about whether he used my ladder last night?"

Hannah saw Armstrong's eyes dart toward Seth in the rearview mirror. "One step ahead of me, Seth. No, not with everyone, just key witnesses, and I don't figure Naomi's fiancé is one, but I've looked into him, too. The Troyers are a wealthy family, aren't they, with owning the big grain elevator and that historic grist mill? Since they offer tours of the mill, I'm not sure if they'd think publicity of a murder around here would be good or bad for business."

Hannah and Seth exchanged lightning-quick glances. This man was suspicious of everyone and considered every angle. If he thought Josh or the Troyers could be involved, anyone could be on his list.

Neither Seth nor Hannah responded. Linc Armstrong's eyes—like those of the eagle on his [thought]—glanced at them in the rear[view mirror] now and then. Could her feeling of being [watched] be a reaction to his FBI surveillance and suspicious nature, no matter how friendly he seemed on the surface? She felt so torn about him, both guarded yet grateful.

When he pulled the car to a stop, almost exactly where her friends had parked at the graveyard on Halloween night, Linc said, "Seth, I'll ask you to stay put until I've had Hannah walk me through things, then I'll have you approach and enter the grounds just as you did that night."

If "stay put" meant stay in the car, Seth ignored that order. He got out and stood near the fence, festooned with fluttering yellow plastic tape with the big, black words repeated over and over: Police Crime Scene Do Not Enter Police Crime Scene Do Not Enter... It was a good thing, she thought, that no one in the church had died right now. Her thoughts went to Kevin and Tiffany, to her other worldly friends who had not been hit by bullets that night. She wanted to write letters to their families. She couldn't call, because Linc had confiscated her phone for now; a phone she'd need to give up, if she stayed here....

Feeling Seth's gaze burning into her back from where he stood at the fence, she ducked under the tape Linc lifted for her, and they went into the graveyard.

"I'm sorry I didn't get here sooner," Jack told Ray-Lynn as he pulled her into the inside back entry to the restaurant, despite the fact she'd just seated a party of six during the lunch rush. "I ran into complications."

"I guess you did. If she's come back to haunt you, she missed Halloween."

"I didn't mean her. Something about the graveyard case with Agent Armstrong. Ray-Lynn, why didn't you answer your phone last night after you drove away? Or come to the door of your house when I knocked on it? Considering how you ran out, I didn't want to just use my key—which I'd left at my house, anyway."

"Where did she stay last night?"

"Not with me. I got her settled in at Amanda Stutzman's B and B."

"Oh, great! Just great. So she's living within walking distance of my house! You told me once she worked as a hostess in this restaurant. Don't you dare ask me to give her a job here, I don't care if you do own fifty percent of it now! You said she used her salary to help pay for your house and the decor, so I supposed you're thinking she still owns half of that. When she took off, you never paid her back because she didn't want your money, right? Bet she thinks that house is still half hers and you're all hers, because it kind of looked that way last night!"

"Would you calm down? I'll work it out. I just didn't want you to be upset."

"I'm not upset. I'm way beyond that."

"I want us to talk this out, but I've got obligations right now, you know that, and you've always understood that. You gotta trust me on this."

"I do—to help solve the graveyard shootings. The other…" She shrugged and fought to keep from bursting into tears. "I've got people waiting, Jack, and you do, too. Duty calls, as they say. Does she—does she intend to stay?"

He shrugged, then nodded. "So she says. Got fed up with a shallow life in Vegas, she said, and—"

"Las Vegas? She's been in Las Vegas and now wants to come back to Homestead, Ohio, in Amish country?

Jack, she may look like a million bucks, but she's probably just broke or running from something!"

"From mistakes, she says."

"Did you tell her about us?"

"Of course I did. Told her not to apply for a job here or even to come in, but she said it's a free country."

Ray-Lynn slapped the extra menus she still held to her chest down on the pile of cartons. "You can't handle her, can you? But you want to, don't you—handle her, real up close and personal? You never got over her, did you?"

"Damn it, Ray-Lynn, just give me some time!"

"Oh, I will. Lots. Now, I've got a restaurant to run and a life to live, so excuse me," she said, and grabbed the menus. She darted past him back into the restaurant proper, put the stack of menus by the cash register and went into the ladies' room, the two stalls of which were blessedly empty.

With stiff arms, she steadied herself against the washbasin, afraid to look at herself in the mirror. She wanted to throw things, to break the mirror, just shatter it and scream. But she ran cold water and dabbed it under her eyes, then went back out and stood near the front door with a smile pasted on her face. The sign over the front door, the one she'd been so proud of, that her very own Amish artist, Sarah Kauffman, had painted so beautifully, really riled her now: Southern Hospitality and Amish Cooking—Y'all Come Back, *Danki.*

No way in all of God's creation could she be glad Lily Freeman had come back.

5

"IS THIS PRETTY MUCH THE PATH THE FIVE OF you took that night?" Linc asked as they walked from the gate up the hill into the heart of the graveyard.

"Yes," Hannah told him. "I don't think we walked in single file, though."

"I believe these are your grandparents buried here," he said, indicating two of the many identical stones laid out in neat rows.

"Yes. You have cased the place, as they say," she said, trying to keep her voice steady. Again, it amazed her how much background work this man had done into her life. Did he think she was somehow the key to what had happened? Surely no one had meant to shoot her that night, but she couldn't accept that someone had been after the others, either. It must have been a random act—except for that slit screen. And was the policeman assigned to guard her hospital room just to keep reporters away? *Daad* had fended the media off, so was the policeman to protect her from someone else?

Linc interrupted her agonizing. "Forensic specialists have gone extensively over this site and that upland woodlot where the shooter stood. So that night you had your friends put down the blanket, the boom box, the food and wine on Lena Lantz's grave, right?"

"No! No, I wouldn't do that. As you said, you shouldn't construe things. That was just chance that Kevin and Mike stopped at her grave, because they knew nothing about Lena or Seth, either. I obviously hadn't been here for her burial, so I was upset when I saw we were near her tombstone. I wanted them to move away, but I didn't want to have to explain why, so I didn't say anything."

Studying her as she spoke, he nodded. She gasped as they reached Lena's grave. Not only was the tombstone a mess but white paint outlined the shape of Kevin's body on the grass. She noted he had fallen sideways over the lower part of Lena's grave. Nearby, small yellow circles were sprayed around what looked to be blood spots.

"Tiffany's blood and yours," he said. "We had it tested. You're type AB, if you ever need to know."

Linc firmly took the elbow of her good arm to steady her. Each time he touched her, even briefly—but especially when he assessed her with that hard stare— she felt heat. No one but Seth had ever affected her that way.

Hannah took a good look at what was left of Lena's tombstone, which, they'd said, had kept her from sustaining a much worse wound when the bullet ricocheted. The rectangular stone was deeply cracked, one corner shattered. One or more bullets had blasted away the word *Lantz* and her death date, so it read only *Lena* and her birth year.

"He— Seth, I mean," she said, "is going to replace it when you let him, when you clear away the police tape."

"So he said. That tombstone definitely saved your wrist, pins in it or not, and it may have saved your life. The shooter took Kevin down in one head shot, and I suspect was pretty skilled, so you and Tiffany were just plain lucky."

"Just plain blessed," she corrected him, then realized how Amish that sounded. "I'm grateful Mike and Liz weren't hit at all. The shooter must have been interrupted or— I don't know. I—I see you have a gun, though your jacket hides it a bit."

He turned her toward him and looked her full in the face. "Affirmative—yes. You're very observant, very smart, Hannah. But this small semiautomatic handgun in my hip holster—I try to especially keep it out of sight among your people—is a far cry from what someone shot you with. That was a high-velocity—that's a high-speed—rifle, probably with a night-vision scope. We've retrieved and tested the bullets, lethal for hunting big game and, obviously, for a person. And I promise you I'm going to find out whether it was a random act, an anti-Amish or anti-goth hate crime, or whether it was some sort of hit with a specific target. Okay, now talk me through what happened when all of you settled here."

She did her best, though she'd done the same when he'd interviewed her in the hospital. Was he looking for discrepancies in what she said? As she told him about Tiffany's wound and screams, Kevin's scarlet bloom of blood, he interrupted for the first time.

"So the two of them were sort of dancing around

and pretending to dig at Lena Lantz's grave with Tiffany's closed parasol when they were shot?"

The dreadful scene she'd been reliving fled. Her head cleared. She simply nodded. Did he think Seth had seen them and been angry? She darted a look down the hill at her former fiancé. He was pacing, not looking up at them, but frustration and anger emanated from the tilt of his head, his hard strides and clenched fists. Yes, she thought, Seth as she once knew him was capable of passion, of sudden swerves from self-control. He might be Amish, but he was only human! She was surprised to realize that her time away from him had somewhat muted her anger toward him.

Afraid Linc would think she was somehow suspicious of Seth—and upset at how much she wanted to protect him—she dragged her gaze from Seth back to Linc's gray-eyed, piercing stare. But he did not pursue what he must be thinking and surprised her by changing the subject.

"One more quick thing before we ask Seth to join us in this reenactment. Can you give me any idea of how long it was between when Tiffany and Kevin went down and Seth arrived to help? Think about the time frame of when you crawled to your purse to get your cell, made the call, talked to the 9-1-1 operator, then he appeared."

"I—I don't know. Time was…strange. Extended, I think. I was in pain, I saw all that blood on them, then on me—"

"Ten minutes? Five?" he probed.

"I'd say two minutes, max, until I made the call, but then don't you have the rest of the timing from the 9-1-1 records?"

He blinked. Not, she realized, because he hadn't thought of that, but because he hadn't thought she would. She'd read his mind, hadn't she?

"I'm not trying to protect Seth in this," she insisted, even as she realized that was a lie. "He couldn't have done the shooting up in those trees, with a gun that didn't match your bullet tests—"

"Forensics," he said, but she ignored him and plunged on.

"And then he didn't have time to run around, down the hill and drive up in his buggy to help. Give that up, Special Agent Armstrong."

"I said before, I admire your backbone, Hannah. You're a fascinating blend of this world and the one you've lived in these past few years—my world. But my world includes solving crimes, and I do what I have to at any cost."

"Then I'll get Seth," she said.

"No, I will. I want him to come over the fence, just where and how he did that night. If you don't mind, lie on the ground as best you can recall where you were that night. Be right back."

Her thoughts racing, Hannah sat, then lay where she was certain she had been hit. She felt cold all over and not just from the chill wind in the shadow of this hill. How had her safe Amish life changed so much that she was a new person now, an alien back where she'd been born?

Suddenly, she longed to see her old friend Sarah Kauffman, who had gone to the world, been shunned, but planned to wed the arson investigator who had solved the barn fires. Sarah had followed her heart, not only with Nate MacKenzie but by becoming an artist who painted scenes from Amish life—with faces on the people. But Sarah was living in Columbus.

This close to the earth, near the grass of Lena's grave, Hannah could see that the edges of the replaced sod had not yet evened out or grown into the other grass. At funerals here, she'd seen the shaved-off sod the grave diggers had set aside so it could be replaced after they refilled the grave by hand. Had Linc and his investigators dug up the edges of the grass blanket over Lena's grave, looking for bullets or digging for more blood spots?

"Okay, please vault the fence just like you said!" Linc's loud voice nearby startled her, and she turned her head to see Seth, one hand on the fence with the yellow tape, clear it easily and land on his feet.

"Hannah, however it happened, I'm so glad you've come home!"

Later that afternoon, her first Amish caller was her close childhood friend Ella Lantz, Seth's sister. Ella was a year younger than Seth and Hannah, the middle child in their family of five children. They shared a hug, and, as ever, Ella smelled wonderful.

Hannah had always thought Ella looked like an angel with her white-blond hair and pale blue eyes. As a girl, she had nearly drowned in the pond at the juncture of the three farms. Sarah and Hannah had saved her and it had bonded them all closer. But from that time on, Ella had changed. She'd buried deep her daredevil streak, become timid, even rigid and judgmental of those who didn't toe the line—and that was Hannah and Sarah now, for sure.

But maybe, Hannah hoped, Ella had learned that

people make mistakes that should not only be forgiven but forgotten. Naomi had told Hannah that Ella had recently broken up with her serious come-calling friend, Eli Detweiler, because he hadn't given up alcohol after his *rumspringa* years.

"I brought you some lavender," Ella said, and held out a basket of sachets and soaps which perfumed the air. On a large lot near the Lantz farmhouse, Ella grew and harvested the fragrant herb. Then in a little workshop Seth had built for her out the back of their family's farm, she packaged her precious plants she sold locally. Each hand-lettered label read Lavender Plain Products, Homestead, Ohio.

"How thoughtful of you!" Hannah said, and inhaled deeply as Ella took a chair at the card table laid out with a half-finished family jigsaw puzzle of the Grand Canyon. "They smell delicious and look lovely," she added, admiring the printed cotton packets that made each sachet look like a small quilt square.

"Some say the scent is good for the heart," Ella said. "I mean, not to cure a damaged heart, like what happened to Lena, but to lift your mood. Oh, Hannah, it was awful that she just fell over like that in their kitchen with the baby there but Seth out on a job. Such a tragedy. But then, you've had one, too. And I...believe me, I remember how it feels to...to almost die."

"I was sorry to hear about you and Eli parting, but at least it was before you got betrothed or married."

"I just couldn't take a chance on him, trust him not to drink," she said, gripping her hands in her lap. Ella's feelings and moods were always transparent. She looked instantly grieved. "Every time he said he was done with drinking, he wasn't. He looked bleary-eyed and was always tired, too, cutting back his work hours. I could smell it on him day or night. I just— I could not trust him to be the father of my children. I guess all of us—you, Sarah and I—had disappointments with men. Though Sarah's gone the wrong way with a worldly man after that mess with Jacob, I'll find someone to build a life with here, I know I will!"

"Meanwhile, you have a sweet future!" Hannah said, forcing a smile and picking up a cotton-wrapped and ribboned bar of soap to inhale the scent. Ella didn't make the soap at home but provided the dried leaves and flowers for it, then wrapped the bars herself.

"Both bed-and-breakfasts in town use my products now as well as the Amish gift shops and Mrs. Logan's restaurant, so that gets me more business. I just came from Mrs. Stutzman's B and B, and she said to tell you that if you want a job you could do one-handed, she needs a half-time housekeeper—dusting, laundry, ironing. She does the cooking and makes the beds. Her half-time girl just quit."

"People have been so kind to offer jobs. They must know it's hard for me to have come home like this."

"I know it, too," Ella said, and reached out to lightly grasp Hannah's good wrist. "At the B and B, you wouldn't have to face a lot of our people yet, since Amanda Stutzman and her husband are Mennonite and their guests are *ausländers*. Oh, and guess who just moved in there for a spell?"

"Not the FBI agent?"

"No. Can you see him with all those ruffled curtains and quilts and teatime? Sheriff Freeman's wife— former wife, like the moderns say—is back in town. I met her there when I delivered the new sachets and soaps I arrange in each room. She's pretty but wears a lot of makeup. She says she's here to stay. I think she's come home, like you."

Hannah remembered how much Ella loved to gossip, almost as much as her best friend, Naomi. Ella was to be one of Naomi's attendants, or sidesitters, in the coming wedding. Would that be hard for her to face since she'd broken up with Eli? But Hannah kept thinking about poor Ray-Lynn Logan. It had been pretty obvious from the sheriff's visit to Hannah's hospital room that he and Ray-Lynn were getting close, and months ago Sarah had told her the same.

"Ella, that job offer sounds good to tide me over, but I don't know if I'll be staying after the investigation of the shooting is finished."

"Oh, but we want you to. Seth docs, I can tell!"

"Now don't you go playing matchmaker for us, or for Sheriff Freeman, either. But the fact that the former Mrs. Freeman is living at the Plain and Fancy means she's a five-minute walk from Ray-Lynn's house."

"That's right. But here's the thing," Ella plunged on, leaning forward and lowering her voice, although they were alone in the living room. "Lillian Freeman's been living in Las Vegas!"

She'd said those words, Hannah thought, as if the woman had just come from the very gates of hell. "But that doesn't mean she was boozing it up, gambling day and night or dancing in a chorus line," Hannah protested.

"A chorus line? Did she try to be a singer, like you? No, she was a hostess in some fancy casino restaurant, I think."

Hannah wasn't sure whether to laugh or cry. She'd

actually forgotten how much she'd learned in the outside world that she'd never known about here in the
shelter of Home Valley.

Hannah knew the November sunset would be early,
so late afternoon, when she heard Seth come into the
house to wash up and get Marlena, she decided to slip
outside. However comforting it was to be near her
family again, she felt cooped up. She'd even helped,
one-handed, with dusting, as if preparing for the job
at Amanda Stutzman's B and B she was considering
taking. She had to do something other than sit around
waiting for Linc to think of some new clue or lead.

Hannah had been racking her brain trying to come
up with the who or why of the shooting. And she'd
shed tears again, writing condolence letters to her goth
friends' families. Worst of all, if she let her thoughts
drift a bit or woke up at night, she saw the shootings
all over again in her head. Her doctor had told her she
might have such spells, like those who'd had trauma
in battle, a stress syndrome.

She swirled her cape around her shoulders, put a
bonnet on—but couldn't tie it with one hand—and
went out into the dying day. The brisk breeze perked
her up a bit, and she inhaled deeply. She needed to
get her strength back, she told herself, so she walked
back and forth along the side of the barn, admiring
the view of gently rolling fields, now bare of crops
but awaiting spring plantings. Partly screened by bare
trees, the pond at the juncture of the three farms looked
as flat gray as the sky. To the west, the newly repaired
Kauffman barn with the bright quilt square Sarah had

painted looked more distant than it really was as the sun sank lower and the hills threw deepening shadows.

Glancing northeast toward the Lantz farm, she admired Ella's little workshop and Seth's small house, neither of which had been there when she left home. She pressed her back against the sturdy barn built after the fire. Had she instinctively taken her walk here because she could see for miles? No high-velocity rifles with what Linc called night scopes could be out there now. Or was it because Seth had helped to build this barn, big and strong?

"You shouldn't be out here in the open, Hannah."

She jumped and her heartbeat kicked up at the voice behind her, as if her thoughts had summoned him.

She turned to face Seth with Marlena in his arms.

"Because I'm in the open for miles around, I feel safe. I refuse to be a prisoner."

"I was up on a roof all afternoon. Someone else could be, too—on one of these roofs, hidden behind a tree, even hunkered down on the ground in camouflage hunting gear. You have no idea the range of some rifles today."

A shiver snaked down her backbone and she pressed tighter to the barn. "I will not just hide. I'm fine, just fine!" Realizing she sounded strident, she stood straight and said in a calmer voice, "I've been waiting for a moment to thank you for all you did that night. I know my family has expressed their gratitude, but Tiffany and I might have died, too, without your help."

"God's will that I came along to help in time—and that it was you. Even through your friend's screaming and your pain, I knew it was your voice. Talking, singing, even shouting, your voice has always been beautiful to me."

She gaped at him, eyes wide, mouth open before she caught herself and, not trusting that voice, nodded. Marlena fidgeted in his arms and sneezed. He cleared his throat.

"That's all I had to say," she whispered.

"It means a lot to me. Can I talk to you a minute before I head home? But not out here, where Marlena might catch cold. Can we step into the barn? I have my buggy there."

She was afraid of the rush of feelings that overwhelmed her near this man, memories, yes, but too strong a reaction to him even now. Distrust, dislike for what he'd done to her, but also raw need, far different from the curiosity she felt about Linc Armstrong. Not moving to follow him at first, she asked, "Do we really have anything but the shooting—which we've been over backward and forward with Linc Armstrong—to talk about?"

"I want to show you—you, not him—something I found stuck or caught in the widow with the slit screen late this afternoon. He didn't climb a ladder to look at your window from the outside so I did."

"Which means now your footprints are probably where you said they weren't!"

"We're both starting to think like him, aren't we?"

"But what did you find?" she asked, following him around the corner of the barn, not that she wanted to feel even more alone with him, but she understood about Marlena. If she had a little girl like that, especially if she was rearing her alone, she'd be so overprotective that she'd be as uptight as Ella.

He went to his buggy, not the two-seat courting one Hannah was picturing. Of course he'd have a family-size one now. He put Marlena on the front seat, where she sat primly, while he reached in past her and brought out what looked to be a big chicken feather, until Hannah noted its strange black-brown markings in the light from the open barn doors.

"That was stuck in my bedroom window?"

He nodded. "So you couldn't see it from inside, or almost from outside, either. Wedged lengthwise with the side of the quill and the outer edge of the feather holding it."

"So, wedged there carefully, intentionally, by someone who managed to open the window itself at least a crack."

"I'd say so. You can see I damaged it a little, pulling it out. If I wouldn't have been nearly on top of it, I never would have seen it, either."

"It's a big one. From…"

"From an eagle, I think. A wing pinion."

"An eagle? Like the American bald eagle?" she said, picturing the eagle with arrows in its talons on Linc's FBI badge.

"I think they're endangered and government-protected. But that kind of eagle is also sacred to Native Americans. I heard the eagle and the panther were special animals to the historic Indian tribe that once lived around here."

Her good hand on her hip, she demanded, "Indian tribe? From long ago? You heard that where?"

"At your father's request, my *daad*'s been reading up on Iroquois and Erie Indian history because of tribal rights disputes to some lands around here—some of our land. We've got to be prepared if there's a lawsuit or more bad publicity. It's all come to a boil since you've been gone. John Arrowroot, their local spokesman, is on a mission about getting Indian land back from people in this valley."

"I remember him. He's a retired lawyer, isn't he? He'd always show up at our auctions or fundraisers, stalking around and looking grim. I used to be scared of him when I was little."

"That's him. He's been a lot louder about it lately, giving interviews in the Cleveland and Columbus newspapers. He has an eagle feather like this one painted on the picture window of his house, like a talisman or a warning. I've only seen it once when I was hunting with my *daad,* and we wandered onto his isolated piece of land. I saw him last in the butcher shop outside of town, in an argument with Harlan Kenton, who owns the place."

"I know where that is. Harlan's the brother of Amanda Stutzman, who runs the Plain and Fancy B and B. Ella says she's offered me a job, which I'm thinking of taking."

"If you do, I'll buggy you there and back, or if I'm working away, get someone else to. You shouldn't be out alone."

"As soon as Naomi's married, she's giving me my old horse and buggy back. By then, maybe all this will be over. By the way, the Plain and Fancy is where Sheriff Freeman's ex-wife is staying."

"Sheriff Freeman's ex-wife is back in town? But the thing is, I've been trying to decide whether to get the sheriff or our mutual friend Linc in on this feather clue or not. I don't want to falsely accuse Arrowroot or get him stirred up again over Indian rights to our land. But this feather says he needs a closer look."

"That's pretty flimsy evidence. Maybe we could talk to him about something else, just psych him out."

"I like the sound of that 'we,' if it doesn't include Agent Armstrong. But no, I don't want you around Arrowroot. Listen. There's more. That day in Harlan Kenton's butcher shop, before their argument, I heard Arrowroot say the large mound—mound, not hill—with the Amish graveyard on it had once been holy land his people used for sacrifices."

"Human sacrifices? Did they bury people there, too?"

"I don't know. But I'm going to find out."

6

THE NEXT MORNING, SETH DROPPED MARLENA off at the Eshes and told Mrs. Esh he'd be back to continue reroofing in about an hour, but he didn't tell her why. He'd decided to talk to John Arrowroot without tipping him off by questioning or accusing him about the feather, let alone about shooting people in the cemetery.

After Seth had questioned his *daad* last night about what he knew of Arrowroot's Erie Indian tribe, he'd come up with a few facts that might point to him as a suspect. Which tribe Arrowroot claimed was a bit confusing as the Erie had supposedly been wiped out years ago by their enemy, the Iroquois. But many of the Seneca tribe were descended from Erie blood, as Arrowroot claimed to be.

The Erie had been farmers and hunters who once flourished in this area, living in small groups. That, Seth thought, sounded like his own people. But the tribe were fierce warriors, known for their skill with poisoned arrows.

So, Seth told himself, Arrowroot deserved watching, not only because he wanted Amish land returned to Seneca-Erie tribal members, but because he could have been the cemetery shooter, especially if that hill had once been sacred to his tribe. Maybe he'd been there for some special, secret ceremony and thought Amish or goth intruders were defiling it. If Seth picked up any proof, he'd tell the sheriff or Linc Armstrong. Right now, he didn't need the FBI Goliath jumping in with both feet and stirring up this man against the Amish again. If Seth could prove Kevin Pryor's killer was John Arrowroot, that would get him out of the way for good.

Seth buggied down the main street of Homestead, getting caught at the single traffic light. He'd seen the Dutch Farm Table Restaurant was busy already. Though he'd fixed oatmeal for Marlena and himself this morning, his stomach rumbled. No way he wanted her hooked on those sugary, boxed cereals just because they were easy to serve.

He turned down Fish Creek Road, passing the Rod 'n' Gun shop, which was attached to its owner's one-floor house. The shop was run by Elaine Carson, a former U.S. army officer who bled, as she put it, "red, white and blue." A big American flag flapped in front of her store with a shooting range out back. Linc had told Seth he'd asked to obtain her list of customers who'd purchased high-velocity rifles in the past two years, but since both Amish and English around here hunted in droves, he'd given up on that tactic.

Seth shook his head as he passed by. His people were grateful for the country that was their home, but too much patriotism spelled idolatry to them. Elaine Carson was way over the line on that, even though

Amish kids loved the fireworks she shot off every Fourth of July. Elaine, he'd heard, thought the Amish, who didn't vote or serve in the armed forces, were ungrateful to the U.S. of A., though she sure tolerated their business.

Seth turned Blaze onto Valley View Road several miles southeast of town and went up and down two hills until he reached the narrow, unpaved road that led to Arrowroot's property, hidden in trees on a hill. That day he and his father had found themselves hunting near the man's house, they'd gone up to the door and asked for permission to be on his property. It was a friendly, common question, since hunters often traveled from farm to farm with, "Mind if we hunt here a bit?" The answer was always "Sure, don't mind a bit."

"Yes, actually, I do mind," Arrowroot had told them, standing in his front door and glaring through thick glasses that magnified his dark eyes. "You Amish have my people's land. Isn't that enough for you?"

"Sorry to bother you," *Daad* had said, immediately backing off. "And sorry you're bothered by our owning land in these parts."

"These parts should be returned to their rightful owners. The U.S. government had no right to sell it to settlers, but there will be a day of reckoning."

"I'm sure there will," *Daad* had replied calmly. It was another of the countless lessons Seth had seen of his people's pacifism, their turn-the-other-cheek philosophy in action. But he figured even then that the day of reckoning his father agreed on was Judgment Day for everyone, not the return of land to a historic tribe of Native Americans. Still, the Amish felt for any group that was persecuted by a government.

"Whoa, Blaze," Seth said, and reined in. At least he'd recalled one other important thing about John Arrowroot that he was planning to use right now. The roof of his single-story, sprawling house needed new shingles. Seth needed the work—and, as Hannah put it, to psych out this man.

Seth wrapped the reins around a low tree limb and climbed down from the buggy. He saw someone glance out at him from behind a dark curtain in the front window, the one with the large, painted feather that looked identical to the one stuck in Hannah's window. He hoped he hadn't made a mistake to try to look into this on his own. But he wanted to help Linc Armstrong solve the shootings *schnell*—that is, fast—so he'd get out of here and leave the Amish—and Hannah—alone.

Ray-Lynn was relieved that Jack came in for breakfast with the FBI guy because then she didn't have to spend time with the sheriff. Until he came to her to explain what was really going on between him and his ex-wife, she didn't trust herself not to just bawl like a baby. Still, his eyes sought her as she bustled about the restaurant doing her best to keep busy away from the men's booth. But when she could, with a swift, sideways glance, she watched him, too. At least Lily Freeman had not shown her face here.

Elaine Carson, who owned the Rod 'n' Gun store, came in, wearing her usual black jeans and leather jacket. The woman rode a motorcycle at times—noisy, darn thing—but Ray-Lynn could see her bright red pickup with the American eagle and stars-and-stripes flag decals parked out in front. Unlike most women, she sat at the counter.

"Hi, Ray-Lynn," Elaine called out. "Got some pancakes and sausage on the griddle for a hardworking woman?"

"I recognize one when I see one. Right away."

"Any more news about the shootings? Kinda miss that newspaper, despite who ran it. Oh, I see the powers-that-be over there, so I'll ask them."

Taking her freshly poured coffee with her, Elaine strode over to Jack's booth. She was tall and angular with straight, short brown hair and no makeup. Ray-Lynn took the opportunity to seat an English couple in the next booth, but she didn't have to strain to hear since Elaine seemed to have one level of volume, and that was loud. Ray-Lynn wondered if she was hard of hearing from her army days or working the shooting range, or if she'd never gotten over the decibel level for giving orders.

"Gentlemen—officers of the law," she addressed the two men. "Sorry my customer list was a mile long, but you gotta understand the culture around here. I'm sure the sheriff has told you, Agent Armstrong. I mean, everyone hunts, Amish and English alike, right, Sheriff? Even kids. 22-caliber for small game like squirrels and coyotes, 12-gauge shotguns for deer, then the high-speed weapons, you name it."

"We understand," Linc Armstrong told her. "Just keep your ear to the ground, then, okay?"

"And my mouth closed, you mean," she said and, with her balled fist, lightly hit his shoulder. He was dressed in a cargo camouflage outfit today. "But I will keep an eye out. They didn't call me Eagle Eye in the old days for nothing. And, you know, Annie Oakley was an Ohioan, though I'm actually related to

Kit Carson. Take care, then," she concluded, and went back to her place at the counter.

Ray-Lynn quit her chitchat with the new couple, whom she suspected were outsiders here just to gawk or newspeople on the sly, and headed back to the cash register, only to have her cell phone play "Tara's Theme" from *Gone with the Wind*. She answered it, stuck one finger in her other ear to cut the restaurant buzz and tried to not look at Jack when he glanced at her. Darn it, let him think it was some other man calling her.

"Ray-Lynn, it's Sarah Kauffman, calling from Wooster. I'd love to see Hannah, but I know better than to try. How's she doing?"

"Good, as far as I hear—mending physically, at least. Not sure about the rest of her."

"I can imagine it's hard for her to face what happened and to be home. I thought we'd have time to stop to see you, but we're here looking for a house to buy or rent."

"You're moving to Wooster?"

"Nate and I are going to be married a week from Saturday, on the thirteenth at 2:00 p.m. It will be a small wedding in a chapel we just booked here in Wooster with a restaurant reception after. The northeast supervisor for the State Marshal's Arson Investigation team has lung cancer, and Nate's going to take his place earlier than we thought. We don't want to be separated and—thanks to you—I can move my painting studio anywhere."

"I'm looking at your latest and my favorite, the one of the kids playing *eck* ball back of the little schoolhouse. Got it hung right on the wall where folks come in, and I can tell your people stop and admire it, painted faces and all."

"Good to hear. Maybe someday…" she said, but she choked up and her voice broke before she cleared her throat. "Listen, Ray-Lynn, I'm hoping you can take a message to Hannah from me, since no way I can get to see her now, and I'm hoping, once we move, you could come and bring her—maybe even for the wedding. I know Ella and my family won't come."

"Of course, I could bring whoever wants to attend! I'm so happy for both of you. Do you—do you want your family to know? I mean, word will get around…"

"Since I was Hannah's link to her family when she was living away, I'm praying she'll do the same for me. So here are the directions to the chapel for you, and what I want my family to know. I hope Hannah can tell them."

Ray-Lynn reached for a pad and pen to take notes. As she did, she saw that Jack was ignoring Agent Armstrong and frowning at her. Maybe, she thought, that was because she'd been smiling at the good news over the phone, when he didn't expect happiness from her right now. She forced a broad smile and nodded as if she'd been asked something delightful, then hunkered down to pay attention to Sarah.

"So," John Arrowroot said as he opened his front door before Seth could knock, "the graveyard hero. To what do I owe this honor?"

"Not a hero in my mind, but I was glad I happened by, maybe scared the shooter off. I'm surprised you know who I am, since I've kept my face out of the news coverage."

"I know who a lot of you are in the so-called Home Valley. My ancestors once called this land Eri'e Rique, 'at the place of the panther.' And you just happened by my remote location today, because…?"

"I recalled your roof could use reshingling, and I'm between big projects. Jobs are scarcer than usual for timber framers right now."

"Ah, yes, the barn builder, the leader of the barn raisings." The man's taut mouth lifted in a little smirk. This close up, Seth saw his black hair, scraped back on his skull in a tight ponytail, was threaded with silver that matched his silver ring and a sort of eagle charm on a leather thong around his neck. He would guess the man's age at sixty or sixty-five. He wore a white dress shirt with jeans, a wide, studded leather belt and Western leather-tooled boots. "Now, that would be different," Arrowroot went on, "to have just one Amish man hanging over my head instead of all of you. I do get leaks in bad storms."

"If you have a ladder, I can go up, measure and give you an estimate," Seth said, trying to keep calm at the man's subtle digs and goading tone. "I left my ladder where I've been working. You ever climb a ladder yourself to look at the roof's condition?"

"Actually, I don't like heights. You sure," he said as he finally stepped outside, "you're not here to spy on me?"

The man was clever, but Seth had known that. But clever enough to kill someone and escape without leaving a clue, at least at the scene of the crime?

"I intend to fix the roof, not drill holes in it and look through," Seth said.

Arrowroot almost smiled. "I have no secrets,

anyway. I've made it clear what my goals are." He led Seth to the detached, single-car garage and lifted the door himself, though many moderns had a button that did that. "So, how did a man as young as you—what, mid-twenties?—get to be a master builder around here?"

"From the age of fourteen I worked with my mother's father, Gideon Raber, who taught me about timber framing. He was also in charge of barn raisings, so I had a nine-year apprenticeship with him before he died. It ended up I knew more than anyone else who'd trained with him. But getting back to your obvious goals, why not just file a lawsuit, since you're a lawyer?"

"The state government's declined to meet with me so that I can pursue my land claims and the feds don't recognize Indian tribes or lands in Ohio, so my lawyer's brain says to go about this another way."

Seth couldn't resist saying, even as he hefted the ladder from the garage—only a tall stepladder, not an extension one, "You mean like do something dramatic to draw attention to your cause?"

"In a way. You think you can reach the roof with that?"

"Over on the slant of hill, yes. What do you mean, 'in a way'?"

"You've heard of 'don't ask, don't tell,' haven't you? Let's just stick to roofing. I appreciate your having the guts to come up here, but if you have the nerve to run into a graveyard where people have been shot, guess this is a piece of cake. You know, most of your people are polite but they treat me like a pariah, or at least a ghost they don't even see."

"My people love and need their land," Seth said, noting numerous photos of what might be aerial shots of this area tacked to the back wall of the garage near a cluttered workbench. He wondered if there was a shot of the graveyard there, or the woodlot above it. If he could get a job here, he'd have time to check. So maybe the Lord had inspired him to come here for more than one reason.

Seth positioned the ladder, then began to climb. He didn't know what a pariah was and he didn't believe in ghosts. But he was starting to think John Arrowroot had a powerful motive, at any cost to himself or others, to shake things up by bringing in a lot of media coverage here. Linc had asked if maybe the Troyers, who lived on land abutting the hill above the graveyard, would take potshots at weird strangers to bring curious tourists in for their grain mill tours. Seth thought that was a crazy theory, but he didn't trust John Arrowroot as far as he could throw his entire roof.

After the noon meal, Hannah went out in the new barn to familiarize herself with it. She'd been horrified that the barn of her childhood had burned, and she'd watched from a distance as the men raised this one, with Seth astride the very peak of it.

She stopped to pat her onetime horse Nettie's muzzle and fuss over her. When she'd left, Naomi had inherited this horse and buggy. Now she realized she'd missed the sorrel mare with three white feet, missed the slower pace of riding in a buggy, when one had time to enjoy the passing scenery which didn't blur by just like life could do.

Every now and then, Hannah peeked out the door

or a window at Seth working hard on the roof. He was almost finished and then wouldn't be around. Would he still leave little Marlena here during the day? Despite the fact she was the symbol of all she'd lost with Seth, the tot was adorable.

She heard a car and glanced out, wondering if Linc could be back. But Ray-Lynn Logan got out of a van and started for the house. Hannah recognized her not only by her distinctive vehicle but by her red hair. She was a real pretty woman with snappy brown eyes and a personality to match. Her Southern drawl was easy and comforting, like she could lull you into trusting anything she said.

"Ray-Lynn!" Hannah called and waved, ignoring the fact Seth stopped his work to peer down at them. "I just wanted to thank you for the oatmeal chocolate chip whoopie pies you sent to the hospital with the sheriff!"

Ray-Lynn turned away from the house and walked toward the barn with another bakery box in her hand. "Got more for y'all," she said in her soft, melodic way, "but got to admit it's a bit of a cover-up. Here," she said, putting the box down on the family sled *Daad* had been repairing, then fumbling in her purse. "I wrote the information down in case I didn't get to talk to you alone. Sarah's going to marry Nate a week from Saturday in Wooster, and I'll take you there for the service and reception if you want to go. I know how much it would mean to her—to you, too, I bet."

"Oh!" was all Hannah could manage at first as she took the note from Ray-Lynn and held it tightly. Weddings! Weddings everywhere, English and Amish. And poor Ray-Lynn looked like she wanted to cry, as well.

"I'd love to be there for her," Hannah said. "Thanks

for this, Ray-Lynn. I'm sorry, I've decided not to take the job the sheriff said you offered me. I just don't want to face so many people right now, be in such a public place, however warm and friendly your restaurant is. I think I'm going to take a part-time housekeeper job at Mrs. Stutzman's B and B."

Ray-Lynn sank onto a hay bale and pulled Hannah down beside her. "My motto is, when you're all shook about the way things are going—with life, with losses, with love—just eat," she said. She reached for the box she'd just given Hannah, opened it up and pulled out two whoopie pies. She gave one to Hannah. Ray-Lynn took a big bite of hers, then talked with her mouth half-full.

"Do me a big favor, Hannah. Keep an eye on one Lily Freeman at the B and B. See what she's like, what she really wants around here."

Hannah swallowed her mouthful of the cookie and wiped frosting off the side of her mouth. "I heard about her. Okay—for Sarah's other best friend, who believed in her art and helped her follow her heart, I will."

"And I'll let you know if I hear anything at the restaurant about the shootings—" she took another big bite "—for you to tell the sheriff, because I'm not speaking to him."

"Oh. Right. We can be allies in this."

Ray-Lynn tapped the rest of her whoopie pie to Hannah's as if they were clinking goblets or shaking hands. "I swear, however different our lives, we women have to stick together," Ray-Lynn said, blinking back tears. "As for men, you can't live with them, can't live without them, whether they're the Ashley Wilkes or the Rhett Butlers of the world."

"The who?"

"Have I got a movie to share with you. You drop by sometime, since the B and B's not far from my house. Listen, Hannah, I don't mean to dump Seth Lantz and Jack Freeman in the same pot, but ding-dang, I think you and I have a lot in common."

She pointed at the box of whoopie pies between them. "So, you want to split another one of these?"

7

AFTER RAY-LYNN LEFT, HANNAH, FEELING ON a sugar-and-chocolate high from the whoopie pies, climbed the ladder to the loft, one-handed. She sat on a bale of straw by the hay mow window to read the information Ray-Lynn had written down about Sarah's wedding and reception.

Sarah and Nate were moving to Wooster! It was not far away, though in the next county. Hannah was soon to begin twice-a-week physical therapy on her wrist in Wooster, near the hospital. Yes, she needed that job at Amanda Stutzman's B and B so she could hire what her people called taxi service, someone who would drive her not only to get physical therapy but the mental therapy of visiting Sarah.

Hannah shifted her position, looked out and realized, from this vantage point, she was almost as high as Seth. He stood now at the top of his extension ladder, evidently surveying his work on the roof. It all looked neatly done to her—and finished. He'd told the family at noon meal he had been hired to reroof John Arrowroot's house and hoped to be able to talk some sense

into him, but Hannah, maybe her *daad,* too, knew Seth
intended more than that. She resisted the temptation to
call to him, as if inviting him to join her here. If he still
had memories of the way they used to kiss and hug in
the old barn loft...

As he climbed down his ladder and went in the back
door of their house, she heaved a huge sigh. Marlena's
delighted squeals sounded clear up here before the
storm door closed behind him.

Hannah folded the note and stuck it in the top layer
of her wrist bandage, then stood and peered out the
four-sided, louvered cupola, which kept the barn cool
in the summer and chilly right now. Of course, the
vistas were much broader than the scenes she'd admired from below yesterday. She could see clear to
the pond and beyond to the brow of the graveyard hill.
She'd meant to ask Seth why the edge of the sod over
Lena's grave was so unkempt, but she was afraid it was
something Linc did and she didn't want the two men
to argue. She couldn't tell if the police tape had been
removed or not because the fence itself looked as tiny
as toothpicks from here.

She scanned a bit farther. The corn maze her male
goth friends had been intrigued by that fateful night
was partly visible over the next slant of the road. Several years ago, her father, as bishop, and the church
elders had asked that its original name, Amish Corn
Maze, be changed. It was run by two non-Amish brothers, George and Clint Meyers—red necks, Ray-Lynn
had called them. She'd had the sheriff haul them out of
her restaurant when they got into a fight with another
patron a couple of years ago.

The Meyerses had refused to call their maze something else at first but had eventually renamed it Amish Country Corn Maze. Most English in the area admired and worked well with their Amish neighbors, but the maze owners still held a grudge over that. What had really annoyed the brothers was that the Amish boycotted the maze when they filled it with Halloween horror tableaus—witches, goblins, vampires, skeletons and fake bloody, dead bodies—so near the cemetery.

Hannah was surprised the maze still stood this late in the fall. Usually, they cut it down after harvest and Halloween, because the stalks were pretty ragged by then, and in colder weather, interest waned and profits dropped. A puzzle of paths, like life, her *daad* had called it once. Suddenly, she recalled something else that hit her like a fist.

She'd never mentioned to Linc or anyone else that the goths had made a brief maze visit. She'd been so focused on what happened at the cemetery and after.

She began to pace, ducking her head when the roof slanted inward. Could the Meyers brothers have heard the commotion Kevin and Mike made as they tore through the maze long after it closed? The Meyers house was just behind the maze. Could the brothers have been angry and grabbed a rifle and climbed that hill when her friends moved on to the cemetery? She remembered how upset she'd been when Linc had first suggested that someone might have driven a buggy or walked to the site to shoot at them, but it was just down the road from where the brothers lived.

She squinted through the louvers at the distant maze again. She could imagine its angular twists and turns and dead ends. It was a good thing she remembered the cell phone number Linc had told her to call if she ever thought of anything else, because she was going to walk to the phone shanty down the road and call him right away. She would insist he return her cell phone, too. He'd said he wanted to have it checked for any strange or suspicious calls she might have received or even background noise it might have picked up during her 9-1-1 call.

By the time Hannah carefully climbed down the ladder and went outside, her concern about Linc and Seth arguing had come home to roost. At least she wouldn't have to phone Linc, because here he was, jawing at Seth just outside the back door of the Esh farmhouse.

"You're withholding evidence with tricks like that!" Linc accused, pointing at Seth.

Hannah stopped on the other side of his car. She didn't want to get in the middle of this, but they were talking loudly enough that she wasn't exactly eavesdropping. It didn't take long for her to figure out what the topic was.

"So what if I got a job reroofing at Arrowroot's? It's what I do between big projects. And if I learn something or get something out of him, fine."

"But why didn't you—or the bishop or Hannah—tell me about this guy wanting the Amish out of here? The sheriff thought of it and went to see him and guess what—Seth Lantz had already come calling. And now you're saying that cemetery was sacred to his people? Yeah, you're obstructing an official murder investigation."

"It's not evidence yet, just facts. It's enough that the sheriff tipped him off he's being watched. And he's hardly going to admit anything if you storm over there to interview him."

"The FBI has assisted western tribes with tracking looted items and ancestors' bones from cemeteries in our art theft program, so I could have used that to get him talking, built a bridge. But now that you've horned in, you're just going to have to report to me—and don't screw it up!"

"You mean like you did when you didn't closely check the exterior of Hannah's window? I did and found an eagle feather stuck half under the sill," Seth told him, not giving ground. Neither man had retreated but stood just a few feet apart. "And I knew that was Arrowroot's symbol, his talisman."

"And, once again, didn't tell me. But if he's the shooter, why would he want to plant that to draw attention to himself?"

"I don't know, but I'm going to find out. He hardly made his cause a secret lately. The thing is, you could have looked up there, but you didn't," Seth repeated, pointing up toward Hannah's window. His voice was strong, like Linc's, getting louder. Although the Amish were soft-spoken, he was more than holding his own.

"And here's what really scares me," Seth added, finally lowering his voice so she could barely hear him. "Did Arrowroot, or whoever wanted to make it look like he'd been outside Hannah's window, only want to leave that feather? Or did he really want inside that window to hurt her but couldn't raise it? And how did he know which was her window?"

"All right, all right, I'm impressed with your thinking it all through," Linc said, holding up both hands as if he were under arrest. "I've considered she might still be a target, too, but see no evidence of that so far, and this is my investigation. Listen. Anything fishy you find out from Arrowroot, you let me know. You got that?"

"He already asked me if I was there to spy."

For some reason, suddenly, as if he'd sensed that *she* was spying, Seth glanced over at her and Linc turned his head.

"Evidently, you heard us," Linc said, walking closer. "Are you in on this?"

"He showed me the feather."

"Well, confession time all around. I thought you said you'd call me if anything else came up, Hannah."

"Maybe now you'll give me my cell phone back. I was just about to call you, but not about John Arrowroot. I thought of something else that probably doesn't mean anything, just a coincidence, but—"

"There are no coincidences in something like this," he said, taking her arm and turning her away from Seth. "Get in the car and tell me," he told her, and opened his front passenger's side door to practically push her in.

As Linc stalked around the front of the car, got in and slammed the driver's side door, Hannah was afraid to look at Seth. But he just stalked back into the house and that door closed, too.

Just when Ray-Lynn was starting to think that at least Lillian Freeman had a shred of decency not to come into the restaurant, she found the woman standing in the driveway of her house when she pulled in after closing up that evening. In the dark, she actually could have hit the woman with her van. God forgive her, she was tempted.

"What are you doing here?" Ray-Lynn asked, rolling down her window.

"I'm at a disadvantage, since you evidently recognize me," Lillian countered. "I just wanted to say a friendly hello. I mean, no bad feelings, okay?"

Although her blond hair was perfectly styled and her makeup intact, including fake eyelashes, the woman looked like she was out jogging—running shoes, sharp-looking gray workout pants and matching jacket with some sweat marks across her chest. Ray-Lynn almost wondered if she'd caught her at something, like a prank or even worse. She killed her headlights and motor, then got out to face her unwanted guest.

"No bad feelings," Ray-Lynn lied as best she could. "No feelings at all."

"I—I heard you and Jack had—have something going. I mean, he mentioned you."

Ray-Lynn bit her lower lip so she wouldn't say what she was thinking about Jack. Mentioned her? How nice! Or was this woman trying to get her even more angry with Jack, to drive a bigger wedge between them?

"Since it's a small town and all," Lillian went on, "I figure we'd cross paths and better get the worst over."

"If this is the worst, that would be great. Will you be staying long? I'd heard somewhere you were fed up with small-town life—and your ex-husband, for that matter."

"Live and learn," she said with a little shrug and her hands on her hips. "And please, call me Lily. I'm back, maybe for good."

Or for bad, Ray-Lynn thought, gripping her car keys so hard they bit into the palm of her hand. Surely this woman, however much nerve she had, wasn't going to ask for her old job back at the restaurant. And, as she suddenly turned tail and jogged away with a jerky little wave, Ray-Lynn had the worst feeling she wasn't going to keep up this polite facade to ask Ray-Lynn to give up Jack, either. Oh, no, she was just going to try to take him.

"You okay about this?" Linc asked Hannah as he stopped his car where Kevin had parked his along the road by the maze the night of the shootings. They'd planned this all out, and he'd explained everything to her parents, but she still felt shaky about it.

It was even a similar night, Hannah thought as she glanced out the windshield, with the moon mostly hidden by clumps of clouds. Just as when she'd been with her friends, she eyed the big maze sign with its rules: No Smoking! Stay on the Paths! Hold Kids by the Hand! Do Not Touch Displays! Enjoy Half Mile of Scary Fun!

"Yes. I said I wanted to help and I do," she told Linc. "I admit it wouldn't be the same in broad daylight. Sorry I didn't think to tell you sooner, but our quick stop here that night—it just slipped my mind at first."

"I understand. I cleared it with the Meyers brothers this afternoon, played up that you didn't approve of Kevin and Mike running through here and that you said they'd have to pay. George and Clint said they'd stay in the house so we could replicate the trespassing. They seemed pretty calm about it, said it's happened before that people ran through without paying and tampered with the displays or the maze itself. The only thing they said I could slightly construe to be self-implicating was that they don't want people to make their own paths because it 'riles' them. 'We laid it out and no crashing through our corn barriers!'"

She had to smile at Linc's mimicking of the brothers. "They're not the usual type of kind English neighbors around here," she explained. "But if they're guilty of the shootings, anything they say isn't to be trusted—such as they'll stay put in their house tonight."

"In my book they're a step down from rednecks, like you said Ray-Lynn called them. But that type doesn't want the FBI breathing down those red necks, believe me. They'll stay put tonight. Besides, they're entertaining a lady."

"I find that hard to believe."

"Yeah, well, the lady's their momma from the other side of town. It's her birthday. They got a cake and all. Listen, Hannah," he added, his voice suddenly much more serious. He turned even more toward her and reached across her to firmly grasp her right upper arm. "I know you're not big on this reenactment tactic, but it may help. You may remember even more."

"But I barely went into the maze that night, just a little ways to yell at them to come out. I went in the entrance and took one turn and it seemed *so* dark. By the time I started walking back toward the car, they came bursting out through the maze wall."

"Anything else you recall, just let me know, honey."

Honey? It was no doubt a slip of the tongue. He's probably meant to say Hannah. But he still held her arm, stroking it with his thumb as if to calm her, but it didn't. It had the opposite effect.

"All right, let's go," she said, and pulled away to fumble with her door handle, which was still locked until he clicked something so she could open it. The big print sign with the maze rules—Stay on the Paths!—was knocking against something in the wind. It scared her when Linc drew his gun, though he just held it down at his side. In his other hand he held a sturdy flashlight with a bright beam. That made her feel a bit better, as had their earlier heart-to-heart talk today.

Trying to figure him out as a person, not just as an investigator, she'd asked him if he had a family.

"Sure—two brothers who live out near Denver, one of them a police chief. I have nieces and nephews galore. But married with kids? No. Came close, but it wouldn't have worked out, anyway. Sometime I work 24/7, seven days a week, then can leave on a moment's notice and be gone for days, like this assignment. Since Quantico—that's our training site in Virginia—I've been busy climbing the Bureau's ladder—that's another name for the FBI. My college degree was in finance, but white-collar crimes bored me stiff."

"So now you're in a group that looks into murders?"

"Right, violent crimes. Amish country is the last place I thought that would ever take me. If I make it to retirement age at fifty, I don't know if I could take a place this peaceful."

"Age fifty? But that's so young to retire."

"Only twelve years away, but I'll find something else to do. Maybe help build barns," he'd said with a chuckle, though she couldn't see what was funny about that. And she thought someone that busy could still be lonely, but she didn't say so yet. Right now, as they approached the maze, that gun was making her feel more jumpy than safe.

"You sure you need the gun?" she asked as her courage wavered again.

"Just a precaution, since I can't see around the next corner. So how scary are the displays in here?"

"I came through once with Seth in our *rumspringa* years, though we weren't supposed to because the bishop—my father—didn't approve of this place with its witches and fake dead bodies. It's not like things jump at you, at least not back then. They're mostly stuffed, but some look real, even though most folks come through in the daylight, unless you make special arrangements with the Meyerses for a group after dark and then they watch you like a hawk."

"Yeah? Then I'll bet they would have been upset at unannounced night visitors, especially weird-looking ones making noise."

Despite fitful moonlight and Linc's flashlight beam, it was instantly darker inside the maze. The dry cornstalks rustled and seemed to press in on them. Shadows leaped from everywhere.

"Okay, so the guys probably turned to the right here," he said, darting his beam into the blackness.

"I'm not sure, but they did eventually emerge from the right side of the maze, over this way. But they were inside here long enough that they could have gotten a lot farther than this."

"The Meyers brothers must know this labyrinth in their sleep. They could have been in here, nearby, and Kevin and Mike wouldn't even have known it."

Hannah gasped when they walked through fake, suspended cobwebs—yarn?—around the next turn, but Linc just shoved them away with the flashlight. The beam bounced across his face. It almost made his features look like a fright mask she'd seen uptown in the drugstore near Halloween. While Hannah hung back a bit, Linc peered around another corner. It was all she could do to keep from taking his arm, clinging to him.

"Don't look here," he said, stepping back almost into her. "It's a gross ghoul or zombie in an open coffin. Tell you what, let's do this backward since you do know where they emerged from. They should hand out maps of these paths."

"They used to. Only, once you got inside and were lost, and opened the map to use it, it was blank. They thought it was funny, but they only got you once with that," she said as they headed back out, still making one wrong turn before they traced their steps out the entrance.

Hannah felt she could breathe again out here, despite the fact the cemetery was not far down the road and, at night, the mere idea of that haunted her. She fought back one of her waking nightmares of the shooting.

"So, over here?" he said as Hannah led him to the raggedy place she was certain the guys had broken out through, once they realized they were thoroughly lost or maybe got scared by something inside they didn't admit to. She wondered now if it could have been the Meyers brothers. Kevin and Mike had run back to the car and headed to the graveyard in a big hurry.

She hesitated at the opening made by broken, shifting stalks. "You know," she said, "you could call Mike and have him come here. He could tell you exactly what happened."

"It's worth a phone call, but he's with his parents in

Michigan and he's still shaky—in shock, can't sleep—like post-traumatic syndrome, his family says. I think they're trying to keep him away from me and hope they can get a lawsuit out of it when I find Kevin's killer."

She said only, "Mike was high-strung and just staring into space that night."

"So what was his and Kevin's demeanor when they got back in the car?"

"Revved up. Excited. Bragging about it was nothing, but they hit the gas to get out of here, sped to the graveyard."

"Okay," he said, taking her elbow and steering her toward the car. "Here's the deal. I'm going to put you back inside here to wait for me—windows up, doors locked. You give me about ten minutes to step through the looking glass into— Sorry," he added at her blank expression. "Didn't mean to play cultural trivia on you. Ever feel you're caught between two worlds?"

"Only every day. I may not know what you mean by through the looking glass, but I do know this corn is a red strain called Butcher Block."

"Yeah? Amish trivia, huh? I'd like to help bridge your worlds, Hannah. Really. I admire your strength after all you've been through. But right now, you just let me see what I can learn inside this chicken outfit," he said, jerking a thumb toward the maze. "Maybe I can figure out what spooked Kevin and Mike—or if they somehow riled the Meyers men into following and taking potshots at all of you."

8

HANNAH SAT IN LINC'S CAR FOR WHAT SEEMED
a very long time, but of course she was nervous, and
that made time drag. She tried to think of other things.
For one, she planned to have Naomi drop her off at
Amanda Stutzman's Plain and Fancy B and B tomorrow morning so she could see about that part-time job.
And she kept seeing Seth, standing up to Linc.

Of course, Seth needed the roofing work at John
Arrowroot's, but he didn't need to get so caught up in
this case. He'd done his best to help out that fatal night.
Was he staying involved because they used to be so
involved with each other? Naomi had said Seth, who
was the *vorsinger,* or song leader at church, had two
maidals who were eager to have him be their come-
calling friend, but Ella had said he hadn't made a move
on them yet.

Her stomach started to cramp. Linc had said ten
minutes, but it seemed like at least twenty. If he didn't
need her now, he should have taken her home, then
come back out here alone. Or did he want her to go
with him to the graveyard again afterward? No, she'd

refuse. Not in the dark. But she would ask what the crime scene team had done to the grass around Lena's grave when they were testing the blood spots or looking for bullets. It was enough that her tombstone had been ruined. Why would the FBI tamper with the sod over her grave?

Glancing out both side windows, then craning around to look out the back, Hannah shifted in her seat. Nothing but dark night draped with pale moonlight. It wasn't that late, she tried to tell herself. Probably right around eight o'clock, better than near midnight on Halloween when her friends had been here. But she'd sure feel better if a buggy would come down the road and stop.

She studied the car's laptop and special equipment—a GPS like the owner of the Cleveland recording studio had and some other stuff she couldn't name. Without the key, the heater probably wouldn't work. It wasn't too cold in here yet, but she had goose bumps. She huddled deeper in her cape.

Where was Linc? Why didn't he come out the makeshift exit Kevin and Mike had pushed through? Was he walking the entire maze, or had he found something?

If she honked the horn, surely he'd hear it and come out. But what if the sound carried clear to the Meyers house? Birthday party for their mother or not, she didn't want them to think she or Linc were summoning them. If he'd left the keys in the car, she'd be almost desperate enough to drive home, then bring *Daad* back with her to search for Linc.

She counted to fifty slowly, telling herself that if he didn't come back by then, she'd get out and shout for him. Forty-eight…forty-nine…

She reached over to the driver's side and unlocked the car, then—before she changed her mind—opened her door, put one foot on the ground and, still in the shelter of the door, stood and shouted, "Linc? Linc! Liiii-iinc! Agent Armstrong!"

She heard nothing but the wind rustling dry stalks. What could have happened to him? Maybe he tripped or something was rigged to swing like that cobweb and it hit him…hurt him. She would bet that the Meyers brothers would not dare to sneak out after promising they would not, but…

She wanted to dive back inside the car, but she had to know what had happened. Maybe he'd twisted an ankle running through these dark turns, or had fallen and hit his head. When she found him, she could use his cell phone to call for help. Thank the Lord, she had not heard any shots.

Instinctively whispering a prayer for protection—*ya,* she was still more Amish than she wanted to admit— she headed for the outside row of broken cornstalks where Kevin and Mike had burst out of the maze, the same way Linc had entered. She'd have to try to trace his steps without a flashlight, but at least the moon was bright and her eyes had adjusted to the darkness.

The paper-dry cornstalk leaves snatched at her skirts as she stepped inside the maze. Shadows loomed, but patches of wan moonlight guided her on. If she got lost, she told herself, she'd just shove her way out through row after row, despite the Meyers brothers' rules. She almost felt she was on FBI business now, trying to help one of their own who was here to help her and her people.

On the only path she could take from here, she

gasped when she turned the corner and saw a body hanging by a noose around its neck. A store dummy, but it looked so real. But what—what if something really terrible had happened to Linc? Did she dare to shout for him again? If someone had hurt him and was still here, wouldn't that pinpoint her position? And if an enemy lurked, would it be the one who had shot at her and her friends?

She scolded herself not to let her imagination run as wildly as she wanted to run to get out of here. Now she knew what Kevin and Mike had felt; at first curiosity and defiance, then frustration and growing panic. Surely she'd find Linc just intent on checking something out. Either he'd lost track of time or she had. With the wind and rustling stalks, he likely hadn't heard her shout. Best to look for him, not call out again yet.

Two more turns of the maze. From here on, she wasn't sure he'd come this way, because there were choices. She turned right because she thought it was closer to the outside of the maze, but suddenly, she wasn't sure of that, either, not certain about anything. It was like getting lost in your own thoughts and fears in here.

The next fright scene was another store dummy made to look like an old-fashioned Indian warrior with war paint and a raised hatchet—no, it was called a tomahawk, she recalled. If John Arrowroot had known about this, would he approve or disapprove?

She dreaded each turn. The Meyers brothers had outdone themselves, but she understood farmers trying to pick up extra money in these tough times. She passed a witch bent over a small pot and took the stick she was stirring with to use for a weapon. The

Amish litany of "harm no one, turn the other cheek, peace not violence" danced through her brain. Some sort of primitive terror consumed her and, one-handed, she held the stick close. Two turns later, a ghost made from a sheet, shifting just enough in the wind to look real, almost swung into her.

Instinctively, she froze, then listened intently. She couldn't believe they would use sound effects in here, but she'd just heard someone moving, walking. Footsteps. And was that other sound just the wind or heavy, ragged breathing? She knew any sound could be faked in a recording studio. But here…no, she did hear a footstep and not from any of the lifeless figures around here.

It must be Linc, but she still hesitated to call out. She stopped breathing, trying to differentiate the sounds of steps from the rustle of stalks, the shifting sheet. It—someone—was coming close, maybe along the path she'd just passed, around the last corner. If it was Linc, he would not expect her to be here, and he had a gun he could shoot in surprise….

She shouldered her way through one more corn wall, but her stick snagged and made too much noise. She darted around the next turn of the path and found she was in a dead end. And the footsteps could not be Linc's, because he was sprawled, faceup, just like Kevin, at her feet.

Hannah sucked in a sharp breath and knelt to feel the side of Linc's neck the way Seth had checked to see if Kevin was alive. Yes, alive. But so still. She patted his cheek to wake him up. His skin was cold, his slight beard stubble raspy against her fingers. Where were his gun and flashlight? She didn't see them, didn't touch them as she felt the ground around him. The footsteps kept coming, someone nearby breathing hard…

Hannah scrambled to her feet and ran. Nightmare! Could this be a horrid dream, like those the pain pills gave her? No—real. All of it real.

She shoved through wall after wall of dried corn shocks. Some of the stalks hit at her, one tripped her. When she went down, and for once wasn't making noise herself, she heard someone crashing after her.

She scrambled forward on all fours, then got to her feet again, holding her pitiful stick, hardly protection if someone had Linc's gun or a high-velocity rifle. Passing through all these corn walls had to get her outside, didn't it? But then she'd be in the open, just like at the graveyard.

She shoved through a line of corn, banged her knees and shins into a long box or chest. No, a coffin with a fake, bloody body that spilled out when it tipped. If this was the scene Linc said he didn't want her to see, it was near the edge of the maze. But she'd just made so much noise her pursuer would know where she was.

She forced herself to halt her headlong flight. Instead, as quietly as she could with her panting breaths, she tiptoed down a path and around one turn, then another. Oh, no—another dead end. And what if it really was that for her?

When Seth heard Marlena call out in her sleep, he threw down the book he'd borrowed from his father on Ohio Indian history and hurried down the hall to look in on her again. She was thrashing in her little bed and had thrown her stuffed horse she called Gaulie to the floor. It must be the familiar nightmare again, though it was less frequent now, and her limited language skills kept her from being able to explain it to him. But he'd guessed it was a dream about losing her mother, because in it *Mamm* evidently "fall down asleep," then go "bye-bye."

He retrieved Gaulie and put it in her arms, stroked her brow and whispered to her until she quieted. He'd do anything to keep her well cared for and happy, and that meant he should find a good mother for her soon, get her some brothers and sisters, too. But, especially now, his heart wasn't in it.

When he saw she was sleeping peacefully, Seth went into his bedroom next door and flopped down, fully dressed, on the bed. He laced his hands behind his head and stared at the white ceiling. Both Katie Weaver and Susan Zook would make good wives and mothers. It was obvious from the flow of baked goods, smiles and the comments of their parents that both were interested in him. Katie, three years younger than he, was a gifted quilter and, a rare thing, an only child, which meant she would inherit her family farm someday. Susan, several years older than he, seemed serious-minded and a bit set in her ways but eager enough to please. *Ya,* he missed a woman in his house and in his bed.

Seth jumped when a knock sounded on his back door, but only because he'd been daydreaming. It wasn't strange for his parents or his sisters Ella or Barbara to visit after dark, since it was a short walk from the farmhouse. He hurried to the back door.

When he was first married, they hadn't even locked their doors, but these past few years, when it seemed some city problems were invading the countryside, they'd all installed bolt locks around here. He pulled the curtain aside and saw the silhouette of a large man. Oh, Harlan Kenton, Amanda Stutzman's brother, who owned the butcher and meat shop outside of town.

Seth unlocked and opened the door. "Mr. Kenton, what can I do for you?"

"Call me Harlan, for one thing. The lights are out early in the big house next door, and I told your dad I'd bring these last of his venison steaks around. Can you stick them in your freezer so I don't have to come back tomorrow? This is the end of the Lantz stash from last season." Many local families had their meat stored in Harlan's large walk-in freezer, and his shop did big business in butchering venison during that hunting season. The Amish had refrigerators and freezers, but few had large ones since they were run by generators.

"My freezer's too small, but I've got a key to the house and can take them over. I'll bet my sister Ella's light is on around back, because she's an attendant in a wedding next week and she's stitching her dress day and night."

"Thanks, if it's not too much trouble. I been so busy I just didn't get it done earlier today. As is, gotta get back now and cut up some chicken for my sister's B and B. Got some fancy new guest there, from Las Vegas, no less. Hear it's the sheriff's ex-wife. She don't like to eat any red meat, almost a vegetabletarian."

Seth decided not to correct the burly guy. He had what some called street smarts but wasn't the best scholar. Eli Detweiler, Ella's former come-calling friend, had worked for Harlan until Eli started slough-ing off. Harlan Kenton was a hard worker and a real go-getter. He'd told Eli once he intended to retire in style down in Florida or out west by the time he was fifty, but that attitude hadn't rubbed off on Eli.

"Okay, then, tell you what," Harlan said. "I'll unload this on the back porch of the big house, and you can take it from there."

When he stepped back a bit into the reflected kitchen light, Seth could see he wore the usual John Deere hat, tipped way back on his head, with the final *e* Xed out, as if he were correcting the spelling. Harlan's ears protruded almost like cup handles on his big head. His beard stubble made him look tough, but he was always kind and polite. He was obviously prideful about his neatly parted, cut and combed brown hair, probably a result of his wife, Clair, working at the Hair Port Barber Shop in town. As usual, he wore a T-shirt under a plaid shirt—no jacket, no matter the cool weather. In fact, he almost looked like he was sweating from hefting all that meat around.

"It's a deal," Seth agreed. "Any charge for delivery?"

"Nope. I just knew it would be too much for your dad to lift and his horse to pull on these danged hills."

"Real neighborly of you. Harlan, I meant to ask you something."

"Shoot."

"Remember the day John Arrowroot was carrying on in your store about wanting the land around here returned to his people?"

"Sure do. I was tempted to shove a frozen ham hock in his big mouth. I'm hoping he's just a crackpot, 'cause I got near four acres over at my place, and it'll be Harlan Kenton's last stand 'fore he gets his hands on it."

"Do you remember him saying something about the Amish graveyard land?"

He paused, removed his hat and scratched his head a moment. "Yeah, come to think of it. Like it was 'specially sacred to his people, 'cause they used to have sacrifices to their gods there or something like that— or maybe buried their own chiefs there."

Seth nodded, though he didn't remember any of that about burying their chiefs. In all the years the Plain People had dug graves with shovels there, as far as he knew, no one had ever turned up a bone or artifact, although plows turned up arrowheads now and then.

Harlan started away, then turned back. "You're thinking it might have been Arrowroot took potshots at those kids?" he asked. "Yeah, I'd believe that. When he goes on a rant, he's hardly the stoic Indian, and I've seen that up close and personal."

"I didn't mean to imply that much," Seth told him. "Thanks again!" he called after him as Harlan headed back to his truck.

Once Harlan drove off, Seth closed the door. He'd have to carry Marlena over to the farmhouse and get Ella's attention with some gravel against her window. Luckily, Marlena slept hard because he'd just pass her off to Ella while he put the steaks in the farmhouse freezer.

Hannah's teeth were chattering, and she was shivering, though she knew it was from stark terror more than the November night. She hadn't moved—had hardly breathed for what she figured must be at least ten minutes, maybe longer. No more footsteps, at least she thought so. The wind, the corn, even the clouds that occasionally obscured the moon, were playing tricks on her. Should she try to find her way back to the safety of Linc's car, or try to locate him again? He must have the car keys on him. She could drive for help or just find his cell phone and call 9-1-1—again. What if he had a concussion or internal bleeding?

She finally got up the courage to move from her position in the dead end. She actually wished the crusty Meyers brothers would come out to their maze, no matter what they'd promised Linc. She wanted help and human contact that badly. Footsteps again, slower now, more deliberate, kind of scuffling. Had someone waited until she moved and was now stalking her again?

It could be the same person who shot at her and her friends. Maybe she was really the one being pursued tonight instead of Linc. Someone had sliced her window screen, so she could be the one someone wanted to harm or kill in the first place. Would Linc, if he was all right, believe that this was evidence she was the target? But who wanted to hurt her and why?

She realized she had two choices. Push through the cornstalk walls of this dead end and give her position away as she ran outside, or stand her ground here. She raised the witch's stick she carried and pushed herself back into the foliage. Her eyes widened as a man's moonlit shadow fell on the ground, growing as he came closer. Her pulse pounded even harder. She'd have the element of surprise, but that was all, especially if her pursuer had Linc's gun or his own. She felt the imagined pain of the bullet slicing through her wrist, saw Tiffany fall and Kevin's forehead blooming blood. She bit her lower lip so hard that tears blurred her view as a big, dark body shoved around the one-way entrance of the dead end and trapped her here.

Blindly, she swung the stick at him, then thrust herself through the corn wall, only to be grabbed by her skirt, then her leg and dragged back.

9

"HANNAH! IT'S ME! I THOUGHT YOU WERE MY attacker—"

"Oh! Linc!"

They were sprawled on the ground, half in, half out of the maze, with him on top of her. His weight was tremendous, but she threw her arms around him and held tight. He hugged her back hard and rolled them over once so they lay side by side.

"But someone else was after me—stalking me," she told him. "Are you all right? I found you uncon—"

"Someone bushwhacked me from behind, took my gun and flashlight."

"When I found you, I couldn't find either of them. He was coming back, he—"

"I just walked most of the maze. I think he's gone. Did you get a glimpse of him? It must have been a man."

"No—heard footsteps, and I think he was out of breath."

"Come on," he said, getting to his feet and hauling her up after him. He staggered against her a bit as they went back to the car. "Got my keys, at least," he muttered. He put her in the front seat, then on unsteady feet, went around, got in and locked the doors.

"We have to get your head looked at," she insisted. "I don't care if you're not bleeding. There's a medical clinic out on—"

"I'm all right, just suckered and furious, with one bastard of a headache. I've had a concussion before. I'll watch myself. That guy knew the maze, but that doesn't mean he's the graveyard shooter, or even that it was one of the Meyers boys. I'm dropping you off, then going to see them, but I swear, if one of those jerks got the best of me, I'll shoot myself."

"Don't talk like that. You— Both of us could have been killed."

"I thought it was safe, but I'm a gung-ho idiot to endanger you. I swear I'll get to the bottom of all this, but I lost control of the situation. And I—" he turned to study her, frowning as if she was to blame for something "—I can't let that happen."

He muttered something under his breath again— curse words, she figured—as he started the car, see-sawed back and forth on the two-lane road to turn around, then drove fast toward her house. She was afraid he'd black out, but he did seem to be in control of his car at least.

"Come in, and I'll wash your head with cool water," she said.

"Sounds tempting, but I'm not bleeding and I've got to visit our maze friends pronto—fast."

"You don't have to translate worldly slang for me."

"Listen, Hannah," he said, slowing the car and reaching out to grasp her good wrist as he turned into her family's driveway, "I'd appreciate it if you tell no one—including your father, including Seth—what happened back there. What we know may come in handy to trap someone."

"I won't lie to *Daad* if he asks what happened. Besides, I'm a mess."

"Yeah, okay. We can't have him think we've been rolling on the ground for other reasons."

She felt her cheeks heat. "I'm still worried for your head. You're saying things you don't mean. What if you're bleeding inside, and it makes you black out again while you're driving?"

"Okay, I'll hit the medical clinic after I drop in on the Meyerses' birthday party. And thanks for being concerned. You ever hear the saying, 'When the going gets tough, the tough get going'?"

"No. Is that the FBI motto?"

"You're beautiful, you know that? And I'm not goofy from that blow to my head."

"Maybe not goofy but gunless," she said as he turned the car around to pulled up close to her back door, "so you be careful!" *Daad* had evidently seen them, because he was waiting at the door.

"You, too," he said as she got out. He waved to her father and pulled away, a man on a mission, she thought, trying to hide how furious he felt. This time, the victim had been him.

When Ray-Lynn opened her front door to Jack that night—he'd called to ask if he could drop by—he produced a bouquet of what must be at least two dozen roses, a rare peach color, too. Her first thought was no way he'd bought those in Homestead.

"How about a peace treaty?" he asked, looking none too sure of himself.

"A temporary truce," she said, accepting the flowers and inhaling deeply of their scent.

He came in and they sat on separate ends of the sofa. She could tell he wanted to touch her but knew better. In a way, she'd put up a barrier by cradling the flowers on her lap.

"Look, Ray-Lynn, I had no idea Lily was coming back or had changed her mind about things."

"Things, meaning living here and with you. Have you changed your mind about us?"

"No, honest to God."

"But you're still carrying a torch for her."

"Don't put it like that."

"How should I put it?"

"It was a shock right in the middle of this graveyard shooting mess, that's all."

"So the graveyard shooting keeps you from making a decision about who you really want to be with?"

"You know, sweetheart, you have a real way with words, with slicing right to the heart of things."

"The heart of things is where we need to be, Jack."

"Things are crazy right now. I'm not spending time with her, either."

"So I can assume she and I are running neck-and-neck in the Who Gets Jack Freeman sweepstakes?"

"Now, there you go twisting things again. I love you, Ray-Lynn. Said I did, still mean it. I want us to have a future together, but you gotta give me some time and some trust."

"I just hope you more than want our future. Wanting's not enough. I've waited for you for months, years, to figure out what you really wanted, and then here comes a real big monkey wrench into the works."

"She is kinda the take-charge type, like you."

"That kind of compliment I don't need. Take it back or you can have these beautiful, sweet flowers back and give them to the monkey wrench."

"I do love you, Ray-Lynn. There's nobody like you. You just put those in water 'fore they hang their heads, and have a good thought for a guy who's sorry this happened, really."

"Me, too. As pretty as these flowers are, they've got big thorns. You just be careful, Jack Freeman, dealing with a killer and an ex-wife, you hear?"

"I know better than to push my luck, but how about a goodbye kiss?"

"As long as it's not really goodbye."

As he leaned closer, she kept the flowers between them, so he wouldn't pull her close, however badly she wanted that, wanted him. And so she wouldn't just grab him, burst into tears and not let go.

The next morning, Hannah had her first buggy ride since she'd been back. She even took the reins from Naomi and talked to Nettie just like she used to when this horse and buggy were hers. It thrilled her that when she blew the mare a loud kiss, she put her shoulder to the traces and sped up. With her foot braced against the backboard, Hannah enjoyed the rock and tilt of the buggy as they clipped along at about twelve miles an hour.

Since she was garbed Amish—one of her old dresses *Mamm* had kept since she'd washed her new one—she wore a bonnet today. Strangely, she missed the familiar feel of the stiff organdy prayer *kapp* beneath it. Or maybe it was just the memory of her father's assessing gaze on her red, short hair—which had pieces of corn tassel in it—when she'd gone into the house last night.

"Ach," he'd said, taking in her mussed dress Naomi had so painstakingly made, "you been rolling down a hill? Now, I don't want to question you or Agent Armstrong, but you all right?"

"We ended up running through the maze to try to figure out what Kevin and Mike must have done or seen."

"And?"

"I fell—as you can tell. And both of us pushed through the rows of dry, rotting cornstalks." There, she thought. She hadn't lied. Linc had told her to say as little as possible about what happened.

She'd steeled herself for more questions, for a scolding. But her father had said only, "You and I—many times since you've been gone, I told to myself, I will not argue with my Hanni again."

She'd nodded. Tears had filled her eyes at the sound of that sweet childhood name he alone had for her, a mingling of her name and *honey*. But Linc had called her honey. Or could he have said, "Hannah," and she misheard—or even heard what she wanted to hear from him? No, she was not going sweet on that man. She'd just been worried about his hard head, that's all.

But last night, though she hadn't hugged her *daad* in years, not even when she came back to the house, she'd hugged him hard, and he'd held her and kissed her cheek.

"Danki, Daad," she'd said as they stepped apart.

She'd always thought he was too stern and judgmental, but now she recognized that, as father and as bishop, he had to hold the line to protect them all from danger. And that's just what she'd brought to this sheltered valley: someone maybe stalking her, wanting to hurt her and others—someone evil.

"I see the Dutch Farm Table's doing big business," Naomi interrupted her agonizing. "I just hope the outside interest in all of us calms down before my wedding day. All we need is cameras in our faces. You said—I heard you tell *Mamm* you wanted to go to Sarah and Nate's wedding."

"She needs at least one Amish attendant, don't you think?"

"Well, it's nice, at least, to hear you think of yourself as back in the fold."

"The truth is, I don't. Not yet. Not until Linc solves this crime that has brought shame and the bad opinions of our people on me."

"See—'our people.' There you go again. Like Agent Armstrong would say—I guess it's Linc now to you—'I rest my case.'"

Hannah smiled and gave Naomi a hug around the shoulder with her good arm as her eyes took in the familiar, two-block-long sight of Homestead stores. It was the first time she'd been back in town. They buggied down Main Street past the volunteer fire department that, thank the Lord, had not been a bit busy since the nightmare of the barn arsons. Linc's car was parked in front of the sheriff's office. Would he tell Jack Freeman that he'd been what he'd called "bushwhacked" and that someone had taken his precious gun?

The newspaper was now closed, but Amish An-

tiques had a few customers looking at the things the
storekeeper had put on the sidewalk. As ever, both
cars and buggies were parked in front of the Homestead Pharmacy and Kwik Stop grocery. Since Amish
women didn't cut their hair, the Hair Port Barber Shop
was patronized only by the English, but its lights were
on. The hardware store and the Citizens Bank looked
as stoic and solid as ever.

It was a bit early in the day for the Hole in the Wall
pizza and subs shop to be open. How she and Seth had
loved to order out there when they had extra money.
Memories assailed her as they clip-clopped past the
McDonald's and Wendy's restaurants facing each other
across the street. Crazy Amish kids—families, too—
she thought. With all the delicious home cooking and
Ray-Lynn's restaurant right down the street, it used to
be such a treat to eat out at those fast-food places. But
now she knew what a really formal, nice restaurant
could be like. In Cleveland, she'd been to several on
dates, and the place their recording studio owner had
taken his staff twice a year was really posh. But she
didn't miss all that the way she had missed this quiet,
little place.

Across a vacant lot and a small stand of trees,
she saw the charming three-story Victorian house
with its wraparound, spindled front porch—Amanda
Stutzman's Plain and Fancy Bed-and-Breakfast. Naomi
let her out, promised she'd be back for her later and
clucked Nettie away.

Hannah had to smile as she walked up the brick-
paved path. The block of houses on this side of town
and the two blocks on the other side were pitiful compared to the sprawl of suburbs encircling Cleveland.

She didn't feel safer here anymore since the shooting and the nightmare in the maze, but still, she felt more at home. With poor Lena gone, she could even partway forgive Seth for his betrayal and desertion. Forgive but not forget.

Rocking chairs sat on the front porch, one of them shifting back and forth in the November breeze as if a ghost sat there. The horror tableaus in the maze leaped at her again. Would the cemetery and the maze always haunt her now? Linc had said her goth friend Mike's family claimed he was suffering from a sort of post-traumatic stress syndrome. Was she, too?

She rang the bell and heard it ding-dong musically inside. Wondering if she'd get a glimpse of the sheriff's ex-wife whom Ray-Lynn had told her to check out, she held her breath as the front door—real pretty etched glass—swept open. It was Amanda Stutzman, pink-cheeked and smiling. Years ago, Seth had said the woman reminded him of a picture of Mrs. Santa Claus he'd seen with her curly, white hair and plump face. She must be in her seventies now, her husband Hank, too. Naomi had said he still worked in the Troyer saw-mill outside of town near the old Troyer historical grist mill, both places owned by Naomi's betrothed's family.

"Oh, Hannah, dear, I was hoping you'd stop by. How are you coming along now?"

Inside, Mrs. Stutzman gave her a tour of the living room and parlor—lots of cubbyholes and figurines of beautiful birds to dust there—and the spacious kitchen where the kindly woman sat her down for tea and sugar cookies, little ones with scalloped edges, not the huge kind the Amish made. But then the Stutzmans were Mennonites, a more liberal group who used electricity and drove cars. Mrs. Stutzman kept popping up from the table because she had another kind of cookie in the ovens, and the aroma was fantastic.

"If my guests wish and are here for over a week, you'll dust their rooms, too," Mrs. Stutzman went on. "Some prefer privacy, others are in and out so fast—several TV reporters lately, but they've left now—that you'd only dust between guests."

"Do you have a long-time visitor here now?"

"You may have heard," she said, lowering her voice, "that the former Mrs. Jack Freeman—Lily—is here now, and for how long, I don't know. She's been out and about a lot, jogging or revisiting places she used to know around here." She spoke even more quietly. "I think she might be writing a book about her adventures in Las Vegas. Spends a lot of time on her laptop and was upset we didn't have Wi-Fi, so just paid us to plug into our cable line—Hank loves his football games, but we don't go online."

Hannah had a hundred questions about Lily Freeman, but she didn't want to be overly obvious or a gossip, however much it was accepted that her people loved *schmatze und klatsche,* eating and talking. Besides, if she took this job, she could check out Lily for Ray-Lynn on her own.

"Will I dust your and Mr. Stutzman's private quarters?" Hannah asked, realizing that the Amish had nothing on Mrs. Stutzman when it came to conversation.

"You know, if you have time, that would be lovely. The older I get, the usual tasks seem to get harder and harder. Listen, my dear, I know you are a talented singer and are used to some sort of office work and that this job is far below your abilities. But with your one hand—and just coming home in transition—I thought this might be a good temp job for you. As a matter of fact, to give credit where it's due, my brother Harlan suggested it."

"I can't thank you and him enough for your thoughtfulness, Mrs. Stutzman."

"You just call me Amanda. Even though Hank and I are Mennonites—my brother Harlan's nothing of the sort, but he and his wife have good hearts—we are blessed to live among your people."

They discussed wages. Of course, the pay also was nothing like Hannah earned in the big city, but she agreed to take the job. "The only thing is, twice a week, I'll need to be driven to Wooster for physical therapy for my wrist. And a week from Saturday, I won't be available at all."

"I heard about your family's big wedding this coming Thursday. I know I can trust you to get things done, even if on a flexible schedule. Your friend Ella has been so helpful, delivering her wonderful lavender products for the guests. Why, come to think of it, she was here when my brother and I talked about hiring you and she seconded the motion. I use her lavender soaps and sachet, as I'm sure you do. Oh, speaking of deliveries," she went on, glancing out a kitchen window, "here comes Harlan with chicken breasts for dinner. Fish or chicken, that's it for my new guest. You want to let Harlan in for me? That next batch of cookies needs to come out."

Hannah went to the back door and held it open for the big man as he carried in two large packages, wrapped with white butcher's paper.

"I'm going to work for Mrs.—Amanda now," she told him. "And I appreciate your suggesting this job for me."

"Don't mention it. Glad to see you're doing okay. What a tragedy. The law getting anywhere solving it?"

"They don't tell me everything," she said as she closed the door behind him, but not before she'd seen a sleek, shiny red car with a Nevada license parked out in back next to his black refrigerated delivery truck. Around here, both vehicles really stood out.

"Man, this place smells good!" he exclaimed, and patted his sister's shoulder. "Heck of a lot better than my butcher shop." Amanda handed him a cup of coffee, and he plunked himself down at the table.

"And," Amanda said, lowering her voice, "my coffee's better than booze any day."

"Never you mind. I hear enough of that from Clair. Oh, meant to tell you," he said, turning toward Hannah and frowning, as if he couldn't wait to change the subject, "Seth Lantz is in his buggy out front. Said his sister asked him to come by for you, take you home."

Feeling like a silly *maidal*, Hannah felt herself blush. "Amanda, I was going to start today."

"No, you go on now, and I'll see you midmorn tomorrow. Just come right in, either back door or front, and I'll have the things you need."

"Glad you're not hurt more'n your wrist, Hannah," Harlan said, his mouth full of a cookie.

"Thanks again to both of you," she said, and went to let herself out the front door. Ordinarily, she'd be upset with Naomi or whoever arranged this switch of buggy drivers, but something had been bothering her. With all the excitement last night, she hadn't asked

Linc how the grass over Lena's grave had been disturbed. At the risk of getting Seth upset at Linc again, she was going to mention it to him and let him do the asking. She wanted to make the mess at Lena's grave up to Seth somehow.

10

ALTHOUGH HANNAH HAD RIDDEN WITH SETH for many years, it felt so strange to walk toward him, waiting in his buggy for her. She pictured again his small, two-seat courting buggy, but his bigger family carriage waited. At least his sturdy mare, Blaze, hadn't changed, as had so much else.

"I hope you don't mind the change of plans," Seth said, and got down to give her a hand up. "Naomi and Ella are into wedding plans at our house," he explained, "and it took longer than they thought. Then they're heading to your house to finalize the food."

Wedding plans...it took longer than they thought. His words snagged in her head. "No, I—I understand," she said. "That's fine. Thanks for filling in." As Seth giddyupped Blaze away, she told him in a rush that she'd taken the B and B job for a while.

"Will you ever be content here again?" he asked. "Maybe you could manage the B and B as Mrs. Stutzman ages. Or once your wrist is healed, you could help Ella with the lavender business or your mother with the *kapp*-making."

"I suppose so, but that would not be my calling, though I'm not sure what is yet, either here or—or out there. Seth, I've been meaning to mention something to you."

His face lit as he turned to her. Sitting to her right as the men always did in a buggy, he was so close she could see herself reflected in his clear blue eyes. She wondered if he hoped she had something personal to say to him, something about them.

"It's about Lena's grave," she blurted out.

He frowned and looked away. "I know you didn't intend to sit there that night. You didn't know where she was buried and probably didn't even see her name on the stone in the dark—"

"Actually, I did, after the guys parked all our stuff there. And to ask them to move—which I wanted to do—I would have had to explain why and that was no one's business but—but mine. However, that's not it. I mean, I am sorry her tombstone got hit, but—"

"I was thinking maybe it was kind of a trade-off from her, like she reached out from heaven to help you, to say she was sorry for what happened. She betrayed you just like I did, but her being buried there, her stone, might have saved your life."

Hannah gripped her hands in her lap and gave a little shudder.

"Are you cold?" he asked. "I have a lap robe here."

"No—no, please just listen for a minute," she rushed on, not looking at him now. "It's not about Lena's tombstone. When Linc had me lie on the ground when we were reenacting what happened that night, I noticed the sod needed to be pressed down or watered or something. I don't know, maybe in the spring it will just all grow together, grow back."

"Hannah, I've been there, even sat on the ground. I didn't see anything with the sod. Of course, when we were there with Armstrong, I wasn't looking at that. I probably haven't really noticed the grass itself since the men shoveled the soil back in on the coffin and replaced the sod."

She turned to face him. "It looks like it could be peeled up. I don't want you to argue with Linc again over anything, but I'm thinking when they measured and circled and dug up the blood and bullets, they cut into and around the sod."

He was silent for a moment. She realized he'd been nervous with her, too, overly talkative, wanting to give her every benefit of every doubt. But now he was in what she used to call his think-time. She studied his profile. He was frowning. More than interested—upset.

"Hannah, I'm due in an hour at the lumber mill to pick out roofing shingles for John Arrowroot's place, but if you have time now, let's go look at it. The police tape was just taken off yesterday, so we're legal. I hated seeing that stuff strung all over, as if the graveyard wasn't really ours!"

Ours, she thought. That was the Amish way. Help for any brother or sister in need, cooperation not competition. Sharing, support and love...

"All right," she said as he sped Blaze up once they passed through town. "Let's look at it, even if Linc will probably have a fit we didn't mention it to him first, either."

When they reached the graveyard, Seth got out. He was really shaken but trying to stay calm. "Stay put there a minute," he said, and took out binoculars to scan the area.

"You never used to carry those in your buggy."

"Not until lately, when someone might be watching you or us from afar. You can climb down now. I don't see anyone but one of the Meyers brothers, plowing under their corn maze."

"Just one of them in sight?"

"*Ya,* can't tell which one," he said as he replaced the binoculars and opened the squeaky gate for them.

Despite his loyalty to Lena, Seth realized it had seemed so normal to have Hannah beside him in the buggy, dyed-red hair and all, though it was smoothed down now and mostly hidden under her bonnet. But to see her close-up without all that garish eye makeup and those black lips—her mouth naturally pink and moist and full...

He thrust those thoughts aside. He wanted to help her through the shame of the shootings for old times' sake, that was all. And he knew that Linc Armstrong watched him like a hawk. Seth wanted to find the guilty one so Hannah would be safe, but also to clear his own name of any FBI suspicion.

They stopped at Lena's broken tombstone, which he was already saving money to replace. "Here," Hannah said, bending down, then kneeling beside the grave. "Here. Look."

He knelt beside her and saw immediately what she meant. Despite the fact the grass was seldom cut, and even then by a scythe rather than a mower amid all these tombstones, there was a real rift between the sod blanket over the grave and the surrounding grass. *"Ya,"* he said, lifting a line of sod, "it does kind of peel away. Maybe this spot had clay-type soil and the roots just didn't grow down after she was buried, but I don't think so."

Hannah moved to the foot of the grave. "Same here. And on this other side. Who else was buried around the same time? Maybe there was something done different when they filled the graves or some weird weather condition that kept the sod blanket from mingling with the surrounding grass."

"It has to have an explanation. Your former friend Sarah's *grossmamm,* Miriam Kauffman, died about the same time. What a long life," he said, trying not to sound bitter, "especially compared to Lena's mere twenty-five years."

"I am sorry about her death, Seth, for you and Marlena. I meant to say that. It must have been awful."

"A huge shock. She'd had the weakness since birth, the coroner said, like a ticking time bomb. At least she wasn't holding Marlena when she fell. He said that it wouldn't even have made a difference if I'd been there—nothing to do to help. Still, I felt guilty for it— like about what happened to us."

He knew this was the wrong time to spill all that, but he couldn't help it. His guilt over betraying Hannah and causing her to leave had eaten at him from that time on. Lena had accused him of still pining for Hannah. He'd denied it, denied it to himself, but she'd been right.

"I'm sorry, too, Seth, but we have to let it go—go on. So Miriam Kaufmann is buried up farther?" Hannah asked as they trudged uphill. He saw her stop and glance toward the trees where the shooter had evidently hidden. She was frowning as if angry, not fearful. He should not have brought her back here and out in the open. Linc Armstrong would have a fit, as she'd said.

"Don't fret," he said, reaching out to give her good hand a squeeze. "You can see no one's there with all the bushes bare and the leaves off the trees."

"I know. But that night—I was just remembering. I stopped and stared up into the trees. It's a miracle I wasn't shot, standing there like that—and then Kevin went down and... Do you think the shooter might have thought I saw him—could even recognize him—and that's why he's stalking me?"

"Has there been something else besides the feather and slit screen? I've got to get you back in the buggy. You'll have to tell Amanda Stutzman you can't work there unless someone comes in a car for you and—"

"No! I won't be a prisoner in my parents' house. I told Linc the same. If I can help him look into suspects, I will."

"Something else did happen besides the slit screen, didn't it? Something that gave Armstrong a new lead?"

"Seth, you used to read my mind years ago, but—" She sucked in a sob. He realized that, if he wasn't so intent on getting her back into the buggy and home, he would have pulled her into his arms. "But—at least on this—you're right."

"So something happened, and Armstrong asked you not to tell me. See—he still considers me a possibility to have shot at all of you, as if I carried two rifles around after dark just waiting for you to show up, then buried the one I shot at you all with!"

"He said not to tell you and my father, and he doesn't suspect my father, so it isn't that. You're over-reacting."

"I always overreact when it comes to you."

They stood on the windy brow of hill among the tombstones of the dead, staring deep into each other's eyes. She broke their gaze before he did. "Look," she said, pointing, probably only too glad to change the mood and the topic. "Sarah's *grossmamm*'s grave has loose sod, too, just kind of patched into the surrounding turf."

Seth picked a corner of it up, knelt down, tipped his head and stared under it. "A crazy idea," he said, "but what if in these tough times, someone is shaving the sod up and burying money or jewelry under here— then getting at it when necessary?"

He looked up at Hannah when she gasped. "And thought," she said quietly, almost to herself, "especially when he or they saw Kevin and Tiffany pretending to dig at Lena's grave with her parasol in the dark, that we were digging up their treasure!"

"Hannah, I want to make a deal with our FBI superman. If he won't tell you to keep things from me—I'm already sticking my neck out with John Arrowroot and reporting to Linc—then we'll tell him about this possible motive for the shooting."

"All right," she said, hugging herself with one arm while her cape flapped like wings in a sudden gust of wind. Seth thought she looked as if she could fly, his beautiful friend and once beloved Hannah, with whom he'd ruined things forever. But at least she seemed to trust him on this much.

When Seth took Hannah home, she saw that, not only Ella's and Naomi's buggies were here, but Linc's car. "Making a deal with him may be easier than we thought," she told Seth as he dashed around to help her down. This time, she noted, it wasn't her *daad* who stood in the door staring out, but Linc.

He opened the door for them. "Just the man we wanted to see," Seth said.

"Really? Naomi said she and Ella asked you to bring Hannah back. But I got a wedding dinner invitation out of all of this," he said with a sweep of his hand to indicate *Mamm,* Naomi, Anna—Ella and Seth's mother— and Ella bent over lists on the table.

"Oh, good, Hannah, you're back!" Naomi cried. "We're planning who fixes what for the dinner after. Will you help oversee the cooks in the wedding wagon? And I was hoping you would be a reception singer, too."

"The wedding wagon?" Linc asked before Hannah could answer.

"Fixing food for about four hundred is more than our kitchen can bear," Hannah explained. "So we rent a trailer that's hauled in with lots of ovens and stovetops. Sure, Naomi, anything I can do with one good hand, I will."

Linc and Seth hustled her off into the living room and Linc produced her cell phone, which she was glad to have back. "Sorry that took a while," he said. "We needed to check your phone records—who called you, who you called—in case it led to anything, which it didn't."

"Small potatoes," Seth said.

"What's small potatoes?" Linc asked, his voice instantly on edge. "Evidently not some special dish for the wedding?"

Hannah didn't like his tone with Seth, but Seth liked to bait him, too.

"We—both Seth and I," she said, "are trying to help with your investigation."

"If you call withholding need-to-know intel help," Linc countered with a glance at Seth.

"But you've asked me to do the same, and I think," she said, hoping she could talk fast enough to keep them from arguing, "since Seth's gone out on a limb to check on John Arrowroot, no one will be withholding more information. But sniping or one-upmanship won't help, either."

Linc's eyes widened. "You told Seth about last night," he said, a statement and not a question.

"What about last night?" Seth asked.

"No, I did not," Hannah told Linc. "But we need to tell him and then we can go on to something Seth and I discovered."

"So this is your investigation now?" Linc demanded, his voice rising.

"It might be my life on the line!"

"All right," Linc said, lifting both palms toward her as if to hold her off. "So what have you two learned?"

"First, we need to tell Seth about last night."

"I said, what about last night?" Seth demanded.

"You drive a hard bargain, Hannah Esh," Linc said, managing to ignore Seth's outburst. "Okay. Maybe he can go reroof the Meyers brothers' house to learn more than I got out of them last night. They—and their momma—swear they never left the house last night or the night of the shooting, though they did hear the shots and didn't know where they were from. So let's fill Seth in, then I want to hear that momentous news."

* * *

Linc agreed their find in the cemetery was momentous. "Pretty weird, too," he'd added, but Hannah could tell he was impressed enough to make a real concession. He'd immediately phoned and summoned Sheriff Freeman. Not only that, but he'd asked *Daad* if he could spare some Amish clothing, including hats for him and the sheriff, to borrow. And he wanted Seth to drive him and Jack Freeman to see the sod over the two graves. Seth agreed, though he was still fuming over Linc taking Hannah into the corn maze. To Hannah's amazement and admiration, he had not—yet—exploded at her or Linc for that.

"But the loose sod was my discovery, so I'm going, as well," Hannah insisted, and so, though Linc made her wear a bulletproof vest under her cape, she did.

Once they reached the graveyard, the three men took turns studying the sod or scanning the area. It reminded Hannah of when geese fed, staring at the ground, one always watched for danger.

Linc kept shaking his head. Lena's grave, Miriam Kauffman's grave farther up the hill, then two more graves of church members buried during the past year, had their sod shaved up, then replaced. The men could almost lift each away as if it were a blanket, though the weight was great and it started to tear and crumble on the edges. By simply peering beneath, they could not see soil disturbed in a pattern to indicate that anything small like a box or chest had been buried.

"The theory of treasure being buried here is farfetched," Linc said with another narrow glance up toward the trees, "but then so is a case where picnickers are shot on Halloween night in a quiet, secluded Amish cemetery."

Sheriff Freeman put in, "And since you and your goth friends were hovering over Lena Lantz's grave when you were shot, Hannah, I say we start there."

"Start there, how?" Seth asked. Hannah could tell he continually positioned himself between her and where the shooter had been, even if she moved a bit.

"I'm going to ask your and the bishop's permission to dig under the sod," Linc said.

"Bishop Esh and the church elders won't agree to that, and I don't like it, either."

"Seth," Linc said, "if someone buried something precious they plan to dig up later, they didn't go down six feet where the coffin would be. We won't need to disturb that."

"Can't you get a short rod and just probe the ground a ways without digging?" Seth asked.

"You do still dig these graves by hand, by shovel, right?" Linc asked.

"Yes, but we won't agree to just dig randomly."

"Then I might have to get a court order—but your suggestion of a probe just gave me an idea. I know how we can take a good look, as deep as we want, in this grave—the others, too—without sticking a rod or a shovel in the ground, yet."

Seeming excited, he hurried back to the buggy and used his cell phone in the wind shelter of it. "Don't worry," Sheriff Freeman told Seth and Hannah as he scanned the woodlot up the hill again. From here, Hannah could see no one except one of the Meyers brothers still plowing the corn maze under, with a snowplow attached to the front of his tractor, no less.

Sheriff Freeman was just trying to calm them down, she thought as he went on. "Agent Armstrong's probably referring to probing with radar or some kind of ultrasound. I've heard of that. If they find something, they dig."

Hannah shuddered, remembering the big backhoes that had dug holes in the street for a new sewer near the recording studio in Cleveland. The machines had made so much noise that she was grateful for the soundproof studio, despite the fact it always reminded her that the demo she'd made there had not brought her a singing career and she'd probably remain a receptionist forever if she didn't move on.

And what if Linc's idea of a probe did lead to digging up these graves? She'd already brought shame and suffering on people she admired and loved. She knew her father, as bishop, would fight any disturbance of the graves and then the tense truce between the Home Valley Amish and the government's FBI would be over. And wouldn't that bring in droves of TV and newspaper people again? Sarah's *grossmamm*'s grave on TV would be a terrible gift to her for her wedding day, and for Seth, the destruction of more than a tombstone. Worse, it would be Hannah's fault again, the rebel, the fence-jumper gone to the world, the grotesque goth, Hannah Esh.

Tears blurred her vision so badly when the three of them started down the hill that she stubbed her toe on the next tombstone and would have fallen if Seth hadn't caught her.

11

ON THE WAY HOME FROM THE GRAVEYARD—
Linc had gone with the sheriff in his cruiser—as Seth's
buggy took them past Kauffman's farm, Hannah asked,
"Can you let me out here? I need to tell the Kauffmans
about *Grossmamm* Miriam's grave possibly being disturbed, and I haven't been to see them yet. Besides, I
need to break it to them that Sarah's marrying Nate
MacKenzie."

Seth's hands tightened on the reins. "She is?"

"And I'm going to her wedding in Wooster next Saturday, so please don't try to talk me out of it."

He shook his head, and she saw his jaw clench
before he said, "I'd like to try to talk her out of it. Love
aside, Hannah, you know it's best not to be 'unequally
yoked,' as your father would put it."

"Love aside? That's pretty hard to do, isn't it? At
least for me, it is. Oh, sure, just put love aside when
terrible things happen and—"

Feeling a furious blush coming on, she shut her
mouth. Was she really arguing for Sarah or still fuming
over her own situation with this man? She couldn't help

it that her long-buried anger for Seth sometimes roared to the surface.

"Just don't try to take Ella with you," he said as he pulled into the Kauffman driveway. "You left before you joined the church, but Ella shouldn't be supporting a fence-jumping wedding or she could be censured. Our family doesn't need her following you and Sarah in rebellion. Look, Hannah, I think a lot of Nate MacKenzie and what he did for us here, and Sarah's a gifted person, but—"

"But I'm supposed to just abandon her? I may be a fence-jumper, too, but people should not betray or abandon someone and then ju—"

Before he could help her down or come to a complete stop, she stopped midword and climbed out of the buggy. She was talking about the two of them again. He made a grab for her arm but missed. She hit the ground in stride and walked quickly away.

"After you've talked to them," he shouted, "don't you be running alone across the fields or walk the road. I'm late to order the shingles for Arrowroot's place and get up there to see him, so promise me you'll have one of the Kauffmans buggy you home."

She turned back to face him and shouted back, "Don't tell me what to do! I'll be fine—just fine!"

Ray-Lynn took the call, standing by the cash register at the restaurant.

"Hi, Ray-Lynn." It was Jack! "I know your carryouts don't have delivery, but Linc Armstrong and I'd be really grateful if you could send a couple roast beef sandwiches over with one of your workers. We're up to our necks in a new development and haven't eaten since an early breakfast."

"Something about the graveyard shooting?"

"Big-time."

"I'm almost on my break. Your office, right? I'll bring it myself."

"That would be great. He'll appreciate it, and it means a lot to me."

His voice had warmed at her reply. He was probably thinking she was dying to see him, which she was. But mostly she was just plain nosy, and she'd promised Hannah Esh she'd let her know if there were any new developments.

Ray-Lynn put Leah Schwartz on the cash register and prepared the roast beef sandwiches on sourdough buns with horseradish and dill pickles on the side, along with coleslaw and four half-moon pies. Jack and Linc were probably mainlining coffee, so she grabbed two root beers to give them a change of pace.

She bagged the food and pulled her coat on. The walk to the sheriff's office wasn't far, so why did she feel she and Jack were worlds apart? She couldn't just worry about that tomorrow, like her favorite character Scarlett O'Hara always did. Ray-Lynn blamed Lillian Freeman, crashing into their lives and into this town, which had enough problems without her.

Ray-Lynn greeted Jack's receptionist at the front desk but walked right on back to his office. The door was open, so she went in and put the food down on the corner of his big, cluttered desk. Agent Armstrong was on the phone, pacing, talking about some sort of machine. Jack took her elbow and steered her back out.

"As the old saying goes," he told her as they huddled in the hall, "you're a sight for sore eyes."

She looked up into those eyes, intense, riveted on her, and felt the thrill race through her she always got near him. She reached up to touch his cheek—unfamiliar beard stubble there—and he turned his head to kiss her palm. That made her tingle clear down to the pit of her belly.

"What's happening?" she asked, hoping her voice didn't betray how his mere presence shook her.

"Something strange is going on at the graveyard."

"Still? Meaning what? Not another shooting?"

"Just consider this a word to the wise. Batten down the hatches—and your restaurant—for another big influx of customers, tourists and media. Now I gotta get back to Linc, but let me pay you for—"

"You will not! I'd rather," she said with a little smile, "that you owe me."

"I do, sweetheart," he said. "And, I promise you, I will happily, privately pay—with interest and with love."

Hannah's legs shook as she knocked on the back door of the Kauffman farmhouse. How many times had she, Sarah and Ella just bounced in this back door, up to something? Anna—who had the same first name as Ella's mother, but many Amish names were common—and Ben Kauffman had almost been second parents to her. They'd taken her into their home when she'd sneaked back once a couple of months ago. She prayed they didn't blame her for setting a bad example for Sarah by going to the world before she did, even if for a different reason. But, even if they welcomed her back now, they could not welcome the news she was bringing them of their daughter's worldly wedding.

"Oh, Hannah!" Gabe, Sarah's younger brother, yelled when he opened the back door. "*Mamm, Daad,* it's Hannah Esh! Come in!" he barely got out before Mrs. Kauffman appeared with her arms open wide to engulf her in a hug.

They both cried a bit as Mr. Kauffman patted Hannah on the back, and Gabe stood on one foot and then the other. "Martha's not here now, but we're so glad to see you!" Mrs. Kauffman said.

How Gabe has grown! Hannah thought. And like her own parents, Sarah's mother and father had aged, though Mrs. Kauffman bustled about to serve them hot chocolate and the half-moon pies the family produced by the scores each day for Ray-Lynn's restaurant. The four of them sat at the kitchen table, as familiar to Hannah as her own, while she answered question after question about how her injuries were coming and her new job at the Plain and Fancy B and B. Finally, Hannah put in, "I have two important things to tell you."

The Kauffmans quieted. Although they'd all been turned toward her, they leaned in even closer now.

"Something about Sarah?" Mrs. Kauffman asked. Both their mothers—Ella's, too—always seemed to have a sixth sense about things.

"Yes, one thing about Sarah. She phoned Ray-Lynn Logan and asked her to tell me that she and Nate are going to be married."

"Ach," Mr. Kauffman said but he managed a nod. "Better than just living together."

His apparent acceptance of the wedding surprised

Hannah. She had expected more of a protest. "They weren't living together," Hannah corrected. "She was living with his stepmother. It—the wedding—will be in Wooster on the thirteenth, because they're moving there. Nate has been promoted to oversee this area for the State Fire Marshal's office."

"I like Nate," Gabe blurted out. "He was always good to me, and he saved our barns and lives."

"But that doesn't mean," Mrs. Kauffman said with a nervous glance at her husband, "we can approve of her leaving—being put under the *bann*—or marrying an outsider, even if he is a good man, and we all know he is."

"I miss her, and I'm going to see her," Hannah said, looking from one to the other of them. Both of the senior Kauffmans were holding it all in. Sarah's mother blinked back tears.

"You mean going to her wedding?" she asked.

"Yes, and to visit them once they get settled. I know it's *verboten* and I'll probably get in even more trouble for it. But whatever I did, whatever she did, she's still one of my two best friends in the entire world, and I've learned lately that life can be cut short, even when you're young."

"You mean, because of what happened to your goth friend—" Gabe got out before a look from his father silenced him.

"Yes," Hannah answered him anyway. "Because of that and missing all of you when I left, as I'm sure Sarah does. The other thing—and I know this will be difficult, too, for you—Mr. Kauffman, your mother's grave, along with Lena Lantz's and at least one other, may have something buried in the ground besides the coffins. The sheriff and the FBI agent found something strange there."

Ben's chair scraped back and nearly toppled as he jumped to his feet. "They are disturbing those graves? Something buried there? Anna, I'm going to see Bishop Esh. Hannah, you want to go home now? If there's nothing else to say, I'll take you."

Mrs. Kauffman was crying quietly now. Gabe jumped up, too, and Hannah heard him pounding up the stairs. "Yes, I—I need to go home now," she said as Mr. Kauffman left the room.

"Good to hear you say 'home,'" Sarah's mother said, and reached over to squeeze her shoulder. "Just a minute now before you go."

She also hurried out, although she went toward the back of the house and Hannah heard her rustling through something that sounded like paper. She came back into the kitchen, glancing around to see if they were alone, with two brown paper sacks in her arms, each filled with a folded quilt that protruded out the top.

"These are two of the four quilts Sarah's *grossmamm* Miriam had in the *grossdaadi haus* when she died. I kept one and saved one for Martha's hope chest, but there were two others. With her Alzheimer's, of course, she never knew what Sarah had done—to leave so she could do her paintings and be with Nate—and so be shunned."

Tears blurred Hannah's vision, and she wiped at her eyes. "One of these is for you," Mrs. Kauffman said, speaking quickly and quietly, "a welcome home gift. The other—I hope you will know what to do with it— give it to a friend, if you wish."

This woman wanted Sarah to have a quilt, a wedding gift, but she could not give it to her daughter directly, oh, no, not under the strict rules of the *meidung*. And it was pretty obvious she feared that her husband would not approve.

Hannah nodded and took the sacks. Mrs. Kauffman hugged her again, crunching the paper and soft quilts between them. When Mr. Kauffman came back into the room, she said to him, "I'm giving two of *Grossmamm* Miriam's quilts to Hannah."

He only nodded and headed for the door as Hannah followed, the precious quilts in her arms.

Seth saw that word had spread quickly by the next morning. Although it was the Sabbath, it was the off-week for the bimonthly Amish gathering at a church member's home. But neither that nor the fact the Plain People did not have phones in their home stopped the shocking news. It didn't take long for an Amish crowd—all men, not even Hannah—to gather at the graveyard where the sheriff had again cordoned off the area with neon-bright yellow police tape. Seth had brought his father. Bishop Esh, Ben Kauffman and the church elders already lined the outside of the fence, with other Amish men behind them or strung out along the barrier. They stepped aside to allow Seth and Eben Lantz to stand near the bishop.

Seth was also amazed at the number of *Englische* who had come out to gawk: Harlan Kenton and Elaine Carson stood lower on the hill along the fence, as did both of the Meyers brothers, George and Clint. Mr. Baughman, who owned Homestead Hardware, was there. And a blonde woman with dyed hair and a lot of makeup, dressed in a pink jogging outfit. He didn't see a camera or microphone, but could a reporter be here already?

Inside the fence, Sheriff Freeman and Linc Armstrong were working hard, along with two men he didn't recognize. Amid the grass and plain tombstones, near some of the graves, including Lena's, they had laid out rows of yellow and orange string. Like the fluttering plastic tape along the fence, it looked so wrong in this graveyard. One of the strangers had a sort of box with an antenna strapped on against his chest, and the other was pushing what looked like a big-wheeled red lawnmower back and forth down the narrow rows between the graves right in front of Lena's broken tombstone.

Once Seth and his father had joined the other men, Bishop Esh summoned Ben Kauffman to stand next to them. Then he called out, "Sheriff Freeman! Agent Armstrong! This is the Sabbath, a day of rest. And this graveyard is the property of the Amish Church of the Home Valley."

Linc hardly looked up, but Sheriff Freeman came over as the bishop went on. "We have here next of kin of Lena Lantz and Miriam Kauffman, and we at least want to know what is going on. Is that contraption a mower or a digger?"

"Bishop Esh, this is government business, out of even my hands, but I assure you," the sheriff said, "that machine merely probes the ground with radar—invisible rays—looking for abnormalities in the soil. There is no digging yet."

"Yet? But if you find abnormalities, you intend to

dig? We need to know more than that. We protest the destruction of these graves."

"Let me explain it to you as best I can, Bishop Esh. I didn't know this would all happen so fast. I decided to stay here to keep an eye on things, so that I could inform you after they found something, if they did."

"Are there any signs at all of abnormalities yet?" Seth demanded. "And we should have at least one observer at the graves, not held off our property by this fence and tape."

"Just a minute. I'm going to tell Agent Armstrong, since Seth and Mr. Kauffman are closest of kin to two of the deceased whose graves are in question—"

"In question?" Bishop Esh cut in.

"—that I intend to bring the two of you and the bishop inside to explain things. It's all new to me, too, but it may lead us to why the shootings occurred here. Just a minute now. I'll be right back."

Seth's stomach cramped as he watched the machine run over Lena's grave, back and forth between the grid lines. When the sheriff motioned the three of them inside, Seth almost vaulted the fence rather than walking through his murmuring people to the gate.

"Bishop Esh, Seth, Mr. Kauffman," Linc Armstrong greeted them and shook their hands. Linc pointed at the man with the computer screen strapped to his chest. He was reading it as he walked back and forth, following the man with the wheeled contraption. "The reader is Mel Pleiss, a geologist from Akron, who works for a company that uses GPR—ground-penetrating radar— which can peer into concrete or soil. It can locate such things as pine boxes in unmarked graves—"

"These graves are all marked—clearly," Bishop Esh

said, but the men went about their business and did not look up.

"Or it can locate underground voids or foreign objects," Armstrong went on. "In other words, even disturbed soil or other things buried will show up as imagery—a kind of wavy picture—on that screen that Mr. Pleiss can read. It can take a long time to process a scene, but this is not clay soil so the GPR can read almost six feet down."

Seth asked, "You're looking for something bigger than bullets you didn't locate before, bigger than a small box of money or treasure?"

"Right, although some of those other items could show up. The truth is we're not quite sure what we're looking for, but as Seth or Hannah can explain since they stumbled on this—"

"Hannah told me last night," the bishop said. "But that does not give you or your people—radar machines or not—the right to disturb our graves."

"I'm sorry, sir," Linc said, staring hard at the bishop, then at Seth. "We have a court order coming that will allow us to get to the bottom of this crime scene, literally. And I regret that word of this will soon get out to more than just your people, and we'll have swarms of media in here again, because they complicate my job."

"We will see about all this," the bishop said, and walked away.

Seth felt guilty he'd helped to cause this latest outrage. In his mind, the first catastrophe was not the shootings, but that he'd let Hannah down when he'd gotten Lena pregnant, though he'd never wish that he didn't have Marlena in his life. He, too, turned and walked away, with a frowning glance up the hill from where the bullets which had changed everything again had come, but, for now at least, had kept Hannah home.

He gasped. On the ground, halfway up the hill between the fence and the woodlot, John Arrowroot sat cross-legged on a blanket, just watching. Was Armstrong too occupied to have noticed the man, or had he not yet met him and so didn't recognize him? The sheriff, at least, should be keeping an eye on him. Seth went out the gate, now guarded by a state highway patrolman, and circled the growing crowd of his people.

Seth strode up the hill toward Arrowroot, but before he could say a word, the man called to him, "Now maybe you people will get what it means to have the government ignore you and have your sacred land violated!"

12

SETH STARED AT ARROWROOT, WHO WENT ON as if he'd said nothing important. "Shouldn't you be up on my roof, starting the reshingling?"

"You know I can't with this going on. I have a feeling you're enjoying yourself here, getting back at us."

"Not really. The last thing I want is the government—and make no mistake, the FBI is the U.S. government—digging up land sacred to the Eries. I'm just waiting for them to turn up one little artifact or ancient bone, and I'll have them stopped like that—and Agent Armstrong knows it, even if he's like a bull in the china shop."

"Stop them how?"

"They're throwing around their terms—GPR, FBI, the BCI. I told him my answer to them—the NAGPRA."

So Arrowroot and Linc Armstrong had had words already. "Which is?" Seth asked. This man obviously liked lording the information over him. Despite Arrowroot sitting there so cockily, Seth sometimes thought he could smell defiance to cover guilt reeking from him.

But for shooting young people he didn't even know and with the intent to kill?

"It's the Native American Graves Protection and Repatriation Act, a 1990 federal law," Arrowroot said. He sounded like the lawyer he was as he went on. "For too long this country has ripped off not only land from Native tribes but their ancestors' human remains, funerary objects, artifacts. But that law says, they turn one of them up—with their radar or so much as a spade—and all digging stops until they get forensic anthropologists and tribal observers out here to preserve and then return everything."

"Mr. Arrowroot, I do feel for Indian tribes losing their land, but my people have dug our graves on this hillside by hand for nearly a century and we haven't turned up any objects like that."

"Not that you've made public, anyway. What about arrowheads in the fields? My people," he threw back, emphasizing each word, "were known for their poison arrows, and they always used a mound like this for burials. You have any idea yet of what they're looking for?" he asked with a tilt of his head down the hill.

Seth had been baited long enough. His *daad* would have come up with a soft answer, but he blurted, "Maybe something you planted there."

"Now, look," Arrowroot said, jabbing the air with his finger, "you want that job on my roof or not? Maybe you should get back to work."

"I can send someone else if you don't want me there, but I can't start when I said I could because of this."

"Yeah, fine. I'd be pretty shook, too, if I thought those bastards were going to dig up my wife's grave."

Seth jerked his head around to glance down the hill.

Armstrong, the sheriff and the two GPR men were huddled in conversation, almost on top of Lena's grave. Armstrong immediately got on his cell phone, nodding and gesturing as he talked while the other three men pulled the GPR machine up toward Miriam Kauffman's grave.

"Let me know what you find out," Arrowroot called after Seth as he hurried down the hill and stood at the highest part of the fence, closest to old Miriam's resting place.

"What is it?" Seth called to the sheriff. "What did you find?"

By the time the sheriff walked up to where Seth stood, Bishop Esh and Ben Kauffman had joined him. Bishop Esh was out of breath. "I'm sorry, Seth," the sheriff said, "but I'm not at liberty to say just yet. You'll be one of the first to know if anything pans out. They need to examine the other graves with the lifted sod."

"Sheriff, just tell me one thing," Seth said, reaching out to grasp the man's shoulder, right above his badge. He remembered how adamant Agent Armstrong had been that Seth examine his FBI badge when he first questioned him about the shootings. Armstrong was a prideful man, but Sheriff Freeman was more approachable. "Lena Lantz is still buried there, isn't she?" Seth asked. "She hasn't been…disturbed, like the sod?"

"Yes, Seth. As far as we—they—can tell, her coffin and body are there intact."

Seth heaved a sigh. "So something else has been put into her grave besides her coffin?"

"Later, Seth. I swear that you, the Kauffmans and

the bishop will be the first to know when we figure things out."

Seth could have fallen to his knees, but he nodded and stood firm. Things could not get worse, he thought, just before a helicopter with Channel 9 News/Cleveland printed on its side circled, then hovered, sucking grit and Amish hats into the air while someone leaned out with a camera.

Hannah, who was helping Amanda Stutzman clean the common rooms of the B and B, first heard about what had happened when Lily Freeman jogged back that morning. She wore a hot-pink running suit with white stripes. Though she was sweating and out of breath—and still looked somehow put together—the moment she came in the front door, she told Amanda and Hannah about the GPR, the crowd at the cemetery and the news media literally hanging over the scene.

"Their chopper was kicking up so much dust and leaves. I didn't need that in my eyes and hair," she told them. "Contact lenses, green-tinted ones at that. I used to wear glasses before I left here, but a lot of things used to be different. So you're the Amish survivor of the shooting," she said, patting Hannah's shoulder. "Thank heavens you're all right. Amanda told me you'd be working here. Despite that wrist bandage, it looks like you're doing well."

"I start physical therapy this week, which I guess is a good sign. But do you know if they found what they're looking for underground at the graveyard?"

"It's driving everyone crazy—the sheriff, too, I can tell, because he's caught between the two worlds involved. I still know that man better than he knows himself."

Well, Hannah thought, there was a quote Ray-Lynn should hear, but it would worry her to death.

What could be buried in those newest graves? Hannah still figured it was some sort of treasure. Who would get possession of it if no one dared claim it without incriminating himself? If it was in Lena's grave, would Seth own whatever they found? The Amish church? As soon as Hannah was finished here today and Naomi picked her up, should she head to the graveyard to see what was going on? Or would that make her fair game for the media visitors she'd managed to avoid before? She could already feel the assessing stares of her own people. In a big way, she was the one who had caused all this, set these terrible events in motion.

Amanda interrupted Hannah's agonizing when she asked her guest, "I suppose you're going back to writing your book, but would you like some tea or a snack, Lily?"

So this woman was writing a book. Was it really about her life in Nevada? Hannah wondered. It could be about the contrast between Homestead and Las Vegas. She sure hoped she didn't see all the events around here as ideas for a murder mystery.

"Coffee, but no more pastries for me right now, thanks," Lily said, patting her flat stomach. "Love your bakery items, Amanda, but I've got to keep my girlish figure and that's not easy in Amish country. Hannah, I see you're keeping it off, though maybe you have your bus to catch, too."

She gave a light laugh, but it seemed to have an edge to it. It actually took Hannah a minute to realize she was talking about men, not buses. So did she mean she was still after Jack Freeman or did she have someone else in mind?

It was almost dark that Sunday night when Sheriff Freeman, with the light bar on his cruiser blinking, made his way through several cars and three TV trucks with antennas and broadcasting dishes lining the road in front of the Esh house. Twice, Hannah's father had gone out to ask reporters to please stay off his property, and their vehicles were now blocking one side of the two-lane Oakridge Road in front of the farm.

The bishop let the sheriff in before he knocked and firmly closed the door behind him. *Mamm,* Naomi and Hannah had been serving cider and doughnuts to the assembled group: Ben and Anna Kauffman; Seth and his parents, Eben and Anna; and several church elders. Hannah saw Seth's shoulders tense. How she longed to be able to stand beside him, to rub his back or at least touch it to comfort him.

Silence fell as everyone clustered in the kitchen to hear what the sheriff had to say. He took off his big-brimmed hat and turned it over and over in his hands. "First of all, I promise you," he began, "as soon as I leave, I will clear out those media vultures, at least tell them they have to keep back a hundred feet, off your property and out of the road."

"We appreciate that," *Daad* told him. "Will Agent Armstrong be coming here, too?"

"He's very busy with the new developments."

"Would you like to sit down? Have some coffee and doughnuts?" *Daad* asked. Hannah almost wanted to scream at the polite chatter, but it was the Amish way.

"No, thanks. I'll need to get back to—to try to keep a lid on things. There's no easy way to say this, after all else that's happened." His eyes met Hannah's before he looked away, back to her father. "The coffins with the bodies of your loved ones have not been disturbed, exactly, so you can rest easy on that."

"Not disturbed 'exactly'?" Seth said. "What did you find with that radar? Is there a pattern in the four graves you examined?"

"The fourth one, Amos Miller's, is so new, we think the sod just hasn't grown back in this cold weather. But in the other three—Lantz, Kauffman and Zook—yes. It appears that there may be a second burial on top of the original coffins—two bodies per grave, the newer additions not in coffins but…in something else, not sure."

Everyone stood stunned. Hannah's heartbeat thudded so loud she thought the others might hear it. Finally, some murmured, waiting for the bishop to speak again, but her father only put a hand on a chair back to steady himself. For one moment, he glared at Hannah, but covered it quickly. Her stomach cartwheeled. Did he blame her for all this, too? Seth folded his hands over his chest, and she heard sniffles as Mrs. Kauffman began to cry.

"But those other bodies are not our people," Seth said. "No one has gone missing or is unaccounted for. Even those who are in their *rumspringa* years or have gone to the world—well, we know where they are. I stood there while four men I trust filled my wife's grave after her death. But your findings mean you will have to dig, to open it again."

"Agent Armstrong has a court order coming that

gives him the right to do so. A backhoe will be here Monday morning—tomorrow—and it shouldn't take long."

Hannah could tell her father was distraught. As usual, he tried to keep control, but she could see his chin quivering. Finally he said, "'For you are like graves which are not seen, and the men who walk over them are not aware of them.'"

The sheriff frowned. "A Bible verse?" he asked. "And a good one."

Seth stepped farther forward and stood beside the bishop. "I've used backhoes to dig foundations for more than one building project," he said, facing the sheriff squarely. "They're quick but, even with a skilled operator, they can really scrape or crush the soil. Those coffins are pine, Sheriff. I would ask, at least on my wife's grave, that a backhoe should be *verboten* and— if the law insists on digging—it be done by hand, by shovels of our own."

"*Ya,* that at least," Bishop Esh agreed. "Our men should dig, not a machine that could hit other tombstones and make them look as bad as the one on Lena Lantz's grave."

Hannah bit her lower lip. Like one stone dropped in the pond where she and her friends used to swim, the ripples of what she'd done had gone out, out, out to more dreadful things. And she was certain that's the way the bishop, her own *daad,* would see it.

"I'll see what Agent Armstrong says," the sheriff answered, "but I will argue for that, Seth, if the others here are agreed." Heads nodded, *ya*s all around. "I'll let you know first thing tomorrow. Right now I've got to clear out those media folks and check with Agent

Armstrong on your suggestion. Makes sense to me, not only to cooperate, but because hand shovels, held by men who are careful and respectful, is the least the government can do if they don't want bad publicity. We may have used new technology to find the hidden graves, but your way sounds best for this. Thank you all—for not fighting this further."

Her father nodded. "We, too, want to find out who would do such a thing. And why bodies are hidden among our own where they should not be."

Hannah forced herself to keep calm as people left for their homes, but once they were gone, she hurried down in the basement to be alone. In the familiar darkness, she went way back in the corner, past the washing machine, past the rows of neatly arranged canned vegetable and fruits that would shine like a rainbow if she lit a lantern. She still knew this black basement well, for it was where she sometimes hid when she was young. She and Seth had sneaked down here one time when there was a singing in their barn for their buddy group. Snatching a few moments alone when one of them wasn't leading the songs and everyone was concentrating on the spread of good eats, in this very spot the two of them had caressed and kissed like crazy until she was downright dizzy.

She sat on an old rag rug amid boxes of borrowed china for Naomi's wedding dinner and started to cry. It felt good—cleansing. Finally, she could let out all the frustration and the pain of failing her people, her mistake of bringing her outsider friends into the heart of Amish land, of abusing the cemetery, and worse—of the fear she still loved Seth.

She sobbed in great, gasping breaths as she had not

since just after she left home, as she had after Seth had told her he was going to wed Lena. Nothing wrong with a good, thorough cry sometimes, she tried to tell herself as she wiped her eyes and blew her nose with her handkerchief. Her father was angry with her, had not forgiven. And here, Naomi's wedding was in three days' time, and she'd probably ruined that, too. The TV and newspaper reporters would not have swooped in—twice—if she had just stayed away. But then, whoever had been hidden in Amish graves needed to have their deaths investigated. Maybe, like Kevin—like she could have been—those people had been murdered.

She froze, stopped crying, even held her breath when she heard a footfall on the stairs, a heavy tread, a man's. Being trapped in the maze flashed through her mind. She didn't want her family—especially *Daad*—to find her this way, but who else could it be? She should just leave the Home Valley, go back to— But to where and what?

"Hannah," came a deep voice. "You down here in the dark?"

Seth! But he'd gone home.

"*Ya,* in the dark, for sure."

She swiped under her eyes, dabbed at her wet cheeks and tried to blink tears away. At least it appeared he didn't have a lantern, she thought as she heard him bump into something and mutter, *"Ach!"*

She felt torn in two again: she wanted to be with him but he was the last person on earth she felt she could face right now.

"I just needed time alone," she added, thinking he might take the hint. He didn't.

"I dropped my parents off," he said as he came

quickly closer, evidently as his eyes adjusted to the darkness, "then returned to apologize to the bishop for speaking out in his place to the sheriff both at the graveyard and here. But he was thankful I did. When I was leaving again, I asked Naomi if she'd fetch you, and she said you were down here. You've been crying. I'm sorry. Sorry for that and for everything—and I'm talking about ruining things for us in the first place."

"Water, as they say, over the dam."

"Is it? I think we're still fighting the rapids, not only of this graveyard mess but of being near each other again after—after everything."

"I was feeling guilty, just terrible that I agreed to bring my friends back here, then the shooting, then the graves being disturbed—but at least, if more people have been shot, we need to know who died and who did it."

"Maybe a mass murderer—that's what Armstrong's thinking, I'll bet, something that can make his career."

"You judge him harshly."

"I know, 'Judge not,' but I think he has designs on you, not just as a witness but as a woman."

"No way!" she insisted, but there were signs, and evidently Seth had seen them, too.

"Let's not talk about him right now," he said, sitting down beside her. "I want to say once and for all that I regret my actions with Lena, regret that they caused you to run away, although I can never regret Marlena."

"I—I understand that. Besides, Lena was also to blame. I know it's best not to speak ill of the dead, but as they say in the world, 'It takes two to tango.'"

"Does the world still hold such allure for you?" he

asked, leaning so close now his breath warmed her cheek. "Could you never be happy here again?"

"I don't know. It's too early, too much—too much going on."

"I talked to the sheriff outside before he left. He says that whatever—whoever—they find in the graves, they're going to check all the graves now. It may take a long time to investigate the additional bodies—to identify them—even with modern science, forensics and all that. I hope, at least, that means you will stay here for a while. And I, for one, don't intend to give up on finding some of my own answers, especially if it takes their modern ways so long."

"John Arrowroot?"

"From him and whatever other leads we—I might get."

He reached out to touch her arm, then slid his hand upward to stroke her cheek. Knowing he'd feel the dampness there, she pulled away.

"It's all right," he said, his voice soothing, yet strong. "All this makes me want to cry, as well. Don't blame yourself, Hannah. I—I hope the bishop doesn't, but I see he's still grim over it all—your leaving."

"Grim—a good word for it."

"But maybe this is all God's will that you came back, that through you these terrible things are being uncovered and maybe, somehow, will be solved, too."

"I'd like to believe that, but then I'd like to believe a lot of things. Like when I was a little girl and hid down here as if something naughty I'd done would not be found out, or that I'd get something I wanted that *Mamm* or *Daad* said I couldn't have."

Seth leaned close again, and she yearned to throw

herself into his embrace, to cling to him with her one good arm and—

As if he'd read her mind, Seth pulled her to him and held her close.

She clung to him, amazed how natural it felt, how necessary. And that scared her almost as much as walking a dark maze or graveyard paths in the utter blackness of night.

13

JUST AS THE FIRST MORNING SHE'D BEEN BACK in her parents' home, Hannah awoke the next day to see little Marlena Lantz in her bedroom. So Naomi was still going to keep an eye on her, at least until the wedding? But why had she let her wander off again?

Hannah saw the door to the hall stood ajar. Marlena had not been watching her sleep this time but was staring up at the doll that had been Hannah's as a child. Standing on tiptoe, the child had both hands stretched upward with fingers wiggling, as if that doll atop the dresser would float right down to her.

"Lumba babba," the little girl said when she saw Hannah was awake. She pointed her chubby finger adamantly now. "I want hold *lumba babba!"*

"I'm in here, too, Hannah!" Naomi's voice came from the foot of the bed. She must be on the floor. "I was trying to be quiet, looking for a box of paper wedding napkins under the bed—oh! Here they are. Believe me, she has her own dolls at home. I think Seth spoils her. She forgot hers today, so I was trying to ignore her. I know that doll is yours."

"Which means I can let her play with it if she likes. I know she won't give it up later, but when she's asleep, Seth can substitute it for her own."

"And have another excuse to see you when he brings yours back," Naomi said with a pert smile, popping up with a cardboard box in her hands. Whatever tragedies beset her people right now, Naomi was so lost in love with Josh Troyer that happiness radiated from her. She spoke softly, with a nod at Marlena, "Seth said she has bad dreams at night."

Hannah nodded. She could sympathize with that. How she wished she could help the little girl, even if she never got over her own hauntings.

"Oh, by the way," Naomi went on, whispering now, though the child surely could not grasp the import of the words, "Seth dropped her off early. He was heading for you-know-where with his brother Aaron and Mr. Kauffman to dig open the three graves."

Even clutching the covers, Hannah shuddered. "Thank the Lord Linc allowed that. He's very used to getting his own way."

"Ha! Do you mean 'Lord' Linc as well as the Lord God? Oh, one more thing I meant to tell you before all of this sadness. I think Ella's going to give you something to take to Sarah's wedding, probably a lot of lavender soap and such. I was really surprised because Ella's such a stick-in-the-mud about people who break the rules." She heaved a huge sigh. "At least you're back with us."

Instead of telling Naomi that she wasn't sure she'd stay, Hannah got up in her nightgown and reached for the doll on the top of the dresser. "I'm surprised Sarah didn't draw a face on this doll, like she did on her own," Hannah mused. "Naomi, I know you're busy. I'll keep an eye on Miss Marlena here and bring her down when I come to breakfast. And I know she'll keep an eye on the doll."

Naomi thanked her and hurried out. Marlena's blue eyes lit to have the doll descend from the heights and fly right into her arms. *"Danki, danki!"* she cried. Hannah lifted the tot up on the bed where she sat chattering to the doll while Hannah got dressed. Now and then she stroked the child's hair and then in her rich alto voice sang a lullaby. Marlena smiled and started to sing, too, pretty much in one pitch. She evidently had not inherited her father's musical talents.

As Hannah took Marlena's hand and they went down to breakfast, she felt she'd done something good. Caring for this little darling was at least one step in forgiving Lena and Seth for what they'd done. Because she really did want the words *Forgive us our debts as we forgive our debtors* to be reality for her. She pictured poor Seth digging Lena's grave, digging up the past. She recalled what he'd said last night: he was going to try to find out who had shot her and her friends, perhaps because the murderer wanted to distract from or keep people away from the double burials. No matter what Linc, the sheriff or her own father said, she was going to try to get to the bottom of that, too—with or without Seth.

Ray-Lynn's hopes that Lily Freeman would not set foot in the Dutch Farm Table Restaurant ended when the woman bounced through the front door midmorning on Monday. What a lousy way to start the week! At least Jack wasn't here.

"Table for one?" Ray-Lynn asked.

"Oh, my, no. Jack said you do carryout sometimes, and I want to order some stuff for him—he-man lunch-type things."

If Jack told her that, had Lily seen him last night? Ray-Lynn wondered. And after he, darn him, had more or less promised undying love? Or since everyone in the restaurant was buzzing about the double burials and exhumations—too many outsiders, as Jack had predicted—did Lily know about that from someone else?

"What will it be?" Ray-Lynn asked, picking up a pad and pencil. No way she wanted to be waiting on or catering to this woman, but maybe she could find out if Jack had asked Lily to bring him food. What if, despite being busy with this big murder case, he was playing things both ways with both of his women? No, she didn't really think he was that kind of man or she'd never have fallen for him.

Lily picked up and scanned a menu, frowning over it. "How about eight Reuben sandwiches and the fixings? It's for those poor Amish men who are digging up their own relatives' graves, and the law enforcement with them."

So, she was up-to-date on all that. Did she learn it directly from Jack? Not by late-night pillow talk, Ray-Lynn hoped.

"Coffee, too," Lily went on. "Oh, never mind that. It wouldn't keep really hot, would it?"

Ray-Lynn figured Lily liked most things really hot.

"Never mind, they'll have water," she told Ray-Lynn. "I thought all that would be a nice gesture."

"Very nice," Ray-Lynn agreed, but it irked her to

no end because she had planned to take her van out there with what the Amish called eats later today. And it really annoyed her that this woman, whom she was starting to think of as the Wicked Witch of the West, had a decent bone in her voluptuous body. But then, if Jack had loved her—maybe still did and didn't even know it—she had to have some redeeming virtues that were more than skin-deep.

"It will take a few minutes," Ray-Lynn told her, and went back into the kitchen. A couple of other things surprised her when she came out with six sacks of food and told Lily the bill would be $78.20. The woman didn't blink a fake lash and peeled off two fifties out of what looked to be quite a few bills. Ray-Lynn helped her carry the food outside, mostly because she wanted to see the snazzy red car Hannah had described to her. Next shock—the vehicle awaiting was Elaine Carson's red truck. And Elaine, in the usual leather outfit, was carrying two cases of bottled water out in Kwik Stop plastic bags and loading them in the backseat, where they put the sacks of food.

"Gotta take care of our very own sheriff and the FBI guy," Elaine said. "Any rep of law and order in the U.S. of A. needs all the support we can give. But Lily and I knew we'd have to feed the Amish workmen, too, or it wouldn't look right," she added with a quick frown that wrinkled her nose. "Thanks, Ray-Lynn. Appreciate it!"

With that, the odd couple jumped in the truck with the flag and eagle decals and roared away.

When Hannah finished a busy morning cleaning ground-floor rooms at the Plain and Fancy B and B, she felt torn about whether to talk Naomi into taking her to the graveyard or just going home. The familiar buggy wasn't here yet, anyway, though Ella had just pulled up in hers. Hannah went out to help her carry her week's supply of lavender products inside.

"How is it going?" Ella asked as Hannah lifted her second basket of goods out of her buggy.

"If you mean here at the B and B, great. Amanda Stutzman is a gem, and her brother even brought me some extra sausages to take home today—says they go great with cold beer, as if we're drinkers like I guess he is. I overheard Amanda telling him his wife would leave him if he didn't let up on that. So, have you been to the graveyard? I need to know what's going on."

"*Daad* said we womenfolk aren't to go because he doesn't know what they will find. But I heard it's packed with outsiders, and there's a helicopter that keeps circling the area. Noisy thing! It scares animals. I hope everyone clears out by Thursday for Naomi and Josh's sake."

"You might know there's a reporter from New York City, no less, staying at the B and B, but of course she isn't here right now."

They toted the baskets in the front door. "In other words, this place is packed with worldly women," Ella whispered. "New York, Las Vegas…"

"And me, from Cleveland."

"I didn't mean that. You're one of us, back home now. Say you are!"

Amanda bustled into the front room from the kitchen. "Oh, Ella, I thought you'd be here this morning. It's fine with me if you just put the things in the two front bedrooms upstairs. No one's here, of course, not with all that's going on. Both rooms are unlocked right now because I was going to take in fresh towels. I'll be in the kitchen if you need me. I'm fixing vegetable pizzas for lunch that can be popped in the oven individually when my guests come back." And she was gone again.

Standing at the bottom of the wide, wooden staircase, Hannah asked Ella, "Mind if I tag along? I haven't seen the rooms upstairs, just dusted furniture and floors down here and the Stutzmans' quarters today."

"Sure. I'll be in and out pretty fast, especially since I don't need to get the key to unlock them."

It wasn't the New York reporter's room Hannah was interested in but Lily Freeman's. Ray-Lynn had been so kind and supportive. Hannah didn't mean to turn into a spy for her, but if Hannah was going to play detective about who did the shooting Halloween night and maybe who buried other bodies in Amish graves, she was obviously going to have to practice getting nosy.

At first, standing in the doorway of the first room Ella entered, Hannah couldn't tell whose it was. It could be Lily's but Hannah didn't ask, just practiced her observation skills. In this charming, country-style room with a quilt on the wall as well as on the bed, she noted a laptop, along with several other electronic devices. One looked like those new eReaders. But a photo of a handsome Asian man and what looked to be twin boys who resembled him on the dresser suggested this was the reporter's room. It didn't have its own bath, so Ella was putting the items out on the dresser.

The larger room across the hall, with the bay window and its own bath, was obviously Lily Freeman's. She would have the larger one since she was here first and was evidently staying for a while. Hannah also saw a laptop, this one on a flat-top desk with a chair in front of the window.

Hannah moved quickly into the room, across the big braided rug partly covering the oak floor. "There's a great view from here," she said, pretending to glance out the bay window while taking a quick look at the pile of papers next to the laptop. On top was a printout of an email of— Why, it was a copy of a news story about Sheriff Freeman calling in the FBI to look into the Amish graveyard shootings! But if Lily wanted to get her ex-husband back, that wasn't unusual. Hannah jumped when Ella spoke.

"Well, that's it, except for the extras I leave with Amanda in case any of the guests want to buy some. What? What is it?"

"Nothing. Just thinking how hard it must be for Mrs. Freeman to be living in this single room when she used to have that whole nice brick ranch house. And, of course, who knows what she was used to in Las Vegas?"

Ella studied her but said nothing. Hannah figured she'd sensed she wasn't telling her the truth. Worse, Hannah realized, if she was going to do some investigating on her own—and she still wasn't sure of whom or how—she was going to have to lie to some of her family and friends, and Linc, too.

Seth was glad the sheriff had produced a tall, plastic, four-sided barrier they wrapped around poles stuck in the ground to give them a bit of privacy while they dug. It rattled in the wind but that sound was mostly drowned out by the helicopter overhead. The crowd had grown larger, including John Arrowroot, who seemed to be camping out up the hill. Seth had mentioned him to Armstrong, who had said he was definitely making himself a person of interest.

Seth, his brother Aaron and Ben Kauffman took turns digging in pairs while Bishop Esh and Armstrong watched. The sheriff and several Ohio Highway Patrol officers handled the crowd. Sheriff Freeman had produced three black plastic body bags and summoned the Wooster coroner, whose van was parked down on the road with two men in it. But Armstrong had pulled rank on the sheriff, telling him that "as soon as the Bureau of Criminal ID and Investigation boys get here, they'll protect and process any findings."

Right now, Aaron and Ben Kauffman stood below in the hole. The mounds of soil they'd dug out lay along each side of the grave to keep the head and foot clear. The sounds of *chunk-swish-chunk-swish* of each spadeful of earth they dug up and threw out of the grave haunted Seth, and each circuit of the TV chopper overhead annoyed him to no end.

They were about four feet deep in the grave and still digging, slower, more carefully now. Guided by the GPR images Armstrong kept studying on a piece of paper, they tried to stand along the edges of their dig to avoid putting weight directly over where the mystery body would be. The helicopter came close overhead again, no doubt taking video because they had no roof on their makeshift shelter.

"Can't you pull some strings and get that helicopter out of the air?" Seth asked Armstrong, raising his voice to be heard.

"Already did!" he shouted back. "It's supposed to be radioed to land at the Troyer grain elevator and mill, where there's a parking lot! It should be soon."

It should be soon. The words rotated through Seth's head. The uncovering of his wife's coffin, defiled by someone who had dumped another body here, should be soon. And whose body? Why?

"Got something, *ya,* not too far down," Aaron said, and stopped digging. "Should we switch to the trowels?"

"I'll do it," Seth said. "Come on up here."

"Seth, you sure?" Armstrong asked. "I'll take over."

Taking one of the four trowels and a hand broom, Seth lowered himself into the hole and boosted Aaron and Ben out. But the moment a space was clear, Armstrong, trowel in hand, came down, too.

"I could order you out," he told Seth.

"I could make things difficult for you," Seth countered.

"Then let's work together. The forensics people from BCI will be here soon. We find something, they'll insist on doing the other digs."

He crouched and, using the side of the trowel, swept soil away, again, again, until he was down another foot. Seth knelt beside him. Gooseflesh covered his arms; his hands shook. It might be best to let others do this, but he still felt he was protecting Lena—and somehow Hannah, too. Had someone shot at her and her friends to protect what was hidden here? And now all that had blown up in the shooter's face. At least, wouldn't these finds make the murderer flee? Or would it only make him—or her—more desperate to stick around to be sure he wasn't linked to serial or mass murders? Surely

the extra bodies buried here could not have died naturally.

"Got it!" Armstrong said, going for his brush.

"Got what?" Seth demanded.

Armstrong cleared the soil with the brush, then both
hands. A sheet of sleek, thick plastic emerged. The sun
was almost straight overhead and illumined what lay
beneath.

Seth saw not only the pine boards of Lena's coffin,
but, within a plastic sheet or bag, a withered hand and
half-rotted arm attached to a corpse lying almost on top
of Lena's coffin, which he'd built with his own hands
and thought he'd never see again.

When Naomi pulled up in front of the B and B,
Hannah popped her head in the kitchen to say goodbye
to Amanda and get the sausages from the refrigerator
to take home. "See you tomorrow, Amanda, and tell
Harlan thanks again!"

"I'll bet everyone's at the graveyard, including
Harlan. Listen, I'll save you a veggie pizza for lunch
tomorrow."

But as Hannah let herself out and headed down the
brick walk, she saw Amanda was wrong about everyone being at the graveyard. A petite, pretty Asian
woman with long, straight black hair, wearing a belted,
red wool jacket over tight jeans tucked into fancy boots
was coming up the walk. "Are you Hannah Esh?" she
asked.

"Yes." *Uh-oh,* she thought. *The reporter.*

"I'm Marcy Shin, East Coast Cable News. I was so
pleased to hear you worked here. I didn't want to get
your side of the story secondhand from Mrs. Stutzman

or anyone else. Could we talk for a few minutes? I'm so sorry about your friends and you being shot by some lunatic. But now, with the exhumations, perhaps we'll all get answers."

"They've exhumed bodies?"

"They're still working at it, but they've dug up one at least. I've got some video of it to file a story, if you'd like to see it."

"I—I can't. I need to go with my sister now."

"I understand your reluctance to talk. I certainly would not show your face on my report, and there's nothing gross on the video—really. If you can just give me a brief statement…"

"My statement is that I really need to go right now."

"Let me show you an example, then," she said, blocking her way and pulling a device that looked just a little larger than a cell phone out of her big purse. "Here, I just shot this footage of Lily Freeman at the cemetery. Lily, as I'm sure you know, is staying here at the Plain and Fancy, too."

Still curious about Lily, Hannah stayed put. Naomi had wrapped the reins around the hitching rail and came to stand by Hannah as Marcy Shin touched the small screen a couple of times. Lily Freeman's face appeared on it with a crowd of people behind her, some English, some Amish.

"I used to live here several years ago," Lily said. Ms. Shin turned the volume up. "But with these terrible shootings, I fear big-city crime has come to the Home Valley. We have a great sheriff here in town who is now working with the FBI, but I'm going to learn how to protect myself just in case. I'm going to take lessons from Elaine Carson, here at the Rod 'n' Gun shooting range...."

"Well," Ms. Shin said, "that comes off as a bit of a promo for the sheriff and the Rod 'n' Gun, but you see what I mean about how easy it is to give a statement? Of course, I'd just shoot from the side—get your bonnet brim or even from the back if you wish—or just use your comments as a voice-over for the crime scene."

Hannah was tempted to sprint for the buggy, but she stood her ground when Elaine Carson's face appeared next on the small screen. "I'll ID them at the bottom of the video when I edit," Ms. Shin explained.

"The ironic thing," Elaine Carson was saying on the tiny screen, "is that the Amish are under attack, yet they're pacifists. Sadly, that means they refuse to protect themselves physically or serve in the armed forces of our country. They do like to hunt, though, and can be very skilled at shooting. I just hope this danger in their backyard makes them realize they need to not only arm themselves against a criminal element, but reconsider serving the country that allows them to have their own opinions and religious freedom. I'm a former officer in the armed—"

Marcy muted the sound and said, "See, you just talk, although, as I said, I won't film your face and you can respond to leading questions instead of just talking, if you'd rather. Also, I can edit out anything you're not comfortable with after your statem—"

"Excuse us, please. I've given my statement in detail to both the sheriff and the FBI special agent, so feel free to check with them. As for being comfortable with this, I'm not." Hannah headed for the buggy with Naomi right behind.

"I know what you mean about not being comfortable," Naomi said, frowning. "Sometimes the wealth and…well, the power of my new family sort of scares me."

The senior Troyers, Levi and Rachel, were influential people with their large holdings northwest of town. Their extensive acreage covered more than a mile in a crescent shape, with the nearest point touching the far side of the graveyard hill. The land housed their historical grist mill on Killibuck Creek, their tall grain elevator, which straddled the railroad tracks, their large home, their four sons' houses and the Troyer cornfields.

They were always ready to support others in the church, but Naomi had mentioned that Josh had said that his family had recently taken financial hits from all sides: the mill needed to be renovated; property taxes were high; their father had set up four sons— soon to be five when Josh wed—with houses, barns and fields of their own; and the Troyers had loaned money to several of the brethren who could not repay right now.

"I vow," Naomi broke into Hannah's thoughts, "if that reporter or her buddies show up for my wedding, I'll just die!" She untied the reins and they climbed quickly in.

"Don't talk about dying, even that way. Let's head home. Nothing else worse can possibly happen today."

But as they pulled into their driveway—at least the media vehicles were at the graveyard now—a small propeller plane zooming low overhead nearly collided with a helicopter that was heading the other way. Nettie, who was never spooked by so much as a semi-truck, shied and reared at the roar, pawing the air and whinnying wildly. The taut reins almost yanked Naomi out of the buggy.

Despite not having the use of both arms, Hannah jumped down and grabbed Nettie's traces and then her bridle to quiet her before she reared again. But her heart was pounding. Someone around here—someone who knew when Amish burials occurred—had hidden their victims there. But what victims and why were they killed? Sadly, the trail had to start nearby, close to home.

"Hannah, thank goodness!" Naomi cried as she got the horse and buggy back under control. "Are you all right?"

"Sure. Sure, everything's fine."

But it wasn't. Seth was determined to keep an eye on John Arrowroot because he wanted Amish land. Hannah could hardly keep a close eye on a man, but with Elaine Carson, who was skilled with guns and held a grudge against the Amish, as well, she had a place to start.

14

HANNAH SAW SETH'S BUGGY COMING UP THE
Esh driveway shortly after she and Naomi returned
home. She'd been watching out her bedroom window
for their father, but he'd not returned from the graveyard yet. She dashed downstairs and ran outside to
greet Seth.

Looking pale and shaken, he climbed quickly down.
Before she could stop herself, she hugged him. His
arms closed hard around her, but only for a moment
before she pulled back, amazed and upset that she'd
lost her head. "It must have been terrible for you," she
told him.

"It was—is. Let's go inside. Your father sent me to
tell all of you, and I still don't want you out in the open
like this."

They hurried inside. Nervous at his nearness and how
she'd greeted him, she talked more than she'd meant to.
"I think you worry for that more than I do. I'll be careful tomorrow, going into Wooster for my first physical
therapy session and to see Sarah and Nate."

She didn't tell him that she also planned to have

her driver stop at Elaine Carson's Rod 'n' Gun on the way back.

While he used their small bathroom off the back entryway, Hannah rushed upstairs to get *Mamm* and Naomi. She found them packing Naomi's hope chest full of quilts and linens. "Come quick," she told them. "Seth's here!"

"Seth, welcome!" *Mamm* said as the three of them came downstairs. "Sit, sit, and we will fix you something to eat. You look tired. Tell us. Is the bishop coming, too?"

"He thought he should stay. The sheriff's ex-wife and Elaine Carson brought them some food, so don't worry about that. It's a nightmare there, but after we opened Lena's grave, he said I should come home. I didn't want to because they haven't refilled it yet. The forensic people just arrived and they're going to sift through the soil. Agent Armstrong called them back in on the case."

"But you found what?" *Mamm* asked. They all stood like statues, staring at Seth.

He pressed his mouth tight, screwed his eyes shut once, then blurted out, "Almost on top of Lena's coffin, a man's decaying corpse in a heavy, clear plastic sack. They don't know yet how he died or why, let alone who he is—was. All that will be discovered by the forensic team and may take a long time. They're digging up Miriam Kauffman's grave now, then will do the Zook grave. I expect they will find something similar."

"At least," Naomi put in, "the media won't be parked out on our road on Thursday. *Daad* said the wedding won't be canceled. I mean, with relatives and friends coming in even from Indiana and Pennsylvania, it won't, will it, Seth?"

"I'm not the one to say, but we all need to be together for a good event. Your wedding is just what we need to lift our spirits."

Everyone breathed and moved again. Hannah hugged Naomi one-handed, and the three women worked together to put grilled cheese sandwiches on the table with applesauce and milk. They all sat down to eat, though Hannah wasn't hungry—Seth wasn't either, she could tell, though he thanked *Mamm*.

"Danki," Seth whispered to Hannah for the slice of pumpkin pie she'd put in front of him. It was laden with whipped cream, just the way she recalled he liked it.

Hannah peeked at him during the silent prayer. All their heads were bowed, and Seth, as big and strong as he was, fingered away tears from the corner of each eye. How she longed to lean forward to take his hand under the table the way she used to, but she had to hold back, had to keep from just climbing onto his lap and hugging him hard, not only to comfort him but herself. Yet she refused to just cower in this house and wait for Linc and his associates to find who shot her friends and her and maybe dumped several strange people bagged and thrown away like trash in someone else's grave.

Hannah felt a bit guilty to be spending the next day, just two days before Naomi's wedding, away from the house, but she had doctor's orders about her first physical therapy session in Wooster. She'd promised Naomi she'd give full attention to the wedding preparations after that. Hannah was grateful to have hired Nelson Sterling, a retired mailman, for taxi service, because he didn't talk much. At least Marcy Shin hadn't tried again to get her to "make a statement."

Her appointment didn't take long, and she liked her therapist, Verna. She left after a half-hour session, where she'd squeezed a rubber ball, which she took with her, picked quarters out of something like clay and worked with huge rubber bands. All of that hurt, but physical pain took her mind off her emotional upheaval.

Then, heart beating hard, she had Mr. Sterling drive her to the large house on a quiet street that her dear friend Sarah and Nate MacKenzie had bought to start their life together. A sold sign was in the yard, and a car was in the driveway, so she had hopes she'd caught them and would not have to just leave a note and stop next time.

When she saw Sarah look out the curtainless window, she told Mr. Sterling in a rush, "I will be at least a half an hour, so if you'd like to leave and come back…"

He said something about going to get something to eat, but she rushed out of the car and hugged Sarah hard on the front porch. It was really strange to see her dressed like a modern, with her honey-hued hair cut to shoulder length. She seemed to glow with happiness.

"It's been so long, and I've missed you!" Sarah said as they both blinked back tears. "Thank the Lord, you weren't seriously hurt in that shooting, and it's brought you home!"

"And look at you!" Hannah said with a sniff. "So *Englische!* And so in love, right? I knew it!"

Nate MacKenzie, handsome as ever with his dark hair and blue eyes, came out and put his arms around both of their shoulders. "It means so much to us that you're here," he told her. "I sure hope you'll forgive me for what happened before."

"Of course I do, as long as you take good care of Sarah."

"Hannah," Sarah said, "is there any way you can come to the wedding? I know no one else will but Ray-Lynn can bring you, and—"

"Yes! I'm coming, and I think Ella's going to send you a gift. I'll ask her to come bu—"

"But we know Ella!" Sarah said with a roll of her amber eyes that took Hannah right back to the old days, at least for a moment.

A silver-haired older woman appeared in the front screened door, a shawl wrapped around her shoulder in the brisk breeze they were letting in the house. "Oh, I didn't know you had a visitor, Sarah," the woman said. "Ask her in right now!"

"M.E.," Nate said, "this is one of Sarah's best friends from Homestead."

"I would guess this is Hannah and not Ella," M.E. said. "You see, my dear, not only has Sarah painted you in many of her works, but she's talked about you, too, about your lovely voice."

"Which reminds me," Sarah said as she linked arms with Hannah, and Nate swept the door open for them, "I'd love it if you could sing a song or two at the wedding. We can hire an organist, but you've always sounded like an angel a cappella."

"And, Hannah," Nate put in, "I'd like you to meet my mother, Mary Ellen Bosley, but we call her by her initials M.E."

"I'm his foster mother, really," M.E. said, but for

some reason Hannah couldn't figure, she had tears in her eyes. Was it just because Nate had introduced her as his mother?

Sarah showed her around the house, which was nearly empty, but for a large sun porch out back that already held two easels and about ten paintings of Home Valley Amish life leaning against the wall, perhaps ready to be hung or sold. Hannah recognized most of the places and people in them.

"They're wonderful," she told Sarah, "faces and all. I see me in almost every one, and there's Naomi! And Seth, too, astride the barn being rebuilt! And Ella—wouldn't she get in a snit if she knew? Oh, Sarah, you've brought it all to life to save the precious times, even if things change or—or go bad in real life."

"The arsons were bad," Sarah said as they walked toward the kitchen, "but I know things are frightening for you now. And I know you well enough to be certain you're going to do something about it, but be careful. Like you, I could have been killed."

Over cups of tea, while Nate made a cell phone call about a moving van, the three women chatted until Hannah saw Mr. Sterling sitting in the driveway. She promised to be at the wedding with several songs to sing. But, despite the last-minute questions about how everyone was—especially Sarah's family—the words that had snagged in Hannah's mind were *Be careful... like you, I could have been killed.*

At John Arrowroot's place, Seth tied Blaze's reins to a tree near the garage. As he surveyed the plastic-shrouded stack of shingles that had been delivered from the lumberyard, he shuddered. They were covered with the same kind of heavy polyethylene that had encased the corpse atop Lena's coffin, but that was hardly a clue to the killer. Hundreds of stores used or sold such material, so he forced his thoughts back to the business at hand. These weren't shake shingles but asphalt ones he liked to use, and the lumberyard was the closest place to order large amounts of them.

"I never thought you'd show up today!" John Arrowroot called from his front porch door.

"I'm already late on my promise to start this roof project," Seth said as Arrowroot walked out to join him.

"Despite our differences, I'm sorry your wife's grave was disturbed," he told Seth. "Maybe you can grasp the feeling I live with about my people's burial places—their very birthright—being stolen and defiled. The tribal nations have kept quiet too long, because we had no power to fight back. So I don't suppose you've seen any of the TV coverage? I know word gets around in town between the non-Amish and your people."

"I haven't seen it and don't want to. Do I have your permission to go in and out of your garage to get the ladder and store my things until I'm done?" he asked, starting away.

"Sure. The thing is, I've managed to get a reporter from a national paper and another from a cable TV station to listen to me. That's really what I was hoping for, not that I was reveling in seeing your pain when I sat there yesterday."

Seth turned to face him again and walked back. From about three feet apart, their eyes locked and held. "I was reading," Seth said, "that a mound or hill sacred to your people, which you claim the hill with our graveyard used to be, was especially important at its highest points—the hilltop."

"Sure. Closer to the Great Spirit. I'm sure you can understand that. So you've been reading about my people just so you could understand me more? How nice," he said, his tone goading.

Seth decided to ignore that. "True about hilltops, then?"

"So the sacred lore says."

"Then I would assume you are familiar with the top of that hill and with the trees from which the killer shot at Hannah Esh and the goths Halloween night. I'm only asking because I'll bet you've been clear up that hill since, and I'm wondering if you spotted anything there on the ground the sheriff or investigators might have missed, something you might even have picked up on your own."

Seth watched as Arrowroot clenched his jaw. A bluish vein in his forehead stood out for a moment, though the man remained outwardly calm.

"I'll take that at face value and assume you're not accusing me of anything," Arrowroot said. "I thought for a second, since you've been hanging out with our illustrious sheriff and the G-man, their investigation and accusation paranoia might be rubbing off on you."

Seth still stared at him. Though he hardly expected this man to confess to anything, what Seth had said was as close—right now—as he dared to try to get a guilty reaction from him. "I'll get to work now. And if you can remember anything about that hill you observed in your graveyard vigil even yesterday, I'd value your help," he added as he started away.

"I was not there that night!" Arrowroot called after him, finally sounding annoyed. "I've been there after dark on occasion, but not that night!"

He had gotten something out of him, after all, Seth thought with satisfaction, so he wasn't going to give up on the possibility he was involved. He felt Arrowroot's eyes bore into him like bullets as he walked to the garage to get the ladder, the garage with all the photos of the area tacked up, including, he saw clearly now, ones of the graveyard and top of the hill.

Despite her fear of guns and Sarah's warning ringing in her ears, once they were back in the Home Valley, Hannah asked Mr. Sterling to stop at Elaine Carson's store and shooting range.

While he waited outside for her, Hannah hurried into the Rod 'n' Gun. She had to admit that it was partly Lily Freeman's testimonial for Marcy Shin's story that had given her the idea of coming here to inquire about shooting lessons, which were the last thing in the world she wanted to take or pay for. But if she came here from time to time for lessons, she could keep an eye not only on Elaine Carson but, for Ray-Lynn, on Lily, too.

No car was in the parking lot or inside, so that would give her time to look around. Through a series of windows at the rear of the building, she could see the gun range with its array of various targets—including the life-size shape of a man!

"Hey, welcome!" Ms. Carson called out from a side room as she came in carrying a carton labeled Winchester Xpert Hi-Velocity Ammo. "Oh—Hannah Esh, in the flesh. I'm surprised to see you here. How's the arm?"

"Coming along, thanks. Would I need both hands to learn to shoot a handgun?"

"No kidding? You want lessons? If an Amish woman shoots—and they're few and far between—her dad or husband teaches her. But I'll bet you don't want to upset your family that you still feel you're someone's target."

"That's true enough. I saw the interview you did for the television reporter. What you and Mrs. Freeman said made sense."

"And since you've been on the receiving end of a hate crime—or whatever it was—well, I applaud your bravery."

Bravery, patriotic bravery, seemed to be the theme of this place, Hannah thought as she glanced around. Of course, she expected this small front store to be lined with glass-covered cases and shelves with rifles and guns of all kinds, hopefully under lock and key. Although the store sold fishing supplies, as well, only a corner seemed to be devoted to rods, tackle and nets. When Elaine had inherited her uncle's store, she'd probably just kept the name and concentrated on what she really loved.

Pictures of Elaine in an army uniform with medals on her chest hung on one side wall with a huge American flag with gold fringe on the other. As Seth and Linc had mentioned, she liked eagles; there was a large picture of one swooping at something with talons outstretched.

Hannah pictured again that eagle feather that had been stuck in her window as some sort of boast or warning. She could picture Elaine hefting a ladder and handling the climb, but she still could not accept that a woman had shot at them. But for a cause…and from a woman who had no doubt shot people in defense of her country, it was possible. Elaine Carson seemed to give no ground on what she believed. A sign on the back of the cash register proclaimed America—Love It or Leave It!

Ms. Carson plunked the box of bullets down on the counter and came closer. "As you may know, Hannah, guns have a big kick—a recoil. Even handguns, especially for a woman, should be steadied with both hands. But I'd love to teach you to protect yourself. Can't promise you'd be able to pick off an attacker in the dark, but close."

Did she mean anything by that? She did have a motive in that she seemed to dislike the Plain People for their pacifism. And, come to think of it, Ms. Carson had once gotten in real trouble with the church elders for putting little American flags in the ground around the graveyard at Fourth of July time—which the church had immediately removed.

"For now," Ms. Carson went on, "why don't you just come observe how I teach Lily Freeman, and then you'll have a head start when your wrist heals. I'm glad you're no longer with those crazy goths, and maybe you'll start a new trend among your women, so no charge for now, how's that?"

"That couldn't be better!" Hannah told her, and meant it. She could keep an eye on both Lily for Ray-Lynn and on Elaine Carson for herself. She asked when Lily would be taking lessons and said she'd join them after Naomi's wedding. After all, she had to put

family first these next two days, until all that excitement was over and she had her horse and buggy back
for getting around on her own, no matter what Seth
and Linc said.

15

THE MORNING OF NAOMI'S WEDDING, HANNAH'S
family rose at 4:15 a.m. *Daad* and the church elders
had finished setting up tables and benches in the living
and dining rooms for folks to eat in two shifts. Hannah
kept an eye on the ovens and stovetops in the house
and the wedding wagon, which were manned—that,
is, womanned—by family and friends. Their task was
to brown, then bake, three hundred pounds of chicken,
peel kettles full of potatoes and make huge saucepans
of gravy. It was an honor to be asked to help at a wedding, whether as a cook, usher, waiter or hostler, who
handled the many horses and buggies. A black sea of
buggies surrounded the Esh and Kauffman houses by
the time the sun rose.

The Plain People always pitched in with preparations for a wedding, but Hannah soon saw she'd have to
work extra hard at this one. Not that almost four hundred guests was an unusual number to handle, since
visitors stayed at other homes and the church service
itself was in the Kauffmans' barn. The problem was
people seemed focused not only on the coming service

and celebration, but on the desecration of the grave-yard. And though Naomi was supposed to be the center of attention, Hannah saw it was often focused on the other Esh girl—her—who had caused such upheaval.

Some folks were happy to see her and to have her back. But Mrs. Zook, whose brother's grave had been disturbed, suggested that since someone had tried to hurt Hannah, she might want to leave the Home Valley for a while, perhaps going to Indiana or Pennsylvania with some of their relatives here for the wedding. Others told her they weren't a bit surprised that the evil of the world followed her back home, and they were praying for her safety.

"All this for a five-minute ceremony after a three-hour church service," Ella whispered to Hannah as they peeked in the window at the line of people greeting the bride and her reddish-haired groom inside the house. It was still dark outside; the line had begun forming at 7:00 a.m. Everyone was dressed in their Sunday best. The bishop welcomed each person at the front door, and after they went through the reception line, they headed for the Kauffman barn.

Naomi radiated joy; Josh looked a bit overwhelmed. The bridal couple were seated at the place of honor, the corner table called the *eck,* where they would preside over the noontime dinner after church. Peering through the window, Hannah could see that, when Naomi and Josh were not shaking hands, they held hands under the table. During their wedding service would be the only approved time the couple would ever publicly hold hands, for unlike moderns, her people were not affectionate in public. And here, she scolded herself, she'd dared to hug Seth out in the yard when he buggied in two days ago! How the world—or desperation—had changed her.

"Someday, it will be our turn," Ella said with a sigh, interrupting Hannah's silent agonizing. "We won't just be outside, looking in—oh, you know what I mean. And then there's Sarah…" Her voice trailed off. "I wish her well, but she's making a big mistake marrying a worldly man."

"I wish you could go to her wedding with Ray-Lynn and me. You know we always promised we'd be together on the days the three of us were wed."

"Hannah!" she said, and tugged at her good arm so she spun to face her. "She's broken her vow to the church, to all of us. Besides, if I went, I couldn't go inside the church, anyway."

"It's a chapel attached to a church of Anabaptists and Bible believers, just like us—well, not really like us. Since she's under the *meidung,* she'll just have to settle for some lavender products from you, then. I know she'll be grateful even for that gesture."

"Are you going to sing?"

"I am. It's the only gift I can afford to give them now. I'm grateful to Nate, too."

They walked away from the window, back toward the wedding wagon with its rich aroma drifting toward them. "Hannah, listen. That FBI man—I heard he's invited to the dinner and reception today."

"My parents asked him, though he may be too busy to stay long."

"I just—I want to be sure you don't make the same mistake with him that Sarah's making—leaving, being unequally yoked."

"What? That's a crazy idea! Did someone say something that—"

"Naomi just thought he really cared for you."

"I should hope a man whose job it is to investigate and fight crimes cares about his victims—I mean, the victims. And I want to help him, but that's all."

"That's how it started with Sarah and Nate. But I think Naomi's wrong to think you'd take up with Agent Armstrong."

"I'm glad to hear you're on my side. If this wasn't her special day, I'd set her straight right now!"

"I still think it's Seth you care for. I've watched you watching him, even when he got out of his buggy today. If you want him back, you'd better not put it off. I don't know if anyone told you, but he has two very willing *maidals* sighing over him—Katie Weaver and Susan Zook."

Hannah fought not to be angry with Ella—and not to care about what she'd just said. "I didn't know, but why should I? Not only have I been gone, but he's an unmatched man, free to do what he wants." But, she thought, of course a catch like Seth Lantz, even with a child, would have a choice of young women. He wouldn't mourn Lena forever, even with his concern for her grave. And now she knew why Mrs. Zook, Susan's mother, had urged her to leave Home Valley for a while, as if Linc or her parents would let her go right now. "I've got to get back to keeping an eye on the food," she told Ella, annoyed when her friend rolled her eyes at the obvious change of topics, "but I am going over to the barn for the service and wedding."

"I'll get you, and we'll go together," Ella said, and hurried off to where she was helping the other sidesitters, named for their places of honor at the reception table next to the bride and groom. They were decorating Josh's buggy out in the barn with hand-lettered signs and streamers.

Fuming at what Ella had said, Hannah headed back into the busy, crowded wedding wagon where the kettles of potatoes had steam pushing out from the edges of their covers. Good, she thought. That way no one would see the steam coming out her ears.

To best fit the shape of the Kauffman barn, the rows of separate benches for men and women were set up at a slant, one set on each side of an aisle, slightly facing each other. Hannah thought that was a good arrangement until Seth sat down exactly in her line of vision. To watch the preaching and the short wedding ceremony at the end, she'd be looking at him, too.

Seth, as the *vorsinger,* or song leader, led the first hymn from the *Ausbund,* the traditional hymnbook. He did not go up in front or even stand, for that would make him too special. Hannah had not heard Seth's deep bass voice and the unison singing of her people for nearly three years, and she blinked back tears. In the world, she'd become used to upbeat, solo, individualized or multipart singing. This was more like a Gregorian chant, and she sang out, blending her clear, alto voice with her people's.

During the second hymn, Naomi and Josh left the service for the Kauffman house with two of the elders. It was usually the bishop who took the bridal pair off for questioning about their preparation and purity for their union, but since the bishop was Naomi's father, they'd changed that a bit. Besides, *Daad* was going to preach today. He focused on faithfulness and forgiveness, citing the trials of several biblical characters, so why did she feel he was speaking to her?

At last Naomi and Josh came back in, holding hands. Over her blue wedding dress, Naomi wore a white apron, which she would never don again until she was laid out for her funeral. Her funeral...Hannah thought, as her mind drifted. She had not been here for Lena's funeral or when they put her in the grave...and then someone dared to—

On the bench beside her, Ella subtly elbowed Hannah. She had no clue why until she saw that Seth, whom she had been trying to ignore, was staring straight at her. Hannah felt her cheeks go hot. She fidgeted on the hard bench. Her stomach fluttered as if butterfly wings beat there, and her thighs, pressed tight together, tingled.

She forced her eyes away from his magnetic gaze, looking instead at the Troyers, the bridegroom's family: his parents, Levi and Rachel; his four brothers and their wives and children. Although all Amish sought to be humble, their special place in the community emanated from them. No wonder Naomi was nervous marrying into such a family. She began to wonder how it would have been to have married Seth, to be truly sisters with Ella—but then cut her own thoughts short.

It was not a day to dwell on her losses, Hannah thought, but rather on Naomi's gains as they prepared to take their final vows. And they would be final, for, among her people, unlike in the world, marriage really was "till death us do part." No rings, no kisses, but permanent promises of love and duty.

Her gaze snagged Seth's again. This time he looked quickly away.

Addressing the bridegroom at the conclusion of the short wedding service, her father's voice rang out, "Do you promise, Joshua Troyer, that if your wife should be afflicted with bodily weakness, sickness or some similar circumstance, that you will care for her as is fitting a Christian husband?"

"*Ya,* I will."

He then repeated the question to Naomi, who gave a louder, "I will."

The bishop put his hands over the couple's clasped hands. "Then I wish you the blessing of God for a good beginning and a steadfast middle time, and may you hold out until a blessed end, this all in and through Jesus Christ. Amen."

It was done, Hannah thought. It was done just as she'd always planned and pictured it would be for her and Seth. Ruined. Gone. Over. And yet...

She hugged Naomi after the ceremony, shook Josh's hand, then almost sprinted back across the field.

To Hannah's surprise, Linc was waiting outside the Esh house. "Hey, good, you're back before the crowd," he said, and steered her into the small space between the house and wedding wagon. "I can't stay long today, got to keep an eye on the team at the cemetery, but I want you to know we have recovered three bodies of unknown—as yet—victims who were in those graves. All head shots, from behind, execution-style."

"Execution? Not a crime of passion, as they put it?"

He looked surprised she'd said that. He took her elbow as if he were afraid she'd bolt. "Hannah, we'll do tests to see if it was the same gun that took out Kevin and shot you and Tiffany. But this is huge—diabolical and huge! Sorry to tell you all that on a day like this," he added when he took in her shocked expression, "but I thought you should know."

"Does Seth know?"

"Not yet."

"Did you ever come across another case like this one?"

"That's my Hannah, ever the clear thinker, even when distracted or in danger. No, I haven't seen a situation where a body was stashed in someone else's grave, but the Bureau has dealt with victims buried a ways from where they'd been whacked."

"Whacked?"

"Hit—killed. In 2004, in a remote vacant lot in Queens, New York, the FBI uncovered a half dozen graves of victims executed by a New York City mob. I doubt if the bodies in the Home Valley graveyard were eliminated in this immediate area—their disappearances or deaths would have been reported. Of course, we're cross-checking in national databases, missing persons in Ohio and the surrounding states, all of that. I'd guess these corpses are the result of some big-money drug deal gone bad in a city, but it's sure unique, even clever, to stash hits here. Hey, here comes the crowd, so let's go in for a while."

"I have to oversee some things," she said, angry with how excited he seemed over all this horror. He'd been so stoic and businesslike before. "Family members at our weddings work hard," she told him as she freed her arm and edged away. After what Ella had said, she didn't want to seem as if she was with him, but she couldn't help asking, "How is it you can just turn from one thing to the other—the terrible things you see in your work and then a social situation? How do you turn it all off to sleep at night?"

His gaze went over her. "I shut it out, a necessity of the job to turn emotions off and on, or I'd never survive. I have pleasant dreams at night. But this investigation has new possibilities now I'd never imagined when I said I'd look into a rural shooting, a possible hate crime—nor that there would be a day where I'd be involved with love as well as hate."

Hannah's eyes widened and her lower lip dropped until she realized he was talking about his invitation to a wedding reception—wasn't he? She turned her head and saw Naomi and Josh's arrival was nearly engulfed by the crowd of well-wishers.

"Please stay as long as you can. You're welcome here," she told Linc as she hurried farther away from him and was swept into the house among family and friends.

The dinner and reception were as exciting as the ceremony had been solemn. The corner table for the newlyweds and their attendants was set with candles and two cakes for the wedding party—the three layers was okay, but no tiers allowed in bridal cakes by church rules, for that would be too worldly and fancy. During the meal, there was teasing and laughter, much getting and giving of small gifts; the larger ones such as money and items for their future home were on display in the guest bedroom upstairs.

Hannah was given a ballpoint pen with Joshua and Naomi's names and their wedding date. She saved one of the napkins which said the same. While their guests laughed and cheered, some of the couple's friends got up to present Naomi with a clothesline and mop, then a bridle for Josh someone suggested he get used to putting in his own mouth, on and on.

The first seating ate and chatted as nearly two hundred guests in three rooms devoured chicken, dressing, mashed potatoes and gravy, coleslaw, applesauce and creamed celery, a traditional wedding dish. Special yeast rolls with butter were distributed by the waiters, who were also friends of the bride and groom. Coffee, tea, pies and cakes came last. Hannah had wedged herself in between Ella and her sister Barbara, who was being courted by Gabe Kauffman, Sarah's brother. Gabe sat on Barbara's other side. The bride had worked hard to seat courting couples together, but Hannah noted Naomi had put neither Susan Zook nor Katie Weaver in shouting distance of Seth.

But Hannah made a mental note that, when she saw Sarah in two days for her little wedding, she'd have to remember to tell her Gabe was still Barbara Lantz's come-calling friend. Sarah had been so hungry for any news of her family.

Hannah was somewhat surprised that Linc sat next to Seth, who had Marlena on his lap. She admired how he had managed to feed himself and her, yet listen to Linc. If that conversation was about people being "whacked" and "hit," she thought, it was the strangest Amish wedding talk of all time.

"Remember how Sarah used to stuff herself with nothings at weddings?" Ella asked, referring to the lightly sugared, fried pastries that moderns called "elephant ears." Nothings were stacked on plates at the end of each table. People usually just broke off a piece but Sarah used to snatch and hoard half a dozen of them.

Amid the hubbub and the laughter, Hannah and Ella stayed silent for a moment, remembering, before Hannah said, "I'll take some and put them out for her reception Saturday."

Hannah was just about to excuse herself and go out to check on the wedding wagon before the first seating was dismissed, when her older sister Ruth appeared over her shoulder and whispered, "Naomi would like for you to sing. The only thing is, Josh also asked Seth."

The room seemed to spin, a blur of noise and movement. Hannah could feel Ella looking at her and Ruth's steady stare. She glanced over at Seth and Linc. Seth hadn't budged, either; he was staring at her with eyebrows lifted as if to say, *Are you game?* Linc, who had evidently overheard, lifted both hands, palms up, and bounced them once as if to say, *Come on! I'd like to hear you sing.*

"For Naomi, of course I will," she told Ruth. "I'll sing first and then Seth can, unless he insists on starting."

While Seth handed Marlena to his mother, Hannah stood and stepped over the bench. This invitation to sing before her people was in her world what Linc had called "huge" in his. She'd jumped the fence to pursue a singing career. Back she had come, shamed and scared. What she'd done was considered to be prideful, although singing at a wedding—the newlyweds never sang themselves because it was bad luck—was encouraged and common.

She met Seth in the corner, behind the *eck* table. Josh turned around with a grin. "Guess you'd better sing fast so folks don't think you have an announcement to make," he kidded them, and returned to talking to his bride and sidesitters.

"Shall I go first?" Hannah asked Seth as they went off into the hallway to talk things over. "We can't sing together, haven't for years, and we don't need any rumors."

"True. There are enough of those winging around today about who was in the graves or who put them there, besides those about the Troyers' financial troubles, today of all days."

"What did you hear about that?"

He lowered his voice, though the noise level in the next room was high and no one could see them here. "That Levi Troyer had some money out to other Amish businessmen that went bad and he's over his head financially with a worldly bank—desperate for cash to prop things up. He's actually talked to some of the reporters in town about doing articles about the mill— said he'll be in them, pictures and all. He's going to hire me to oversee the reconstruction crew for the mill, and I can't turn that down—if he's financially stable."

"Better make sure you get paid some up front. But wait till *Daad* hears all that. Mr. Troyer will get a warning or worse if he shows his face in the papers or on TV. But what are *we* going to do?"

"About the singing or something else? Okay, you go first. We can't just do a duet. But I'd like for us to— sing like the old days, I mean."

"The old days are gone. You killed them, and I did, too."

"Then we should try to make new ones."

She didn't know what to say. Her heart was thumping harder from that than from anything today. Seth was not so much as touching her and she yearned for his hands on her, his mouth covering hers.

They planned their songs, then she darted away, but he stayed by the door while she asked Josh to tap his cider glass for quiet and make an announcement. "My wife's sister Hannah is going to sing, and after that, our own *vorsinger,* Seth Lantz."

Hannah had been rehearsing several *Englische* songs for Sarah's wedding, but she knew this audience would like one of them. Her voice rang out, almost shaky at first, but then in control and conviction. The lyrics were from the *Book of Ruth* in the Bible with the chorus:

Whither thou goest, I will go.
Whither thou lodgest, I will lodge.
Thy people will be my people, my love,
And thy God, my God.

When she finished, everyone sat quiet, as if stunned. It wasn't their way to applaud, anyway. Tears in her eyes, Hannah stepped back, then moved away as Seth sang two songs in German, one a hymn and one a rollicking song about a horse that pulled a buggy all the way home when the suitor fell asleep after visiting his beloved.

Just hearing Seth's voice and recalling how he used to sing love songs for her alone shook Hannah to the core, more than her own song had. Afraid she'd be silly enough to cry, she slipped out into the kitchen and pushed past the volunteer cooks who had stopped preparing food for the second sitting to crowd in the doorway, in order to see as well as hear Seth. When he finished, Hannah ducked out on the back porch and sucked in a huge breath to steady herself.

She heard the door open, a man's heavy footfalls on the porch boards behind her. He must have followed her out, but she couldn't bear to face him right now. He'd see the need for him on her face, and she couldn't just act like a coward.

From behind her, he put his hands on her shoulders. Trembling, she put her hands over his and—not Seth. Not Seth's hands. She spun to face Linc.

"I've got to go, but I had no idea," he said. "Your voice is fantastic—unique! You must have had some idiot for an agent. I know getting a foothold can be tough, but I can't believe you couldn't make a go of it. I swear to you, once I've solved this case, I'll stake you to a new beginning and find you some contact that will get you a start. I know nothing about the music biz, but, for you, I'm going to find out!"

All afternoon, people said their thanks and good-byes, especially the dairy farmers who had to go to milking. That evening, the Troyers provided the repast, starting with snacks of all kinds, then cold cuts of ham and beef with mounds of potato salad and cookies. Hannah saved some nothings to take to Sarah and gave herself a sugar and caffeine buzz eating chocolate chip whoopie pies.

You might know, she thought, she got the piece of bride's cake with the little wedding ring favor in it, the only piece of jewelry an Amish woman ever bought.

Unfortunately, it meant the recipient would be the next to wed. When she saw its cheap golden gleam peering out from her piece of cake, she'd been tempted to just hide it, but Naomi would have had a fit, and it was her day.

Dusk was descending outside when Seth suddenly appeared at her shoulder with a sleeping Marlena in his arms. They stood in a corner of the kitchen, which was temporarily deserted while the cooks ate their bride's cake in the dining room.

"I hope what I said about us making music together didn't upset you," he said.

"No, I— We have some good memories of that. So how's it going with John Arrowroot?" she asked to shift the subject.

"I told Linc he admitted he's been to the hill above the graveyard after dark at times, and he's got blown-up photos of that area in his garage. I'd like to get into his house—farther than his back bathroom—but that's risky if he's guilty. You know, I do feel for his cause and understand it. Well, I've got to get my little angel home and in bed. Hannah, your song was beautiful. Are you singing it for Sarah's wedding?"

"Yes, that and several others. Ray-Lynn Logan's taking me."

"Give Sarah a kiss for me and my best wishes for their happiness."

"I will. She'll be glad to hear that."

"And you and Ray-Lynn be watchful if I don't see you before then." He studied her face, then stared at her lips, almost as if he would give her that kiss to pass on. But he didn't. He moved away before turning back. "And thanks for loaning Marlena your doll. I'll get it back to you soon. She sleeps with it, and it seems to help her bad dreams."

"Then let her keep it for a while."

"I think there's an *Englische* song about 'I'll see you in my dreams.'"

"I've heard that one."

His smile caressed her. Somehow it was as if he touched her all over. He put his hat on and went out into the darkening night.

16

THE NEXT MORNING, HANNAH NOT ONLY DUSTED
and straightened things in the Plain and Fancy B and
B common rooms but, one-handed, helped Amanda
change beds upstairs. But she didn't learn anything
new from another close observation of Lily Freeman's
room, except that she hadn't removed her makeup at
night and had thoughtlessly smeared rouge or powder
on her pillowcase. And the paper pile and laptop had
disappeared from the desk.

All Hannah really learned about anyone was that
Amanda was worried about her brother Harlan's drinking and thought his wife, Clair, who was a hairdresser
at the Hair Port in town, talked about it to too many
people. Hannah kept her mouth closed on that because
here was Amanda telling her about it.

"There are some around here," Amanda muttered,
"who just won't want to store or buy their meat from a
man who drinks. And what if he drives that new refrigerator truck of his around with a bottle of that rotgut
stashed in it?"

"As long as he doesn't hit something, I doubt if the

sheriff has time right now to arrest someone for not passing a sobriety test," Hannah said.

"Harlan's a very hard worker and has done well for himself, especially lately," Amanda went on. "But I told him things will go downhill fast if he doesn't give up drinking. And I shouldn't have said 'rotgut,' because he says he buys only the best Canadian or Scotch whiskey, as if that makes a difference, because booze is still booze!"

Rather than staying for lunch after her work was done today, Hannah excused herself and headed Nettie toward the Rod 'n' Gun. She surprised herself with how excited she was to have her old buggy and horse back. It gave her a heady sense of freedom, despite the fact that her family and friends thought she shouldn't be out on her own. But nothing had happened since that night in the maze, and Linc thought that was probably an attack on him, not her. Besides, there was safety in numbers, and other buggies were on the road. Some drivers or riders waved to her, though maybe they thought at first she was Naomi. However much the horses and buggies looked alike to outsiders, her people could identify them by their gait and appearance.

When she reined Nettie in on Elaine Carson's property, Hannah heard a sudden, loud noise and hit the buggy floor. Gunfire! Nearby! Then she felt like an idiot and sat up fast, hoping no one had seen her. That was just the flapping of the big flag in the stiff wind, and besides, there was a shooting range out back.

She saw Lily's red car was already here. Maybe, since she knew her room would be cleaned today, she'd taken her laptop and papers with her. A quick glance in the back and front seats showed nothing, but someone who'd been living in a big city must know to hide important things in the trunk, even around here.

As she went inside, Hannah had to buck herself up to stand her ground. The *bang-bang-bang!* of gunfire from the range out in back was barely muted by the rear wall and window.

She moved to the back window and watched Elaine work with Lily on the shooting range with their backs to her. Both wore large, black earmuffs. The range was built to avoid the wind and weather with separate booths that opened toward a variety of targets at varied distances, some strung on lines to be moved sideways. Only Lily was shooting, holding a pistol, stiff-armed, straight out with both hands. That reminded Hannah of Linc's handgun. The loss of that had shaken him as much as getting hit on the head, but she'd notice him wearing another one, even yesterday. Why didn't he just leave it in his car? Did he think he was going to have to arrest someone at an Amish wedding celebration or draw it in the graveyard when he rushed back to be with his BCI team of forensic specialists?

Suddenly, Elaine turned her head and saw Hannah. She gave a thumbs-up. Lily turned, too, and nodded, but went back to shooting—this time at the man-shaped target—while Elaine came out into the store.

"We're about ready to take a break," Elaine told her, now wearing the earmuffs around her neck. "Want some coffee?"

"Oh, sure. Thanks."

"She's going to work with a moving target after, so that will be new."

"It's all new to me."

She thought at first that Lily might not want her here, but it just seemed that she was really intent on the shooting lessons. It was obvious, at least, as the three of them sat in Elaine's small office—lots of photos of her life in the army there, too—that Lily was concerned about crime coming into the Home Valley.

"It's just terrible what you had to go through, Hannah," she said. "It's what convinced me to learn to protect myself. I supposed I should have done this when I lived in Vegas, but I guess I still had a bit of the small-town girl in me then, like nothing bad could happen. Why, before I left the Home Valley you never so much as heard about someone smashing a pumpkin at Halloween! I hope the sheriff and Agent Armstrong are getting somewhere in their investigation. Even when I wine and dine the sheriff, he's so close-mouthed. But they surely don't think it's someone Amish or even from around here, do they?"

"They have to look at all possibilities, of course."

"I know there are some unstable characters, like the Meyers brothers and that pro-Indian-rights guy—what's his name, Elaine?"

"John Arrowroot. I'm for individual rights, but he's really going overboard when he tries to claim our land for those long dead and gone. He's sure as heck not gonna get my property!"

Though nothing Elaine had said was enough to put her on Linc's list of suspects, at least Hannah had picked up on one thing from Lily to help Ray-Lynn. She'd been wining and dining Sheriff Freeman? But how and where? For sure, not in the restaurant he and

Ray-Lynn coowned. At his own—Lily's old—house? Ray-Lynn would have what she called a conniption when Hannah told her what the woman had let slip.

"It's nice that you and the sheriff are still friends," Hannah told Lily. "I know it's been tough for me, coming back after I left, to patch up some relationships."

"Don't I wish! I swear, it must have been early menopause talking when I was so mean to Jack and took off. I should have had my head, not my rampant hormones, examined. But at least I'm back and making some new friends, like Elaine and Amanda—and you, too, Hannah. You're welcome to come to my shooting lessons, and I hope your hand—and heart—heal fast."

That insight and kindness softened that very heart toward Lily Freeman, Hannah realized, but she was still going to report into Ray-Lynn.

Saturday morning, after dressing for Sarah's wedding, Hannah tiptoed downstairs, surprised that *Mamm* wasn't already bustling about in the kitchen. She was wearing the new emerald-green dress Naomi had made for her but would take her bonnet off inside and go bareheaded. The opposite of many worldly women, she had not dark, but blond roots, and she was starting to wish her bright red hair would grow out fast.

The house seemed extra quiet without Naomi here. As was tradition, she and Josh were spending some time at the Troyers' before they would live here for a few days, then be off to visit other family and friends. It would be late summer before they moved into their own place, which Naomi said Mr. Troyer would hire Seth to build at the edge of the family's holdings.

In two big shopping bags with handles, Hannah carried a wrapped box of Ella's lavender products, the Kauffman quilt she'd also wrapped and a bakery box of nothings she'd saved from Naomi's wedding. These gifts would mean so much to Sarah. Weddings, Hannah thought, Amish and English, here and there, but not hers. Maybe never hers.

She carried the bags out into the small pantry off the kitchen so they wouldn't get in the way at breakfast—or upset her mother. She decided she'd have time to fix breakfast for her parents; she'd heard *Daad* go outside a while ago.

From the three walls of shelves, she took down a carton of oatmeal, then looked for raisins and honey. She heard the back door open and then men's voices in German, close by—*Daad*'s and one she couldn't place. Someone must have buggied in and joined her father in the barn. Would a guest be staying for breakfast? It probably wasn't Seth because Marlena was going to stay with Seth's mother and Ella now when he went to work. Hannah thought she'd better let her presence be known—but it was too late.

"I'm doing what I can, Joseph, so I don't think we need this discussion again. I've confessed as much as I can both to you and to God."

It wasn't Seth. Embarrassed to be overhearing a private, spiritual discussion, Hannah quietly closed the pantry door and stayed put, though she was surprised that she could still hear their impassioned words.

"Do you admit at last that you have overstepped?" *Daad* asked. "Is there any way you can pull back from all your investments before disaster befalls? And what's this about publicity for the mill?"

Mr. Troyer! The visitor was Levi Troyer, Naomi's father-in-law.

"You know, Levi," *Daad* went on, "that *ausländers* 'devise deceitful matters against the quiet ones in the land.' So have you been too prideful in your dealings with outsiders? And now, Seth says, you might borrow money from them to hire him to help rebuild the mill and to build Naomi and Josh a new house."

"I have been dutiful, not prideful."

"*Ach,* I just mean you are overextending your God-given funds and letting worldly men hold the purse strings. And that means you must owe and rely on— give power to—those who do not honor our ways."

"I'm committed now and won't go back on my word. I'll be able to work my way out of this debt, I vow I will."

"Do not become desperate, my brother. Desperate men do desperate deeds. Believe me, I know and have confessed such to the Lord not long ago, for a rash act I committed and am still paying the price for."

What, Hannah wondered, was her father referring to? What desperate deed could he have committed not long ago?

They evidently got whatever they had come in for and trooped out again. The back door closed, and their footsteps sounded across the back porch boards as their voices faded. Hannah opened the pantry door and got the oatmeal for three to cooking. When *Mamm* came downstairs, she told her, "*Danki,* Hannah. I was just so tired this morning after the wedding. Now here you

go to another. I saw Levi Troyer's buggy in to talk to
your father again."

"I think they're still talking out back."

"Well, whatever is amiss, the Troyers are family
now."

"*Mamm,* has something been bothering *Daad* lately?
It isn't my fault still, is it?"

Mamm kept busy fixing toast to go with the oatmeal
and didn't turn to face her. "The graveyard shootings
upset him real bad, worse than he let on, I can tell.
He stopped sleeping well, walked the floor after that,
no doubt because his Hanni could have been hurt. He
wanted to go to help right away that night, after he
came in from taking a walk and we heard the sirens.
At least our lives changed for the best to have you back
again."

"What? He was walking outside that night?"

"We'd had a coyote in the area, so he was keeping an
eye out for it with his gun. It killed some of the Lantz
chickens, and the men were all determined to get rid of
it. Now eat that oatmeal fast, because I see Ray-Lynn's
here. I can't approve of your going, my girl, but I am
proud you are loyal to your lifelong friend."

Hannah quickly downed the rest of her breakfast,
kissed *Mamm*'s cheek on the way out and grabbed Sarah's gifts. But something had grabbed her, too, out of
everything said this morning. Her own father had been
outside, maybe walking the fields with a rifle the night
someone shot at five goth kids disgracing themselves
in the graveyard. And he, the shepherd of his flock,
was not only angry with her for something unspoken

but maybe sorry for something desperate he had done. He might have confessed it to God, but he sure hadn't told anyone else.

"I did kind of get something out of Lily Freeman at the shooting range," Hannah told Ray-Lynn once she'd filled her in on Naomi's wedding.

"I'm listening and promise I won't steer off the road."

"Well, a couple of things, I guess. She actually blamed rampant hormones and early menopause for being mean to the sheriff and taking off."

"If she's gone through menopause, she's taking designer hormones, because she looks darn good—too good. And?"

"And she said the sheriff wouldn't tell her anything about the shooting case even when she wined and dined him."

Ray-Lynn hit the steering wheel with a fist, once, twice. "What? Wined and dined? Like where around here? He's been too busy, unless they've gone out late at night and not around here! Maybe she means at his house. Hannah, I hate to ask you this, but can you find out at the B and B if Lily's been coming and going late at night?"

"They don't sign out or anything like that, and they all have their own keys, but I'll keep my ears open."

"Drat, I hate to have you playing spy for me. I take back what I said. That was wrong of me, so just forget further snooping. I'll level with Jack, ask him. If she's telling someone like you she doesn't know all that well, who knows who else she's told?"

"Maybe Clair Kenton at the Hair Port?"

"Good idea! I heard Lily gets her hair done there. Clair talks to everyone about everything, and I need a cut and color, anyway. Yeah, if it doesn't work to ask Jack, I might just try that. You know, I wish I could say all this was the least of my worries, especially since I left my restaurant in the hands of four Amish waitresses today. Listen, Hannah—if you choose to stay in Homestead, I'd like you to consider helping me run the restaurant. I should have a manager or assistant, but I never quite found the one I thought could handle both the locals and visitors. I know you could."

"I have no background in business, and I don't think you want a singing greeter."

"I'd train you, of course, and you could work into it. Just a thought—just a real, good thought. That's all contingent, of course, on my getting out alive in this mess with 'the other woman.'"

"Don't joke like that—getting out alive."

"Sorry. Let's just concentrate on making this a great day for Sarah, whatever we're both going through."

Hannah was surprised that there were about sixty people at Sarah's wedding, though most were Nate's coworkers and M.E.'s friends. Still, several artists attended as well as the couple who ran the art gallery in Columbus where Sarah was going to have her first art show this summer. And, of course, Hannah and Ray-Lynn were there to support the bride, though that was a sad representation for all of the Homestead area. Ray-Lynn sat with her friends who ran the art gallery whom she'd introduced to Sarah. Hannah stood in front to sing, almost as if she were a bridesmaid or sidesitter, since neither Sarah nor Nate had anyone stand up with them.

Although Sarah had said the organist could accompany her two songs for the wedding, Hannah sang a cappella, just as she had at Naomi's. Besides "Whither Thou Goest," she sang "The Lord's Prayer" at the end just before the final blessing—no different from the Amish one, Hannah thought, until she realized that Sarah must have written the traditional one out for this minister, word for word.

Like Naomi, Sarah radiated joy, though it seemed to her that this was the marriage of a man and a woman instead of a girl and a boy who would grow into those roles. What made the difference? Worldly experiences? Suffering? If so, Hannah figured she was a prime candidate for marriage.

During the reception at a charming restaurant, Hannah found herself again, if for different reasons, a center of attention, especially after the meal when she sang "Wind Beneath My Wings" and "We've Only Just Begun." An artist friend of Sarah's whose name Hannah had forgotten, a woman with corkscrew-curly hair and huge eyes, dressed something like a gypsy— she stuck out here as much as Hannah did—came up to her with a glass of champagne in her hand.

"Here's a toast to you, as well," she told Hannah with a little lift of her glass. "You know your voice is quite unique, kind of reminds me of Karen Carpenter. She made that song famous, you know, 'We've Only Just Begun.'"

"That's a very nice compliment. I've heard her music, I think. But nothing new lately."

"Oh, she died years ago—young, too. Anorexia, kind of like she killed herself. Well, keep up the good work, and don't let anyone turn you into Lady Gaga. Mind you, she is a work of art deco with all those splendid outfits and dancers. They're even too avant-garde for a Paris runway. Speaking of which, did you hear Nate's taking Sarah to Paris for their honeymoon?"

"Paris? No!" That sounded about as far away as Mars. And here, she'd been thrilled to see Lake Erie!

"I guess it was a secret until today. Nate's never been there, either, but he's taking her to see the art of the Impressionists, even though that's not her style. Sarah's art is wonderfully primitive."

You might know, Hannah thought. With that, the woman's eyes went over her hair, apron, long dress, black stockings to flat, black shoes. But she seemed only curious and interested, not disdainful.

Finally, Hannah got a few moments alone with Sarah and dragged her over to the wrapped gifts on the table. "You have to open these so I can report in," she said, and pushed the box of lavender products at her first.

"Is it—I can smell what it is. Did you buy these for me from Ella?"

"No, she chose and sent them. There's a card in there for you, too, warm wishes from her."

"I could not have hoped for more from her. I miss her, too."

"And these are from Naomi's wedding, your favorite nothings. Ella and I decided you should have some."

"Mmm," she said, diving into the sack and breaking off a piece, which she munched on with her eyes closed as if she could transport herself in time or place. "Don't think I won't do some traditional cooking and baking just because I'm not in an Amish family anymore!"

"And this one—it's from your mother for you. Your father doesn't exactly know. It's—well, it was *Grossmamm* Miriam's."

Sarah's teary eyes met hers. "Oh, Hannah, I hated to leave *Grossmamm,* even though she was off in another world most of the time. And now, here I am, off in another world all the time. Thank *Mamm* for me and tell her I cried and cried when *Grossmamm* died!" She pulled the paper away, hugged the quilt to her, then put it down and hugged Hannah.

"Sure I will. And that reminds me, Seth said to give you a kiss, so there!" she said, and pressed her lips to Sarah's teary cheek.

"Then I'm going to give you a kiss and hug back to give him. And you see that you do!" she insisted as they hugged each other again, both trying to stop threatening sobs.

When they stood apart, Nate was there, watching them both swipe tears from under their eyes. "Tears of joy," Sarah told her new husband.

"Hannah's always welcome in our home," he said, putting a hand on Hannah's shoulder and the other around his wife's waist. "So, did you make that beautiful quilt, Hannah?"

"Sarah's *grossmamm* did," Hannah told him. "The pattern is Wedding Ring, and her mother sent it."

Nate bit his lower lip and nodded as his blue eyes misted, too. "Maybe someday…" he said, but his voice trailed off. "We hope the sheriff and the FBI agent are making progress on the crimes," he rushed on. "Above all, in case someone thinks you know something—even if you don't—be on your guard, and leave the investigations to the experts."

"In other words," Sarah put in, leaning her head on his shoulder, "do as he says, not as I did, even if you and I have always been birds of a feather."

Sarah's and Hannah's eyes met and held. *She knows me,* Hannah thought. *She knows that, no matter what, I'm jumping in with both bird's feet and feathers flying.*

17

RAY-LYNN ALWAYS CLOSED THE RESTAURANT on Sundays, despite how she could use the profits. She wanted to honor the closed-on-the-Sabbath, no-Sunday-sales beliefs of the Amish. Today she had Jack coming for lunch to her house and, hoping they could start again from how things were between them before Lily showed up, she'd fixed that same meal she'd left at his house that night: meat loaf, mashed potatoes and his favorite raisin cream pie.

"Wonderful food, wonderful cook—wonderful woman," he told her as they finished their coffee and pie, sitting catty-corner from each other in her dining room.

"I know you're working hard—late nights, too?"

"You asking me to come back later?"

"I just want things to be honest and open between us. Lily's been telling folks that she's been wining and dining you."

"What? We met once at the fast-food place up the street, 'cause I know you don't want her in your—our—restaurant."

"It's a free country, and I took personal care of her the one time she came in. But I thank you for not bringing her there."

"As for the bit about her wining and dining me—like where and when? Oh, that's why you asked me about working late? Ray-Lynn, wining and dining's just a figure of speech. She's just bragging or it's wishful thinking."

"So it's not true?"

"Did you just hear me? Look, honey," he said, rising, and pulling her to her feet, "I know my temper's short, but you gotta trust me or not. No more cold shoulders, no more fancy put-downs like you're so good at. You believe me or not, you want me or not, and I'll settle things with her either way. You and me—yes or no? I'm aching to put my hands all over you, carry you upstairs to bed, but I'm not gonna do any of that right now, and you're going to give me an answer and stick to it!"

"Yes. Yes!"

He hauled her hard against him, and she held tight. His kiss was demanding but giving, too.

"Then you're gonna have to let me go—leave, I mean—right now and you're gonna have to be strong," he told her. "You *are* strong, Ray-Lynn, just be strong *with* me and not against me."

"I said yes, and I meant it. I trust you, but I don't trust her."

"I said I'll take care of it—then, after this graveyard case and ID search for three John Does is over, I'll take care of you, honey."

He kissed her again, thanked her for the meal and apologized for running, but he'd told her he couldn't stay long when he'd accepted her invitation. She peeked out through the drapes as he backed out of her driveway and his police cruiser's red taillights disappeared into the night.

Monday afternoon, two days after Sarah's wedding, Hannah headed Nettie and the buggy away from the B and B. Marcy Shin had checked out. Lily Freeman was not in again, but Amanda had mentioned that Lily had come in late at night a couple of times, without saying where she'd been. Once, when Amanda had gotten up to see if she was all right, she'd said something about being at the Rooster Roadhouse. Amanda called it a watering hole, though Hannah knew they didn't sell water there. She'd heard about the place from a couple of her running-around friends during their *rumspringa*. But unless Ray-Lynn asked her direct, Hannah was not going to volunteer that information and get more involved. She didn't want to make the sheriff her enemy or Ray-Lynn's, either.

According to the conversation at church yesterday, after four days of searching for evidence, the opened graves had been closed again and at least some of the media visitors had gone home. *Daad* had told the congregation that gawkers were still stopping to look at and tramp around in the graveyard. Having that as an attraction was not the way they'd hoped to bring more visitors into Eden County, he'd said. Hannah had not yet dared to ask him anything about his being outside with a gun the night of the shootings.

Honk! Honk! sounded behind her. She nearly jolted out of the buggy, even though Nettie didn't break stride. Hannah twisted around and saw it was Harlan Kenton's truck. Though she wasn't certain if he knew it was her, he was waving. He evidently just wanted to pass and was giving fair warning.

As no one was on the road but them, he pulled up beside her and slowed down. He rolled down his passenger's side window, so she reined in. "Hey, sorry I missed you at Amanda's just now," he called to her, leaning over toward the window. The fact he was in a truck made them almost eye to eye. "I left some cold cuts for you there, but you can pick them up tomorrow."

"That's so kind of you, Mr. Kenton, but you don't have to do that. You've been very generous."

"Least I can do for someone who's been through what you have and is friends with Amanda, too. In case you're wondering, I had to use some raw steak on my shiner, here," he added, and turned more toward her so she could see the left side of his face. He sported a black eye. He must have thought she could see it and was curious.

"What happened? I think my mother has an herbal wash that could help that."

"Naw, I'll be fine. Indian Chief Arrowroot and I just have a continuing discussion on things, that's all."

"He hit you? You should tell Agent Armstrong or the sheriff!"

"I hope they're on his case already. Naw, I just turned away from him and knocked right into the meat locker door at my shop. I may look like a bruiser but 'Peace and Plenty,' that's my motto. Here comes a car. You take care now," he said, and pulled away.

The other car passed with tourists, at least five of them, peering at her through their car windows. Despite not wanting to go back to the graveyard again, decided to drive by it before her next errand. M just seeing it looking normal would help. She had a box of Naomi's clothes she was going to deliver to Troyers' place. She had finally convinced her parents they could not keep her in the house, at least in broad daylight.

Several cars, including the one that passed her, were parked at the graveyard with outsiders looking in and several more inside. Linc should have left the police tape up for a while. It looked to her, at least from this distance, as if the BCI people had filled in the graves pretty well, though the sod over them was now ragged from being taken up. Linc had ordered every grave to be probed with the radar machine, so at least there would be no other grotesque surprises buried here.

She giddyupped Nettie faster, taking the curve of road and slight downhill quickly toward Troyer land. The stretch of their acreage lay before her, woodlots, fields, houses, the old wooden grist mill on Killibuck Creek—which was really a river—attached to the mill by a chute and a walkway, their three-story grain elevator straddling the railroad tracks. Two boxcars, without the rest of their train, sat under the storage chute, waiting to be loaded.

To her left, just beyond a copse of bare trees, she could see one of the two, old, barnlike covered bridges in the area, the one they'd called "the kissing bridge" in her *rumspringa* years. Held up by stone tresses, it spanned Killibuck Creek. Even as she flushed with the memory of how she and Seth went there more than once to smooch, she saw a familiar buggy coming toward her as if her thoughts had called him. Seth! She'd thought he'd be at Arrowroot's place on the other side of town. On opposite sides of the road, they reined in.

"What are you doing way out here?" he asked, much too sharply, she thought.

"It's not 'way out here,' and I might ask you the same. I thought you'd be up on Arrowroot's roof."

"I was, but needed to meet with Levi Troyer about plans for the mill and Naomi and Josh's house. I'm almost done with the roof."

"I was just taking a box of her extra clothes to Naomi. Seth, are you sure Mr. Troyer can pay you?"

"He's evidently got outside backing from investors, though he didn't want to give their names. There's a big meeting at the mill tomorrow, but he said I shouldn't be there. I'd like to be, though. Why don't you let me take the box to Naomi and you head home?"

"You're worse than my parents! I want to see my sister. Thank you for your concern, but I'll be fine," she said, getting even more annoyed when Nettie insisted on nuzzling his horse, Blaze.

"You always were stubborn."

"And you weren't? Bullheaded, more like."

"Shall we argue? How about we get off this road for a few minutes and just talk?" he suggested, his voice maddeningly calm when she felt so riled up near him.

"Have you learned something else at Arrowroot's?" she demanded.

"Ya, I have."

"I've learned something about him, too—from Harlan Kenton, of all people." She could see a tour bus—those were few and far between lately—cresting the hill beyond the mill, coming this way where their buggies were blocking the road. "All right," she said, "for a couple of minutes. We don't need to be sitting here."

Seth buggied down the lane toward the bridge to give her room to turn around and follow. To her dismay, he drove clear up onto the bridge, but then he was always worried about her being out in the open. It was possible someone could come this way, but the road beyond the bridge was seldom used anymore. She reined Nettie in just behind his buggy, and he helped her down.

"You go first," she said, stepping back against her buggy, though he didn't budge, and they stood so close she had to look up at him.

"Both of the Meyers brothers came storming onto his property when I was in the garage getting more nails this morning. They pounded on his door, and he was crazy enough to let them in. I could hear yelling inside, so I went to his front door—I've been in his place only to use the john by the back door—and called in, 'I'm going back up on the roof, Mr. Arrowroot!' just to let Clint and George know someone had seen them go in the house. They left shortly after, looking upset, but Arrowroot seems to revel in that kind of confrontation, and he's pretty good at talking angry people down."

"If they were there to rough him up—I'm sure they're as shook up as everyone else about Arrowroot saying their land shouldn't be theirs—you shouldn't have let them know you'd be up on the roof. Easy pickings with a gun!"

"Now who's worried about who? And who's telling me where I should and shouldn't go? But I'm starting to believe it's not Arrowroot's style to be shooting at anyone, not when he's got such a high boiling point and seems to enjoy verbal combat so much. But then again, sometimes—maybe like between us lately—that leads to something else, something more."

He tilted his head in a beseeching way and put his hands lightly on her shoulders. From where his palms touched her, even through her cape and gown, sparks shot clear down to the pit of her stomach. She tried to keep her mind on her words. "I just talked to Harlan Kenton, who says he'd argued with Arrowroot recently, too, and is sporting a black eye."

"Really? Then the lawyer might be rougher than I th—"

"Which Harlan says Arrowroot did not give him, that he ran into his freezer locker door. Harlan also claims his motto is 'Peace and Plenty,' whatever that means. Amanda says he's doing really well financially, though, so maybe that's the plenty."

"One of the few around here on a roll right now."

"What about Mr. Troyer's financial ties to outsiders— Linc thinks outsiders planted the bodies here."

"You know," Seth said with a shake of his head, "I think Levi Troyer has a couple of his sons going everywhere with him now, almost as if they're bodyguards. I saw one of them put a rifle inside his buggy. I'm going to ask him a few more questions before I agree to work for him. But tell me about Sarah's wedding. I knew asking about that at church yesterday was *verboten*. So, did you give her a kiss for me?"

"I did," she admitted, refusing to say Sarah had told her to kiss Seth back. But he stepped even closer. He was staring not into her eyes, which was enough to curl her toes, but at her lips. It was getting harder to talk, to stay on track.

"Well," she told him, "it was a lovely wedding and

reception.... She was really thrilled about the gifts from here, Ella's and her mother's—even the nothings I took her from Naomi's wedding. She said she was deeply touched."

"That's good—that's really good," he said in a raspy whisper.

Deeply touched... Seth's hands slid from her shoulders, down her arms, then parted her cape to rest on her waist. Oh, no. She shouldn't have agreed to come here with him, not here. His thumbs were stroking her flat belly while his fingers at her waist tugged her closer. *Ya, ya,* she was falling back in time, falling for him, falling into his arms....

He lifted her up against him as his mouth descended to take hers. Like a madwoman, she parted her lips for him, savoring his taste and touch. He smelled of sharp pine and the outdoors. His arms around her back and waist were like steel bands, binding her to him. The kiss turned breathless, wilder, deeper, and went on and on as they breathed in unison, her breasts flattened against his hard chest, her thighs tight to his hips, so she knew his need for her.

Danger. Insanity. And yet she wanted more as her arms grappled him to her. When he put her down, she stood on his booted feet so she whirled with him when he turned them and he leaned back against her buggy. They rocked the frame of it. They rocked the frame of the entire earth.

He lifted her and laid her back on the floor of her buggy in front of the seat, then climbed up to wedge in beside her. His hands went wild along the length of her, kneading her back, cupping her bottom as they lay pressed together. At last, they came up for air, gasping, stunned.

"You're so beautiful and so strong, my love," he whispered.

"Don't say that—call me that."

"I need you. I need another chance, Hannah!" His breath was hot against her throat where he ran his lips and the tip of his tongue up and down as if he would devour her.

"I—I can't, might not stay here—Home Valley after, after it's over."

"Yes, you will! Say you will!" he insisted, and kissed her hard again.

She was suddenly terrified she would promise him anything, do anything he wanted. *Ya,* she knew how it happened, the blinding passion between him and Lena, the moments that made Marlena and ruined her own life. But, oh, how she wanted him to hold her, to master her, to take and keep her forever.

"Seth, Seth!" she murmured when she could catch a breath again. Her heart was pounding so hard it alone could shake the buggy. "You— We have to stop!"

"For now. But I can't help what I've been thinking and wanting."

"We have— I have other problems."

"Then they are mine, too, have been from the first, more than what your friend Agent Armstrong could ever know."

He sat up, got out of the buggy and lifted her down. She locked her knees to steady her legs. While she shook her skirts and cape out and straightened her bonnet they had smashed, he retrieved his hat from under Nettie's feet. He brushed it off before helping her back up into the buggy.

"You—you can't just turn your feelings off and on, then?" she asked, remembering what Linc had told her about his own emotions.

"Not about you or Marlena, anyone I love. Especially not at night. You're costing me a lot of sleep."

Love. He should not keep using that word. But how different Seth was from Linc. Thanks to Seth's caresses and kisses, she almost didn't need the buggy to drive away from their old haunt, the kissing bridge, because she could have flown.

Hannah was happy to see Naomi. Her younger sister had a certain glow to her, even four days after the wedding, though perhaps it had something to do with the slight beard burn on her throat and cheeks. Josh was growing his married man beard, so Hannah didn't say a word about that. In a house without mirrors, maybe Naomi didn't even know her skin was glowing from her new husband's loving. As they carried the box of clothes into the house, Hannah also noted that the Troyer men, Levi and all five sons, were huddled in conversation out by the barn.

When the men didn't come in, Naomi's mother-in-law, Rachel, fixed chicken salads for the three of them, and they reminisced about the wedding.

When Naomi walked Hannah to her buggy and fussed over Nettie, who was also glad to see her, Hannah said, "The men seem to be preoccupied today."

"I guess you know about the financial situation. Josh says everyone's worried, but his mother and I aren't to worry, that everything will be just fine. They're having a big meeting with his investors from Detroit at two o'clock tomorrow at the mill, so that's supposed to solve everything, I guess. You know, in getting married, you kind of marry the whole family, their joys and problems, too. Oh, and *danki* for bringing me the extra clothes."

But Hannah wasn't to be deterred. "From Detroit? Couldn't he get anyone from Cleveland or Columbus? Why Detroit?"

"Detroit is not a foreign country! And I'm not even supposed to know that much, so don't worry about it."

"I just don't want my sister's new family to have money problems, that's all," Hannah insisted, knowing full well she was lying again.

They hugged and Hannah drove the buggy out the long paved driveway to the road. And there were the Troyer men, all six of them, Levi using the phone in the shanty on the road, which was permitted as long as no wires went into the house. The five younger Troyers, Josh included, were standing close around him. Josh waved.

She waved back, but her thoughts were spinning. She was looking beyond him, past the big barn and fields to the old grist mill even as she turned away from it and headed home.

18

THE NEXT AFTERNOON, HANNAH LEFT immediately after work at the B and B. For the first time, she only had an ache instead of pain in her wounded arm, even off the pain pills. Maybe, she thought, it was because she was not only practicing her physical therapy exercises at home but starting to use her hurt hand at work. It was a good sign for a good day—at least, she hoped so, because she was going to do something really risky.

Keeping an eye on the clock, she grabbed a quick salad at the Dutch Farm Table Restaurant, where Ray-Lynn told her that she'd decided to trust Jack. Hannah didn't tell her friend that Amanda had said today about Lily coming in late at night. Ray-Lynn seemed determined, and Hannah didn't want to upset her with more suspicious news about Sheriff Freeman.

Hannah headed the long way around—not going past the Yoder houses—toward a spot on Killibuck Creek about two miles from the kissing bridge and a half mile from the old grist mill. In a sheltering patch of pines, she tied Nettie to a tree with a good amount of rope where she could graze and be protected from the wind. Shaking, her stomach upset, Hannah was so nervous that she fell back into her old habit of talking to her horse. Her family, Linc and Seth would have her head if they knew what she planned. She was going to sneak into the mill the back way, just as she, Seth and other young folk had years ago when it was derelict. And she was going to eavesdrop on the meeting there.

"See, Nettie," she said as she patted the horse's flank, "I think for Mr. Troyer, this is the perfect storm. I saw a movie called that when I was in the world, a tragedy where everything just came together the wrong way, and some people died."

Nettie snuffled into her hand, then, disappointed not to find a carrot or apple, started to graze. "I'm sorry Naomi's in that family now, but at least Josh is the youngest and may not be involved. Here's what I think," Hannah went on. "Levi Troyer is in debt to evil worldly men, so he's forced to do what they say or he'll have no heritage to leave his sons and their families. So he agrees to let those men hide people they killed— maybe they're the mob, like Linc mentioned. Or else, he doesn't know what they're doing and they thought of the burials themselves. But either way, what better place than a rural Amish graveyard near Troyer land, because no one will ever know, and it won't really disturb the dead—that's probably what Mr. Troyer told himself if he knows. All I need is some kind of proof, then I'll let Linc take over."

Hannah took it as another good sign when Nettie whinnied and bounced her head up and down. With a pat on the horse's haunches, Hannah, cape flapping, bonnet brim pulled low, headed into the sweep of wind toward the mill.

A blast of frigid air burst from the walk-in locker door behind Harlan Kenton's stainless-steel worktable as Ray-Lynn entered the Kenton Meat Shop and Storage midafternoon. Caught between that blast and the cold air from the door behind her, she shivered.

"Yo, Ray-Lynn."

"Hi, Harlan." She watched as he emerged from the freezer, carrying what looked like a big haunch of venison on his shoulder. It must be heavy, but he put it easily on his worktable. "I'm a bit early, but is the extra ground beef I ordered ready?" she asked. "Can't turn down those sale prices."

"I told you I'd deliver it. Yeah, it's ready. You wait here, just a sec and I'll get it for you, help you carry it to your van."

As he went back into the meat locker, a puff of white air swallowed him. That might feel good in summer's heat, but she pitied him right now. Still, not much seemed to bother the man. She'd made an appointment with his wife to get her hair cut and colored, and she hoped the conversation could be focused on Lily Freeman, not Harlan. Ray-Lynn figured Jack would never know about some girl chat in a salon.

She walked slowly along the array of fresh meat Harlan had displayed in his glass case. She was almost never in here, because he did deliver, but—

The store door opened, and the person she wanted to know more about but never wanted to see again strolled in.

"Well," Lily said, "we simply must stop meeting like this."

If that was supposed to be funny or cute, Ray-Lynn didn't laugh. She nodded and said, "Are you buying your own meat? Amanda's such a good cook."

"Oh, no, but Amanda's gone out of her way to cater to my fussy eating ways, so I'm going to treat her with some salmon Harlan said he got in—he stops in almost every day to see her, you know. But I wanted to give it to her, not have him bring it over."

The woman was generous, at least. And she seemed to have discretionary funds. "When did you give up red meat?" Ray-Lynn asked.

"When I first moved to Vegas and decided to get rid of my change-of-life—literally—love handles," she said with a pointed glance at Ray-Lynn's midriff. "I was the hostess at a really glam, chichi restaurant and had to look good. Fabulous Asian fusion food. Now don't you think I'm casting aspersions on your and Jack's restaurant—he told me he owns half now—a mutually satisfying partnership, I'm sure."

Why did this woman have to be so subtly insulting and yet seem so chipper? And what was taking Harlan so long? The freezer door was ajar, but barely, so it wasn't noticeable except for a thin slit of white air.

As if Lily had read her mind, which annoyed Ray-Lynn even more, Lily said, "Harlan's here, isn't he? He said he would be."

"In the frozen north," she said with a nod at the freezer. "I'm about ready to go in and get my order myself, or see if he's turned to a block of ice."

"Oh, he'll be right back, I'm sure. I'll bet that's his inner sanctum—no one else allowed."

Their back-and-forth suddenly ran dry. Ray-Lynn had a hundred questions, but Jack might think she was horning in on dealing with Lily when she'd vowed she would not. She bit her lip to keep from blurting out a hint for this woman to leave town like, *Don't you miss Las Vegas?* or *What do you plan to do here for a career after hostessing in a glam, chichi restaurant?* But what came out was, "So you evidently like to gamble."

Lily gave a little laugh. "So many people stereotype Vegas that way, but there are plenty of other places— closer places—to gamble these days. No, I just wanted to see all the shows, the night spots and get away from the wretched winters here. And in the summers, no humidity, when you're all sweating bullets. Besides, life's a gamble, isn't it?"

The meat locker door opened with another icy cloud. "Sorry, Ray-Lynn but I mispla— Oh, Mrs. Freeman—I know, call me Lily. I wasn't expecting you until later," he said, bringing out Ray-Lynn's four large, wrapped packages on a tray.

"Later is now," Lily said, "but please, take care of Ray-Lynn first."

Harlan bit back a grin, though Ray-Lynn wasn't sure why. Something she'd missed? The last thing in the world she wanted was to like anything about this chatty, attractive woman, because that meant she could understand why Jack would, too.

Evidently her timing was good, for Hannah saw only one large buggy in the mill parking lot and no cars yet. She did not approach directly but kept to the path down along the stone-sided creek in case someone glanced out the windows of the mill. Its three stories made it and the grain elevator, to which is was attached by a covered walkway and a slanted chute, the tallest buildings in the area.

The Troyers' historical grist mill had perched on the stony, elevated riverbank since the mid-1800s but had fallen into disuse years ago. She could understand why Levi was proud of it, despite the strictures that the Amish must not be prideful. It had been passed down to him for generations, perhaps even more precious than a barn or a field, a piece of beloved furniture or a quilt.

If he could restore it, maybe with Seth's help, the mill could become a tourist attraction that would benefit everyone in the area. But had he gone about it wrong? She recalled a sermon *Daad* gave once, warning against trusting the rich and powerful of the world, for "pride serves as their necklace and violence covers them like a garment." Was Levi Troyer in the mire with men who buried their enemies in borrowed graves? If so, she could only pray that he did not know a thing about it.

The empty flume chute and twenty-foot wooden mill wheel loomed over her. It was through the two doors next to the wheel that she and her friends used to enter the derelict building and run around inside, playing hide-and-seek amid its grinding stones and storage bins. The mill's interior was a forest of old machinery and crisscrossing wooden trusses on all three floors. It was full of cobwebs, gray dust and white flour dust, which had made them look like gray ghosts when they'd emerged. Once they'd even gone into the creek to wash off on a warm day, and she'd held on to Seth in the current and they had kissed and floated...

"Oh, no!" she muttered when she saw the door they'd once used was completely boarded up. She should have realized that some barriers had been built to keep out vandals or someone who could be injured.

Was the Lord warning her away? Eavesdropping, spying, was wrong, but then, so was murder. If she could learn anything that linked these Detroit outsiders to the secret burials or shooting, she'd let Linc take over from there, no matter what trouble she got in with him for risking this. But the worse fallout would be from ruining the Troyer family's reputation. Naomi's future could be shattered. She could still hear *Mamm* saying that the Troyers and Eshes were one family now. Yet Hannah felt this was the right thing to do.

She craned her neck to look up. The second door wasn't boarded shut, but she would have to climb the big cogs of the mill wheel. She hiked her skirts and up she went. *Ya,* this door, despite the big X of boards nailed here, had a broken lock. Sweating, panting, she pulled the latch on the door and shoved, then had to kick it inward. She boosted herself and belly-crawled through the X. Inside on the second floor, she closed the door behind her. Surely the men would be meeting downstairs. She remembered how well sound carried here, for holes were cut in each floor for the diagonal chutes and grinding poles that operated the three sets of millstones.

She heard voices below in German, so no *Englische* here yet. She hoped Josh had not come along on the first week of his marriage, but as she tiptoed toward the front of the mill and squinted out through a dusty window, she saw he'd been left outside with the buggy, probably not to guard it but to wait for their guests and guide them in. *Ya,* exactly! A big black car was pulling up.

She stepped back a bit and caught her heel in a broken floorboard, but righted herself without a sound. No wonder the Troyers needed Seth's skills to rebuild this place. She could see a sag in this part of the floor where sacks of grain had once been piled.

Four men got out of the car, and Josh led them in. From this height, she could not see their faces, although one of them looked up and she jumped back from the window. He had silver hair and looked heavy and jowly. They were dressed rather formally; all wore tan or black overcoats but only two wore hats. The minute Josh led them inside and Levi greeted them, she could hear clearly. This was going to be much easier than she thought!

"Quite a place," one of the outsiders said. "But it sure needs a lot of work."

Hannah wished she could find a location to watch as well as hear them. She tiptoed across the floor and peered through a hole cut around a grain chute but she could only see one outsider and Levi.

"I've driven by here more than once and admired the place, so I hope this works out," the same man went on. "We've appreciated your cooperating with our earlier business, Levi."

Hannah's heartbeat kicked up. *Bingo!* as Linc sometimes said. Not only did that man admit he'd been in the area before, but "cooperating" with what earlier "business"? Could that be a code for providing a place to stash bodies?

She heard voices from outside and tiptoed back to peer out the dusty window again. She'd like to wipe it off with her apron, but that would be as bad as waving, because all five Troyer sons now waited outside by the buggy. If things were on the up-and-up, wouldn't Levi have let them stay inside? They'd been sticking tight to him earlier, so this gave her hope they didn't know everything their father was up to.

As she tiptoed back to the vantage point, her thoughts raced. From the first, Linc had thought someone had climbed up the back of the graveyard hill to shoot at them, and that was Troyer land. These men or someone who worked for them—surely not Levi himself—could have been there to shoot at her and her friends that night because they wanted to bury another body or they didn't want the ones they'd already stashed discovered. It flashed through her mind again that she'd have to ask her father if he knew anything that might incriminate his friend Levi on the same night *Daad* was outside looking for a coyote with his rifle.

"You do realize, Levi," another of the outsiders said, "that it will take close to a hundred thousand dollars to restore this mill properly, let alone get approval for a state historic site? The fact you'll use the Amish barn builder and your carpenters rather than outside unions with their higher bids and wages will help, but we're still talking megabucks here."

Could those be union leaders in those graves? Hannah knew the worldly builders unions were sometimes angry at the Amish for asking fair prices, bidding lower than they could. What if these Detroit moneymen had eliminated some of them? But wouldn't they have been missed?

"I realize it will be expensive," Levi said, "but it

will be worth it to the Home Valley community. Jobs for the rebuilding, jobs down the road when it becomes a living museum, more tourists to visit our stores and shops. Besides, I have three local investors interested, too, so that will help with funding. Harlan Kenton, a local meat store owner, is willing to pay for an Amish sandwich shop here on the first floor. And, for a healthy investment she's willing to make, a former Las Vegas restaurant manager will run that restaurant and a gift shop."

Hannah gasped. Lily sure got around! That's what she was planning to do with her future here; she and Harlan had more in common than frozen salmon and Amanda. Maybe Hannah would tell Ray-Lynn about Lily's plans, since it didn't involve her love triangle with Sheriff Freeman.

It bothered her that Levi sounded like he was boasting as he went on. "I've even got a local American Indian who will pay me to include a display about his tribe which once lived in this area. But besides funding, I got another problem. The bishop and the brethren been fretting over my doing publicity for this, *ya,* even appearing in the newspaper and TV ads like you said."

"That publicity should be the least of their worries!" the first speaker insisted. It was the silver-haired man who had looked up toward the window when they got out of their car. "After what's been going on around here, they're worried about publicity for this? Burials of executed victims being uncovered, *that's* publicity we don't need!"

Was that a confession? Someone below started sneezing, so she had trouble hearing what they said next other than, "God bless you." How dare these men so much as mention God and blessings if they were involved in sinful schemes!

They moved out of her sight, and she tiptoed to another vantage point. It took Hannah a moment to realize the men were coming up the stairs to the second floor. They must have asked for or arranged a tour of the mill. She should have thought of that. She couldn't go out the way she came in, because the stairs were between her and that door. She'd have to go up.

The steps to the top floor looked rickety, but she hurried up them, steadying herself with her hands. Cobwebs—real ones, unlike in the corn maze—laced themselves across her sweating face. A splinter from the hand rail. *Ach,* a dead rat with maggots on the step! And the floor up here under the eaves was much more rotted than below, so she'd have to be extra careful where she stepped. If they came up this far, she was trapped unless she could wedge herself back under the slant of eaves, and who knew what creatures made their nests there?

Levi was telling them about how this mill used to be a mechanical marvel in its day until steam-powered wheels made it obsolete. "Renovation will be a challenge," he went on. "The Amish timber framer I will hire is young but skilled. He's overseen the raising of huge barns, even a large lodge in a state park. We'll replace these hand-hewn timbers, use mortise and tenons to form joints just as when my great-grandfather built it. Look out this window. The mill wheel is called an overshot wheel because the power that turned it and the millstones came from water shot through a wooden flume above it, which we can get to work again."

"What about pouring a concrete base to hold all this up?" one visitor asked.

"I'd like to buttress the original stone instead, *ya*, keep it authentic," Levi said. "It needs to be done right. I know that will take a larger loan, but once the mill is open, I can begin to pay you back. I don't want to be beholden to you like before. It isn't our way."

"A lot of things around here aren't your way, Levi, but I like it that you can face facts and go along with what needs to be done."

Why didn't they just say Levi had agreed to planting bodies in the graveyard, or were they afraid the walls had ears, as indeed they did? Hannah finally found a long crack in the floorboards she could peer through to see them as they moved below her.

As she stepped back, bending down to miss the slanted roof, her bottom bumped against it. No—a person! Her inside cartwheeled. An arm pinned her wrists to her sides, and a hand clamped over her mouth as she was jerked off her feet and dragged back into a corner.

19

HANNAH WAS AFRAID TO FIGHT HER ATTACKER, or she'd give herself away. Or was it a guard they'd sent ahead? No, Amish arms. Someone working with Levi?

"It's me," he whispered. "Don't cry out."

Seth! Here doing the same thing she was?

He loosed and steadied her as they strained to hear what was being said below. She had a hundred questions but kept quiet. Besides, Seth looked furious. They glared at each other as they heard Levi say, "All right, if you want to see the top floor, that's fine, but watch your step, 'cause it's dangerous up there."

So much to say but no time to talk. Seth pulled her away and across the floor. Despite the sound of footsteps on the stairs, she heard something skitter across the floor behind them. A rat? An entire den of rats here, human ones?

"We can't go out a window this high," Hannah mouthed to him, but he pulled her on.

"The connecting chute to the grain elevator," he whispered, pointing.

"We can take the walkway."

"Too long—might be seen. Windows. Chute faster."

He was right. The walkway had light slits cut in it, but the grain chute would be dark. Maybe Seth had been here recently to assess both for the restoration. She had to trust him.

The stairs creaked as Levi came up, then called down, "All right, one at a time and be careful!"

Hannah saw the entry to the chute was unblocked, but the door to the walkway was closed, maybe locked. Seth must have known that. The slant of the chute hadn't looked this steep from outside, a black throat waiting to swallow them.

Seth boosted her up, then hoisted himself up beside her. With her good hand, she held to the mouth of the chute. She might reinjure her wrist going down, but they had no choice. What she could see of the inside looked coated with dust and grain chaff.

What would they hit at the bottom and would they be trapped below? If Seth had toured the place, he must know. "Protect your injured arm," he mouthed to her as if he'd read her thoughts.

The last thing she saw was Seth with one finger over his lips as if to say, *Don't scream!* She had screamed and screamed that time years ago, when they went on a roller-coaster ride at the county fair. Seth had laughed and thrown his arms up in the air, but she'd hated every minute of it, out of control, her stomach dropping away, her head whipped around and...

Too late. Too late for so much... Seth pulled her good hand away from the edge, held it tight and they careened together into utter blackness.

* * *

Seth tried to hold her tight to him as they slid down, down, but she slipped sideways, then away before he grabbed her again. At least the chute was only about two people wide. He didn't think they'd slide this fast. Grappling Hannah to his side, he fought to keep them going feetfirst. He'd seen the grain spew out of a spout over waiting boxcars—he felt like that. When Levi had showed him around, he'd said there was still some corn below, but that was more than two weeks ago. He prayed it would cushion their fall—and not bury them.

They didn't make a sound until they hit the corn. Both of them went in thigh-deep, their upper torsos thrown across the bed of kernels. Breath whoofed out, and they lay panting and stunned in a cloud of chaff that made them sneeze and cough. It was dim here but, even with watering eyes, so much better than the pitch-dark chute.

As Hannah tried to right herself, he saw her cape and skirt were up to her waist, showing her black stockings, panties and white thighs. That sight froze him for a minute, then he moved, thrashing about, trying to get up while Hannah pulled herself out and straightened her clothes. Her bonnet hung by its strings around her neck. He'd lost his hat in their wild ride. He spit out several grains of corn.

Hacking at the chaff, he said the obvious, "We have to get out of here."

"I hope we weren't wrong to leave Levi with them."

"You mean because he's going to agree to their terms again and get in even deeper?"

"No, what if they harm him—throw him down through the broken flooring and tell his sons it was an accident? They must be killers, and he knows what they've done."

"Hannah," he said, grabbing her arm to turn her back to face him, "they're loan sharks. They don't want him dead, they want him paying them back at a steep rate for years, partnership in the mill and who knows what else he owes them already. His biggest worry is the church will put him under the *meidung* when they find out, if you ask me."

"But I heard some things that suggest those men could be the ones who put the bodies in the graves. So they shot at—or, more likely, hired—someone to shoot at me and my friends. Couldn't you hear them from the third floor?"

"*Ya,* from the beginning, when they came in the mill. Did you come in here thinking they might be the killers, and you're spying on them and could have been caught? I couldn't believe it when I saw you creeping up the steps to the third floor!" Their raised voices echoed in here.

"You should talk!"

"Levi gave me permission to come into the mill whenever I want, so I had that excuse. I was only trying to find out if they were usurers or on the up-and-up, so I could decide whether to agree to oversee the rebuilding project. But you're playing judge and jury on more than that!"

"Of course I am. I'm going to tell Linc!" she insisted, shouting so loud they got back the echo *Linc... Linc...Linc...*

Seth lowered his voice. "Look, we don't need Attorney Arrowroot here to tell us that anything you tell Agent Armstrong about what you overheard is what they call hearsay, maybe entrapment. You're way out of line and out of your league again. He will hit the ceiling for more than one reason."

"And you and I have hit rock bottom," she insisted as she glared at his grayish-white clothes and brushed madly at her own. She half stumbled, half swam through the pile of corn, then said over her shoulder, "How do we get out of here?"

"Assuming your comment about rock bottom refers to our relationship as well as this mess, my answer is the same. We're going up."

He pointed to a metal ladder attached to the far side of the dim storage bin, then slogged toward it himself. This was hard enough going, so he was grateful it was too late in the season for more wagonloads of grain waiting to be dumped into boxcars from here.

"You go up first," he told her. "In case you fall, I'll be just behind."

She glared at him again. He wanted to grab her and kiss her, but there couldn't be a worse time or tactic.

"At least," she told him as she began to climb, "this will let us out on the far side of the elevator, and I can walk the tracks back near where I left my buggy."

"You're not going anywhere alone. All you do is get into trouble. And, in the long run, Linc Armstrong is not the one to help with that."

"Really?"

"Really," he said as she climbed carefully out on the high ledge that girded the elevator. He quickly followed. Swinging their legs as they scooted along toward the ladder that led down, he blurted out, "I love heights. What a spectacular view of our valley."

She turned to face him, frowning. "I don't know if

it will be my valley in the future, or if I'll try a singing career again. Linc likes my voice."

"Who doesn't? But I imagine he likes a lot more than that, you have to offer."

"I haven't made any offers, so take that back. He said he'll find someone to get me a new start with a singing career, stake me to it."

"Oh, great. Then he'll have sway over you just the way these money lenders do over Levi—only with a different payoff with interest."

"You would say that!"

"Of course I would. I'm still in love with you. I can't give you the world, but I would give you love and loyalty here for the rest of our lives."

"Loyalty? I can't trust that from you! And I guess love was never enough!"

He felt she'd slapped him. But he had betrayed her— betrayed both of them, and in a way, Lena, too, since he'd never really loved her. Fighting for self-control, he said, "Let's not argue here and now, or anymore. I deserve some of that, but people change, Hannah. You know that. Let's get down so I can walk you to your buggy and go get mine. Let's just not say any more if all we can do is hurt each other."

Biting her lower lip, with tears in her eyes, she waited for him to start down the last ladder and followed him. Silently, they trudged along the railroad tracks to a pine stand where she'd left her buggy.

"Thanks for rescuing me," she said, her voice choked and whispery. "I could have been trapped there if it wasn't for you."

"You could have been a lot of things if it wasn't for me, Hannah. Wife and mother, content, I hope, even happy. For once and for all, I ask your forgiveness for betraying your trust and hurting you. Except for Marlena, I'd take it all back, wipe it all out."

They stared at each other. It was all he could do not to just grab her, make love to her, hold her. He loved the stubborn Hannah Esh, always had, and he probably wasn't going to be able to keep her.

"Be careful going home," he said. "Be careful wherever you go...."

He turned and headed away. He realized it must sound as if he'd just said goodbye, and he almost wondered if he had.

Late that afternoon, Hannah called Linc on her cell phone and told him she had some information. It turned out he was back from Columbus and at the sheriff's office in town, so he said he'd be right out. *Daad* had gone to an elder's house across the valley, and *Mamm* was working in her *kapp*-making shop, but Hannah didn't want to invite Linc into the house in case *Daad* came back or *Mamm* took a break.

She quickly washed up, changed her clothes and went outside to wait. It was cold in the barn. She paced but not to get warm; her frustration with Seth and having to tell Linc what she'd done had heated her up.

When Linc pulled in, she called to him, and he strode toward her. He was dressed in what looked like army combat gear except for a jacket with the FBI script on the front. His olive-green cargo pants looked bulky with so many pockets; any pockets were *verboten* for her people. He'd gotten a haircut—even shorter than usual, but his ears still looked like they were glued to his head. He whipped off his wraparound sunglasses as he came into the shadows of the barn.

"What happened?" he greeted her, then lifted a quick hand to cup her chin, to tilt her head up to study her face. His eyes went over her, all of her, then he let her go. "Tell me," he ordered when she hesitated.

"All right. I had an opportunity to overhear Levi Troyer talking to the investors for his grist mill restoration project, four men from Detroit, and I remember what you said about the killers maybe being big moneymen from a city. These men fit the bill. I don't know how they got their hooks into Levi, but he's asking them to finance somewhere around a hundred thousand dollars and his land—"

"Yeah, his land backs right up to the graveyard hill. I talked to him early in the investigation but nothing about him seemed suspicious."

"Well, see, maybe it is. I've been praying he's not really involved with what those men might have done. He's family now and—"

"Where did you overhear this? Were you visiting your sister?"

"No. I mean—I *have* visited Naomi. I saw Levi and his sons huddled in conversation at their farm and then he made a phone call."

"Hannah, *where* did you overhear this? Did you get any names?"

"I thought you'd have a way of finding that out without telling Levi I was eavesdropping. It was in the mill, where they were looking around. I knew a back way in. Seth was there, too, because he needed to find out if the men were on the up-and-up before he signed a contract—although ordinarily, we don't have worldly legal contracts among ourselves—about heading up the restoration of the mill."

Linc took her by the upper arm so hard it hurt, but she didn't flinch. "Seth took you into that situation and let you eavesdrop?"

"No. They didn't know he was there, either. We just— We ran into each other."

He loosed her and smacked both hands on his thighs. He muttered a curse, then another. "Do you want to get yourself killed?"

"So you do think they could be behind everything?"

"I didn't say that. But if—huge *if*—these guys have anything to do with the graveyard killings, anything's possible."

"I know the mill well. I knew there were lots of holes in the floor and old chutes where I'd be able to hear." She almost told him how they had to leave the mill in a hurry, but she didn't want to upset him more.

"I ought to lock you up."

"Stop sounding like everyone else! Besides, you made a mistake to take me into the corn maze, didn't you? You understand how desperate someone can get to check something out, no matter the risk."

"That's my job, but *touché*," he said. She thought he'd translate that for her, but he rushed on. "Yeah, I lost my gun and my head that night. The thing is, you're screwing things up when you're supposed to be cooperating and complying with my orders. I need a promise that you will not try again to do my work for me."

"But I've given you a good lead!"

"And I'll look into it. But how am I going to help

you get a great singing career going if your parents—
after all you've put them through—have to bury you
in that cemetery?"

"You're trying to play on my guilt and scare me."

"Damn right, I am. Hannah, if these people pan out
and their sharp lawyers start taking me—or you—
apart in court, this initial info you've risked your life
for could possibly be thrown out as hearsay or entrapment."

Hannah gritted her teeth, not just because she might
have risked a lot for nothing, but because Seth had
been right about that. "Then tell me what you're doing
to find the killers," she said, her voice much too loud
and strident.

"Some I can tell you, lots you wouldn't understand."

"Don't fall into the trap of thinking the Amish aren't
intelligent."

"Oh, honey, I don't. You want to hear about DNA
matching, facial reconstruction? Okay. The bones of
the deceased have been X-rayed, measured and photographed to determine height, weight, race and ethnicity
by forensic scientists. It's laborious, detailed and takes
a long time. They've entered evidence into state and
national databases, including the National Crime Information Center database run by the FBI, which has
descriptions of thousands of un-ID'd persons whose
bodies have been found. But until we ID the three
bodies from the graveyard, we can't do much else."

"Thousands? That many?" She knew he was trying
to shock her by throwing all of that at her, but it did
comfort her to know they were working on it. Only,
still, not fast enough.

"We do know that the killers were careful, clever professionals," he went on, "because the three corpses had their fingerprints burned off with some sort of acid. The BCI has an Automated Fingerprint ID system, but that's out of the picture. The FBI's National Crime Information Center has gun and missing-persons files, but that hasn't helped yet. And while all that's going on, I'm still rattling cages around here to see who turns up as persons of interest."

"But now you'll have even more of those."

"Listen to me, Hannah," he said, seizing her wrist and pulling her closer. He lowered his voice. "You're a person of interest to me and not because I suspect you of foul play. I want to protect you and help you after all this is over. Maybe with a singing career, maybe in other ways that I can't get into now."

"Well, later then, because you can turn your feelings off and on like tap water!" she accused, realizing too late her voice was sharp, almost goading.

To her amazement, he put his other hand behind her neck to hold her still and dipped his head to kiss her. Quick. Once. Hard. It happened so fast that she had no time to react.

"You drive me nuts in more ways than one," he said, frowning, completely back in control as he released her and stepped back. "Call me if anything else comes up, but quit looking for trouble or you're going to find it. Here's the deal—your illegal breaking and entering at the mill never happened. That kiss never happened. Stay the hell home and away from Seth Lantz until I get this taken care of."

She was sure she had a hundred retorts, but nothing came to her as he stalked away. Funny thing, too. Her head was spinning, but only with what he'd said about his investigation. Her lips tingled, but her heart did not.

20

THE NEXT MORNING, IN THE VERY PLACE THAT Linc had warned Hannah to stay out of his business, she found a chance to take care of some business of her own. As she went out to harness Nettie, *Daad* was in the barn, putting the bridle on his buggy horse. Finally, she thought, she could learn more about the night she was shot.

"How's working for Mrs. Stutzman at her B and B going?" he asked. "She's Mennonite, but her parents were Amish. She left before she was baptized, other side of Wooster, so she wasn't shunned—just like you."

Hannah decided to ignore the *just like you*. He still hadn't gotten over that she'd left her family for the world. "She's been very kind, her brother, too," she said only.

"*Ya,* good sausage from his meat market. And the Plain and Fancy's a good place for you to work for now, my plain Amish but fancy worldly daughter."

There was an edge to each thing he said, but she tried to just stay conversational, keep heading toward what she wanted to ask. "A nice enough job until my wrist heals, but Ray-Lynn Logan has offered to train me to help her manage the Dutch Farm Table if I stay."

"*If* you stay…" he echoed, but did not finish that thought. "That job you would like more, but Mrs. Logan is not so good an influence on you. A nice lady, but modern and worldly."

"Ray-Lynn loves the Home Valley and its people!"

They looked at each other over the backs of their horses. Now or never, she thought. She had to risk changing the subject before he finished harnessing and was on his way.

"*Daad,* I'm still trying to sort through what happened the night of the shooting. *Mamm* mentioned you were outside that night, looking for a coyote."

"I told Agent Armstrong that, too. I told him the coyote must have moved on because we never saw it again."

"But did you hear the shots from the graveyard? I know when we hear hunters those sounds carry pretty far in the valley."

He frowned, as if trying to recall—or was he upset with her for bringing that up? He had told the congregation that God's justice would be served and they must go on with their lives despite the terrible upheaval surrounding them. He had said they must live in the valley of home and hope, *not* the valley of the shadow of death.

"Best that night be forgotten, my Hanni. Let worldly men fret over that, but you put it behind and look ahead. God will punish the wrongdoer—probably already has."

"You mean, 'Justice is mine, sayeth the Lord'?"

"Ya," he said as he pulled his horse's reins into the buggy and got in.

But she couldn't let it go. "So you didn't know anything was amiss until you saw the lights of the emergency vehicles and buggied over with *Mamm* to try to help?"

"Did you not hear what I said about moving on? Agent Armstrong asked all these things. He said to me that you must learn to let him do his work. Now, let it be, so you can heal, body and soul! And me, too!"

Her always steady, calm father's voice broke. She stood stunned at the anger that suddenly flared from him. Without another look or word, he snapped the reins and pulled out of the barn.

Puzzled and upset, she had barely finished hitching Nettie when she heard a buggy. *Daad* must be coming back! He felt bad he'd cut her off or meant to tell her something else. She ran to the barn door—just in time to see Seth get down from his buggy with her childhood doll in his hand.

"I was hoping to catch you before you left for work," he said, noticing her. He strode over, though he stopped a good six feet away. "I felt I should give this back. I took it from Marlena when she was asleep. She's upset, but I made her a horse on wheels she can pull by a string, so she's distracted for now." Stiff armed, he extended the doll toward her.

"No, I want her to have it. Fathers and daughters— best to be friends." Her voice caught and she blinked back tears as she darted a glance at her father's buggy disappearing down the road.

"You and the bishop…" he started to say, but cut himself off. "I don't mean to pry into your personal affairs anymore. You obviously want a break between us, so I will honor that."

"I don't know what I want! Other than to have Kevin's murder solved, find out who defiled those graves, get peace back in the valley, in our families. And I know I want Marlena to have my doll. Please, keep that for her."

She yearned to throw herself into his arms. She knew from the past that being away from him would not ease the agony she'd lived with since they'd stood at the pond that terrible night and he'd told her he was going to marry Lena.

For a moment, she thought he would not take the doll back, but he did, cradling it in one arm as if it were a living thing. The silence stretched between them. She wanted to say so much, but what came out was, "Are you going to take the Troyer job offer for Josh and Naomi's house and the mill restoration?"

"Their house, *ya*. The mill—I'm not sure. I haven't seen Levi since what we overheard. John Arrowroot sent me word this morning that he'd like his garage roof done, too. It won't take long, but I need to measure it for shingles. I'm going up there now to see him and better get going. For Marlena, *danki* for the *lumba babba*. For me, I still meant everything I said yesterday, but until I hear from you, I'll stay away."

He turned and strode for his buggy.

She wanted to call after him, even run to him. But she only stood in the barn door and waved, though he didn't look back.

When Arrowroot didn't come out to greet him, Seth went to the garage to get the ladder and climbed up on the roof. He knew this garage like the back of his hand now: a few basic tools, a ladder and those aerial photos of the valley and graveyard tacked on the walls. None of that was enough to charge him with anything. Seth no longer believed Arrowroot had slit Hannah's screen and left the eagle feather—it just didn't seem something he'd do. Linc had questioned the man again and come up with—as he put it—"diddly-squat," so Seth planned to abandon his earlier suspicions and keep out of the case. And keep out of Hannah's life.

He paced off the roof area to get an estimate. Pretty much what he'd thought. At least, since Arrowroot wanted this roof done, too, it must mean he approved of the job on the house. And the money had been really welcome until he got that down payment from Levi Troyer for the newlyweds' house. Of course, he'd see Naomi quite a lot while he built it. Maybe Hannah would come to see it, too....

Ach. He had to stop thinking about her.

The November wind was biting today, so he hustled. He recorded the measurements, climbed down and put the ladder back in the garage. While he'd been up and down his own ladder during the roofing of the house, he'd been able to peer into a window or two, but had mostly seen his own reflection. Though he'd used the bathroom by the back door, Arrowroot had always been close by so, other than a glance in his kitchen, Seth had given up on spying on the man. Given up on a lot lately.

But he was puzzled now. Arrowroot had sent him a note telling him to be here at this time. Why didn't he come out? Maybe he was on the phone. Seth scribbled his calculations down—amount of shingles, cost per bundle, his labor costs—and went up on the front porch. He knocked on the door.

No answer. No sound.

"Mr. Arrowroot! Seth Lantz here!"

He knocked again, then tried the door. Locked. He walked the length of the porch, shading his eyes to look in the front windows. He couldn't see around the large painting of the eagle feather very well, but not a thing inside looked disturbed.

He walked around to the back door. It, too, was locked. But the man's truck was in the garage, so he had to be here. Seth looked in the back kitchen windows and knocked on one. No sound but the cawing of crows in the bare trees as if they were arguing. What if Arrowroot had had a heart attack or had fallen and knocked himself out?

Seth did a quick search in typical places to hide a key. Under doormat, flowerpot, ledge above the window—yes!

He unlocked the back door and called, "John Arrowroot! It's Seth."

He felt it now, an icy shiver up his spine, the sense that something was very wrong. He closed the door behind himself and put the key on the butcher block wood counter. After a quick peek into the small half bath, he hurried down a short hall into the living/dining area. He opened two closet doors, then pounded up the stairs, not trying to be careful anymore.

The first room was obviously an office. Drawings of Native Americans, including one of Arrowroot in Indian garb, covered the walls. The closet was full of extra filing cabinets. Next the bathroom, empty: he hadn't fallen in the shower. Next, his bedroom. Indian designs and one wall painted bloodred, with real arrows and feathers mounted on it—eagle feathers, of course—in some intricate, probably sacred design.

And—in the middle of the bed—a big eagle feather, which looked identical to the one stuck in Hannah's window, along with a piece of paper with the word *Guilty* circled on it. Next to that lay a handgun and a rifle.

Seth backed from the room, ignoring the phone on the bedside table, and nearly tripped on the stairs going down. He grabbed the key, ran outside and relocked the door. Arrowroot had to be somewhere in that house, didn't he? He'd never leave such damning evidence for someone to see if he was going to flee. And flee how, with his truck still here?

Rather than go back inside to use Arrowroot's phone to call 9-1-1—and get his fingerprints on it—Seth decided to get Linc Armstrong and the sheriff without leaving the property. Until help came, he'd act as the men he'd watched at the graveyard, cordoning off and guarding a possible crime scene. Maybe he'd been wrong about Arrowroot; maybe that was the rifle that shot the goths.

He grabbed his pencil and pad and scribbled a note to the sheriff, who would probably be a lot easier to find than Agent Armstrong. Seth ran down to the road and waited for a buggy to come by—even knew the family, who were going to town. He gave them the note, then ran back up the hill and, from a stand of trees where he could see the front and back doors, hunkered down to wait.

* * *

"Thanks for seeing me so early for this cut and color," Ray-Lynn told Clair Kenton. Clair was a cute blonde who still teased her own hair into a bubble. That went to show how well Homestead's hairdresser kept up with the outside world. The woman was friendly and talkative but not the sharpest knife in the drawer. "I'll be back in the restaurant before the lunch rush, so thanks for working me in," Ray-Lynn told her.

"No problem. Hey, I sure love your pun'kin pie at the Dutch Farm Table. You know the recipe offhand? It's the spices make the big diff'rence."

"All the pies are made by women in the area, so I don't have the recipes. The one I'm thinking you mean is actually made from scratch, from her boiling and mashing the pumpkins right out of her garden," Ray-Lynn said as Clair painted the dye on her hair and wrapped each area in tin foil.

"So, any new customers lately?" Ray-Lynn asked, hoping to bring up Lily Freeman. "We've had an avalanche of them, but most come and go too fast to stop here."

"Sad but true. At least my downtime lets me really read these celeb magazines we buy. I sure do wish the Amish ladies around here would cut their hair. Imagine it being clear to their waists and they only take it down at night for their husbands. You know, if Amish women had their hair done for all the weddings around here, like reg'lar women do, I'd be rich. At least Harlan's been doing really well the past few years. He says we can both retire young—well, kinda young."

Ray-Lynn did not want Clair to get on Harlan's drinking or money or anything else. "I've met Sheriff

Freeman's former wife a couple of times," Ray-Lynn said. "Have you?"

"Oh, yeah, a real breath of fresh air. But don't take that wrong, 'cause you're the best, Ray-Lynn. I sure hope for your sake she don't have designs on the sheriff, but a word to the wise, she seems real int'rested in him. Says she missed Ohio and is back to stay."

Ray-Lynn gripped her hands in her lap under the plastic cape. "She was telling me some about her life in Vegas."

"Oh, yeah. You know, she's not like those TV ads, 'What happens in Vegas stays in Vegas.' She told me all about the posh restaurant where she was the hostess."

"She told me, too. So had you even ever heard of Asian fusion food before?"

"I don't know about that. She said it was a steak house, where à la carte started at something like fifty-dollars for Western-bred beef. À la carte and fifty bucks for the meat alone, can you imagine? And she loved to gamble in her free time, liked blackjack better than the slots or faro or anything else."

Ray-Lynn sat up straighter. She was going to correct Clair but then it hit her. Lily might have worked in more than one restaurant, but her comments about gambling couldn't have been that different—could they?

"She must still be something of a night owl," Ray-Lynn said. "I think she still likes the bright lights, but I don't know where she'd find them around here."

"Harlan said he saw her once at the Rooster Roadhouse when he was out for poker night with his buds."

"That's kind of a man's place—a little rough, isn't it? Was she alone?"

"I think he said the sheriff checked it out from time to time to keep a lid on the place. I told Harlan he'd better just drink at home or I was gonna pour that fancy stuff he buys in the creek, but he said..."

Clair's voice went on and on. While Ray-Lynn was sitting, waiting for the dye to take, she formed a plan. Somehow, despite what she'd promised Jack, she was going to just check out who he was keeping an eye on at the Rooster Roadhouse, where his ex had gone at least once. It seemed Lily really did like to gamble, so Ray-Lynn was ready to risk some high stakes, too.

Seth saw Linc get out of his black unmarked car behind his buggy. No sheriff in sight, so he walked down out of the trees to meet him.

Linc, jacket open and hand on his gun, called to him, "Sheriff got called out on a domestic before your note came to his office. I called him, and he'll be here soon. Can you can get me inside without breaking and entering?"

"I found the back door key, went through the place looking for him. I checked the bathroom in case he fell and in a few closets, but didn't search the basement or much else. Thought I'd better leave that to professionals."

"It seems you're at the center of the action once again," Linc said as they walked toward the back door. Seth didn't like the tone in his voice or the narrow-eyed look he gave him. "Yesterday, there you were with Hannah in her escapade at the mill. She told me about it, but you should have, too."

"I haven't seen you, like she obviously has. Besides, she's seeing bad guys behind every tree. You want to deal with this, or shall we wait for the sheriff?"

"Yeah, we're going in. No note from Arrowroot on the premises?"

"A message, in a way. The thing is, he said he'd be here," Seth said as he retrieved the key again and unlocked the back door. "It's really strange—especially what I found on his bed upstairs—that's the message."

"Which is?" Linc demanded as they walked through the first floor, then started up the stairs.

"I guess what you might call incriminating evidence, at least for leaving a feather in Hannah's window. And a rifle that may link to the graveyard shootings. There's a paper he cut or tore out from somewhere with the word *guilty* circled on it. And he left a pistol there that looks like the one you carry."

Linc's head jerked up and his eyes widened. His hand jumped to his gun again.

"In here," Seth said, and pointed at the items on the bed.

"You didn't touch anything?"

"After all your earlier suspicions about me? No. And I don't like the look you gave me just because I happened to be here. He sent for me. I have his note at home."

Linc leaned over the bed. Seth thought he'd check out the rifle first, but he picked up the pistol with a ballpoint pen stuck through its trigger guard. "Yeah, it's the one taken when Hannah and I checked out the corn maze."

"You took her in the corn maze and someone took your gun?"

"I thought she'd told you. You mean, for once, she did what I said?"

"What happened in the maze?"

"I said, someone took my gun. Please stand out in the hall while I call in a forensic team," he said, and dug his cell phone out of his jacket pocket.

Seth stepped out into the hall but asked, "You sure it's the gun you lost?"

"You want to quit playing FBI agent here?"

"I'm only playing concerned citizen. So what happened in the corn maze? You obviously didn't think it was Arrowroot or you would have arrested him. If there was violence involved, I'd say it wasn't him. He's prideful and hostile, but he uses words, not guns."

"I said I'll handle this. I need to make this call!"

Linc turned away and Seth backed off, but he could hear most of what he said. He asked for a search warrant and a BCI team. He said that it was possible he had a suspect in the Halloween shootings and in the professional hits found in the graveyard. And that it was also possible there was another victim.

21

RAY-LYNN HAD JUST FINISHED TALLYING UP
the day's receipts in her office when she heard a rap-
ping on the front door of the restaurant. Her employees
were long gone. She stashed the money in her little safe
and peeked out to see who was there.

Thank heavens—Jack! She hadn't seen him all day,
but there had been restaurant buzz that John Arrowroot had gone missing. Folks who came in from over
by Valley View Road said there was an army of outside
law enforcement in the area. She hurried to unbolt the
door.

"Did you all find him?"

"I knew word would get around," he muttered as
he stepped inside. "No. It's like he vanished right
out of his locked house, which has been thoroughly
searched by Linc, me and the BCI team. His truck's in
the garage. No signs of violence or foul play—nothing
but some stuff I can't talk about."

She saw he had some big pieces of cardboard in his
hands. Oh, missing-persons posters. He put them down

on the counter and pulled her into his arms behind the counter in the dimly lit front dining room.

She held tight, her face pressed against his black padded jacket, which was damp.

"Don't tell me it's raining outside," she said.

"Spitting snow. Wish I could stay, but I've got two more stops to make with these posters. I talked Linc into letting me organize a hunt for Arrowroot tomorrow, especially up in his neck of the woods. Under normal circumstances, we'd never search for a missing adult for days, but he's got information we need about the murders, at the least. Can you put up a poster on both sides of the front door? Hope to have several search parties ready to go out by 9:00 a.m. Gathering place will be the parking lots of the sheriff's office and fire department."

"Of course," she said as they stepped apart. "I'll be there with coffee and doughnuts. Leah Schwartz can take over the restaurant briefly. She even has a key, though I'm hoping to train Hannah Esh as my new assistant. John Arrowroot's not the most popular man in the county, but folks will pitch in, even the Amish."

"You bet they will, though he's harassed them for years. I'm going to stop by Bishop Esh's to ask him if he can get the word out to his people, then stop a few more places—the gas station, the Roadhouse."

"The Rooster Roadhouse?"

"Yeah. Jake Johnson, the owner, is a nice guy. He owes me for dropping in there once in a while, just so his patrons know to behave. He's got lots of contacts, and we'll need some big bruisers to cover some of that hilly, wooded terrain up by Arrowroot's place. We'll fan out from there."

"If Arrowroot had anything to do with the grave-yard shootings or hidden bodies, maybe he thought he'd better just get out of Dodge, make it look like someone took him," she suggested.

"If so, he's been planning it for a long time because it looks like he took nothing with him, even his precious tribal art. His wallet's there, money found in a drawer, and he hasn't touched his savings account at the Citizens Bank, not that he couldn't have something stashed elsewhere."

"It— What if it's a suicide? You said there were some things you couldn't talk about—like a suicide note?"

"Not exactly, but he's got to have some answers we need. As crazy as he was about the old Indian ways, I half wonder if he hasn't gone out to live in the wilds the way his people did once. But in this weather…? Look, honey, much as I'd like to stay with you, I've got to get going to set all this up tonight."

"You just be careful if the roads are getting slick. The Rooster Roadhouse is a ways out."

"Just a couple miles. Ray-Lynn, I can't wait till this is all over and we have our town, our restaurant, our lives back. You be careful driving home now, hear?"

"Sure. And I'll get your signs posted and talk up the search with the early-breakfast crowd, too."

He pecked a hasty kiss in the general area of her mouth and was out the door, which she locked behind him. It sounded like he knew the owner of the Road-house pretty well. If he stopped to see Bishop Esh first, he was going out there pretty late tonight. Couldn't he just call Jake Johnson to put up a hand-lettered sign and tell his patrons about the search tomorrow?

She picked up the poster and read it carefully. He had even come up with a photo of John Arrowroot, maybe one they found when they searched his house. "Missing. John Arrowroot, age 60. 6' tall, medium build, 185 pounds, black hair, brown eyes, wears thick glasses." At the bottom in smaller print was "Contact Sheriff Jack Freeman" and his phone number and email address. Then, "Outdoor search party members needed, Thursday, November 17, 9:00 a.m. All day or anytime until dusk. Meet at Sheriff's Office in Homestead."

Ray-Lynn hurried back to her office and phoned Amanda Stutzman at the B and B. "Hi, Amanda. Ray-Lynn here. Listen, I thought you, Harlan, Clair and Lily ought to know there's going to be a volunteers' search for John Arrowroot, who has disappeared or wandered off from his property."

"Wandered off? You can't tell me that quick-witted man had Alzheimer's!"

"No, it isn't that, but maybe he fell and is dazed or something. I know you're pretty tied to your place, but I thought Lily might have some extra time. She's such a great jogger that tramping through the hills might be her thing, even if the weather's a little iffy." Then she asked the first question about what she really wanted to know. "Is she there right now?"

"She went out just a few minutes ago, but I'll let her know when she gets back. I might not see her until tomorrow morning, though, since she said she'd be in late."

"It's spitting snow out there, so the roads might be slick. Hope she's not going too far."

"I think to that sports bar out on Troyer's Mill Road, but she's lived around here long enough to know how to drive on icy roads."

That sports bar out on Troyer's Mill, Ray-Lynn thought, and stamped her foot. Spitting snow be ding-danged, she was getting spitting mad about being taken for a ride. So she was going to go home to change her clothes, then just take a little ride herself.

Hannah was in the kitchen getting a bedtime snack about nine. Her reflection in the window—like a black mirror—bothered her. Her hair was growing out, so that was good, but her image made her feel caught between two worlds. Her once-spiky red hair was brushed smooth, so it would look strange to the goth world she'd grown used to, though never really felt a part of. She suddenly missed the sweet shape of a white prayer *kapp* like the ones *Mamm* made so beautifully. Which was it going to be in her future, worldly living or Amish life? If Linc offered to loan her money for another try at a singing career, what should she do?

She bent closer to the window so she could see out through her own shadow. A few snowflakes swirled down outside, the first of the season. Now and then a gust of wind whipped them sideways. A car pulled in at the back of their house, its headlights illumined the dancing dots. Linc? No, it was the sheriff.

Her heartbeat kicked up. What if something had happened to Seth, like he fell off a roof? What if the sheriff had already been to Lantzes and thought he'd best tell the bishop, too? She left her half-moon pie and milk on the counter.

"Daad," she called toward the living room where the three of them had been playing Scrabble, "Sheriff Freeman's here!"

She opened the back door for him. He had several big pieces of paper in his hands. *Daad* and *Mamm* both came into the kitchen, concern written on their faces. The sheriff took off his hat, which was wet with melted flakes. "Bishop, Mrs. Esh, Hannah. Got us a missing person, and we're organizing a search tomorrow." He put what appeared to be three posters down on the kitchen table. John Arrowroot! Hannah realized she'd been holding her breath.

"Seth went out there this morning to give him an estimate on doing his garage roof," the sheriff explained, pointing at the picture. "Seth has a note to show Arrowroot asked him to come out. But our Indian activist was not home, not anywhere, like he just vanished right out of his house. The FBI and the forensic teams are assisting on the case."

"You know we will help," *Daad* told him. "No matter who, we will always help our neighbors."

"Here's the info on the meeting time and place," the sheriff explained, pointing to the bottom of the top poster. "I knew you'd help, Bishop—even if the person hurt you or your people. Well, gotta get going."

Hannah kept quiet, though she had a dozen other questions. Why an immediate search for a man who was not only in his right mind, but clever and careful? Had they found proof that John Arrowroot was involved in the Halloween attack or the double burials? She'd alienated Seth, but she'd sure like to know what he knew. But then, maybe Linc would tell her.

* * *

Seth figured he was blessed Arrowroot had paid him for roofing the house, but his disappearance, perhaps set up and timed so that Seth would find him missing, really baffled and bothered him. As he told Marlena a bedtime story about horses pulling little girls on sleds in the snow, and then tucked her in, his mind raced. Though Linc had been busy all day, he'd asked for permission to drop in tonight. Seth was expecting more than what Linc had referred to as a debriefing. He figured it would be like an interrogation.

Seth could tell that Linc was getting desperate. Maybe his reputation was at stake, or it was a personal thing to a driven man. Seth remembered seeing an old movie on his employer's TV during his *rumspringa* years, about World War II general Douglas MacArthur. A graduate of West Point, the general had seemed obsessed with loyalty to "the corps, the corps." It was like that with Linc, always thinking about the regulations and reputation of the FBI, which he called the Bureau.

Just now Linc was furious someone—evidently Arrowroot—had taken his gun, then left it there on the bed with a guilty plea and a possible murder weapon. Linc had not liked it that Seth had made him look bad by finding the feather stuck in Hannah's window. He was angry that Seth had admitted he'd been watching Arrowroot on his own, and then had defended Arrowroot for not being capable of violence. *Ya,* Seth had been through Linc's questioning after the graveyard shootings, and he didn't want to be his target again. But he'd tell him to keep his voice down, because Marlena was sleeping.

Seth let Linc in the back door about ten minutes later. "Don't like driving hills when they're slippery," Linc muttered as he came in and slung his damp FBI jacket over the back of a kitchen chair. The man looked bad, with dark circles under his eyes and his cheeks shadowed with beard stubble. He had a thermos mug of what smelled like coffee in one hand, which shook.

"Maybe you should switch to a horse and buggy around here, if you're going to spend the winter," Seth said. "Slower. Safer. You can do other work while the horse handles long stretches."

"Very funny."

They sat in the small living area, Seth in his favorite chair, Linc in Lena's. Linc put his mug down, leaned forward and propped his elbows on his knees as if to hold himself up. "Okay, here's the bottom line, because it's going to get out, anyway. The word *guilty* he had circled was on a page torn from a law handbook in the house. And ballistics just called to tell me that the rifle on the bed was the one which killed Kevin Pryor and wounded Tiffany Miles and Hannah, but probably—just probably—not the one that executed the three buried victims. Only Arrowroot's prints are on the rifle. So far, we can't find that the rifle was his— who it's registered to at all—but it could have been bought black market. The pistol was mine, taken from me when he knocked me out in the corn maze."

"While Hannah's life—yours, too—was in danger. So you obviously have checked out the Meyers brothers and couldn't find anything on them."

"I swear, I should hire both you and Hannah. Yeah, I talked to them immediately after, but they came up clean and had an alibi from their mother, though I supposed she could have lied for her boys. Listen, Seth, I know there are a couple of hundred people around here who must have hated John Arrowroot."

He shook his head and slumped back in the chair. "You know," Linc went on with a bitter laugh, "the sheriff's receptionist said she thinks Arrowroot's just gone to join his ancestors or the Great Spirit or something like that. Next, it'll be he was abducted by the same aliens that make crop circles. She's wacky, of course, but I'm so sick and tired of what I thought would be a quick open-and-shut case that her theory doesn't sound so bad."

Surprised by a calm demeanor he hadn't expected, Seth said, "You can eliminate my people from doing anything to harm him. It's not our—"

"I know. It's not your way. I'm looking into a few others," he said, staring at Seth with bloodshot eyes.

"I think this is a dead end—well, I shouldn't put it that way—but I once saw Harlan Kenton really argue with him."

"Okay. Annie Oakley, alias Elaine Carson, has also been really vocal about Arrowroot wanting her land, and I'll have to interview George and Clint Meyers again after what you told me about their going to his house earlier. Unless Arrowroot took off and is just setting us up."

"I know Arrowroot was publicity-hungry for his cause, but this kind of stunt? Can't see it," Seth insisted.

"But he managed to get some TV and newspaper coverage during the graveyard exhumations. There may be a lone wolf out there somewhere who decided to set him up or shut him up. Then that would mean the lone wolf was the one who shot at the goths and followed us into the corn maze to hit me on the head and take my gun. But lone wolves committing random crimes? Coincidences in police work? Rarer than rare."

"Someone thinks he or she is pretty smart. Someone enjoys playing games," Seth muttered.

"At least Hannah doesn't seem to be a target anymore," Linc said.

"Not of the killer, I hope, but how about yours?"

Linc sat up ramrod straight. "What's that supposed to mean? You should talk. You both just happened to be in the old Troyer mill when their patriarch met with some investors from Detroit. I've got to check them out, too."

"I didn't take her there. I ran into her there. But you evidently took her to the corn maze. I think she's your target—and not for questioning about a crime. You've been stringing her on about a music career or more."

"I'm out of here," Linc said, grabbing his coffee mug and thermos and getting to his feet. "After how you screwed up her life, I don't think you're the man to throw stones about giving her a reason to leave here."

That hit Seth hard, like a fist to his gut. He had no answer for that, no right to argue about Hannah. And Linc had surprised him tonight. Despite the fact Seth had been the one to discover that Arrowroot was gone and that Seth had his fingerprints on the doorknobs and in the downstairs bathroom, Linc hadn't accused him of anything. He'd kept calm, calmer than Seth felt right now.

After he let Linc out and locked the door, he went back to check that Marlena was sleeping soundly. She was, with Hannah's doll in her little arms. If someone could disappear right out of his locked house—of course, he'd probably just locked it after he'd left—he had to keep an eye on his little girl. But how he also longed to keep an eye on Hannah Esh, ever the rebel, the one he'd always loved and could not bear to lose again.

Ray-Lynn tried to tell herself she wasn't jealous of Lily, that she believed in Jack, that she shouldn't be driving around on a slippery country road on a pitch-black November night. Sure, Jack was busy and under pressure, but might stress and exhaustion entice him to make a bad decision? She'd promised to trust him, but she didn't trust that woman—the "other woman" in his life.

At home, she changed into black wool slacks, a black turtleneck sweater and her black raincoat. She pulled on high, leather boots. They were her new, fashionable ones instead of her mudders, but she wanted to keep warm. She tugged a knitted hat down over her newly coiffed hair. As she walked to her garage, the wind seemed brisk but the snow was not heavy. Still, once she was through town and out on the rural roads, there was a glare on the pavement. Her headlights illumined each snowflake, making them seem to fly at her. She knew she should go back, but she gripped the wheel and drove on. Just like Jack, she needed answers once and for all.

She came to a sign that read Bridge Ices Before Road, so she hit her brakes to test them. Not too bad so far. She slowed for the short bridge that crossed Killibuck Creek, a river that wandered through the area. A ravine with the river at its bottom ran along the right side of the road here.

She was careful at stop signs, drove a little slower now, however much she wanted to rush there, get this over. What really was eating at her was that she and Jack had gone to the Rooster Roadhouse once, eaten greasy burgers and shot pool. It was early in their dating. He'd helped her make a couple of pool shots by bending over behind her, his hands on the cue stick near hers, breathing in her ear, pressing himself against her bottom so that her pelvis pushed against the wooden edge of the table....

Darn! She had to keep her mind on the here and now.

The bright, blinking neon sign for the sports bar came into view in a blur through the wet windshield. She'd have to get her wiper blades changed at the gas station. The *swish-swish, swish-swish* was driving her crazy. The lousy winter weather was one bad thing about living in the "valley of Eden."

As she pulled into the parking lot of the place, the reflection of the orange neon words Rooster Roadhouse and the red, orange and yellow rooster, with its head going up and down as if it were crowing, lit up the entire interior of her car. She squinted at the vehicles parked here. No sign of Jack's, though she saw what must be Lily's with its Nevada license plate. Yeah, as Hannah said, it was a flashy car. She recognized Elaine Carson's truck, too, with its flags and eagle decals. Bad sign both women had their vehicles—they hadn't come out here together.

She spotted the truck that belonged to either George or Clint Meyer, the only one in town with a red rebel stars and bars flag stretched across its back window, like so many she'd seen down South while growing up. Under the flag, the cab sported an empty gun rack. All those two needed was a couple of coonhounds baying in the bed of their truck, and they'd be ready for hunting in the haunts Ray-Lynn's granddad had loved.

She drove around to the back, so Jack wouldn't spot her van when he came in. She supposed she could concoct a cover story, but he'd never believe it.

Ray-Lynn got out and locked the van. Out here, surrounded by miles of open fields, she felt the snow sting her skin. Maybe it was turning to ice pellets. She'd peek in the ample windows in front, then get out of here, hopefully before Jack even arrived. She'd been foolish to venture out, at least on a night like this.

Keeping an eye out for approaching cars, she sidled along the front of the building and peeked in. With all the lights and action inside, she hoped no one noticed or recognized her. At least she was partly sheltered from the wind here and there was no moisture on the window glass. She had a clear view of the inside, as if the window were a huge high-def TV screen. Speaking of which, four large TVs mounted over the long bar were carrying different basketball games.

There were ten or twelve patrons she didn't recognize, despite how she knew most of the people living in the area. But there were some she sure did. Elaine Carson, looking like a biker babe in black leather, was shooting pool with George and Clint Meyers. Yeah, she could imagine all three of them being regulars here. They had beers they drank from nearby bottles from time to time. The two Meyers men looked so much alike, with their big heads, brown hair and eyes and beefy frames, that she could hardly tell them apart. They weren't twins but might as well have been. No wonder they never married when they had each other.

You might know, Harlan Kenton sat at the bar, facing this way, but looking up at a TV screen. Poor Clair and Amanda, who were obviously so worried about him. She hadn't seen his truck out front, but maybe he'd driven a car she didn't know. And at the far end of the bar was Lily. Sitting in profile to Ray-Lynn's position, Lily was also alone—ding-dang, probably waiting for someone. She seemed totally out of place with some sort of a fancy red drink in front of her, maybe a cosmo. Besides, she was dressed way too nice for here, dark slacks, some sort of bright green silk blouse and big, gold earrings. An alarm went off in Ray-Lynn's head. Lily must know Jack was coming, even as she got up and sashayed away from the window toward the back of the place.

There was a video game room in that direction, Ray-Lynn recalled. Maybe video games were the closest thing to slot machines around here. Why had Lily told her and Clair Kenton different things about her past? Was there some good explanation, or was she lying and why?

Headlights slashed through the darkness, and Ray-Lynn hustled off the porch and around the other side of the building from where she'd parked. Yes, Jack's cruiser! Holding a couple of posters, he bent against the snow and wind to walk inside, but she could see him take a look at the vehicles parked close to the building. It had been a good move to leave hers around the other side. And she had to get out of here. Her insides were tied in knots. But she still crept back around the corner and peered in the window again.

Harlan had downed his beer and was shuffling off toward the bathrooms. Jack was talking with the bartender, probably about the poster he showed him. The others came over, but Lily did not reappear. Elaine went into the back room, then Clint and George followed, maybe to bring her out or tell her about the search for John Arrowroot tomorrow. At least Lily wasn't running out to greet Jack.

Ray-Lynn jumped back when she saw Jack turn around and glance at the front door, scan the windows. That was his way, even in their restaurant, always keeping an eye on who could be coming in. What if he spotted her or just saw a form looking in? As much as she wanted to keep an eye on things, she'd best get in her van. It would be warmer and she could wait a bit to see who left together—unless Jack drove through the entire parking lot when he left. Jack's house wasn't far from here, if he—or he and Lily—drove around by Troyers' old mill.

Though the shorter way back to her van was to walk in front of the building, Ray-Lynn didn't dare push her luck. Besides, it was getting more slippery, so she should go home. Well, maybe just a few minutes sitting in her car to see who left together, or if not in the same car, then nearly at the same time.

Around the back of the roadhouse, she bent into the wind. Oh, Harlan's truck was behind the restaurant, back up by the door, so he'd obviously been delivering meat. The blinking neon sign threw garish colors on top of the van and the wet pavement. Her fingers were numb; she should have brought gloves. She fumbled for her car key in her pocket, pulled it out and pushed the button that would unlock the van.

Its interior lights came on, though she wished, for once, it just stayed dark. She opened the driver's side door, and heard something—someone?—behind her. Had Jack spotted and followed her? A form, a blur...

Pain crashed through her head, and everything went black.

22

NEARLY ELEVEN O'CLOCK THAT NIGHT, *MAMM* had gone up to take a shower, but Hannah and *Daad* still sat in the kitchen talking. He had listed information for who he needed to tell about the search for John Arrowroot in the morning. He'd drawn arrows to show how that word would be spread from farm to farm among the brethren. They'd been talking about who would have to leave the area for work, who should stay home with children, who was incapable of a strenuous search. It all reminded her again of how close-knit her people were—yes, she still thought of them as her people.

Tomorrow morning, Hannah planned to stop by the B and B only long enough to tell Amanda she would need to miss work tomorrow to volunteer for the search and to ask her if she and Lily could help look for John Arrowroot, too. Hannah was achingly tired, but here she sat, for she could tell something besides the search was bothering her father. The burden of being a bishop—a position decided by the drawing of lots, not a popularity vote—weighed him down at times, but this seemed something beyond that. Twice he had started to say something, then had stopped.

"You feeling all right, *Daad?*"

He frowned, reshuffling his papers. "You know, Hanni, it would help if you could leave just a bit early tomorrow morning. You could buggy over to tell the Lantzes and make sure Seth and his family know all the details of the search before you go to the Plain and Fancy. It would save me some time, *ya,* it would. We should make a good showing at 9:00 a.m. and that's pretty early for word to spread."

"Seth probably knows about it from Agent Armstrong. Seth and I aren't exactly speaking—kind of a mutual decision, for now."

"*Ach!* Aren't *exactly* speaking? Kind of? For now? Sounds wishy-washy to me. Hanni," he said, leaning over the corner of the table to cover her hand with his, "I was praying you and Seth would patch up the past. Perhaps the Lord brought you back for that purpose. There are many reasons for you to choose to stay home after this is over, and he's a big one."

"I struggle with that—my relationship with him. I felt so betrayed. He ruined my plans, my life. I can't forget and struggle to forgive. Sometimes I feel so desperate."

"Your leaving ruined my plans for you, the life I saw you could and would lead among your people. And now with your friend Sarah jumping the fence and Linc Armstrong tempting you about a worldly singing career... I just don't want you to follow in Sarah's footsteps."

His eyes became glassy with tears. He took out his handkerchief and blew his nose. "I—I know desperation, Hanni, felt it when you left us, my sweet, bright girl. One of four daughters, *ya,* but somehow special in my heart."

Hannah's lower lip dropped. No one Amish was considered individual or special. Cooperation, not competition, was what mattered, for all were equal in God's eyes. *"D-daad,"* she said, stammering because she was shaking so hard, but she had to get this out, "something has been bothering you since I came back—since my friends and I were shot."

"Ya," he said only, then, after a pause, took a deep breath and went on. "I did something sinful, but I wanted bad to bring you back, keep you here."

Surely, surely, she thought, he could not be about to confess the impossible, what she had feared so deeply she had never voiced it even to herself. Her father, the bishop, had been outside with a rifle looking for a coyote Halloween night when she and her friends were shot. Had he seen something, had he...done... something?

"I been lying, Hanni," he said. "God will forgive me, but will you? And if you can't forgive Seth, I'm not hoping for it."

Her entire body tensed. She held her breath.

"I lied to your mother the day I hired taxi service. Told her it was to see an old friend."

She shook her head in bewilderment. "You are upset because you lied to *Mamm* about something? About Halloween night? Or the night Linc and I went to the corn maze?"

"No, way before all that. Sarah told her mother who told your *Mamm* that you were going to sing for a man who owned a music company. She told me the man's name, too. Jason Flemming. I went to Cleveland, found him, talked to him."

"What?" Hannah jumped to her feet, grabbed the back of her chair for support. "You went to Cleveland and talked to Jason Flemming before I auditioned? He listened to me but turned me down, told me to go home until I was better. I had to get a job as a receptionist in another recording studio just to pay my bills, and no one would give me an audition after that! You—that's one reason I turned goth, because they befriended me, got me that job."

"Mr. Flemming didn't turn you down because he didn't like your voice. He'd already heard some recording of it and said it was good, very good. I told him you were bad sick and would have to come home for treatments."

Hannah just gaped at him. Again, she had to remind herself to breathe. "You— I can't believe it!"

"It's true. I didn't kill your friend in the graveyard to keep you home if that's what you were thinking, but I killed your plans, your dream. I want to be sorry, but I feel I saved you, saved you for the family, your people—Seth."

"Did he—did he know anything about what you did?"

"*Ach,* no. No one, not even your mother. But it has eaten at me and I had to get right with you, with the Lord. I'll make a church confession. They may want me to resign. I pray it won't make you want to leave again. Stay with us, Hannah, sing to your and Seth's children, teach us to sing in our hearts—"

Hysteria flooded her. "I— How can I stay in a place where the two men I loved and admired most in my life betrayed me?" she shouted, and ran sobbing from the room.

Ray-Lynn swam upward through the dark fog of pain and confusion. She felt terrible. A heart attack? No, her head hurt, not her chest. Was she home in bed, trapped in a nightmare?

She tried to lift her head from—from a steering wheel. A car accident? She could not recall—needed help. Where was she? Bright, gold lights around and behind her, in the rearview mirror when she opened her eyes. And her own lights were on, illumining bare trees but nothing else beyond.

Her van lurched forward bit by bit. Something was pushing it! She tried to turn to see but the headlights behind blinded her. She only caught the words on a sign beside her van as it moved jerkily, slowly past: Bridge Ices Before Road. But that sign was out by Troyers' old grist mill between the road and the river ravine!

She fumbled for her car key in the ignition. Not there! She felt so woozy. She tried to focus on the console with the gear stick—in neutral, jammed in neutral! Her leg hurt but she moved her foot, tried to find the brake. Tried to push it hard, but the van still moved, slowly, jerk by jerk, not even enough to put a dent in the bumper. Out. She had to get out.

With one hand she tried to unfasten her seat belt, with the other fumbled for the door lock. So dizzy, but Jack would come to help her. Why was she out driving? It was snowing. Why—

Another jolt against the back of the van, gentle but stronger. A sapling bent ahead of her front bumper. It would never hold. It snapped and the van tilted, throwing her forward, jerking her hand from her seat belt lock.

Then she remembered. She'd gone out to see if Jack and Lily were together. John Arrowroot had gone missing and now—and now...

She tried again and got her seat belt loose. Unlock the door, get out! She was going to fall, roll over the edge. Cell phone, call Jack, but no time to find her purse. Behind her in the glare of high headlights—a van or truck?—she thought she glimpsed a dark form, a driver. Who and why?

The front of the van, the whole thing tilted downward, slamming her against the wheel, the dashboard, then throwing her into the backseat. Next, blessed blackness.

Shortly after a cold dawn, Seth saw cars and buggies had begun to assemble in Homestead. They filled the small parking lot behind the sheriff's office and the volunteer fire station and parked along both sides of Main Street. Hannah had stopped by their farm this morning to tell him and Ella how the search would be organized. Since he and his father knew the immediate area around Arrowroot's house, they would lead volunteers closest to that site while others fanned out farther. He'd been glad to hear that Hannah and Ella would be together because he didn't want Hannah around Linc Armstrong.

The sheriff seemed to be running the show, although Linc and Bishop Esh were also moving among the volunteers and passing out papers with rules and directions. Seth glanced over at the Dutch Farm Table and wished he had time to go in for coffee and doughnuts. By the time he had fed Marlena and delivered her to his mother to watch today, he'd eaten only a Pop-Tart washed down by orange juice. But there was no time for a hearty breakfast now. He, like many others John Arrowroot had threatened or abused, were giving up their time to search for him.

He saw Hannah had arrived from telling Amanda Stutzman she couldn't work today. She'd left her own buggy somewhere and climbed up into Ella's. The sheriff had suggested that those who were searching farther out than Arrowroot's immediate neighborhood go in pairs. Lily Freeman jogged in, despite the slippery sidewalks, then climbed into Elaine Carson's truck with its flag and eagle decals.

Evidently Homestead storekeepers were closing up for the morning to help, too. Seth saw Mr. Baughman, who owned the hardware store; one of the bank tellers; and Tim Green, who managed one of the fast-food places. Clair Kenton was with her husband, Harlan. He had his motor running to keep them warm inside, but that was fogging up the area with its exhaust. The Meyers brothers, George and Clint, were there, bleary-eyed and unshaven, looking like they'd been up all night, standing by their truck.

"Seth, you clear on who's going with you?" the sheriff asked. "And you and your father mind going over there in Linc's car instead of your buggy? He's still got the place taped off for a possible crime scene, so he insists on going to stay on the property there."

"*Ya,* fine. I'll tell *Daad.*"

"One more thing. I thought sure Ray-Lynn would be out here with her usual coffee and doughnuts, so you mind checking to see what's keeping her? We've got to get this show rolling."

"Happy to," Seth said, and he was, because he'd grab some coffee while he was there.

But the moment he went into the warmth of the restaurant, he sensed something was wrong. Of course, fewer folks were inside than the usual breakfast crowd, but the Amish waitresses seemed rushed, almost frenzied. And no Ray-Lynn in sight at her usual post of hostess or cashier.

"Leah," he said to the Schwartz girl as she raced past, "where's Mrs. Logan?"

"Late. Not here. I think she's sick or something. I opened up like she said to do if she's late. I phoned her house and no answer, so I thought she'd be here soon. Then I—a couple of us—figured she was out with the crowd, the sheriff and all. Did you see her out there?"

He shook his head and, forgetting the coffee he was craving, hurried back outside. Sheriff Freeman was huddled with Linc, but he barged right in.

"Sheriff, Ray-Lynn didn't come in this morning and she's not answering her phone. Leah Schwartz figured she was on her way in—Leah has a key with orders to open up—but no Ray-Lynn." Seth was going to ask if the sheriff had seen her at all this morning but the alarmed look on his face answered that.

Frowning, the sheriff asked, "And her girls weren't told she was off on one of her missions of mercy—coffee and TLC for anyone else?"

"They seemed at a loss for—"

The sheriff spun away, leaving Seth and Linc standing there.

"It's probably nothing," Linc said. "But things get complicated when hearts get mixed up with heads, right?"

"You ought to know," Seth countered. "What about driving past Ray-Lynn's place on our way out to Arrowroot's?"

"Not with a car full of volunteers. I don't want it to look like some kind of a crisis. I argued we should keep a low profile when Arrowroot went missing, but the sheriff may have a point with all this. It's FBI gut instinct, but I think, if Arrowroot's fled the coop, he's working with someone who picked him up and this is another ploy to get publicity for his cause. We'll see."

Seth did see one thing. The sheriff was aching to go to Ray-Lynn's house to check on her, but he was caught here in charge of all this. He was talking to Amanda Stutzman, who had just driven up. He took a key off his key ring and gestured in the general direction of Ray-Lynn's house as he handed her the key. Amanda immediately backed up, turned, then drove quickly away, heading down Main Street, away from the swelling crowd.

By noon, Hannah and Ella were exhausted and chilled, despite the fact that they occasionally got out of Ella's buggy to tramp into thick copses or bushy areas along the river above the ravine. She peered over the side now and then at Killibuck Creek. The breeze was still stiff so both wore their boots and stayed bundled up under the buggy blanket.

Hannah had been upset they had been assigned to

an area a good distance from Arrowroot's house, not far from where she'd left her own buggy that disastrous day she and Seth had spied on the outsiders from Detroit at the Troyer grist mill. She'd told Ella nothing about that and evidently Seth hadn't, either. For more than one reason that day brought back bad memories.

"Let's eat," Ella said, handing the reins to Hannah and reaching behind the seat to bring out a sack of peanut butter and jelly sandwiches and a thermos of hot chocolate they'd already been into. "You might know the menfolk would get the places Arrowroot might actually be found, closer to his house. If he's living like his ancestors in these woods, he's frozen stiff anyway by now. Do they think he'd scalp us if we were the ones to find him?"

"Not funny," Hannah said. "But do I hear Ella Lantz even slightly criticizing the way things are around here, the decisions the men make? It's my *daad,* our brilliant bishop, who decided who looks where—and decides most else in our lives."

"Hannah! How can you talk like that? And I was not criticizing, just mentioning. I know we have to go the extra mile even for an enemy. I'm cold and hungry, that's all—but glad to have some time with you. Seth's pretty upset about your not forgiving him," she added hastily as Hannah pulled them into a little clearing along the road not far from a bridge—a modern one, not one of the nearby covered bridges.

"Did he tell you that?" Hannah demanded. "Besides, even if I forgive, which I do, I can't forget."

"He's never stopped caring for you."

"Ella, please don't play matchmaker!"

"I'm not. It's just you'd be so perfect together. I hope

Marlena's not a reminder of Lena to you. The little sweetheart even named the doll you so kindly gave her after you—'baby Hannah this, baby Hannah that.'"

"Did you or Seth suggest the name?" Hannah asked as she savored the hot chocolate. She pressed her gloved hands to the cup, but it was plastic and not that warm. Still, even talking about Seth, she felt warmer inside.

"Not me."

"Meaning Seth did?"

"Or else maybe he just told Marlena the doll was *from* Hannah and she thought that was the doll's name. See, you do care about him, about all of us. I've been praying you'll stay home after this is all over."

"I don't know." They both bit into their sandwiches. It was hard to talk with a mouth full of peanut butter, but then her thoughts about Seth and staying here were just as gummy. "I think I have another chance to have an audition, not sure when or where."

"My dear friend, just because God gave you a beautiful voice, doesn't mean He thinks you need to give it to the outside world. Maybe He meant it for a blessing to everyone here, our people."

There it was again—*our people*. That echoed in Hannah's head and heart as they finished their lunch and drove on toward the bridge. It was starting to spit snow again like last night, and the wind was from the north. She could barely feel the tip of her nose. This snow would add to the scattered coating of it on the ground, where the flakes had mostly stuck to grassy spots but melted off the roads to make them a bit slick. Only on the north side of the trees had flakes snagged in rough tree bark, and they clung to stop signs or the Bridge Ices Before Road sign just ahead.

"You want to stop at the Troyers' and see if Naomi's there?" Ella asked. "I didn't see her or Josh in the crowd in town this morning, but they could have come in later. I mean, it is their honeymoon period, but I think he's going to keep her close to home, anyway. At least a Troyer wife doesn't have to work and she'll be busy with their new house Seth's going to build them and then with her family."

"Sure, let's stop there. Anything to get warm for a minute," she said, but she was thinking it would give her a chance to learn from Naomi, or maybe even the Troyers, whether those Detroit men were for sure going to control the mill project and who knew what else?

Ella snapped the reins to move her horse fast, but Hannah grabbed her wrist. "Ella, wait. Look! See those car tracks in the grass there? Someone could have slid off the road."

Ella reined in and leaned over Hannah to look, too. "But I heard Seth say John Arrowroot's car was in his garage. And you can see where the car stopped in time and then backed out."

But she pulled over, and they climbed down. Hannah gasped and Ella gave a little scream when they saw saplings snapped off and tracks that went over the side of the ravine.

Seth, his *daad* and their crew made their last circuit of the hills surrounding Arrowroot's property and met down where the lane to the property entered Valley View Road. Linc and his party, which had stuck closest to Arrowroot's house, were not yet in sight. Seth had been uneasy all morning, after he'd heard Ray-Lynn Logan was evidently unaccounted for, too, but the sheriff had asked him to start the search, anyway. Now here he came, roaring down the road, no siren but light bar flashing. Maybe they'd found Arrowroot—or Ray-Lynn.

Seth hurried to the cruiser, and the sheriff rolled down his window. "Just heard from Linc's. No Arrowroot. You neither?"

"Not a sign. What about Ray-Lynn?"

"Amanda Stutzman checked her house, and I've been looking everywhere she could be. She's been upset with me off and on, but she'd never just disappear, leave the restaurant. I nearly slugged Clint Meyers when I heard him joking to his brother that she obviously ran off with Arrowroot. I have a key to her house and I'm gonna go through it with a fine-tooth comb, so I wanted you to know Linc's in charge. I asked him to head back to town to oversee things from there. I'm grateful for your efforts and those of your people, so please pass the word on suspending the search for now. I—I can't believe she's missing, too, on top of all this...."

"Sheriff, I'm sure Ray-Lynn's all right, but if you need us—"

"Yeah. It can't be something bad—just can't." The sheriff thumped his steering wheel with both fists, rolled up the window and roared away.

Seth knew from Ella, who had heard from Sarah before she'd left the Amish, that Jack Freeman had been sweet on Ray-Lynn Logan. The man's deep concern for her was not just because he was her partner in the restaurant. No, he saw in his face the same pain and fear Seth felt when he thought of losing Hannah again.

* * *

Holding on to trees on the slippery slope above the ravine, Hannah and Ella peered over the edge. Ella shrieked, and Hannah sucked in cold air. A van that looked just like Ray-Lynn's was nosedown against two big trees almost in the fast-flowing water.

"What if John Arrowroot walked into the restaurant after she closed and made her take him somewhere?" Ella choked out. "Then this? It—it is her van, isn't it?"

"Yes. I wish I wasn't so Amish today—I left my cell phone at the house. I'm going down to look inside."

"You can't! You'll fall. Too steep here. If we go closer to the mill, we can hike back up along the river."

"You've got to go for help. Take the buggy. Use the phone on the road in front of the Troyer farm."

"Hannah, you can't go down there! Your wrist—"

"She's my friend. I'll be careful. Go. Ella, go! Call 9-1-1, the sheriff's office, and they'll find him. Go!"

Hannah could see the path of the car's plunge from the broken saplings. She held to those or ones along the side of that path and, ignoring the snow-studded grass and slick rocks, started down the incline as she heard Ella drive away.

23

IT SEEMED TO HANNAH THAT ALL SOUNDS stopped. The ripple of the river below, the wind, her own rapid breathing—but her thoughts and then her desperate cry screamed at her. "Ray-Lynn! Ray-Lynn, are you down there? It's Hannah!"

She half fell, half skidded from tree to tree, using them for handholds. It was extra hard because she still tried to protect her injured wrist. Saplings dotted this part of the hill above the ravine. She was soon sweating and gasping. At least the embankment was not too steep to handle here, but without the trees, she'd tumble down to the river for sure. How could this have happened? Ray-Lynn must have skidded off the road in the snow. What if Ella was right and Arrowroot had forced Ray-Lynn to drive him somewhere and they struggled in the car? If Arrowroot was not involved, why would Ray-Lynn be out here on the road near the Troyers'?

"Ray-Lynn! Ray-Lynn!"

Hannah fell, nearly straddling the next tree trunk. Her skirt ripped up to her hips. The tree bark snagged her stockings and scraped her thighs. She shoved herself up, balanced, then went down again. How long would it take Ella to get help here? She should have told her they'd need an ambulance, too, but would they? She had to be alive! Maybe she'd walked away from this, was following the river to get help.

Fighting panic and tears, Hannah neared the back of the van. Although she'd only used her left arm to push off and balance, not to grab trees, pain shot through her injured wrist. Her heart thudded so strong she shook even harder. A big tree nearly at the river's edge had stopped the van's fall, crunching in the front fender and hood. It looked balanced against that tree. If she held to the car or opened its door, would that shift its weight and slam it into the water?

Cracks cobwebbed the front windshield, but it was not broken out; the other windows were intact. Trying to find a foothold on a large embedded rock, Hannah leaned closer to look into the van. At first she saw only her own reflection. She looked frazzled and frenzied with her bonnet ripped back and her hair wild. She bent closer and, through the shadow made by her own face, peered into the driver's seat.

No Ray-Lynn, no John Arrowroot. An empty driver's seat and passenger's side, so maybe she did get out and go for help. The two nearest places were the Troyers' and that sports bar down the road a ways. Ray-Lynn's purse was snagged between the side door and the seat. She wouldn't leave her purse, would she? But if she was dazed or seriously hurt...

This time she screamed toward the river. "Ray-Lynn! It's Hannah! Raaaay-Lyyyyyyn!"

She inched up along the cold metal and carefully grasped the handle of the backseat, trying to keep her herself from leaning against the van. At this awkward angle, she could see straight across the rear seat, even into the back storage area where the third set of seats was down. She saw no one, though some things were thrown around, caught against the back of the middle seats—including a single boot.

She glanced down. A leg sticking up, no shoe, bare foot. A body wedged behind the driver's seat! Thrown onto the floor, not moving from that awkward position, was Ray-Lynn!

The other Amish searchers had left in a buggy, but Seth was sitting next to Linc in his car, heading back toward town, when Linc's cell phone sounded. He fished it out of his pocket and punched a button. The voice at the other end was so loud that Seth could hear every word.

It was the sheriff, yelling into the phone.

"Linc, meet me out on Troyer's Mill Road now! Near the new bridge, just west of it. Ray-Lynn's van's in the ravine there! Ella Lantz and Hannah stumbled on the wreck."

Seth tensed and turned toward Linc, not even pretending he didn't overhear.

"Roger that. She all right?" Linc asked.

"Don't know. Hannah went down to check, and Ella called from the Troyers'. I've got paramedics coming, too. I'm almost there."

"On our way!" Linc said, and punched off. "You heard?"

"*Ya*. Turn left at the next road. Not paved but a shortcut."

"I thought he was going to say he found Arrowroot. Jack's in love with Ray-Lynn, you know."

"I do know," Seth said, hanging on as Linc took the sharp turn much too fast. Despite the snow glaze on this road between fallow fields, at least it was a straight shot from here.

"You might know, Hannah's in the mix again," Linc said, voicing Seth's fears. "And you love her."

"Always have, no matter how much I messed things up."

"You should let her go, let her have her chance with a music career. She bombs, she'll come back—maybe."

"*You* should let her go," Seth threw back at him.

"It's not like that," Linc insisted. "At least not around here."

"You get her out in the world again, you think you'll keep her, want her for good? It would be bad for her. Turn right, and we'll be almost there."

Linc careened around the last corner, but slowed as he saw the sheriff's cruiser off to the side, light bar blinking, no one in it. Seth was out of the car before Linc could kill the engine. A taut rope tied to the cruiser's back bumper draped over the side of the ravine. Seth looked over the edge as Linc joined him. The sheriff was only partway down, and he didn't want to alarm him by yelling that they were here. Seth gasped and Linc swore when they saw Hannah far below, balanced on a rock, leaning toward the upended van.

When Hannah saw the sheriff was taking too long, she dared to try the back door of Ray-Lynn's van. She was surprised it was unlocked. Maybe the jolt of the accident had sprung it loose. Bracing herself against the weight of the door, she carefully opened it. Ray-Lynn lay sprawled on the back floor, her body twisted and wedged in at a funny angle with one leg and one arm up. So pale, unmoving. No blood on her that Hannah could see. Though she didn't wake up or move, even when Hannah shouted her name, she thought—just maybe—she might be breathing. Hard to tell with that bulky coat she wore. She had one boot on, but her other bare foot looked so strange with bright red polish on her toenails.

Hannah dragged her gaze away from Ray-Lynn as Sheriff Freeman came down the slant of the ravine, holding on to a rope as if rappelling. "She there?" he called from about twenty feet away.

"Yes, but she's...unconscious, I think. Not moving, won't wake up."

He stopped his descent just above the van by putting his foot on a sapling. It bent, unbalancing him, but he held on, righted himself, swung a bit to the side. "I got help coming," he shouted, but his voice shook.

Those words...a friend not moving...fear...his voice... It was not the same, not that time, but pictures flashed through Hannah's mind of the night in the graveyard when Kevin was killed, when the sheriff came and she was so afraid, when the squad was coming...but Seth was there then. But now—did she hear his voice above? Could he be here this time, too?

She remembered how Seth had touched Kevin's neck to check his pulse to see if he was alive. She had to know. She reached out and put her hand under Ray-Lynn's coat collar, beneath her turtleneck sweater. Her skin felt so cold but she had not gone stiff. Yes! A faint pulse, though not regular.

"She's alive, alive but so hurt!" she shouted as the sheriff stopped himself a few feet above the back bumper of the van. She could tell he'd been tempted to put his feet on it, then had backed off.

"Thank God! You sure?" he cried.

"Yes. Yes, I feel a neck pulse!"

"I didn't see from up there that the van's wedged against a tree. I'm gonna have to go around a little. Here, take this, push the green button and tell the medics what you know, what you see," he said, and dropped what she'd call a walkie-talkie to her.

She did as he said, surprised that a rescue medic was already on the line. She told him how Ray-Lynn was positioned and about her jerky neck pulse and that there was no blood, and that she wouldn't wake up and—and that reminded her of the 9-1-1 call she'd made the night of the shootings, too. A nightmare. A nightmare she couldn't escape.

But when Linc and Seth rappelled down ropes closer to the path she'd taken, even as she heard the screech of a distant siren, her past horror became that of the present. The sheriff was yelling orders. Mr. Troyer's voice from up above rang down, asking what he could do to help. Linc was looking in the van without touching it, telling the sheriff not to touch or move Ray-Lynn. At last a medic rappelled down and a rescue basket on ropes bumped over the side, snagging now and then against the trees. But Hannah was suddenly in Seth's arms, holding tight to him, shaking all over as they leaned off to the side against a tree as big as the one that had stopped the van.

Here she was, Hannah thought, in the arms of the man she'd asked to stay away, the man who said he would. It had taken this terrible accident, on top of the earlier tragedy, to bring them together again. Was that a message from on high? But all that mattered now was that Ray-Lynn be helped and saved.

Such joy she was yet alive—such hope! Yet the grim expressions on the two medics' faces and the ashen look on Sheriff Freeman's said it all. Though she didn't trust Mr. Troyer anymore, Hannah had no choice but to let him and two of his sons pull them up, one at a time, after Ray-Lynn had been strapped in the basket and lifted. As limp as the rag doll Hannah had given to little Marlena, as cotton-white in her blank face, the once-vibrant, vital Ray-Lynn didn't seem to be there at all.

Up on the road, in the EMR vehicle, the medics fought to do what Hannah overheard them call "stabilize the victim." Hannah's trembling increased as Seth and Ella wedged her in between them in Ella's buggy where they were trying to keep warm. "I'm all right. I'm not in shock," she told Seth more than once as he held and chaffed her icy hands. Somehow down there, she'd taken off her gloves.

Hannah could see the EMR vehicle was preparing to leave. "Ray-Lynn doesn't have any family except cousins down south," she said. "Maybe I should ask if I can go with her."

"I think the sheriff will take care of that," Seth said. "If—when she's conscious, we can have women go and sit with her. Then you can, too."

The sheriff strode over to the buggy. "Thank God you found her, Hannah and Ella. Can't thank you both enough for what you did. I'm going to the Wooster hospital with her. Hannah, she told me just yesterday she was hoping to hire you as an assistant and have you work your way up at the restaurant. You do me a favor, go close it up today. Take a key home with you and go on in tomorrow, see if you can help out there. Mrs. Stutzman will understand—if it's okay with the bishop."

"I make my own decisions now." She could tell her declaration of independence from her father surprised Ella and Seth, but she plunged on. "I'll do it for Ray-Lynn. She's been a good friend to Sarah and me."

He started to say something else but choked up and turned away. He jogged back to his cruiser where he said something to Linc and got in to follow the EMR vehicle away, both with their lights blinking in the wan early-afternoon light dusted with snow.

Linc came over to the buggy. "I'm going to stay here and survey the scene. I've got help coming from the State Highway Patrol, a tow truck to retrieve the vehicle. Even though first responders compromised the area above the accident site," he said, turning back and pointing, "it looks like there are two sets of tire tracks, in addition to my car and the sheriff's cruiser's treads and your and Troyers' buggy wheels. I'm starting to agree with him—nothing's coincidence around here, so you be careful."

"You mean someone did this to her deliberately?" Hannah asked. "And it might be related to the grave-yard shootings?"

"No conclusive evidence. Sorry, that's FBI talk."

To Hannah's amazement, Ella piped up. "In other words, the proof is in the pudding? That's Plain People talk."

Finally, realizing Seth still held her hands, Hannah pulled them back and gripped them in her lap. She and Ella shared the buggy blanket but she was still shivering. "Is Ray-Lynn going to be all right?" Hannah asked. "What did the medics say?"

"She's comatose and barely hanging on. The sheriff's insistence on a search for Arrowroot may have bombed, but it paid off big-time with your finding her."

"God works in mysterious ways," Ella put in. Linc nodded but didn't glance her way as his sharp gaze pinned Hannah where she sat.

"So we're still looking for Arrowroot," Linc went on. "Not sure how, but he could be connected to this. Hannah, when I get finished here or can turn it over to others, I want to depose you—an interview about your being the first on the scene here."

"I'll be at my parents' after I close up the restaurant for Ray-Lynn. But if you don't find any evidence of Arrowroot in her car, that means someone else lured her out here at night and then ran her off the road."

"No jumping to conclusions, but I hear you. But other than answering my questions about finding Ray-Lynn, you're not going to help out with this investigation anymore. Got it, Hannah?"

"Now I hear you."

"Seth? Same for you."

"Then solve it fast, Special Agent Armstrong."

Linc looked as if he'd say something else, but, as if Seth had bested him, he turned and walked away, pulling out his cell phone and punching something into it.

Ella whispered, "Maybe he was secretly recording your words with that little machine. Like he wanted to have it on tape that he warned both of you to keep out of his way, which I wish you would. What he said scares me."

Everything that had happened scared Hannah and, as they buggied back toward town, she sent a silent prayer heavenward for Ray-Lynn's recovery and her own protection from whoever had injured her. Yet, wedged in warmly between Ella and Seth in the buggy, she felt strangely safer than she had in days.

24

"ANY WORD ABOUT RAY-LYNN?" HANNAH ASKED Linc the moment she opened the back door for him that evening.

"Bishop Esh, Mrs. Esh," he said with a nod as they rose from the kitchen table to greet him. "She's still comatose. Two major blows to her head, at the back and at her forehead. If she was driving when the van went over, a forehead blow is common. Actually, the back blow was a lot like mine in the maze, though since she was knocked around in the car when it slid over, more than one contusion is possible. They're trying to stabilize her, can't tell how much damage was really done until she wakes up. She has a broken arm and shoulder but seems to be holding her own. Bishop Esh, I hope you don't mind if I interview Hannah about finding Ray-Lynn."

"No, sure," *Daad* said as he and *Mamm* took their coffee cups from the table. "We'll be in the living room. Time for more prayers, for Ray-Lynn. For you and the sheriff, too, Agent Armstrong."

"Much needed," Linc said. While Hannah poured

a cup of coffee for Linc and cut him a piece of spice cake, her father lingered at the door, so she wondered what else was coming. Her wrist was paining her again. She knew she'd set her recovery back today, but it had been worth it to help. In the three-way awkward silence, Linc took his leather jacket off and draped it over a chair, then sat with a sigh across the corner of the table from her.

"You know, Bishop Esh," he said, "I never used to give prayer much time or thought until I was attacked in the maze. I guess it's made me empathize with victims more."

Daad nodded. "'The dark places of the earth are full of the haunts of cruelty,'" he recited. "Written long ago, *ya,* but true today. And some of those haunts are in evil thoughts and sinful deeds, mine included." He looked at Hannah, hopefully, she thought. She had hardly spoken two kind words to him since he'd admitted to sabotaging her singing career, though in front of *Mamm* she went through the motions. "I will pray you find and stop the one or ones you seek, Agent Armstrong," *Daad* added, and left the room.

Linc took out a pad and pen. With all of his tech toys, it calmed her that he was going back to basics. "So you and Emma just stumbled on the scene?" he began.

"We pulled off near the bridge to eat a sack lunch. We were thinking of stopping at the Troyers' to see my sister. I spotted tire marks in the frozen grass and mud, kind of like skid marks in the snow that had caught there."

"Skid marks of one vehicle?"

"I know you said you saw two. I didn't notice that

at all, so I think tires from a second vehicle were lined up pretty much with hers, like they were wide enough apart to be another van or a truck. You probably shouldn't have said that about two, right? Like leading the witness."

She could see him grit his teeth, then fight to calm himself as he took a sip of coffee. "Hannah, just answer my questions, all right? If you were watching lawyer or detective shows on TV when you lived away—"

"*Perry Mason* reruns, old ones, I guess, but they were good."

He muttered something she couldn't catch, then added, "Better than those current shows, where the forensic team solves crimes and nails the criminals, too, in a couple of days. Like I told you before, to ID those bodies in the graves—all this takes time."

"The thing is, we don't have time. Terrible things keep happening!"

"Tell me something I don't know. So, once Ella headed to the Troyers' for help and you got down to Ray-Lynn's van, what did you notice first?"

"Crackled front windshield but not broken out. She wasn't in the front seat. Even though the van must have fallen—or been pushed—nosedown, stuff had mostly been thrown into the back. And, oh, yeah, her purse was caught inside, so if things were intact in it, that means no robbery was involved, right?"

"Just go on."

"I was afraid to put too much weight on the van. Did you get it hauled up so you can get a closer look at it?"

"Who's asking and who's answering here? Yes, I did. It's being towed to the sheriff's garage at his house so we can process it without gawkers or gossipers. Go on, I said."

"I was both relieved and scared to see she wasn't in the driver's seat. I had a wild idea John Arrowroot might be there, too—you know, if he'd forced her to take him somewhere. Could you tell if her seat belt didn't work or she wasn't strapped in? Oh, sorry, that's a question. One thing that might be important is that, when I saw her in that terrible position on the back floor and opened the door, it wasn't locked. I can't believe she'd have her car doors unlocked out at night after she closed up the restaurant, especially if she took the day's money with her—which is why she could have been a robbery target. Maybe the force of the van going into the ravine sprung the locks. I'd ask if that's possible, but that would be a question, Agent Armstrong."

Linc rolled his eyes upward and raked his free hand through his short hair. "I've said it before, and I'll say it again, you're beautiful, Hannah. And in more ways than one. Darn right, that door's being unlocked is important because it could mean that she could have been put unconscious in the vehicle, especially with that double hit on her head when it should have only been a frontal blow. In that case, her doors would not have been locked, because someone had to put her inside to push her over. Her car key was found under her on the floor, so it's a puzzle how it would have been thrown out of the ignition if she was actually driving."

"But why Ray-Lynn? You finally figured out Kevin, Tiffany and I were shot because the grave digger thought we were going to disturb those graves and find what he or she hid there. But Ray-Lynn hasn't been a part of this investigation at all."

"The sheriff's on that, working from the hospital. Ray-Lynn phoned your boss, Mrs. Stutzman, that night to ask if she and her roomer, Lily Freeman, could help with the search for Arrowroot."

"But so what?"

"So Amanda Stutzman told her Mrs. Freeman might have gone out to the Rooster Roadhouse on Troyer's Mill Road. Got any other ideas why Ray-Lynn then evidently headed that way?"

Hannah swallowed hard and tried to keep calm. Ray-Lynn had it in for Lily, didn't trust her, but she'd said she had decided to trust Jack—unless she'd found something out from talking to Clair Kenton when she got her hair done. But if Hannah told Linc all that— that Ray-Lynn had a separate investigation of her own going—how would that help?

"Hannah, what?" he demanded.

How to answer this truthfully? When she'd gone into the Dutch Farm Table this afternoon to close it up and post a sign that said Closed But Will Reopen Friday Morning, she'd felt such a sudden rush of responsibility for the place. It was the Home Valley meeting place for Amish, *Englische* and outsiders alike. It was warm and welcoming, an extension of Ray-Lynn's personality and hospitality. She and the sheriff co-owned it, and Ray-Lynn's dream was for them to be partners in life, too. Over the door was a sign Hannah's dear friend Sarah had painted, and soon some of Sarah's paintings would be on display there. And if there was anything that would keep Hannah in the Home Valley and living independently of her father and Seth, too, it was working with Ray-Lynn at that restaurant.

Fighting to keep her voice calm, she said, "Ray-Lynn and the sheriff are sweet on each other—you know what I mean…"

He leaned closer to her. His eyes held hers. "Yeah, I do."

"Seth said the sheriff was going out to the Rooster Roadhouse to pass out more posters about the Arrowroot search. So maybe she thought she could help him with that."

"After he'd just left her with some posters and told her to be careful driving home in the increasing snow? You're a clever woman, Hannah Esh, but don't try to cover for Ray-Lynn, even though we're all pulling for her. Could she have driven out there to tell Lily Freeman, in front of Jack, to keep her hands off him? I get the idea from Jack that Ray-Lynn had more or less told him that in private. So now I've got to talk to him, then help him interview the Rooster Roadhouse crowd who might have seen her or her van that night. However much he cares for Ray-Lynn and wants to be with her right now, he's going to have to get back to work. But I know how conflicted he feels, torn between the oath he took to do his job and yet wanting to just chuck it to be with the woman he wants."

He stood. Hannah felt a big blush coming. Not because she'd lied to him, or at least how she'd tried to slant things. Not only because he'd looked at her so intensely when she'd talked about being sweet on someone—and now, he almost looked as if he'd devour her. But because Seth was right. This man didn't just want to help her, he wanted her.

"I'm hoping," Linc said, putting his paper and pen in his shirt pocket, "that Ray-Lynn comes to without a damaged memory and can fill us in. Meanwhile, for her sake and the sheriff's, too, let's not any of us put words into her mouth or thoughts into her head."

He was letting her off. He'd caught her in a lie, but he was giving her a pass. He stood, shrugged on his jacket, took a final swig of coffee. "My offer still stands to help you get an audition. Professional singing is a very cutthroat, worldly business, where you're going to need advice and backing you can trust. But first, let me do my job and, like I said, steer clear of any more involvement with the investigation."

"What if something falls in my lap?" she blurted.

He looked down at her hips, her lap, then slowly ran his eyes up past her waist and breasts to her face. "Such as?"

"I'm going to oversee the Dutch Farm Table for Ray-Lynn until she's better, at least for a while."

"The sheriff said he asked you to. At least that's a public place."

"But that's it. I might overhear something. Ray-Lynn sometimes did."

"And it might have gotten her hurt. If you hear something about either of these pending investigations, you call me. You'll have a phone there. I'll be in touch."

She was very certain he was going to touch her, kiss her. Her eyes widened; she took a step back. *Daad,* who had always seemed to sense when Seth was leaving during their courting days and who often came in to say *gute nacht,* and keep them from too much smooching and more, walked back into the kitchen.

"Finished?" *Daad* asked.

"Yes, sir. For now," Linc said, picking up the piece of cake he hadn't touched and moving toward the door instead of toward her. He turned back. "And the help of your people today was greatly appreciated. I know I can call on you again."

"For finding someone who is lost, *ya,* sure," *Daad* said with a frown at Hannah. "And hopefully bring them back," he added, though Linc had gone out already, so those words, Hannah knew, were meant for her alone.

At the Dutch Farm Table Restaurant, Hannah felt exasperated but excited at overseeing the many tasks she was not familiar with. She loved greeting and seating people, but behind the scenes she realized she knew next to nothing. Working the cash register was new at first, but she caught on fast. The three Amish cooks and most of the waitresses were willing to take her orders, especially when they heard she might be helping Ray-Lynn in the future when—if—she came back. Only Amy Zook seemed to resent her and acted a bit snippy.

"I hope you aren't serving our guests with that frown," Hannah finally remarked to her, which probably didn't help, but she had to exert herself here. Could Amy's attitude be related to the fact that her older sister Susan was sweet on Seth? At least, that's what Ella had said.

Finally, in a public place and way, Hannah came to terms with her shame over becoming goth, then bringing those friends to a party in the graveyard with disastrous results. But the many locals who came and went, ones she knew and a few she didn't, seemed friendly and all were concerned when word spread about Ray-Lynn.

She was polite, too, but didn't chat much with outsiders after seating them, just in case they were media people who could recognize her. That is, she steered clear of outsiders, until Levi Troyer came in followed by three of the men she'd spied on and overheard at the mill. "I'll help by covering table twelve," she told Leah Schwartz, "though you can bring their orders and get the tip."

As she went over to their table, she saw Harlan Kenton drag himself in. *Ya,* that was the word for it, she thought as the bedraggled-looking man plopped himself on a stool at the counter, but she went back to focusing on these men who could be involved with more than investments in town.

"Hannah, any word on Mrs. Logan?" Levi asked as the men slid in the booth, the two outsiders facing their Amish host.

"Holding her own," she told him. "They're hoping she comes to soon and remembers something about what happened."

The minute that was out of her mouth, she regretted it. If these men had anything to do with evil events around here, she didn't want to put Ray-Lynn in danger. At least the sheriff was with her there. When Hannah had talked to him early this morning—he'd been at Ray-Lynn's bedside all night—he'd said he didn't think she'd been out to the Rooster Roadhouse; at least, he hadn't seen her there. If that was true, could she know something about the Troyers and was in the neighborhood to check up on them?

"Mike and Steve Collister, this is Hannah Esh,"

Levi said. "She was one of the women wounded in the graveyard shootings. My youngest son, Josh, just wed her sister Naomi little over a week ago, a nice event it was, too."

"Glad to see you're doing well," the older, silver-haired man—Mike—told her. He glanced at her wrist, which she'd wrapped again with an elastic bandage after hurting it yesterday. He frowned. "That shooting was not the kind of publicity this area needs. I'm sure we can do better," he said with a glance at the one named Steve, who nodded. The two *ausländers* resembled each other. Maybe brothers, years apart, but more likely father and son. Now she had names to give Linc so he didn't have to upset Levi Troyer by questioning him. He said to phone him if she learned anything, and she'd do that as soon as she could.

She wanted to start a chat with these men about the mill, but she figured it would look too obvious—and Linc would kill her. So she poured their coffee and took their orders, planning to hover a bit to overhear what she could. True, Linc had told her to keep out of the investigation, but she'd told him that if something fell into her lap, she'd call him. Maybe she'd just help Leah take their orders to their table, as well.

The next time she had a free moment, she went behind the counter to pour Harlan more coffee. He'd been so kind and generous that she decided she would cover his bill herself as a thank-you. He had a plate of easy-over eggs and sausage he was picking at.

"That's your meat, so it's got to be good," she told him.

"Don't suppose you got a headache chaser?"

"There's probably some aspirin out back."

"Just kidding. It's a hangover, and I'm in the doghouse, with not only Clair but my sister. At least the coffee here's almost as good as Amanda's. Word's all over about Ray-Lynn. How's she doing?"

"I think she has to come to before they know. Harlan, by any chance were you at the Rooster Roadhouse last night?"

His head jerked up. "I delivered meat there and had a coupla beers. Why? Amanda tell you to scold me, too?"

"No, but you know she loves you. She and Clair are just afraid you're going to drive drunk and—"

"That wasn't why Ray-Lynn went off the road, was it? Drinking?"

"Of course not! But I—I supposed they'll test her blood level for it, for everything. Did you see Ray-Lynn there?"

"No, and that's not her kind of place. Man, I'm bummed out," he said, shaking his head. "I gotta stop this, I know it. If I'm not careful, I'll slice off a finger or something when I'm dopey. Don't want to lose customers, either, even if I am the only frozen meat locker and refrigerated truck in town. Have fresh or frozen meat, will travel."

"I was going through Ray-Lynn's records since I'm taking over for her for a while, and I saw she buys all her meats from you. You deliver them, right? Our storage freezer here's not that big."

"Yeah, though if she wants something special, she stops in or lets me know. I'll be dropping the weekly delivery off Saturday, a lot of bulk country sausage and other cuts." He started to eat his eggs. "Got fences to mend at home," he muttered.

She almost told him that he'd better concentrate on mending his bad habits. She saw now how Ray-Lynn was not only restaurant owner but confessor and counselor around here, and she kind of liked that.

Ray-Lynn drifted from dreams to memories. Mama's honeysuckle vines and azaleas were ablaze with color and scent. She was at home, with her parents sitting on the front porch, but she was running around in the yard with the next-door neighbor kids chasing her, pushing her, playing tag.... Her friends were screaming in delight.... She was careering down a slide at her old grade-school playground with the wind and snow in her hair....

No, it didn't snow in Georgia; well, at least it never stuck for long to make things slippery. But the ground was so slippery here...

Then Daddy was teaching her to drive, trying to keep his temper, she could tell. He was talking to her calmly before her first solo drive. "You come back now, Ray-Lynn. You're going to be all right, honey. I love you and want you to come back to me." Well, ding-dang, where did he think she was going with his car? Clear to Atlanta instead of just around the block?

She felt very afraid then, but she wasn't sure of what. That there wouldn't be enough money to buy the restaurant after Charles just dropped dead? They'd had a good marriage, had their whole life planned out, a restaurant in Amish country instead of Cleveland, so many pretty hills, but sharp ravines, too—with trees that had branches like tentacles, reaching out...

She tried to open her eyes but her lids were so heavy. Her head hurt, especially hurt trying to figure out if she could run the restaurant alone.... But maybe Charles was back with her, hadn't died, because he was holding her hand, talking to her about coming back, waking up, that he loved her and no one else....

She wet her dry lips with her tongue. Her mouth hurt, she hurt all over. "I love you, too, Charles," she whispered, and slitted her eyes open.

Oh! Not Charles, but a policeman, one leaning close with tears in his eyes. He was holding her hand.

"Ray-Lynn, it's me. Welcome back, honey! I got to ring for the nurse. They come in a lot, but they said to do that if you woke up. You—you know who I am, honey?" His voice broke. "I'm—I'm not Charles."

Honey? And she could see he wasn't Charles. Yes, she remembered now. Charles had died. She wet her lips again as a nurse came in even without being called.

"Is she responsive, Sheriff?" the woman asked.

Sheriff? What had happened? What could she have done?

25

AFTER THE EARLY BREAKFAST RUSH, THE restaurant turned into a who's who of Homestead, Ohio. Elaine Carson was eating alone at table twelve. Hannah's parents came in with Naomi and Josh. *Mamm* kept beaming proudly at Hannah, probably thinking this job would keep her home no matter what else happened. When Levi Troyer and his guests were on their way out the door, Hannah overheard Seth's name. So maybe the renovation deal for the mill was on—and what else, she wondered, for the men had stopped all conversation each time she'd filled their coffee cups.

Clint and George Meyers came in, all upset. "If Ray-Lynn don't get better," George told Hannah as she seated them at what they considered to be *their* table, "we're gonna lose one of our homes away from home."

"Right," Clint added. He often finished George's thoughts and vice versa. "If we lost this place or the Roadhouse, we'd be up a creek without a paddle."

They evidently thought that was funny or clever, because they high-fived each other. She was tempted to ask them if they were at the Roadhouse last night, but she had to try to keep her promise to Linc that she'd stay out of this. She had, however, phoned him with the names of the two Detroit men, Mike and Steve Collister.

"Phone call for you." Leah Schwartz hurried over to tell her. "It's the sheriff."

"Hey," Clint said, "maybe good news."

"Or not," George muttered as Hannah dashed for the phone in Ray-Lynn's office to get some privacy.

"Sheriff, it's me," she said, out of breath. She leaned back against Ray-Lynn's desk.

"She's conscious, Hannah. Just thought you should know."

"That's great!"

"She's got some short-term memory loss."

"She can't recall what happened?"

"No. And she doesn't know me."

"What? How much short-term loss?"

"Back to when she bought the restaurant. She's been talking about her dead husband Charles's recent death."

"Recent? But it's been years!"

"Don't mean to dump this on you, but…now I guess I know how she felt when Lily came back to town."

"With more rest, more treatment, she'll remember."

"Possibility of that, according to the doctor. Maybe soon or it may be a long haul."

"But that means she won't know me, either. Did she ask about the restaurant?"

"Not a word. She looked scared and upset and went back to sleep. They said it's common for a person in a wreck not to recall it, but—but this is more."

She could not picture Sheriff Jack Freeman sounding so shaky. "The restaurant's doing okay," she assured him, "so you stay there as long as you need to."

"Since I upset her—which upsets me—no reason to stay. I'll be back to town pretty soon, keep coming back here when I can. Gotta call Linc and wanted you to know. Thanks to you and Ella again. Tell Seth if you see him, but don't make all this common knowledge, okay?"

"Sure. Keep your spirits up now, for her, for both of you."

Back out in the restaurant, she told people who asked about Ray-Lynn only that she had regained consciousness. Clint and George asked her if the sheriff had said anything else. She'd have to remember to tell him and Linc that they seemed overly concerned. And then, as if she could wish him here, in came Seth with Marlena in his arms and Hannah's old doll in hers.

"I'm glad you're here!" she told him.

"I like the sound of that. Marlena, do you remember Hannah?"

"Hannah my baby," she said, and cuddled the doll closer. Hannah would have liked to have thrown herself into Seth's arms as she whispered what the sheriff had just told her.

"I keep thinking things can't get worse," he said.

"Mr. Troyer and his Detroit friends were in and seem to have struck some kind of deal. I heard your name. Let me seat you. Are you meeting anyone?"

"Only came to give you support," he said. "And to get some good home cooking I don't get much of unless I eat at my mother's table, which I don't like to overdo."

"I heard somewhere that there are a couple of *maidals* who would like to change all that."

"I hope you're one of them."

"Flattery will get you nowhere but table two in the front window so Marlena and her Hannah can look outside while you eat. Amy will be your waitress."

She had no more seated them and taken their order to help Amy than her sister, Susan Zook, came in alone and spotted Seth and Marlena. Or had she seen them through the front window? Bad idea to put them there. Susan was almost as tall as Seth and seemed self-conscious about it, stooping a bit when she walked.

"I heard you have been asked to babysit the restaurant while Mrs. Logan's away," she told Hannah. Like her mother's voice at Naomi's wedding reception, Susan's was icy. "I hope she's well enough to come back soon. After all you've put people through, you surely don't intend to make a career of this. There has to be a good reason Seth changed his mind about you years ago, and you'd be no good for him or this place now with one foot in the world."

Hannah just stared at her. It was so unusual for one of the sisters to be cruel. How many others saw her as one who'd betrayed her people and did not want her back?

"Oh, there's Seth and little Marlena!" she said, glancing over Hannah's shoulder. She walked around Hannah and seated herself across from them. Biting her lower lip, Hannah didn't give her a menu but put it back on the hostess stand. One sideways glimpse at Seth's table revealed that Susan was now all smiles, as Amy hurried over to wait on her older sister.

Surely Seth had not arranged that to make her jealous. But she was. Sheriff Freeman's hurt voice when he told her that Ray-Lynn had asked for her dead husband

and didn't even know him came back to her. Blinking back tears, she was tempted to hide in Ray-Lynn's office for a few minutes, but she stood her ground, only to see Lily Freeman come through the front door.

"Hannah, Amanda tells me you're in charge of the restaurant until Mrs. Logan is better. I'm here to help, and I don't expect to be paid."

"Help how? I'm fine. The sheriff asked—"

"He asked me to stay away while Ray-Lynn was here, but now she isn't, and I know how to run a place like this. I have a lot of experience in some very busy, lovely restaurants, and this will be a piece of cake—proverbial Amish cake—at least until she gets back. Surely you can't oversee everything, ordering, payroll, et cetera, on your own."

"I will and can. I'm sure you can understand that Ray-Lynn would want this run her way. She had asked to train me as assistant manager before she was hurt."

"How hurt is she?" she asked, propping her fists on her hips. "What happened is just dreadful! I was at the Rooster Roadhouse last night with Elaine." She waved to her friend. Perhaps that's who Elaine had been waiting for. "Jack phoned both of us to ask if we saw Ray-Lynn there, but we didn't. The point is, he said it was up to you if I pitch in for a few days. He knows how to be sensible about this, especially since he's part owner."

Hannah wondered if Lily was lying, or at least putting her own slant on what the sheriff said. Or was he so upset that Ray-Lynn didn't recall their relationship that he figured Ray-Lynn no longer had it in for Lily?

"Sorry, Mrs. Freeman, but I'll have to honor Ray-

Lynn's wishes with this. I have faith she'll make a full recovery."

"You're way out of your league, you know that?" Lily demanded, leaning close and lowering her voice. "And you're an ingrate. I told Elaine I'd even pay for your shooting lessons if you were serious about that. Here you drag your goth friends back to your people's sacred place, then manage to drag your family and church through the mud of all this ugly publicity. Friendly, gracious, forgiving—baloney, if you're the example of an Amish gone astray come home! We'll just see about this."

Hannah jolted when another voice close behind her chimed in. She had not seen Elaine approach. "You'll regret turning Lily down," she said, shaking a finger nearly in Hannah's face. How long had she been standing there? "Forget free shooting lessons. I thought you people were pacifists, but if you want to make something over this, that's fine. I fight fair, but I fight!"

"I'm not the one making something over this, Ms. Carson. I'm just doing what I think Ray-Lynn would want."

Elaine slapped her bill and ten dollars on the hostess stand and walked out with Lily right behind her. Seth got up, leaving Marlena at the booth with Susan, and came over to Hannah.

"Sorry about Susan charging in here," he said. "And what was that all about? You all right?"

"I haven't been all right since the night I stupidly brought my friends to the Home Valley and my world exploded. Thanks for caring, though. I need to do some things in Ray-Lynn's office."

Those things were to close the door, lean against it

and have a good cry. Then she wiped her tears, looked over the list of supplies from various vendors, wiped her eyes again, bowed her head for a quick prayer for Ray-Lynn and forced herself to go back out into the restaurant with a smile.

The sheriff stopped in the restaurant just as Hannah was closing up. Leah Schwartz, who was getting to be her right-hand help, and Seth were both there. Seth had come back to make sure things went well, because it was after dark, and he'd said he'd follow both Leah and Hannah home. Leah lived the first farm out, so it was easy for her to come and go quickly.

"Sorry I couldn't check on things sooner," the sheriff told Hannah as the two of them went into Ray-Lynn's office.

"Any change in Ray-Lynn?" she asked.

He shook his head. He didn't look like himself with beard stubble and dark circles under his eyes. His usual stiff stance seemed deflated as he sank into a chair across from Ray-Lynn's desk.

"I'm just praying," he said, "that next time she wakes up she's herself again—knows me, knows about us."

"Mrs. Freeman was in here today, volunteering to help and saying you more or less said it was okay," Hannah told him.

"Less, not more, would be the truth on that. She phoned me, and I told her it was a generous offer, but I didn't think it was a good idea. It's like no one's listening to me anymore, like I'm not even there—here."

"I told her thank-you but no and she was pretty upset. Her friend Elaine Carson, too."

"Lily's been itching to find something worthwhile to do around here. I thought her buying into the gift shop they're going to put in with Harlan Kenton's deli when they renovate the Troyer mill would keep her going...."

He put his palms over his eyes and rubbed them. "Hannah, you were right to tell Lily what you did. I'll talk to her when I can, but she's down on my list of things to do. Gotta get going. Glad Seth's here since you're closing up late."

He stood and stretched. "You just close up early so you aren't out after dark," he went on. "You do what you have to here to keep things going, change some things if you need to. I trust you and know Ray-Lynn would, as well, and I'll be sure you're paid well."

"Sheriff, I love Ray-Lynn. I'd do this gratis for her."

"I love her, too, Hannah. All this— It took this to make me realize how much. Maybe being away like you were and then your tragedy has settled things like that for you, as well—living here, supporting your father in his important position. And big decisions about you and Seth—or going back to the world again. Gotta go," he repeated, and was out the door at a faster clip than he came in.

After they saw Leah to her driveway, Hannah went on with Seth right behind her. Maybe it wasn't safe on the roads, she thought. She would have argued about that a couple of days ago, even after the graveyard shootings, after someone slit her bedroom screen and terrified her and Linc in the corn maze, but now, with what had happened to Ray-Lynn...

She thought Seth might head on home when she turned up the lane but she should have known better.

He brought Blaze and his buggy right beside hers when she went into the barn. He had a lantern lit and hung on a beam before she could wrap the reins and climb down. While their horses munched hay and occasionally nuzzled each other, he helped her unharness Nettie and stow her gear.

"Sorry about that scene with Susan Zook today," he said again. "I didn't know she was coming, maybe even followed me."

"She made it pretty clear she thinks I'm a bad influence on you. She said there was obviously a good reason you'd chosen someone else before."

Seth sucked in a sharp breath. "She's sealed her own future with me, or should I say, without me. The moment you came back, there was no one else. God's truth, before my mistake with Lena and from the moment she died, there has been no one else I've wanted. And I don't mean that Marlena was the mistake. I'd die for her—for you, too, Hannah. I need you in my life. I need you."

He pulled her into his arms. Not only did she not resist but she held to him in the dim barn, her arms tight around his neck as he lowered his head to meet her lips.

It was a mutually devouring kiss, openmouthed, moving, deepening. His arms around her waist pinned her against his hard body, then his hands dropped to cup her bottom, lift her closer. Her breasts pressed flat against his chest. She raked her good hand through his crisp hair. His hat flew off; he shoved her bonnet back and fastened his fingers in her hair as if to hold her mouth to his forever. How he must hate her hair, half real blond and half dyed red, his girl with one foot in each world as Susan had accused. But he hardly hated her. The kiss went on and on as they breathed in unison until they were nearly panting.

When they broke the kiss, he sighed, and his big frame shook. She put the top of her head under his chin, pressing her lips to the side of his neck, and they just held on as if the earth was quaking under their feet.

"I want you and love you, Hannah, and always will," he whispered. She could feel the sinews of his neck move when he talked, the pulse of his life there. "Now, as much as I'd like to follow our horses leads and just lie down with you in the hay, it's cold out here and I think you'd better go in."

"Cold?" she said, her voice quavering. "I need a fan and some ice."

He chuckled and she could feel the rumble of that against her cheek. "Listen," he went on, holding her back at arm's length, "I'm heading out to the sawmill before dawn to draw up some specs for the Troyer mill project, so I'll pick you up to take you to the restaurant, then pick you up when you close tomorrow so we don't have a parade of buggies. *Ya?*"

"*Ya.* I'd like to be at the restaurant by six-thirty, though. So much to do and learn, especially about ordering supplies and food. Harlan Kenton's going to drop off our meat supply sometime tomorrow."

"I'll leave Marlena with Ella and be here just after six. I can see your father in the back doorway, so I think what we just shared will have to pass for our good-night kiss. He always was touchy about that. I'll bet he used to really smooch your mother good when they were courting and can't get past worrying how a come-calling friend wants to do more than just that with his *maidal*."

Come-calling friends, smooching, *maidal*. This safe, sweet, sure life awaited her just for the taking, for the staying. But would she then forever be content to have given up her chance to sing for a living and a lifetime, and for others beyond her family and friends?

Hannah took the lantern Seth had lit and walked toward the house as he buggied down the lane. *Daad* held the door open for her. She wanted to tell her father she forgave him for ruining her chance for an audition, but the words stuck in her mouth. He had told her and *Mamm* that he was going to confess that sin in the next Sabbath service, but that wasn't until next week. Hannah answered his questions about how the day had gone, then went to find *Mamm*.

To Hannah's surprise, since her mother seldom worked after dark in her *kapp*-making shop, she found her there in the light of three lanterns. *Mamm* was bent over bolts of white organdy she was fusing with interfacing to make the *kapps* stiff. A little row of others were lined up by the pleating machine. As usual, *Mamm* kept the *kapps* for the New Order Amish, with fewer creases, separate from the Old Order ones with more creases, for each church district chose its distinctive style. Over on the side table were the little black caps young girls like Marlena wore—white ones spray-painted black. None of the *kapps* had strings, for the owners sewed those on themselves.

Her mother looked up as Hannah stood in the doorway. "Come in. Just a minute and I can give you a big hug for how good you did today. I was proud of you, my Hannah. Perhaps a future path for you here, *ya?*"

"Maybe. But four daughters and none to carry on this work for you. I always felt bad about that."

"To each her own path but within the Amish way."

Mamm finished fusing the materials, put her iron aside and came around the table to hug Hannah. "Any time you are ready to put a prayer *kapp* back on, with all it means, I have one for you—there, see?"

She pointed to the top of her storage cabinet and there it stood, seeming to stare down at Hannah in its pristine whiteness. Hannah knew what that meant: returning to the *ordnung* rules, joining the church, renouncing the outside world and a professional singing career. But at least it could mean marrying Seth and mothering little Marlena.

"But then," *Mamm* went on as she returned to her work, this time cutting each *kapp* to fit a pattern, "you must be sure you would stay and make up with your father for what he did. If the Lord forgives him, you must, too."

"I think the Lord has more strength and power than I do, *Mamm*."

"Such things you say sometimes! And what about you and Seth?"

"We're close again, but I don't know. Some things I guess I've set in motion have to be settled and solved first."

"Agent Armstrong said to leave things alone, and I pray you will."

Hannah sighed. The smell of starch in here always tickled her nose, so she pressed her finger under her nostrils so she wouldn't sneeze.

"What happened to your friend Ray-Lynn may be a warning, Hannah, and you out early and late on the roads, and in a buggy, not a car."

"Seth said he'd take me to and from the restaurant, at least tomorrow."

"Good, or your father would have." She straightened, a big spray can of starch in hand. "Hannah, your *daad* loves you, wants only the best for you. We both want you to stay, not to follow your friend Sarah across the fence to the world. But I know you, most of all of my four God-given daughters, have a stiff neck and will make your own way. Whatever you do, your father and I will always love you, but it is best to be like this piece of material in life, fitting to our ways."

Mamm picked up a piece of organdy stiffened by the interfacing and pressed it gently around the head-shaped form, sprayed it with starch, then placed it with the others in a line waiting to be pleated, glued and sewn. Hannah glanced up once more at the prayer *kapp* waiting for her atop the cabinet, kissed *Mamm*'s cheek and beat a quick retreat.

26

LINC WAS THE FIRST CUSTOMER IN THE DOOR when Hannah opened the Dutch Farm Table on Saturday morning. He sat on the farthest tall, rotating stool at the counter.

"Coffee and something quick," he said after she greeted him and asked for his order. "The Bureau—my boss—is sending a small airplane for me in about a half hour, landing, ironically, on the road in front of Troyer's mill. I'm going to Detroit to personally check out and interview the Collister Company execs you gave me a lead on. The Bureau office there has already done some checking. Michael Collister's the CEO, Steve, his son, the financial affairs man, and they've been into some borderline shady projects, buying up large, foreclosed properties. I just hope my investigation and, hopefully, interviews of them doesn't screw up funding the mill project Seth's so gung-ho on. He's going to need something to take up his time after you leave."

She was tempted to argue that, but of course she would have to leave, at least for the audition Linc had promised. He downed coffee and multigrain toast with peanut butter, then got up immediately, leaving his money on the counter. "For once, I'm glad you've got Seth bird-dogging you," he told her. "I passed him on the road, and he said he's taking you to and from the restaurant. I hope to be back by midday tomorrow."

"I just know you're going to get answers soon. I have a feeling about those men—maybe helped by Levi Troyer, though I hate to say so."

When he smiled, she realized she'd seldom seen that from him. "Your belief in me when this has been one heck of a case means a lot. Then we'll look into an audition, I promise. And other things."

"Including the Meyers brothers, maybe even Elaine Carson?"

"Including us," he said, and he hurried out.

When the restaurant mail arrived, Hannah found a beautiful postcard for her and one for Ray-Lynn from Sarah—from Paris! Paris, France! The glossy pictures on the cards were paintings, both by an artist named Monet, one of water lilies and another of a lake with a bridge. Hannah skimmed both cards. They were very happy. Paris was wonderful. They ate snails here. The faces of the people were very different from Amish faces. They were going to look at more paintings. Some of the dancers and singers here performed nearly naked, which they called nude. She was so in love.

Hannah took her friend's boldness to follow her heart as a sign this would be a good day. She sighed as she put Ray-Lynn's postcard on her desk and put her own in one of the pockets of Ray-Lynn's apron. Hannah wanted to see Ray-Lynn soon, and she would show her the cards, talk to her about Sarah, about the restaurant. She would remind her how hard she had worked to get Sheriff Freeman to care for her. She felt hopeful she could help Ray-Lynn. For some reason, today she felt hopeful about a lot of things.

When Ray-Lynn awoke the second time, it scared her to be in a hospital room. A nurse was checking the IVs in her arm. And the other arm—her shoulder, too—was in a huge cast!

"Why am I here—and where am I?" she asked the woman.

"You were in a car accident five days ago, Mrs. Logan. Your vehicle skidded over the edge of a ravine on a slippery road over in Eden County. You're in Wooster. You have a broken right arm and shoulder and a severe concussion. You have a little short-term memory loss but you're doing just fine."

Tired, so drowsy, but some of what the nurse said made sense. Wooster was the biggest city around, the closest with a hospital. And Eden County. Yes, where she had bought the restaurant in Homestead a few days ago. But she recalled nothing about an accident. And why was the road slippery in the summer—well, maybe rain or oily pavement. And her short-term memory...what did that mean?

"You just relax," the nurse said, "and I'll call the doctor in to see you. We're very pleased you are awake, and I'll let Sheriff Freeman know, too. He's been gone for a while, but I believe he's back on the grounds somewhere now."

Ray-Lynn struggled to remember. Oh, yes, the man who was sitting by her bed. Had he been waiting to question her about the accident? But he'd been holding her hand, had tears in his eyes, she recalled that for sure.

"Wait! Please," Ray-Lynn said as the nurse started out of the room. "Did I— Was someone else hurt? Why was the sheriff here?"

The nurse came back, opened her mouth once, closed it, then told Ray-Lynn, "He said to tell you if you awoke that he's a friend. You're not under suspicion or arrest for anything, so don't worry. I'll be right back with Dr. Blackstone."

Why couldn't she remember more about the sheriff? Ray-Lynn's heartbeat kicked up. Something—something about the sheriff. So many things—pieces of her thoughts—seemed to be broken or missing. The words the nurse had said—*You're not under suspicion*—that meant something, didn't it? Why did the sheriff want to interview her? And it occurred to her for the first time that she'd have to interview Amish girls to staff her restaurant, get that going, if she could find someone else to invest in it now that Charles was gone.

Tears blurred her eyes and ran down into her hairline as she stared up at the white, pockmarked ceiling. The doctor came in and leaned over to take her hand. She remembered his name was Dr. Blackstone even before she read it scripted above the pocket of his white coat he wore, so her memory was all right, wasn't it? So why couldn't she even remember the name of that sheriff, because if he was a friend, he must mean something to her.

Midafternoon of that second day in the restaurant, Hannah was pleased that Seth stopped by for an early lunch. Things were going pretty smoothly at the Dutch

Farm Table. Seth told her he was going right back to the sawmill, that Abe Mast was helping him figure out estimates of amounts, types and cost of woods for the Troyer mill project. The Detroit investors wanted him to sign a contract when he proposed the specs. Amish workers hated to sign anything that smacked of lawyers, but he sure wanted the job. He told her that two deputies from Wooster had come in to get wood to board up John Arrowroot's house so it would be protected against vandals or thieves, since he'd had a lot of enemies. Like Linc earlier today, Seth ate quickly. Before he hurried out again, he promised, "I'll pick you up before seven. And every day for the rest of our lives, if you stay with the restaurant—and with Marlena and me."

As rushed as he was, the lingering look he'd left her with still promised more than good-night smooches. It made her decide she would tell Linc that if there were strings attached to his offer for a loan and contact help for an audition, she'd have to just save her money. How she'd love to try professional singing once more. If the Lord opened a door there, she'd walk through it. If Seth loved her, he'd understand and accept that she wanted both a life with him and her people but singing for others, too. The world had come to the Home Valley in evil ways, but in good ways, as well. The "be ye separate" command her people clung to was so hard to live by.

Late afternoon, Ella popped in with sachets and soaps to replace the small display of them Ray-Lynn let her keep on shelves near the front door.

"Everything all right?" she asked Hannah as she

shuffled the older products toward the front and filled in behind.

"Better today. Yesterday I had three women tell me off, but not for bad food or service. Oh, there's an envelope I saw under the till with your name on it." She retrieved and extended it to Ella. "And here's the extra from a visitor who just bought some things," she said, digging in one of the pockets of Ray-Lynn's calico print apron.

"Great. Thanks. They say this winter's going to be hard on bedding flowers so I'm going to hill my lavender up well. I'll put this week's money away to buy more plants if need be. I'm just going to pop on over to the Plain and Fancy to replace my things there."

"I feel really bad I let Amanda down by leaving that job so soon," Hannah confided. "She and Harlan have both been really good to me."

"I'm sure she knows you're more needed here—not that dusting and cleaning isn't important and *so much fun*," she said with a little laugh.

"Ella," Hannah said, snagging her wrist before she could leave, "one of the people who told me off on Friday was Lily Freeman. She wanted to help me here, probably take over, but to honor Ray-Lynn's feelings I turned her down. She tried to give me the idea the sheriff wanted her here, but he said no. Since she worked in some big restaurant in Las Vegas, I'm sure she could have been of help. In case you run into her at Amanda's, I just wanted you to know she's probably about as angry with me as she is with Ray-Lynn. I suppose Ray-Lynn overreacted somewhat around Lily, but I can understand her fear that Lily would like to get back with the sheriff."

"Do you think she's upset enough with Ray-Lynn she'd shove her off the road?" Ella asked wide-eyed. "I can take a look at Lily's front bumper if it's parked behind the B and B, see if there are dents or scrapes."

"I didn't tell you all that so that you'd put yourself in danger. Besides, Linc thought the other tires belonged to a van or truck." She sighed. "I'm starting to sound like Linc, who's always telling me to stay out of his investigation, but just be aware and careful."

"Tell you what," Ella whispered as more folks came in for lunch. "I'll stop back in if there's anything to tell—if I see or hear anything about Lily."

As she went out and Hannah picked up menus to seat a foursome, the very scent of the new lavender products calmed her. Linc was going to get answers in Detroit. The graveyard shooting must have been done by an outsider. At least Ray-Lynn's tragedy hadn't killed her, even if it had killed her memory, her immediate past and maybe her love for Sheriff Freeman.

Ella was back about an hour later, fussing with her products she'd already arranged, giving Hannah tilts of her head and sideways glances that must mean she had something to tell her in the back. It was a busy time, but Hannah put Leah on the front door and doubled Amy's station. If Amy balked—which she didn't, just glared at Hannah—it would be a later excuse to replace her.

"I don't put it past Amy Zook to be spying on Seth and me for her sister Susan," Hannah whispered to Ella as they hurried back to Ray-Lynn's office.

"Speaking of spying, that's what I have to tell you. Amanda's completely understanding about your leaving the job there, but I overheard Lily on her cell phone and she was so mad she was talking pretty loud, like she was ready to lose her temper."

"About my not letting her work here?"

"No, about convincing someone that she is not after Jack—that's what she called the sheriff."

"She can't be talking to Ray-Lynn, can she?"

"No way. She's talking to someone where it's eighty-six degrees today. I overheard that, too, right through the door of her room upstairs at the B and B."

"Maybe it was a friend in Las Vegas. But that sounds like the person she's talking to cares for her—you know, might be jealous if she's after another man. Maybe someone she dated there knows her ex-husband is here and available. I'm going to tell Linc all that when he gets back, even though I've learned your information is hearsay and maybe entrapment. And now she's angry with me for siding with Ray-Lynn and having the job she wants here."

"I don't like the sounds of all that. Especially because she's so tight with Elaine Carson, and that woman loves guns more than people. She's probably be a great shot, even after dark, even if people moved among tombstones. Then what if she planted the rifle she used and a fake note at Arrowroot's house after she lured him out somehow?"

"And did what with him? Murdered him in cold blood? More like, she admired him for standing up for his rights as an American. I should have asked Linc *who* left the Rooster Roadhouse *when* that night, someone who could have seen Ray-Lynn on the road or in the parking lot and then followed her. He's interviewed folks who were there then. Like I said, he thought the vehicle that ran her off the road was a van or truck—big tire tracks."

"Which Lily doesn't have—"

"But Elaine does," they finished in unison.

"Well, if either Lily or Elaine comes in here, I think you should call Linc immediately," Ella said.

"He's not even in the vicinity right now, but no one is going to gun me down or run me off the road in a busy restaurant, and Seth's coming in plenty of time to take me home."

"Is it home to you now, Hannah? Can it—we—all be your family, your friends again? You and I—Sarah, too, of course—always felt like sisters, so if you'd just stay and make a life..."

"I've got to get back out front. Thanks for telling me what you heard. Want something to eat before you go?"

"I'd better head home. I told *Mamm* I'd take care of Marlena. She needs a mother, Hannah, just like Seth needs a wife. I'm hoping and praying, no matter what happened before, that will be you."

Hannah closed up a bit early to be sure all the customers would be finished eating by the time Seth came to get her. It wasn't even dusk, so she sent Leah home shortly after the other waitresses and cooks left. If Ray-Lynn was away for long, Hannah would keep Leah as her second in charge. It was good to have a new friend.

She surveyed the restaurant with her ears attuned to Seth's buggy out back. Nothing yet, but it was a bit earlier than she expected him. Instead, she heard the purr of a motor and a knock-knock on the back alley door.

"Who is it?" she called through the door.

"Harlan. Got the week's restaurant meat. Sorry I didn't get here sooner!"

She unlocked the door and let him in. Wearing gloves while he handled the frozen meat, he nodded and came in with a huge sliced side of bacon over one shoulder. She hurried ahead of him into the kitchen, clicking on electric lights, and opening one of the side-by-side doors of the large stand-up stainless-steel freezer for him. Cold air swirled from it to chill her.

"These are cut in five-pound sections, so you'll defrost about four a day," he told her, all business. She was tempted to ask him how he was doing and if he'd cleared the air with his wife and sister, but she didn't.

"If you can hold the doors for me, that's good," he told her. "Fifteen-pound boxes of beef and sausage coming next."

He came back and forth, hefting two cartons at a time. The man was even stronger than he looked. He grunted as he stacked them inside the freezer, the tops of the boxes toward the front, clearly marked and sealed with black duct tape. "Side of beef next—cut up, so don't worry about the space you got left."

As he slid the remaining box out of the back of his vehicle, she saw the restaurant must be the last of his deliveries he planned to make today. The truck interior was refrigerated and wafted out cold air. He also had several dollies within and an array of ropes and canvas cords. A big roll of dark duct tape lay there, too, the kind he'd sealed the boxes with.

Should she ask if he'd seen Ray-Lynn at the Roadhouse two nights ago, or would that remind him of his drinking? He seemed pretty sober now, both kinds of sober, off the booze and serious about his work.

"There you go," he said as he carried the last load in. He wedged the box of plastic trays of meat into the freezer and she closed the door. He seemed awkward and nervous alone with her.

"Thanks, Harlan. I see Ray-Lynn pays you on the fifteenth and the last day of the month, so I'll be sure to take care of that."

On the way out, she sensed he was going to say something else, but he didn't. At the back door, he stepped out into the gray dusk and looked both ways, tugging his leather gloves tighter up his wrists. She turned in the doorway to go back inside.

Suddenly, he reached for her from behind, one leather-covered hand over her mouth, one shooting around to pin her arms to her sides.

In a swift, strong movement, he lifted and slid her, facedown, into the back of his truck with his hand still over her mouth. Cold metal, cold air. Shocked, but not into submission, Hannah tried to kick and scream, but he duct-taped her mouth shut, then tied her wrists behind her with rope while she thrashed her skirts up to her knees before he could get her ankles tied. Ray-Lynn's ring of keys rattled in the pocket of her apron.

Trapped, trussed, she stopped struggling. Her mind began to work again when her limbs and mouth could not. Seth would be here soon. Find her gone. Search for her. But even if someone had seen this truck, so what? Linc out of town...told Leah to go home...sheriff where? Just calm down, just breathe, pray.

This was not happening. Not possible. Not Amanda's brother! He had been kind, helpful.... John Arrowroot missing...now her, too? Seth, come back early!

Come here now! Someone in the alley, see or hear…
someone!

He rolled her in a blanket she hadn't seen. It actually felt good. Her bonnet and cape were inside the restaurant. Hard to breathe in the blanket with the gag.
Breathe. Just breathe.

"Got orders to clean things up," he muttered, out of
breath, as if trying to convince himself. "Just doing
what I been hired to do. Don't fight, 'cause it's not
gonna help. Just accept it. You Amish are good at that.
The Indian, too."

He got up into the bed of the truck—it bounced
under his weight. He pulled her farther back in, rolling something big and cold against her, one of the dollies. The truck bounced again as he got out, slammed
both doors and shot a bolt or latch. The sound echoed
in her soul. Though the next noises were muted, she
was pretty sure he closed the back door to the restaurant, then opened and closed the driver's side door of
his truck cab in front.

Had he hurt Ray-Lynn, too? Was he going to drop
her over a cliff? And he'd mentioned the Indian. He
must have taken John Arrowroot. But who had ordered
him to "clean things up"?

The meat storage truck, with Hannah in its cold
belly, rumbled to life and drove smoothly out onto
Main Street.

27

IT WAS QUITE DARK A LITTLE BEFORE SEVEN when Seth knocked on the back restaurant door and waited for Hannah to open it. He knocked again; then, thinking she must be in the front and didn't hear him, he left Blaze and the buggy and went around to look in the windows facing the street.

Dimmed lights. Empty of people. No Hannah or Leah. He knocked again louder on the door and on the long glass window, right over the table where he'd eaten yesterday.

He pounded on the front door, then ran to the side of the building and knocked on the office window in case she'd fallen asleep on the couch there. She'd been exhausted. Curtains drawn, the office dark, but his noise would wake her up. Surely she hadn't forgotten he was coming to get her. If only cell phones weren't *verboten!*

Instead, he ran for the sheriff's office just down the way. The small building was dark. A phone—he needed a public phone. In Amish country, pay phones in town were almost as common as the phone shanties on farm roads. The nearest one was down in front of the Kwik Stop grocery. Linc was out of town, so he'd call the sheriff.

Rather than take the time to get the buggy, he ran. Thoughts and fears pursued him: the shooting in the graveyard, a man killed, Hannah and her friend hit. Arrowroot missing, Ray-Lynn hurt. But where was the pattern? Where was the evil doer and where was his Hannah? No way she would have gone with Linc, even if he'd come back for her, promised her the moon—a singing career. Was there?

He had memorized the sheriff's cell phone number, Linc's, too, hoping he'd never need them. Since he had no pockets in his clothing, he kept coins jammed in his hatband.

He slapped three quarters into the slot, punched in the sheriff's cell phone number and heard the phone ring, ring. Why didn't he answer? It would take too long to drive out to his house right now. He had to get in the restaurant, look for Hannah. He hit his fist against his thigh as the sheriff's voice-mail recording came on. He should have just broken into the restaurant. The sheriff would understand; Hannah and Ray-Lynn would give their permission.

"Sheriff, it's Seth," he said at the beep. "Hannah didn't answer the door at the restaurant when I came to take her home. I'm going to break in, gotta find her fast."

He slammed the receiver down and ran down the street. He ignored the few folks who stared at him. Most were home eating suppers in their houses, safe and happy. Why couldn't it be that way for him and

Hannah? His gut churned with raw terror at the thought of losing her again.

What if she felt ill, went home with Leah and left him a note that blew away? What if she just stepped out in town to get something, then planned to be back when he arrived? He was a bit early. What if…what if…

Would a burglar alarm go off if he broke a window to get in? He wasn't sure if Ray-Lynn had invested in that, considering where they lived. Few crimes until recently, the world pushing in on the Home Valley. If an alarm went off, maybe that would bring the sheriff. He must be taking a shower at home, making noise somehow so he hadn't heard his cell phone or had turned it off. He'd check his voice mail, he'd be here soon. Seth knew he should have called Linc, as well, but Hannah said he was out of town today, so the sheriff could do that.

Panicked, Seth lifted the big ceramic pot of geraniums, frost-tinged, that sat near the front door. He moved away from the long picture window and lugged the pot around the side of the building to the smaller office window.

He heaved the pot against the glass. Both shattered, but shards edged the window like jagged jaws. He put his hat over his hand and knocked them out. No alarm sounded. Even before he shoved open the curtains and climbed in, he shouted, "Hannah! Hannah! You here?"

He stumbled across the room and flicked on the light, blinking in the sudden brightness. Her bonnet lay on Ray-Lynn's desk. She didn't wear it in the restaurant, looked strange in Amish garb without a prayer *kapp,* but she wouldn't leave that here, not if she went out in this weather—went out of her own accord.

Worse, her cape was draped over the hook on the back of the office door. Linc had surmised she was safe when he didn't make an immediate arrest of the graveyard shooter, which would have shown she knew who that was, had seen him or her that night on the hill above the graves.

He tore through the place, turning on lights, looking under tables, in large kitchen cabinets, in store rooms, even the big freezer, but it was packed with boxes of meat. He went down into the basement, several storage rooms with stacks of place mats, napkins and who knew what else. No Hannah. Upstairs, the back door of the restaurant was locked, as was the front. Bile rose in his throat, and fear gnawed at his self-control. Leah Schwartz's home was close by. He'd go ask her if she knew anything, if Hannah had received a phone call or someone had been here—and why had Leah left early when she was going to wait to be escorted home?

He jumped into his buggy and got Blaze going at a near gallop toward Leah's.

Hannah tried to remember each turn the truck took. Left onto Main for a ways, then up a hill, out of town for sure. Another left, not too far from Homestead. She counted two more hills before a left turn onto gravel. Harlan's meat shop? It was on a rural road between now-barren fields. Surely he couldn't have driven out to Troyers' mill or the ravine already. What if this was the truck that had pushed Ray-Lynn's van over the side?

Since he'd made no pretense of hiding his identify from Hannah today—no knocking her over the head from behind—he must mean to kill her. But if Harlan was the Halloween night shooter, why? He must know by now she had not recognized him that night. Was he acting because of someone's orders, as he'd mentioned? She had heard that Harlan had boasted of retiring early and living well. For him, was money—and liquor— the root of all evil? She could see his wanting to set up John Arrowroot to take the blame, but why hurt Ray-Lynn—if he had?

The truck came to a stop, and he killed the engine. Nothing happened for a moment. Her pulse pounded so hard she heard drums in her ears. It must be dark by now. Perhaps he'd gone into his store to get something. Seth would be distraught when he arrived at the restaurant and didn't find her, especially since he'd discovered John Arrowroot missing. If outsiders saw Harlan make his weekly delivery after closing time, no one would suspect a thing or know where she'd gone. She should never have sent Leah home early, but then, he might have hurt her, too.

It seemed an eternity before the back door of the truck opened. Harlan slid her out and threw her, like a slab of meat, over his shoulder, still wrapped in the blanket. His shoulder pressed into her stomach and made her feel even sicker. She couldn't throw up with this gag or she'd choke.

Yes, looking down at the ground, she could see it was dark outside now. She caught a glimpse of a back door stoop, the base of a glass meat counter. They were in his store. He closed and locked the door behind them, walked six steps, then opened another door.

Were they going outside again? So cold. A slap of chill air wafted over her, despite the blanket. He clicked on a light and she saw a concrete floor stained with red juice or blood.

His walk-in meat freezer? He was going to put her in his freezer? At least she had a blanket, but no one would ever find her here. Or since he was a butcher...

He laid her down on a shelf amid frozen haunches of meat and pulled the blanket from her. He arranged her on the deep shelf, her hands still bound in back, facing away from him on her side, her knees pulled up in a fetal position.

He flapped a sheet of thick plastic open over her. Was that like what Seth said the extra graveyard corpses were wrapped in? He covered her with it but didn't wrap it tight. Inches from her face, a stab of light reflected off two big, round eyes glaring at her from within the large, wrapped haunch of meat next to her. She screamed right through her gag when she realized she was looking at the frozen corpse of John Arrowroot with his thick glasses still on his face.

Harlan moved away, turned out the light and slammed the door.

Leah was no help to Seth. Instantly upset, she said she knew nothing that hinted where Hannah might have gone. She told Seth that Hannah had sent her home early, that she'd said he was coming to get her, and, after all, Hannah was in charge now. No, no personal phone calls she knew of during the day. Yes, the Meyers brothers had been in as usual and hung around a bit late. Yes, Levi Troyer was here for a while. No, not Mrs. Freeman or Ms. Carson. His sister Ella had stopped in twice and once they'd gone off to the office to talk about something private. A few delivery people came by today. She wrote down their names for him. The girl had tears in her eyes as he left, blinking back his own.

Seth wished he'd left a note for the sheriff on the back door of the restaurant, but he was heading for Bishop Esh now. He hated to alarm them, but they had to be told, maybe knew something. Then he'd check with Ella. She'd been in the store today, perhaps had spotted someone—something!

Bishop Esh, ever vigilant about Hannah since she'd been back, stood in the door as Seth's buggy raced up the lane. Mrs. Esh came up behind him and peered around his shoulder. Seth would have given his life right then if Hannah had come home somehow, even if it meant she never wanted to see him again.

He did a U-turn with the buggy and reined in. "Have you heard from or seen Hannah?"

"*Ach,* no. She said you'd bring her home," the bishop shouted.

"She wasn't at the restaurant, but her cape and bonnet were. I called the sheriff but didn't get him. Agent Armstrong's not around today, even out of the state. I'm checking on who's seen her, going to check with Ella."

As Seth snapped the reins and sent Blaze back to a trot, he could hear Bishop Esh praying and Hannah's mother's sobs.

Pitch-black in here and so cold, but that made her even more desperate to do something before Harlan came back. Or would he not return until he knew she was frozen to death? She supposed this was an indirect way of killing someone without putting a bullet in them. Harlan must have given the graveyard murder weapon back when he took John Arrowroot. She had no time to look at his stiff body, could not stand to— nor could she see a thing in here.

She scooted away from his corpse. Had Harlan killed him just so he could make it look like Arrowroot was the killer? Again, she tried to reason out who pulled Harlan's strings, but she had to get loose somehow, stay warm, stay alive. Find some way out.

The big piece of plastic slid off to the floor as she rolled over her tied hands and struggled to sit up, bumping her head on the shelf above. She shivered despite her frenzy, just as after she'd helped recover Ray-Lynn, but then she'd had Seth and Ella beside her. She'd have to keep moving all night, get out of these ties. She scooted carefully to the edge of the storage shelf. What about oxygen in here? Would she pass out before she froze? How large a freezer was this?

She had no choice but to try to find out, and in the blackest black she'd ever seen. It was like being in a tomb in the cold ground.

Praying she would not stumble or fall, she decided to hop until she found the wall and the door and hopefully the light switch, because she was pretty sure it was inside the door, not out. She got to her feet but, instead of hopping, she could only shuffle in tiny steps.

Twice she bumped into cold metal shelves or racks, went down an aisle to the wall and had to reverse her steps. Could she be going in circles? Now this reminded her of the corn maze. Harlan must have been after them there, too. At last she bumped into a wall of cold metal. She shuffled along it, hit a corner, went back. She was certain he'd carried her in through a door over here. Yes, not a round door-knob but a long one!

She put her ear to the metal door, but could hear nothing through it. Maybe the whirring of a fan some-where in here. It seemed to come off and on, blowing out extra cold air into the already frigid room. She pressed her trembling body along one side of the door, then the other. Her breast scraped over something, maybe a light switch. She ran her face down the wall to it and flicked it up with her nose.

Light flooded the room, making her squint. *Thank You, Lord, for this much. Please protect Your own,* she prayed. As she surveyed the room, she was surprised at its small size. She blinked away tears, only to real-ize they were freezing on her cheeks.

For once Seth did not scoop Marlena up in his arms as she ran to him, but only patted her head.

"Hannah's missing from the restaurant!" he blurted out, lifting Ella to her feet where she'd been playing on the floor with Marlena and both her dolls.

"Hannah here, *Daadi!*" Marlena said, tugging on his coat, but he ignored her.

"But I saw her there twice today," Ella cried. "I went to drop off the lavender and went back after I overheard Mrs. Freeman at the B and B. She was talk-ing about Sheriff Freeman to someone Hannah thinks she must have been in love with in Las Vegas. Hannah said Lily's probably not only mad at Ray-Lynn but at her for not letting her work at the restaurant."

"Could Lily Freeman have come by to argue with her again?"

"Maybe, since they had words yesterday."

"I know. I saw it." He picked Marlena up in his arms, bounced her but ignored her babbling. "All I can think of to do is go to the B and B to see if Lily's there. Then I can check out the Meyers brothers. Linc never did trust them."

"Can't the sheriff help?"

"I'm hoping he shows up. If he doesn't soon, I'm going to phone Linc Armstrong, even if he is in Detroit. Thanks for staying with Marlena," he added, and thrust the child into Ella's arms. He was out the door in a sprint, wishing for once he wasn't Amish. Because he needed a phone and something faster than a horse. Because he was going to use violence, if he must, to shake some answers out of people.

With her exertions, Hannah was having trouble breathing. Mucus from her crying was starting to freeze in her nostrils. She had to get her gag off, had to free her hands. Wouldn't a butcher have a knife nearby?

She shuffled slowly around, down a narrow aisle of shelves. Nothing she could see but stacked meat, much of it wrapped in cloudy plastic. Would the edge of one of the bolted uprights that held the metal shelves saw through the ropes around her wrist? She had to try.

She backed up to a corner shelf and started rubbing her ties up and down. It was exhausting work, but it kept her a bit warmer. She thought she was making progress, but her hands were numb, her fingers, too. From the bonds or from the cold? So cold.

She thought the ties loosened a bit. Sawing harder, pushing against the metal, praying, thinking of that time she and Seth had their legs tied together for a

church picnic in a three-legged race. They had won a
watermelon they and their friends devoured...so warm
that day...so...

It startled her when her bonds popped free. Free!
Free and in the light! *Thank You, Lord, and for that
warm memory of Seth.* When he'd looked at her, even
then, she'd felt the heat of the sun, so golden and
warm....

*Stop it! Concentrate! Keep warm, keep moving,
think about getting out of here!* she screamed at herself as she ripped her gag off.

She sat on the floor to untie her ankles, but her fingers didn't work right. Fumbling, she picked away at
the knots and felt the rush of blood into her feet. Now
to get out of here. Surely Harlan must have gone home
for the night, especially if his wife and sister were
upset with him lately. All that heartfelt confession to
her in the restaurant! And no doubt planning then to
get rid of her as he had John Arrowroot, and maybe
those strangers buried in the graveyard. Maybe tried
to kill Ray-Lynn, too. Well, he wasn't going to kill her.
If he came back to wrap her in that plastic shroud, she
was going to hit him over the head with a piece of his
own frozen meat!

That is, if she could keep her fingers and hands
warm enough to hold it, her feet and legs steady
enough, for she was shaking uncontrollably. Her brain
seemed to drift, as well. *Please, Lord, not like Ray-
Lynn where she'd lose her memory, go unconscious,
Lord, help...*

She wanted to sing to keep her courage up, but what
if Harlan was still here, heard her and came in before
she was ready? Besides, she shouldn't take in more

cold air. She'd just sing in her head, talk to those she loved, *Mamm, Daad*—what if she didn't get a chance to tell him she forgave him? She'd pretend to talk to Seth, of course, Ella and Sarah, little Marlena and her *lumba babba* named Hannah. Talk to Linc, tell him to get here fast from far away—was he in Paris? *Seth, please come find me....*

She was going crazy from the cold. Did she hear faint voices in her head—or were they real?

28

"LILY'S NOT HERE, SETH," AMANDA STUTZMAN told him as she stood in her front door. "What's the matter? Come on in."

"I can't, Mrs. Stutzman. I need to find Hannah."

"But why are you here? Do you think she's with Lily?"

"I doubt it. Lily's angry with her for not letting her help at the restaurant. And with Ray-Lynn injured..."

Amanda stepped out onto her front porch and pulled her wool shawl closer around her shoulders. "You don't think that Lily had anything to do with that, do you? I had the idea Lily wanted her ex-husband back at first— I mean, I just couldn't believe she really missed small-town life enough to return and face everyone, and neither did I come to believe she was writing a book. It just isn't her, if you know what I mean. And then, when I heard the sheriff and Ray-Lynn were close— well!"

"Is there anything else you learned about Lily that didn't sit right?"

"She goes out jogging and driving at strange hours.

I'm sorry I can't be of more help. You know, she really puts up walls, despite how she seems so open and friendly. I was just talking about that with my brother and his wife the other night, and they both agreed."

"Please don't be angry with Ella, but when she was here today, she accidentally overheard Mrs. Freeman talking to a man, probably in Las Vegas, someone who seemed jealous of Sheriff Freeman. Have you picked up on any of that?"

"Well, lots of phone calls, but she was very private about that. You know, maybe if Jack Freeman didn't want to take her back, she wanted to make things hard for him around here by riling up Ray-Lynn. But by pushing her off the road into a ravine?"

"She'd have to be crazy."

"Which she isn't. She's very bright, very focused, but more and more antsy around here, I can tell. Two places you could check, of course, if you must talk to her—you could use my phone—would be the Rooster Roadhouse and Elaine Carson's place. Thick as thieves, those two. I almost wondered at first if they weren't actually attracted to each other—you know what I mean—but not if Lily has someone back in Las Vegas. Now, I must admit Harlan has been out to the Road-house a time or two also, drinking, playing the video games there—even went to Las Vegas once to gamble on their machines. He won a trip on the radio, all expenses paid, so—"

She went on and on. The Lily and Harlan link to Las Vegas might mean something, but that wasn't what hit him now. Hannah had mentioned that Harlan Kenton would make the restaurant's weekly meat delivery today, but Leah had not included him on the list of vendors who had stopped by. He'd stuck the list in his hat, but he pulled it out and tilted it to the wan window light. No, Harlan Kenton's name was not on it, and yet the restaurant's freezer was full of meat. He must have stopped by after Leah left. He'd have to talk to Harlan but without tipping off his sister about it, in case she'd phone him.

"What is it? Where are you going?" Mrs. Stutzman cried as he thanked her, then started away.

He didn't know whether to trust her or not. He had been going to ask to borrow her phone to call Linc and to—as she'd suggested—phone Elaine Carson and the Roadhouse, but he'd better not do any of that here. Could he even trust her to call the sheriff for him?

"I just decided to let the sheriff handle this," he lied. "Thanks again for all your help!"

He was off at fast clip toward his buggy and exhausted horse. Where would Harlan be this time of night? Since Hannah had said he was on the outs with his wife for drinking too much, he'd probably be home after dark. Yeah, he'd get to a pay phone and try calling Harlan's house, then his shop, then the Roadhouse to find out where he was so he could confront him.

The voices made Hannah more alert. They must be real. When the cold air stopped blowing in for a while, they were louder. Maybe coming through an air vent in here somewhere?

She looked up, all around. She hated to do it, but she clicked off the single bare lightbulb on the ceiling and saw wan light up high on the wall that must adjoin the shop itself. If it wasn't so small, she might have found a way to unscrew the grated plate or knock it out. When

she blinked she could tell there was something like
snowflakes on her eyelashes.

She turned the light back on and shoved a heavy
box labeled Zook Family Venison over to the wall and
climbed up on it.

"You've what? You've blown it now, ruined everything!" a woman's voice shrilled. "You're an idiot! You
can't keep making people disappear like a second-rate
magician in a show on the Strip! And your drinking's
way out of control!"

Lily? Hannah's head hurt so much from the cold.
Her teeth were chattering, and keeping her ear close
to the vent in order to listen meant she got a cold blast
right in her face when the blower kicked on again.

"You sound like my wife and sister, and I can do
without both right now," Harlan shouted. "Mr. Davis
told me to clean things up, so I am. Give that bright,
snoopy little Amish chick a couple more days and
she'd remember or figure out it was me trick-or-treat-
ing Halloween night, to bury another of your boyfriend's bodies. They're not buying that Arrowroot's
the shooter, or the FBI guy would have cleared out of
here."

Hannah's hand flew to cover her mouth, but her co-
ordination was off and she hit her palm into her ice-
cold nose. It stung, but not as much as knowing the
supposedly kind, generous Harlan was Kevin's killer
as well as John Arrowroot's. He might not have killed
those extra people in the graveyard, but he must have
put them there. Surely Amanda Stutzman—or his
wife—didn't know. But Lily, in on all that?

The shop phone rang, once, twice. "I gotta get that,"
Harlan said. "Might be my wife. Told her I'd be working

here late, then get right home, no Roadhouse delivery tonight. Hello?" Even louder: "Hello! No one there."

"I swear there's no one there in your brain half the time," Lily started in again.

"Speaking of my wife—you're a worse henpecker than she is! You oughta show a little gratitude I got rid of Ray-Lynn and shut up Hannah Esh for you. They've both been trouble, even if in different ways. Here I drove Ray-Lynn's van out and hid it on a dirt lane, had to hike back to get my truck at the Roadhouse in the snow and cold, then get her van all set so I could push it off. Just lucky it was a back country road where no one came along. A big gamble—and you know all about big-stakes gambling. So I got rid of your competition with the sheriff as a special favor, and don't you forget it, just like I got rid of that sharp little Amish cookie who would have tracked us both down, give her time with that FBI guy."

"But you screwed that up, too. I only okayed your slitting Hannah Esh's screen and leaving that feather to make them suspect John Arrowroot. Fine that you took him and made him look guilty, but it didn't end things, did it? As for Ray-Lynn, I'm not rid of her. As a matter of fact, Jack Freeman seems to be spending day and night at her bedside!"

"Good. Gets him out of here. And I should've gotten rid of the FBI guy instead of just knocking him out, but I didn't need swarms of them rushing in here."

"You're supposed to be taking orders from Trenton through me. I didn't ask to have Ray-Lynn hurt. Seeing if I could break her and the sheriff up was just a diversion while I was here. She can have Jack and that two-bit restaurant. But you've run amok. Planting Trenton's enemies in the Amish graves *was* my idea, but that's all you were supposed to do. Trenton Davis told you to keep your nose clean, not to clean things up by putting people on ice—literally."

"Tell him I want my pay, and I want both of the special deliveries in my freezer planted in one of his other drop spots, a nice rural cemetery somewhere else, as far from here as he can get them! I'll move out west, in case he needs me to clean up other problems, like I said, but that's it. I'm done here!"

"You very well may be."

"Call him, smart mouth! You call him all the time, anyway. If he really cared for you, you think he'd send you here to Podunk to keep an eye on things for a while?"

"Keep an eye on you, after you shot up those kids, and then you go kill-crazy! It reflects on me, too, you know!"

"I can't wait to blow this place for good, leave my wife with my sister for all I care. I liked the way I was treated in Vegas. Mr. Davis took care of everything even you, till he got tired of you!"

There was a crack—maybe a slap. A single gunshot? Their voices had been fading so maybe they went outside. But what if both of them came in here?

Hannah jumped down from the carton to scramble back on the shelf, but when her feet hit the concrete floor, she realized too late they'd gone numb. She tripped and stumbled, sprawling, hitting her head on a metal shelf. She lay on the floor for a moment, flat on her stomach, stunned by the blow, by what she'd heard. Dizzy. She was dizzy, floating, back in the dark maze with Linc again, trapped...no, she was careering down the old mill chute holding on to Seth...spinning into the cold, cold fear that she now knew who the killer was and who had pulled his strings for money, a new truck, an early retirement...and she would never live to tell anyone. She'd end up wrapped in plastic and put in someone else's grave somewhere when she wanted to sing...to love...to live....

She turned over on her back and smiled. The snow under her, around her, falling from the sky was lovely. She was making snow angels with Sarah and Ella, while Seth pelted them with snowballs, so happy in the cold....

Ray-Lynn was awake when the sheriff came into her hospital room. His name, the nurse had said, was Jack Freeman, Eden County's sheriff. Yes, Ray-Lynn remembered his name now and meeting him when she came out of the Citizens Bank where she'd gone to apply for a loan. It encouraged her to know she was remembering the names of places, now recalled this handsome man, too.

"How you feeling, Ray-Lynn?" he asked, sitting on the edge of the chair beside her bed, not touching her this time. He kept rotating his big-brimmed hat in his hands between his splayed knees as he leaned toward her. "I've been in the hospital chapel praying, and I fell asleep. Thought I'd stop by before I head back to Homestead. Got a lot to do, make my rounds, check my phone messages—I'll keep an eye on the Dutch Farm Table, too."

"Thank you. I'm very excited about getting it up and running. Homestead needs a well-run, 'down home' restaurant."

She thought she'd said something nice, but he looked so sad.

"Sure we do—also need you back."

"My next step is to move out of that mobile home and into a nice house, but first things first."

"That's for sure," he said, but his voice caught, almost as if he'd cry. He stood, looking down at her.

"I was afraid at first," she told him, "when I saw you sitting there I'd done something wrong, Sheriff."

"Call me Jack, okay?"

"Sure. Of course."

"No, you didn't do anything wrong, Ray-Lynn, but someone else did. Now don't you worry about a thing and just know you've got a good friend here and waiting for you at home."

She looked up into his intense brown eyes, and something sparked between them. The look lasted for a moment too long, and yet it was comforting and exciting. Was she crazy? He said his goodbyes, told her he'd be back and bring some Amish women to sit with her when she wasn't sleeping so much. His words went past her as she tried hard to recall if she should remember more about him—about them.

She saw him stop at her door and punch some buttons on his cell phone. He looked at his little screen, and she heard him mutter something so low she couldn't catch the words. Then he leaped to action, careered around the corner, and she could hear him actually running down the quiet hospital hall.

Seth reined Blaze in half a field away from Harlan Kenton's meat market, got out and pulled the horse and buggy off the road, way into the barren field where headlights on the road wouldn't spot them. He tied Blaze to an old fence post. She was exhausted, wheezing, and he needed to approach quietly. When Harlan had answered the phone here, something had told him not to give himself away. Even if he had caller ID, Seth was using the pay phone in front of the bank.

He was tired, too, running on panic and fear, but still running. He was glad the field was frozen since that made sprinting toward the meat market easier. He had tried to think what was in his buggy to use to protect himself if need be. Nothing, really. A buggy whip against that big man? His tape measure? No, but he might use a lure or distraction. He'd grabbed the folder with all the supply and price estimates in it, some of the basic sketches and layout of Troyer's mill. The man might be a big bruiser but he was going to answer Seth's questions, or else—or else what, he wasn't sure.

But as he approached the meat market, he had to throw himself flat on the ground. There was a second vehicle there beside Harlan's truck, a car backing out. Not the one he'd seen the Detroit men in. Much smaller, low-slung—and red. Lily Freeman's?

Its headlights swung over him, past him, as the car turned out onto the road and roared away. The door to the market opened, and Harlan's bulky form was silhouetted for a second as he carried a small box out and put it in the front seat of his truck, then headed back inside. Now or never, before he locked up and drove away.

Cutting from the field into the parking lot, Seth called out, "Hey, Harlan. It's Seth Lantz. I was coming out to see you with some good news, but my horse threw a shoe, and I had to walk a ways."

"Be glad to give you a ride back to town if you need to get a blacksmith. So what's the good news this time of night?"

"I've got some specs to show you about your deli space for the mill renovation," he rushed on, holding up his sheaf of papers. "Can I come in for a minute? Wait till you see these plans. I've been at the sawmill all day working on them."

"Well, I gotta get home. I'm late for dinner already."

In the reflected light from the store, Seth could see Harlan had a huge black eye forming up—fresh. Would Hannah have struck him? More likely Lily, but that meant they had something going on between them, and it sure wasn't a secret love affair, not between her and Harlan.

Seth could sense that the big guy didn't want him to come into the store. More than once his eyes darted to the door. Seth had to get in there, look around. His blood pounded so hard in his head that, years of Amish training aside, he almost leaped at the man.

Instead, he surprised him by pushing past him into the store. Seth shoved the door into him, slammed it and locked from within.

He knew Harlan must have another key, so he looked around *schnell* for something to jam the dead-bolt lock he shot closed. One of the carving knives in the rack on the wall? He heard Harlan roar in anger outside, then start cursing. He yanked the door handle, which rattled and shuddered. Tossing his papers on the counter, Seth grabbed a long, thin metal rasp used to sharpen knives and jammed it there.

"Hannah! Hannah, you here?" he shouted.

No sound inside, but pounding on the door outside.

Could he have locked him out without a key? There was a ring of them on the counter. But nothing else in here looked out of place. He raced into Harlan's small office. Looked behind and under the counter, picked up a phone lying there to try to call the sheriff again. He punched in the numbers and, despite Harlan's noise, heard Jack Freeman answer. "Harlan, that you? Caller ID says—"

"It's Seth at Harlan's meat store! I think he took Hannah, might have her here. I'm locked inside but he's trying to get in and—"

He thought the sheriff shouted, "I'm ten minutes out!" but he wasn't sure because the front window shattered; a big rock slammed through it, spewing broken glass onto the floor. Still cursing, Harlan vaulted in. The big man looked enraged, out of control. Was that how he'd been the night he shot at the goth kids?

The meat freezer? His only chance!

He ran for it, opened it. The light was on inside. He tried to pull the door shut, but Harlan leaped at him, stuck his arm in the door. Seth slammed it, anyway, once, twice. Harlan howled, while Seth shoved his hand out, shut the door, braced himself to hold it shut. Looked like it didn't lock from this side. At least a broken wrist or hand would slow the man down. In a moment's silence, Seth lifted box after box to make a barrier in the doorway, then saw another box across the way under the air vent, went to get it—Hannah! Hannah on her back, not moving!

He knelt and cradled her, so cold. But alive. He held her closer, trying to warm her, chaffing her hands more desperately than he had above the ravine when they'd hauled up the unconscious Ray-Lynn. He tore off his coat, wrapped her in it. Her eyelids flickered. She slitted them open, blinked off what looked like frost.

"Hannah! Hannah, it's Seth, sweetheart. Hannah, wake up. I'm going to get you warm, keep you warm forever, I swear it."

He carried her down a narrow aisle between shelves and leaned her in the corner. He stood in front of her as Harlan opened the freezer door, then—from the sound of it—shoved and toppled the boxes out of his path. Praying he didn't have a gun, Seth knew he'd get one chance to hit him with something, and lifted a package of what looked to be a frozen roast he could heave at him. *Do no harm...violence is not our way...turn the other cheek.* The words darted through his head.

Harlan roared, "Now you're both gonna freeze and end up in someone else's grave somewhere! You and your horse and buggy just gonna disappear!"

Seth shouted back, "I'm glad you got the door open and broke the window out, too! That makes it easier to hear the sheriff's siren getting closer! I called him. He knows all about you, Harlan. Better get running, if you can! Hear the siren?"

It was true. The distant shrill sound came louder, closer. Hefting the roast, in case Harlan came at them, Seth blinked back tears of relief and joy as he heard Harlan turn and run, cursing, falling over boxes in his scramble toward the door.

Harlan slammed it after him, muting all outside sounds.

"I didn't tell the sheriff we were in the freezer," he told Hannah as he picked her up in his arms again. "And I'll bet this phone won't work in here."

Her lips were so stiff that he had to interpret what

she said. "When the sheriff—comes in...store—get on box an' yell—through air duct. That's how I heard all—what Harlan did—an' Lily."

He did as she said, standing on the box, but it took a while for the sheriff to come in, hopefully because he was arresting Harlan. Seth almost didn't mind the wait, because Hannah was alive and seemed to be thawing out fast, despite murmuring about three-legged races and snow angels.

Finally, the sheriff heard Seth's shouting and banging and opened the freezer door.

"Thank God you two are all right!" he said as Seth stood there with Hannah in his arms, and the sheriff led them quickly out of the freezer. "His hand and wrist are broken but I cuffed him, anyway. He's in the cruiser, but I'll bet he didn't act alone, did he? Soon as I lock him up and read him his rights, I'm gonna go make a call on Elaine Carson!"

Hannah shook her head against Seth's shoulder. Love was blind, she thought, even a former, deserted love. "Sorry, Sh-sheriff," she said, wishing her mouth worked better. "It's Lily. I heard them argue. The bodies in the graves—people her Las Vegas boyfriend—name's Trenton Davis—wanted hidden. John Arrowroot's here, too—frozen, just how Harlan meant to get rid of me. Tell Linc—that plastic around the corpses—it's all over the place—in the freezer."

At that, all three of them stood like frozen statues. Seth saw the shock, the pain, on Jack Freeman's face. He hadn't moved since Hannah had said Lily's name.

"I've got to get Hannah warm," Seth said. The wind was blowing through the broken window but it felt so much warmer here. He'd wrap her in his buggy blanket, get her home. He started for the door with her in his arms.

"Wait a sec," the sheriff said as he went back into the freezer, then came back out and closed the door. "Arrowroot's in there, all right, ready to be stashed in someone's grave elsewhere. But not here. Not here. Seth, I need to make a call in to the Highway Patrol to secure this crime scene and guard my prisoner for me, 'cause I have another arrest to make. I been played for a country bumpkin—we all have. Hannah, can I call an ambulance for you?"

"I just want to go home and get a warm bath and bed," she said. Seth thought she sounded better now, not slurring her words so much. And how much he'd like to help with that bath and bed.

While he retrieved his buggy and got the blanket, Hannah told the sheriff all that she could recall that had passed between Harlan and Lily. While they waited for help, Sheriff Freeman went back and forth to his cruiser, where he said Harlan was finally settled down to a sulk after demanding they call someone in Las Vegas named Trenton Davis to get him a good lawyer.

"More like, this Davis guy—evidently Lily's lover's—gonna need one himself," the sheriff told Hannah and Seth.

Each time he returned to where Seth was holding Hannah, she resumed her story of what had happened from the time she opened the restaurant door for Harlan's weekly meat delivery.

"Maybe you should just keep control of Harlan yourself and let one of the other officers arrest Lily," Seth suggested.

"Nope. That's one thing I absolutely gotta do myself.

Seth, I'm asking you to take the assignment of keeping our heroine from being the center of any more crime scenes—got that, Hannah?"

"Yes, Sheriff. You know, that sounds like what Linc asked and I didn't—couldn't—do. I'm wondering whether he'll be happy or sad all this got settled without him."

The sheriff just gave a snort, then hurried outside when he heard the shrill of sirens. Seth decided that, though Hannah's lips were working better, it would be a good idea to warm them. Her tightening hold on him—she'd always had a hold on him—showed that she couldn't agree with him more.

29

THREE MONTHS LATER, IN CLEVELAND, ON Saturday, March 12, 2011, to be exact—Hannah hoped this day would be a momentous one in her life—she sat in a soundproof recording booth with earphones on so she would hear the orchestral accompaniment for her demo audition when it started. She would be singing "Wind Beneath My Wings," the same song she had sung at Sarah's wedding reception and two Amish weddings since. In the Home Valley Amish church she was preparing to join, she was getting to be known as the "Wedding Singer."

It had been a hectic three and a half months since Harlan Kenton, Lily Freeman and Trenton Davis III had been arrested. Hannah would honor her people and not testify in court, but had given Linc her affidavit for the three upcoming trials. Davis was a well-to-do restaurateur in Las Vegas who just happened to be into the semilegal fifty-million-dollar prostitution business there. Linc said that operated in a legal gray area where they greased law enforcement palms, much as Trenton Davis had greased Harlan's.

Harlan had not won a radio competition for a free trip to Las Vegas but had been recommended by Lily, who used to buy meat from Harlan, to her lover. Harlan had agreed to be the go-between to hide the bodies of Trenton Davis's competitors and whistle-blowers where they would never be found. That was her idea, too, Lily had admitted, because she'd do anything to help the man she was desperately in love with, and that sure wasn't Jack Freeman.

When Ray-Lynn had returned home, Hannah had become her right-hand helper, moving into her house, telling her about her past, introducing her to people she could not recall and running the restaurant. Living with Ray-Lynn had given Hannah space to find herself, too, while she and Seth grew closer and she came to really know and love Marlena. She was just getting ready to accept Seth's proposal when Linc kept his promise to set up this audition for her. She'd told Seth and her parents she could not resist knowing if she could yet follow this dream.

"But there's no way you can have both dreams—us together, Amish, and that worldly career," Seth had argued, while her *daad* had seethed—silently, this time.

"But I have to know. I'll never be really settled if I don't."

"In life, sometimes, my sweetheart, you have to choose between two ways of life, between two men. I don't want just half your head and heart. Do what you must, but come back to me and Marlena only if you can really be all ours."

Without a goodbye kiss or another word, he'd turned away and headed back to working on the mill project.

He and Levi had talked the Collister Company investors into trusting them to do the work without signing a *verboten* contract. Unfortunately—she hoped Linc hadn't scheduled this audition now on purpose—the official kickoff for the work on the mill was this afternoon with a picnic, something like a barn raising, and she hated to miss it. But Jason Flemming, whom *Daad* had told that she was gravely ill, was here today and couldn't make it at another time.

She jolted when she heard a voice in her earphones from the sound engineer. "Almost set, Ms. Esh. I'm gonna leave the studio audio on till I give you the go-ahead, then you'll hear the intro just like we practiced. Mr. Armstrong has a couple of possible investors here, too."

Her palms were sweating. Her heart was thudding. She had the sheet music in front of her but preferred to close her eyes when she sang. It was a song she knew by heart…by heart…

She felt so closed off in here in this booth, just as she had in the meat freezer, so afraid. And like that horrible night Harlan tried to kill her, she could hear the voices—Linc's, those of the others he'd brought in.

"I can see us packaging her as the Amish Angel," someone said.

"She looks like one—or will when that chin-length, blond hair grows out more."

"We won't want to go with that shapeless, long gown and apron she's got on, though. A glistening, sequined, white, tight-to-the-body gown, maybe slit thigh-high? Even wings in the background. We'll have her knock off fifteen, maybe twenty pounds so she looks other-worldly, get some pale makeup on her. Mr. Armstrong, it's not true about the Amish not wanting their pictures taken, is it? Because that's something we can't work around."

Linc said something, but he must be sitting farther back from the mic. Her head was spinning. The singing wasn't all they'd want from her, of course not. They'd change her name, her clothes, her body, her life. Without ever being formally put under the *bann,* she'd be alienated anyway by her parents and her people—yes, *her people!* And when they saw how she was "packaged," she'd be shunned for sure.

The music started. They'd paid to get an orchestra recording at a Nashville studio just to suit her voice range. This audition was her big chance, and she'd been told by Myron Jenkins, her old boss, that her voice would take her far.

But suddenly, she didn't want to go far. And old Nelson Sterling was waiting outside for her in her hired car to take her home. Home. The Home Valley, and she was going now, not looking back, just like Seth didn't when he told her she must choose and walked away.

She took off her earphones and said into her mic, "Sorry to bring all of you here, but I can't do this and have the life I want. I apologize to everyone, especially you, Linc. The Amish Angel is flying the coop right now."

She ignored their protests as she stepped out of the booth and pushed her way through the men. The only one she owed something to was Linc, and she didn't owe him what he'd been hinting at with his looks earlier today.

"Linc, I'm sorry," she said when he caught up with her. "I'll repay you whatever this cost, though it might take me a while."

When she kept going, he seized her arm to spin her back toward him.

"Hannah, whatever this cost is not just the outlay for this audition. What about me—us?"

When she didn't budge but to gently disengage her arm from his grasp, he said, "I was afraid they'd get to you—Seth, your family."

"This is my decision. Seth said it was mine—even my father said that, when I finally found the strength and faith to tell him I forgave him for ruining my audition last time. And he's right. It was for the best."

"You've lived away from them long enough to realize what's going on here!" he insisted, his voice rising. "It's an old tribal trick—the family and friends use whatever's at their disposal to control any person they perceive as a threat to the tribe's primacy—all that togetherness stuff instead of individuality."

"That from a man who seems to worship at the altar of what he calls the Bureau? I need to go, Linc. Thanks for all you did to help set this up and find the murderer."

He gave a bitter laugh. "Which you and Seth handled when I was miles away on a wild-goose chase, thanks to you. But knowing you and your people has been worth it, Hannah Esh."

She grabbed the big purse she'd brought with her and ran for the door.

Mr. Sterling was willing to drive clear out to the Troyer mill when she told him that's where she was going, but she had him stop at her parents' home first. Though they were at the kickoff for the mill renovation, she used her key to get in, hit the bathroom, then rushed into *Mamm*'s *kapp* shop to take the prayer *kapp* that was still waiting for her atop the cupboard. She fastened in her still-too-short but all blond hair with a couple of bobby pins from the desk drawer, put her bonnet over it, then darted out to the car again.

After all she'd been through, she thought as Mr. Nelson drove as close as he could to the sea of buggies and cars and let her out, this was really what it meant to be coming home, returning to the grace and love of her people. Tears blurred her eyes when she saw Seth standing on a plank platform with Levi Troyer and his sons beside him. They had a bullhorn and were addressing the assembled crowd of workmen, their families and the larger family of the church and the neighbors.

At the back edge of the crowd stood Ray-Lynn, her red hair in a splash of sun, her right arm and shoulder just out of the cast. She was standing next to Sheriff Freeman. They were dating now, though taking things slowly, however much that frustrated the sheriff as much as it used to annoy Ray-Lynn. Bless the man— just like Seth—he'd been willing to court her and wait.

As Hannah walked forward, she saw Amanda standing with her sister-in-law, Clair Kenton, who had moved into Lily's old room at the B and B. Hannah heard someone whisper in German, "There's the wedding singer! I want her to sing at Mose's and my reception!" Susan Zook, standing with her younger sister Amy, turned to look at Hannah. Her face fell, but she lifted a hand in greeting. Susan had apologized to Hannah for her nasty comments earlier, a good Amish woman despite her faults, a woman who had not run when she'd lost Seth Lantz. It was what Hannah knew

she should have done. But, after all, look how the Lord
had worked things out.

She saw her parents standing with Naomi and
stopped to let them see the *kapp* was on her head under
her bonnet. She grasped their hands. Naomi hugged
her. It surprised her that her father cried but *Mamm*
just said, "*Ya,* you go get your man."

Hannah skirted the crowd to where she saw Ella,
holding Marlena up so she could see. "What happened
in Cleveland?" Ella whispered.

"I told them all *nein, danki!*" she said as Marlena,
with her Hannah doll, held out her arms and Ella
shifted her over into Hannah's embrace.

"Let's get closer to *Daadi,* tell him we love him,"
Hannah told the little girl as Ella clapped her hands
loudly enough for some folks to turn around right in
the middle of Levi Troyer's telling everyone that this
project would "bring more folks into our area to buy
more good Amish goods!"

Seth saw her and jumped down off the side of the
platform. "How did it go?" he asked, putting his hands
on her shoulders. "I thought they might sweep you
away right then."

"I decided not to sing for them, only here," she told
him, cuddling Marlena so close she squirmed. "I've
already been swept away by a timber framer who has
promised me a new house someday if I behave—oh,
yes, and if I marry him."

"You're wearing your prayer *kapp.* But, my Hannah,
I don't think you will ever behave, and I don't want a
wife who behaves in bed. Then you will marry me?"

"I will."

It just wasn't done that the Amish couples showed

affection in public, but that didn't stop them from smooching, partly hidden from the crowd behind their hat and bonnet, pressing Marlena between them. Nor did it stop Ella and Naomi from giving a little cheer and clapping louder, which the crowd picked up, thinking it was for the Troyer mill. Her parents came closer, too, and the applause swelled, led by Bishop Esh. Her people's love was the most beautiful song Hannah had ever heard.

* * * * *

AUTHOR'S NOTE

Even when I am writing novels that don't have Amish settings, I visit Amish Ohio country on a regular basis. I find the people fascinating and admirable. I've heard a saying from them: "It's not all cakes and pies!" (I've also heard "It's not all quilts and pies!") This shows the Amish are very aware that their endeavors to keep separate from the world are becoming an increasing challenge. Especially during the teen years of *rumspringa*, some of the youth become snared by the world in ways that lead to big problems. Yet the Amish manage to keep a large percentage of their children.

Another danger is that crimes that used to be urban are now becoming rural. When such crime encroaches, that often means the enemy is us—rural neighbors. It's partly for those reasons I like to set my stories in small towns, not urban centers where most people expect impersonal crimes to happen. Sherlock Holmes's observation in the Sir Arthur Conan Doyle short story "The Adventure of the Copper Beeches," states this well: "The lowest and vilest alleys of London do not present a more dreadful record of sin than does the smiling and beautiful countryside." (*The Adventures of Sherlock Holmes,* 1892.)

On a lighter note, the whoopie pies that Hannah so favors are becoming very popular in the world. Long a regional and Amish favorite, sometimes called gobs, these look like large, puffy Oreo cookies, but are actually cakelike desserts. Such places as Bird-in-Hand Bakery in Bird-in-Hand, Pennsylvania, bake them by the dozens, and a state legislator in Maine recently proposed that these become "Maine's official state dessert."

Places to get whoopie pies abound in the Holmes Country area of Ohio where I do most of my research. There is even an Ohio company making "gourmet" whoopie pies, which they ship by the dozens in many flavors. (Want to read more about them or order some? Check out www.granvillewhoopiepies. com.) Even the ubiquitous Starbucks is getting into the act with whoopie pies in their minidessert line of Petites. Also, look for Hannah Esh's favorite kind of whoopie pie, oatmeal chocolate chip, on my website, www.KarenHarperAuthor.com.

As ever, I am grateful to the Amish of Holmes County who answered my questions. As I mentioned in book #1 of this series, *Fall from Pride,* Ray-Lynn's Dutch Farm Table Restaurant is partly inspired by Grandma's Homestead Restaurant in Charm, Ohio, and partly on the Ohio-based Dutch Kitchen restaurants. For background knowledge of Seth's timber-framing career, I thank the Amish barn builder, or timber framer, who was kind enough to speak to me about his work. Again, thanks to Shasta Mast, Executive Director of the Holmes County Chamber of Commerce and Tourism Bureau.

Finding Mercy, the next book in the Home Valley Amish Trilogy, will focus on some new main characters and some old, as Ella Lantz takes center stage and learns that the strict rules she's tried to live by and has preached to others sometimes don't work when danger comes calling. Also, you are invited to Hannah and Seth's wedding and to see whether Ray-Lynn and the sheriff can finally get together.

I hope you'll enjoy these future Amish stories and have a chance to read the past ones if you haven't already. Previous books include The Maple Creek Amish Trilogy: *Dark Road Home, Dark Harvest* and *Dark Angel. Down to the Bone* is a stand-alone Amish story about a group of Plain People who have left their large Amish community to find more affordable farmland among *Englische ausländers*—and its heroine faces solving a murder and her own forbidden love story.

Also with authors Marta Perry and Patricia Davids, I have an Amish novella-length story, "The Covered Bridge," in an anthology called *Dark Crossings*, available July 2012.

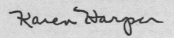

REQUEST YOUR FREE BOOKS!

2 FREE NOVELS
FROM THE SUSPENSE COLLECTION
PLUS 2 FREE GIFTS!

YES! Please send me 2 FREE novels from the Suspense Collection and my 2 FREE gifts (gifts are worth about $10). After receiving them, if I don't wish to receive any more books, I can return the shipping statement marked "cancel." If I don't cancel, I will receive 4 brand-new novels every month and be billed just $5.99 per book in the U.S. or $6.49 per book in Canada. That's a saving of at least 25% off the cover price. It's quite a bargain! Shipping and handling is just 50¢ per book in the U.S. and 75¢ per book in Canada.* I understand that accepting the 2 free books and gifts places me under no obligation to buy anything. I can always return a shipment and cancel at any time. Even if I never buy another book, the two free books and gifts are mine to keep forever.

191/391 MDN FEME

Name	(PLEASE PRINT)

Address	Apt. #

City	State/Prov.	Zip/Postal Code

Signature (if under 18, a parent or guardian must sign)

Mail to the **Reader Service**:
IN U.S.A.: P.O. Box 1867, Buffalo, NY 14240-1867
IN CANADA: P.O. Box 609, Fort Erie, Ontario L2A 5X3

Not valid for current subscribers to the Suspense Collection
or the Romance/Suspense Collection.

Want to try two free books from another line?
Call 1-800-873-8635 or visit www.ReaderService.com.

* Terms and prices subject to change without notice. Prices do not include applicable taxes. Sales tax applicable in N.Y. Canadian residents will be charged applicable taxes. Offer not valid in Quebec. This offer is limited to one order per household. All orders subject to credit approval. Credit or debit balances in a customer's account(s) may be offset by any other outstanding balance owed by or to the customer. Please allow 4 to 6 weeks for delivery. Offer available while quantities last.

Your Privacy—The Reader Service is committed to protecting your privacy. Our Privacy Policy is available online at www.ReaderService.com or upon request from the Reader Service.

We make a portion of our mailing list available to reputable third parties that offer products we believe may interest you. If you prefer that we not exchange your name with third parties, or if you wish to clarify or modify your communication preferences, please visit us at www.ReaderService.com/consumerschoice or write to us at Reader Service Preference Service, P.O. Box 9062, Buffalo, NY 14269. Include your complete name and address.

SUS11

"She goes out jogging and driving at strange hours."